The *Forced Redundancy* Film Club

BRIAN FINNEGAN

HACHETTE
BOOKS
IRELAND

First published in Ireland in 2012 by
HACHETTE BOOKS IRELAND

1

Cataloguing in Publication Data is available from the British Library

ISBN 978 14447 4291 6

Typeset in Sabon and Dancing Script by Bookends Publishing Services.

Printed and bound in Great Britain by
Clays Ltd, St Ives plc

Hachette Books Ireland policy is to use papers that are natural,
renewable and recyclable products and made from wood grown
in sustainable forests. The logging and manufacturing processes
are expected to conform to the environmental regulations of the
country of origin.

Hachette Books Ireland
8 Castlecourt Centre
Castleknock
Dublin 15, Ireland

A division of Hachette UK Ltd
338 Euston Road, London NW1 3BH
www.hachette.ie

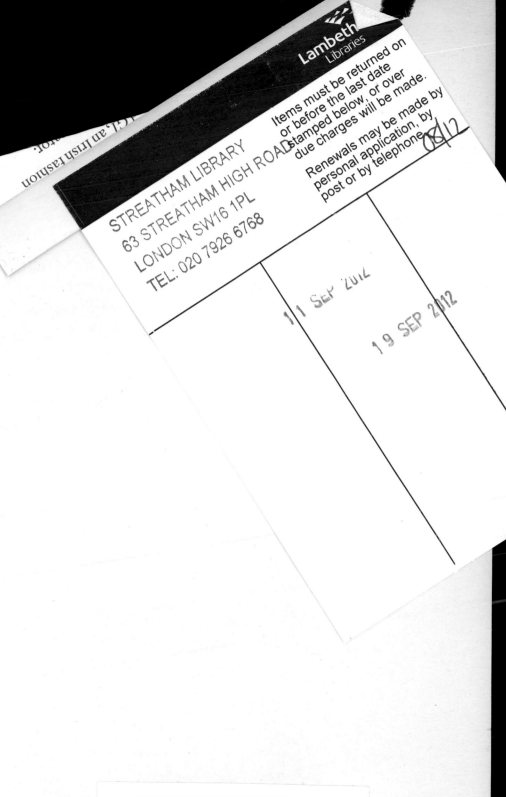

Brian Finnegan is editor of Irela... to that he worked at *In Dublin* magazine and and lifestyle magazine where he was editor and co-crea...

He edited a book of short stories, *Quare Fellas* (Attic Press, 1994), and a non-fiction humour book, *Camp as Knickers* (Marino Books, 1995).

Over the past 15 years he has been a regular contributor to many of Ireland's newspapers, magazines, radio and TV channels, writing and broadcasting on gay politics and culture. He is currently a regular columnist with the *Evening Herald*. He has also ghostwritten a number of celebrity autobiographies.

The Forced Redundancy Film Club is his first novel.

www.brianfinnegan.ie
 @finneganba
 brianfinneganauthor

For Joan, my ever-loving Mam.

Acknowledgements

First and foremost, I would like to thank Ciara Considine, my editor, mentor and friend. Your help in bringing this novel to fruition from the moment I told you the concept has fulfilled a lifelong dream for me. It would not have happened without you.

To the team at Hachette Ireland who got behind my dream, thank you.

The idea for this book came on a Dublin street one day when my partner and I bumped into Lisa Manselli, who told us about the book club she and her friends had formed after they were made redundant. I named the character of Lisa after her, although that's where the resemblance ends. I want to thank the real Lisa for kick-starting a concept that I could get my teeth into.

To everyone at the Tyrone Guthrie Centre in Annaghmakerrig – thank you for providing me with a wonderful space where I could immerse myself in writing; for great food, great company and some great parties, which added to the experience in a very special way.

I would like to thank my readers who gave me honest and very helpful feedback – some of my oldest friends, Maggie Breheny, Eilish Kent, Louise Mitchell and Adrienne Murphy. Your constant support and belief in me is a fundamental part of this book, and my life.

Thanks to Freda Donoghue, who spent valuable time helping me with the plot and to Roisín Meaney who gave me a writer's professional feedback. Thank you too to Pete Reddy and Hazel Orme.

I thank Deirdre Buckley who has been a support to me

throughout my adult life, both personally and in all my creative endeavours.

Thanks also to our beautiful son, Colum, who helped me with the title and is always happy to talk plot with me.

Over the past two years, much of my free time has been dedicated to writing this book. Special thanks go to my wonderful partner in life Miguel Gernaey, who has not once complained about my dedication to getting it done, has read through and given me feedback that I couldn't have done without, and has bolstered me up throughout all those times when I had the fear that I couldn't get it done, always making me laugh along the way.

'Remember, no man is a failure who has friends.'

It's a Wonderful Life
Frank Capra, 1946

January

First Films First

'I don't know how to feel.
I can't feel anything anymore.'

E.T.: The Extra Terrestrial
Stephen Spielberg, 1982

1. Birthday Girl

Katherine Casey's thirty-sixth birthday turned out to be the worst day of her life.

Or the second worst.

So far.

It had begun promisingly enough. When she got out of bed and pulled the curtains, she was greeted by a clear blue sky, the first after weeks with banks of grey cloud sealing the city like a Tupperware lid.

Because it was her birthday, she allowed herself time to sit and eat some breakfast, looking out of the patio doors at a pair of robins pecking from the bird-feeder she'd put up before winter had set in. It was still January, but the morning had a feeling of spring about it.

She was putting the final touches to her makeup in the hall mirror when two envelopes popped through the letterbox. The first was from her mother, bearing a Spanish stamp, the second from her sister Lucy, her childish handwriting instantly recognisable. 'Many happy returns, Katherine, from your ever-loving Mum,' her mother's card read, the same message she always wrote, year in, year out. Lucy's was stuffed with two pictures of Disney's Little Mermaid, coloured in by Kitty, 'Happy Birthday, Auntie Katherine. I love you'. Lucy's message was typically loaded: 'Happy birthday, big sis. Only four more years till forty!'

'Four years,' Katherine said to her reflection. 'That's not so bad, is it?'

There was no card from Barry. He had been particularly busy, she supposed. He'd probably call later, when he was on his break.

She took a lipstick from her bag, touched up her lips and checked to make sure her foundation was covering the pimple that had appeared on her chin last night.

She was tempted to drive the car to work with the top down, but it was still very cold, despite the bright sun, and the wind would wreak havoc with her hair. She tuned in to 4FM for a change, drumming the steering wheel with her leather-gloved fingers and humming along with back-to-back seventies songs that spoke of sunshine and lollipops rather than the wall-to-wall recession, euro bail-outs and rising unemployment figures on the news channels she usually chose.

As soon as she arrived at her desk, she knew something was terribly wrong. Silence floated in the air above the rows of cubicles. Not a phone could be heard ringing, not a person talking.

The dreaded day had finally come.

Alice Little appeared beside her as she was peeling off her gloves. She had a habit of doing that, Alice, silently materialising out of nowhere like a wafer-thin ghost. She looked paler and more drawn than ever, her lank brown hair pinned up to one side with a plastic grip in the shape of a yellow butterfly. It was the only thing of colour about her. 'Mr Maguire would like to see you in his office right away,' she said, her eyes on the floor.

As Katherine followed her to Maguire's door, she had a vision of a prisoner being led to the dock. Above the walls of the cell-like cubicles, anxious eyes followed her progress.

When she walked into his office, Maguire was standing at the window, focused on something in the far distance. 'Good morning, Eamon,' she said, taking a seat.

'Ah, Katherine,' he replied. 'Not such a good morning at all.' He pulled a handkerchief from his trouser pocket and mopped the back of his neck. 'I'm afraid I've got some bad news.'

Katherine tried to smile reassuringly as he turned to her. 'Eamon,' she said, clasping her hands in her lap. 'Everyone's known it's been coming for a long time. It's not your fault.'

'I wish I could be as confident about that as you are.' He sighed and sat down at the other side of his vast, polished oak desk.

'How many are we going to lose?' Katherine asked.

Now Maguire met her eyes. His brows arched, and something seemed to dawn on him. He turned back to the window. 'I'm afraid we're going to have to let you go, Katherine,' he said.

It was a few seconds before what he had said connected itself to her.

Back in August, when the Polish deal had been done, Maguire had called her into his office and told her hard times lay ahead, but he could assure her that her job was safe. There was possibly a less home-based promotion for her in the European sector next March. He would keep her updated on developments as they unfolded, but in the meantime she should put her shoulder to the wheel and double her efforts.

And now he was giving her the sack.

While Katherine struggled to take it in, Maguire mopped at his forehead and talked on. He'd done everything he possibly could and it killed him that he was losing her. Times were extremely difficult; he hated having to do this. He was sure she had nothing to be worried about, with her qualifications and experience …

Katherine realised he had trailed off. She sat staring at him in mute horror.

'I really am sorry,' he said.

He was sorry?

'The European job,' Katherine said. 'You told me it was mine.'

Maguire stood up again and went back to the window. 'I did no such thing,' he said. 'You wouldn't have been suitable for it at all.'

'But after all the work I've put in,' Katherine said, her voice going up a register. 'I did it because you said I was in line for promotion.'

Maguire turned back to her, his watery grey eyes unreadable. 'We're offering a month's salary for every year worked at Qwertec. You may also qualify for statutory redundancy pay based on your years at Henderson. But I'm sure you'll have a new position in no time.'

She didn't know what to say. To stand up and walk out was to admit defeat, but what else could she do? Get on her knees and beg?

Maguire walked over and held out his hand to shake hers. She stood up, but didn't take it. Instead she composed herself, looked him in the eye and said, 'How long have you known about this?'

He looked exasperated. 'It's not my decision, Katherine. You know that.'

'But how long have you known?'

'As you are fully aware, the redundancy plans were drawn up over the past three months.'

'And you let me work myself to the bone on the European deal, knowing all the time I was getting fired.'

'It's not like that. I thought you had the best credentials for the work involved. You should be proud of the part you played.'

'The best credentials for the work involved, but not the best credentials for the actual job.'

Maguire pulled himself up to his full height, which was almost as tall as Katherine. 'We felt the position was more suited to someone else. That's the way the company works, Katherine. You, above all people, should be aware of that.'

'And tell me this, Eamon, is the person best suited to the position a man?'

'As it happens, yes. But that's neither here nor there.'

Katherine's fist balled, her nails digging into her palm. She imagined smashing it directly into his bulbous, overripe nose. It wasn't the first time she'd had the urge. She might have been at Maguire's beck and call since the day she'd started at Qwertec, but that didn't mean she had to like the demanding, ungrateful prick.

'You don't happen to play golf with the man who's getting my job, do you?' she asked.

Maguire brushed past her to the door and held it open. 'Send Lisa Fingleton in on your way out, please,' he said.

2. Hot Sweet Tea

On exiting Maguire's office, Katherine bumped headlong into Martin Brady. He was coming back from the kitchen carrying a full cup of coffee, which spilled out over the top.

'Fuck!' he said. 'I didn't get you, did I?'

Unable to speak, Katherine shook her head. Her heart was flapping against her ribcage, like a panicked bird. What she had feared secretly since her first promotion in her first job had finally, inevitably, happened – she had fallen from grace. It was like being pushed off the top of a skyscraper.

'Are you all right?' asked Martin, scratching his ginger stubble. 'You're white as a sheet.'

Still speechless, Katherine stiffened. She tried to make her expression smooth and impassive, but the muscles in her face wouldn't follow suit. Instead her chin bunched and, for a horrifying moment, she thought she was going to burst into tears.

'Come on,' Martin said, touching her arm and gesturing towards the kitchen station at the end of the row of cubicles. 'I'll make you a cup of coffee.'

Katherine found her voice. 'I've got work to do,' she said.

Martin smiled at her, his blue eyes crinkling up at the corners. 'Ah, c'mon, Katherine. There's no work happening here today.'

Not knowing what else to do, she followed him, eyes fixed on the creased shirt-tail hanging out from the back of his trousers.

Katherine had been poached by Qwertec from Henderson Consulting exactly thirteen months ago, which meant a redundancy package of one measly month's wages. Fourteen years of working her arse off to build a career, of taking all the right steps, and now she'd been thrown on a massive scrapheap with just four weeks' salary for her trouble.

How would she manage the mortgage? How would she pay for the car, and the loan she and Barry had taken out to refurbish the house?

Katherine stopped in her tracks. The space between the edge of the cubicle bank and the wall seemed suddenly too small, as if she was being pressed in from both sides. Martin was waiting at the coffee dock, beckoning her to follow him. But she couldn't walk.

She pushed at the wall with the flat of her hand. Tiny pricks of sweat popped out on her forehead.

Martin walked back towards her. 'You'll be all right in a minute,' he said, and she allowed him to take her arm.

He led her to one of the two high stools that had been placed beside the coffee dock and told her to sit down. On her perch, Katherine tried to pull herself together as she watched Alice usher the permanently exhausted Lisa Fingleton into Maguire's office. With three children under the age of four, Lisa already had her work cut out for her without the demands of Qwertec. That was the reasoning Katherine had given to Maguire when she'd added Lisa's name to the redundancy list she had been asked to draw up last October.

Martin made tea instead of the rotten coffee the machine produced and, without asking her how she liked it, put in sugar and milk.

'Hot sweet tea,' he said, handing her the polystyrene cup. 'My mother thinks it's the cure for everything.'

It wasn't how Katherine liked it, but the syrupy-sweet liquid was comforting, the way hot lemon and honey was when you had the flu. Mercifully, Martin sat in silence. She avoided his eye, concentrating on her cup as if tea leaves might float to its surface and reveal her future.

'I haven't been called into the old bastard's office yet,' Martin said eventually. 'Any minute now.'

Katherine closed her eyes. His name had been the first on the list.

'Jamie O'Donnell said there's TV cameras outside the front doors,' he added, after another moment of silence. 'He's in the toilets getting ready to star in *TV3 News*.'

Katherine smiled ruefully. 'There's nothing more depressing than people crying on news reports because they've lost their jobs,' she said.

'We'll sneak out the back, you and me,' said Martin. 'Out of the way of the roving reporters.'

Katherine's eyes met his and she had a ridiculous vision of the two of them, hand in hand, running through the car park, Martin's shirt-tail flapping in the wind. Shaking it out of her head, she looked back at her cup.

'Maguire had me making lists of people to be let go for the past three months,' she said. 'I never imagined I'd be on one of them.'

Martin opened his mouth to reply, but then Lisa appeared, her round cheeks burning, her wide eyes wet and puffy. 'Maguire asked me to send you in,' she said to Martin, pushing her jet-black bob behind her ears.

'Here we go,' Martin said, sliding off his stool. 'Dead man walking.'

'Good luck,' Katherine called, as he ambled down the corridor. She was immediately filled with regret. What a stupid thing to say.

'I think they've given Alice the chop too,' said Lisa, wiping her eyes as they watched Martin go into Maguire's office. 'When I passed her cubicle I could hear her bawling her eyes out.'

'I can't believe Maguire would agree to that,' said Katherine, although now it seemed that anything was possible. 'It'd be like cutting off his right hand.'

'She's in an awful way,' said Lisa. 'Will you go and talk to her?'

'Why can't you?'

'Look at me. I'm a mess. I don't think I can cope with Alice right now, on top of everything else.'

Katherine drank the last of her tea and stood up. Everybody on the sales floor avoided Alice like the plague, but it wasn't right to leave her alone today.

The sound coming from Alice's cubicle was more like a kitten mewing than someone bawling. Katherine put her head around the corner of the partition and saw Alice slumped at her desk, her head in one hand, the other clutching her phone.

'You're not being let go too, are you?' Katherine said.

Alice looked up and shook her head, wincing. 'It's my mother,' she said. 'She's dead.'

3. The Bell and Castle

By noon it was all done and dusted – 180 people let go to join the thousands of unemployed already on the dole queues. It took a three-interview shortlisting process to get a job at Qwertec, but only minutes to be told you didn't have that job any more.

The sales floor emptied. Nobody from middle management told Katherine where they were going, and hardly anyone from the ranks below talked to her as they abandoned their cubicles.

Katherine didn't care that no one here liked her. She had done her job to the best of her ability, and if that had made her unpopular, so be it. It was the price you had to pay for success in business.

But today of all days it would have been nice not to be left out.

She was sitting at her desk, staring listlessly at her computer screen and wondering whether or not to go home, when Martin popped his head over the divider wall. 'We're going to the Bell and Castle if you want to come,' he said.

'The Bell and Castle?'

'I know. It's a dump. But they pour the best Guinness in town.'

'Maybe not,' said Katherine, turning back to her screen. 'I still have a few things to finish up here.'

'Suit yourself,' said Martin. 'You know where we are if you change your mind,' his disembodied voice called, and Katherine heard the lift doors open and close.

The last time she'd gone to a pub with him she'd barely been in the job a month. She'd had to take to dinner some Japanese clients from the largest telecom company Qwertec dealt with, and even back then, without fully knowing the lie of the land, she was surprised Maguire had chosen Martin to go in his place.

He'd come to the restaurant in jeans and an open-necked checked shirt, ordered his steak 'like shoe leather' and wolfed it down as if he was eating in a trucker's diner. Katherine had tried her best to maintain the formal tone of the occasion, but Martin had chatted away as if he was entirely immune to the cultural differences it was so important to observe. Yet somehow it didn't bother the clients, who seemed to relax in his company and even enjoy it, as he regaled them with stories of how he had broken his wrist pretending to be the Karate Kid when he was eight. Despite herself, Katherine, too, had relaxed.

Later, when they'd waved the clients off in a taxi, Martin had insisted on bringing Katherine to what he called the smallest pub in Dublin. She'd refused to go at first, but with a few glasses of wine on board, her defences were down.

The pub was a claustrophobically narrow room with just a line of scruffy brown leather stools at a bar and an old, grey-haired man quietly polishing glasses behind it. She'd asked for a half of lager, but Martin had bought her a pint. Somewhere in their conversation he'd begun doing imitations of the Japanese clients that were as startlingly good as they were politically incorrect. Katherine had laughed, against her better judgement.

And then he'd done impressions of Katherine's excruciating efforts at conversation with the clients, and she'd laughed harder. Tears had rolled down her cheeks and her stomach hurt. She'd pleaded breathlessly with him to stop, but he wouldn't let up. She'd reached out and grabbed his knee in a desperate attempt to shut him up and both of them had fallen instantly silent. After a moment, she'd excused herself and gone to the Ladies to check her mascara hadn't run. But then she was giggling again at how he'd taken her off . . .

Now Katherine stood up.

'Wait!' she called, into the empty silence of the office floor. 'I'm coming!'

The Bell and Castle was one of those bars that had all but disappeared during the super-pub boom, flock wallpaper and Axminster carpet, the red velvet banquette seats faded and shabby, a distinct smell of cigarettes eight years after the smoking ban had been introduced.

Two decrepit men nursing pints of Guinness at the bar eyed them as they walked in. One raised his stubbly grey chin to Martin in silent greeting.

'Right,' said Martin, rubbing his hands together. 'Who's for what?'

'I'll have a white wine spritzer,' said Lisa, who had perked up considerably since Maguire had given her the bad news. Her cheeks were still spotted red, but she had a kind of giddy energy, as if she might tip over into an uncontrollable fit of giggles at any moment. Sometimes Katherine wished she could be more like that. Lisa had no internal editor. She was forever laughing and blurting out the first thing that came into her mind and she regularly put her foot in it, but everyone seemed to like her.

Jamie O'Donnell looked up from his mobile phone to survey his surroundings. 'What a dump. I'll have a Coors Light.'

Katherine ordered a gin and Slimline and wondered what she was doing there. Apart from that one time with Martin, she had never gone out with any of this crowd. Back at Qwertec she'd known of her reputation as a slave-driver. In fact, she'd fostered it in an effort to replace what she saw as a general lack of ambition with a clear work ethic.

Not in a million years would Lisa or Jamie have asked her out for a drink, and Martin was only taking pity on her now. She felt mortified, and told herself she'd just have the one and go, although she hadn't the foggiest where to. Uncomfortable as she was, there was nowhere else she wanted to be.

Barry still hadn't called to wish her a happy birthday, and she was reluctant to phone him. In Barcelona they wouldn't have heard about the Qwertec lay-offs yet, so he was blissfully unaware. She wanted to leave it that way for the moment.

'Shove up,' said Jamie, when Katherine sat into the banquette. He was still engrossed in his phone, his dark eyebrows knitted, like two question marks. Katherine's hand made contact with something sticky on the seat as she pulled herself in to make room for him.

'This is lovely, isn't it?' said Lisa, beaming from ear to ear, her midriff pushed up against the table.

'Yeah,' said Jamie, 'if what you mean by "lovely" is a normal person's worst nightmare.'

'Don't mind him,' said Lisa, with a conspiratorial roll of the eyes for Katherine. 'He's just pissed off because of what Maguire said.'

'A disappointment,' said Jamie, finally putting his phone down. 'That's what he called me. I bet he said nothing of the sort to any of you.'

'He didn't get a chance,' said Martin, putting the tray of drinks on the table. 'I was in and out of there like a hare. "You're firing me? Right. See ya."'

Katherine did her best to smile along with the others. They all knew she was the one who had put their names on the redundancy list. How couldn't they when she'd been Maguire's clear confidante for the past six months?

'What about you?' said Jamie, turning a cold eye on her. 'I'm sure you didn't see that one coming.'

Katherine sipped her gin to clear her throat. 'It was a bit of a surprise, yes,' she managed.

'I'll bet,' said Jamie. He took a slug from his beer bottle and looked away again.

There was a loaded silence until Martin broke it. 'Let's not talk about Maguire,' he said, raising his glass, 'or Qwertec, or any of it. Let's just get plastered.'

'Oh, no,' said Lisa, her heavy rings clinking against her glass as she lifted it. 'I couldn't go home to the kids drunk. I'll just have one, that's all.'

Three rounds later, they were still there. As the alcohol coursed through her veins, Katherine felt more stunned than relaxed, weighed down and barely able to speak. She sat nodding as the conversation turned from the snow at Christmas to bank managers' overblown bonuses to the new season of *Mad Men*, trying at least to look as if she was contributing. But with each sip of gin her insides seemed shrivel, leaving only an outer shell to keep up appearances.

Martin was holding forth about his favourite film ever, his speech a little slurred at the edges. 'It was the first film I remember watching from beginning to end,' he said. 'I could see *E.T.* a million times and never get tired of it.'

Katherine felt it was time either to enter the conversation or to leave the pub. 'I don't think I've ever seen it.'

'Jaysus,' said Martin. 'Where did you grow up? The gulags?'

'In Dublin. We just didn't go to the pictures that much.'

Martin took a swig of his pint. 'Seriously, you must be the only person on Planet Earth who hasn't seen *E.T.*'

Katherine prickled, although she couldn't say why. She fixed a smile on her face, battling down her irritation. 'I'll rent the DVD,' she said. 'That should make it the full quota for Planet Earth.'

'Same again, everyone?' Lisa asked, wobbling a little as she stood.

'Anyone who hasn't seen *E.T.* hasn't lived,' Martin said.

Katherine got to her feet. 'It's my round,' she said.

As she waited at the bar for her order, one of the old men leaned over and said, 'Soft day, thank God.' His breath stank of stale cigarettes and alcohol.

'It is,' she replied, trying not to recoil.

'From around here, are you?'

Katherine willed the barman to hurry up. 'No,' she said shortly. The man shrugged and went back to his pint.

When she returned to the table with the drinks, Martin was talking about *Star Wars*. 'I don't care what anyone says,' he said, 'Princess Leia is one of the most the most beautiful women in the history of cinema.'

'The woman had Danish pastries for hair,' said Jamie. 'She was the princess that style forgot.'

Martin flushed, as if they were talking about a real live person. 'No way!' he said. 'Leia was a total ride!' He took a swig and swallowed almost half of the pint Katherine had just bought for him, then wiped his mouth with the back of his hand. 'You have to admit, she looked smokin' hot in that gold bikini.'

'Not to my eyes,' said Jamie.

'Well, you're gay,' said Martin, 'so it doesn't count.' He pulled a cigarette packet from his pocket and held it aloft. 'Anyone care to partake?'

'Maybe I'll have just one,' said Lisa, pushing her fringe out of her eyes. She'd dyed her hair from platinum to black just before Christmas, telling Katherine she thought it made her seem younger, but now her head looked too small for her big-boobed frame.

'That'a girl,' Martin said. 'Come on, so.'

'Wait up,' said Jamie, grabbing his mobile phone. He followed them to the back door of the pub, leaving Katherine alone at the table.

4. Tune-in Time

The smoking area was a few beer barrels topped with planks of damp wood to sit on, wedged against a wall under the Gents' windows. Through them Lisa heard a man – probably one of the friendly old lads sitting at the bar – clear his throat, then a heavy stream hitting a urinal interrupted by a loud fart. She blushed hotly but, thank goodness, neither Martin nor Jamie noticed. Anyway, her face was most likely bright red from coming into the freezing cold air, which was probably doing her capillaries no good. Not that smoking was good for them either. This was her last one, absolutely. She'd get mints on the way home so Patrick wouldn't smell the nicotine off her breath.

'Can you believe that cunt said he was firing me because of my lack of productivity?' Jamie was saying, pulling furiously on his cigarette and exhaling without breathing in any of the smoke. 'It beggars belief.'

Lisa made an empathetic sound, although Jamie had worn it as a personal badge of honour that he came at the bottom of the sales sheets at the end of every month. Maguire had said more or less the same thing about productivity to her. Even though she had fully intended to take voluntary redundancy if it had been offered, she'd found herself crying before he opened his mouth to tell her she was no longer wanted. When he was holding his office door open on her way out, he'd handed her a tissue to mop up the tears that wouldn't stop coming. She'd been daft enough to say, 'Thank you.'

'So, what was the first film you remember watching from

beginning to end?' Martin asked them, still trying to steer the talk away from that morning's events.

Lisa took a deep, satisfying drag of her cigarette. 'I think mine was *Chitty Chitty Bang Bang*.'

'Come get your lollipops, all free today,' Martin said, in a singsong voice. His eyes bulged, capturing the Child Catcher perfectly, and a shiver made its way down Lisa's spine.

Jamie's mobile phone bleeped another text alert and he pulled it out of his pocket. 'No rest for the wicked,' he said, and gave her a wink.

'I had nightmares about the Child Catcher for months,' said Lisa. 'I can't understand how any adult would let a child watch something so terrifying.'

When she thought about it, Lisa was shocked she had been let see *Chitty Chitty Bang Bang* at such a young age. But then again, her mother was from a different generation. They knew hardly anything about rearing children properly. 'Can you imagine the effect seeing the Child Catcher would have on Theo?' she asked.

Jamie looked up from his mobile phone and smirked. 'It would probably do him the world of good,' he said. 'That kid needs a good scare to keep him in check.'

'No, he does not. He's got a bit of separation anxiety, that's all. Lots of children with two working parents get it.'

'He got separation anxiety when they cut the cord,' said Jamie, dropping his half-smoked cigarette on the ground.

Lisa knew she should be pissed off when Jamie was sarcastic, but she never was. It was impossible to get annoyed with him. When she'd first met him, she couldn't help harbouring fantasies about him, even after she discovered he was gay. Despite his goatee, he looked not unlike Superman, with his glossy black hair, broad shoulders and chiselled features, yet something about his wide, baby blue eyes brought out maternal feelings. All the women in the office had hovered around his desk from the day he'd started at Qwertec, vying for his attention. They all wanted to take care of Jamie.

'I should really get home soon.' Lisa sighed. 'The au pair will be wondering if I've run away with the circus.'

She always felt guilty leaving the boys with Sofia for too long, but from next month that would be a thing of the past. After eleven years with Qwertec, her redundancy package wasn't to be sneezed at. It would bolster Patrick's earnings for the best part of two years, if they were careful, although he'd have to continue working all the hours God sent.

And at last Lisa could be a stay-at-home mum. She was free to give her boys plenty of Tune-in Time. *Getting Down With Bringing Up Kids* was, Lisa thought, the best book about the toddler-to-six-year-old stage. It said that most modern children suffered long-term psychological effects from having had too little Tune-in Time, with so many parents forced to work full-time.

She was sure that her presence at home would stop Theo being so aggressive and help Ben start sleeping through the night. And Aaron might be less clingy, if he knew she was going to be around whenever he needed her.

5. Get Back in the Race

Alone at the table, Katherine pulled her phone out of her handbag and dialled Barry's number. There was no point in putting it off any longer.

Barry was always going on about how at least their jobs were secure, how they'd made all the right moves in their careers to insure themselves against the disgrace of the dole queue.

The man at the bar who had spoken to her gave her a wide grin as she held the phone to her ear, waiting to get through. She averted her eyes.

'Babes, I'm in a meeting,' Barry said, by way of greeting.

'Sorry,' said Katherine, feeling a stab of irritation. 'I can call back later.'

'Hold on,' he said. She heard his hand go over the mouthpiece of his phone and some muffled voices. Then he was back. 'One of the guys here told me they announced the redundancies at your place this morning. It's all over the net. Two hundred, he said.'

'A hundred and eighty,' said Katherine.

'Fuck. That's some heavy shit. You doing okay?'

'Barry … I was one of them.'

'One of who?'

'I've been let go.'

There was a silence that went on too long.

'Are you still there?' said Katherine. The old codger at the bar was still smiling at her, making her feel oddly exposed. She crossed her legs and turned away from him.

'They let you go?' said Barry. 'Are you sure?'

'What kind of a question is that? Of course I'm sure.'

Barry was quiet for another moment. Katherine could hear him breathing and again her irritation flared. Why hadn't he wished her a happy birthday yet? The day was bad enough as it was.

'Look,' Barry said eventually, 'I have to go back into this meeting. We can talk about it when I get home tomorrow, okay?'

'Okay,' said Katherine, her eyes alighting on a fly-paper hanging from the ceiling above the pub's flashing poker machine. Its sticky brown surface was dotted with the carcasses of flies that had probably died slow, agonising deaths there the previous summer.

'If anyone can get another job, it's you,' Barry said. 'You're well able to get back in the race.'

'What if there are no jobs?'

'There will be, if you look hard enough.' Barry didn't sound convinced.

When she'd phoned, she hadn't really known what she wanted him to say. Maybe she'd just needed him to listen for a few minutes, even though *she* didn't really know what to say. Maybe there was too much *to* say. She was devastated. She was scared. She was angry. She was humiliated. Every time she contemplated the future, panic rose in her throat, like bile.

'It'll be all right, babes,' Barry said. 'You know it will.'

Before he hung up, Katherine said, 'Aren't you forgetting something?'

Another silence. 'No,' said Barry. 'I don't think so.'

'It's my birthday,' said Katherine.

'Fuck, sorry! Happy birthday, babes. You're looking good on it.'

'You can't see me,' Katherine said. 'I look awful.'

'Babes, I'm sure that's not true,' said Barry, 'Look, I have to go. I'll pick you up something nice in the airport on the way home. We can celebrate at the weekend.'

As Katherine put the phone back into her bag, Martin, Lisa and Jamie came in from the smoking area. Passing the two men at the bar, Martin stopped to talk to one. He was introduced to the other, who shook his hand vigorously and leaned over to say something under his breath. All three laughed and turned to look at Katherine.

'What were you talking about with those guys?' she asked Martin, when he squeezed in at the table, her irritation now in full bloom.

'Nothing much,' said Martin. 'The weather. That's all they ever talk about in here.'

'I'm sure,' said Katherine, gritting her teeth. She got up to go to the toilet even though she'd been avoiding it all afternoon. It probably stank, considering the state of the bar.

'Right, everyone, who's for a round of shots?' she heard Martin say, as the door swung closed behind her.

Instead of going into a cubicle, she went to the washbasin and turned on the cold tap. She wanted to scoop up a handful of water and bathe her face, but that would ruin her makeup, so instead she let it run and stared at herself in the cloudy mirror.

A loose strand of hair that just wouldn't stay in place was hanging down over the middle of her forehead, and the spot on her chin was red raw. In her determination to get away from Martin, she'd left her handbag behind on the seat. She wished she had her make-up with her so she could touch up.

Listening to the running tap, she held the tips of her fingers to her temples and took a deep breath.

Katherine had once read a book by a financial guru who said that your forties were the years when you earned the most money of your career and fully came into your own. But here she was, stopped in her tracks in her mid-thirties. What did she have to look forward to?

She turned off the tap, went into the cubicle and hovered over the stained toilet, her Alexander McQueen pencil skirt hitched up around her hips.

Barry had the right attitude. She had no choice but to pick herself up and get back in the race.

'You can do it,' she whispered, as she let go into the bowl. 'You know you can.'

6. Science Fiction

Martin's eyes kept being drawn back to the door of the ladies' toilet. Katherine was taking ages in there. He was beginning to get worried about her. She hadn't deserved to be fired, even though Martin knew for sure she had probably marked his own yellow card. She'd been itching to get rid of him. Any dumb arse could see that.

When he'd bumped into her outside Maguire's office just after she'd been given her marching orders, he'd experienced a wave of what he'd felt way back in the early days: stupidly he'd wanted to protect her.

He'd been surprised she'd accepted his offer to come to the pub with them, but he'd felt sorry for her sitting alone at her desk, abandoned by all those shits in management. Now here she was, hardly opening her mouth except to claim she hadn't seen *E.T.*

She was doing it for effect, Martin was sure of it. Putting herself above the whole conversation, which he'd only instigated to stop them all moaning on about fucking Maguire and fucking Qwertec, the fucking recession and the fucking government. There would have been no end to it if he hadn't forced a change of subject.

Paddy Mac, sitting up at his usual perch by the bar, kept turning round to check Katherine out, taking her in from head to toe with his half-pissed eyes. The guy with him – introduced to Martin as 'Frank McGinty's brother, Jim' – was doing the same. And who could blame them? She might be a pain in the hole ninety-nine point nine per cent of the time, but there was no denying she was drop-dead gorgeous.

She had class. Not the kind that came with money and grooming, even though she was always perfectly turned out, but the kind that was inbred. A heightening of the chin, a lifting of the cheekbones, the delicate movements of her long fingers, a general holding of herself that made her a cut above the average Jane. Even the tiny bump on the tip of her nose seemed perfectly placed.

Sometimes he tried to imagine her sprawled in front of the TV in sweatpants and a T-shirt, her dark-blonde hair loose around her shoulders instead of scraped back from her face into a tight bun, but the picture refused to form in his mind's eye. The Katherine he'd known from the moment she came to work at Qwertec just over a year ago, was always tailored, always flawless and in control, except for the night they'd gone to dinner with the Japanese clients. He could still remember the surprise of her laughter. It wasn't the delicate peal of bells he'd imagined but a loud, honking guffaw that shook her whole body and wouldn't stop. He remembered his chest all but puffing out with pride that he could make her laugh like that. Back then he'd thought he was in with a chance, but how wrong he'd been. What had happened after the Christmas party had proved that.

'I'm trying to think of the first film I ever watched,' said Jamie, 'but it could be any one of a dozen. I remember seeing *E.T.* in the cinema with my brothers, though. I hated every last minute of it.'

Martin gaped at him. 'There's something wrong with you, mate,' he said. 'Nobody could hate *E.T.*'

Jamie finished one bottle of Coors and lifted another. '*Star Wars* was ten times worse. How come all heterosexual males are obsessed with science fiction?'

'*E.T.* is a children's film, isn't it?' asked Lisa.

'Same difference,' said Jamie, as his phone bleeped another text message.

Although he didn't say so to the present company, Martin didn't give a shit about being sacked. He'd kind of drifted into Qwertec after college and the only thing his job had come to mean to him was a paypacket at the end of the month.

When people had asked him as a child, 'What do you want to be when you grow up?' he'd never had an answer. He was good with cars and had liked messing around with the engine of his mother's white Ford Fiesta when he was a teenager, but the expectation that he would follow in his father's footsteps and work in the family business after he'd finished school gave him no joy.

Now he had little choice. With the way things were right now,

Martin figured he was lucky to have the choice to work with his father. Nell had been urging him to do it for months, ever since Dad had had his 'turn', as their mother called it. So, really, he had the luxury of walking out of Qwertec and into Brady's Motors. Even if it didn't feel like a luxury.

7. Jamie's Choice

Of all the days, in all the months, in all the years, why, Jamie wondered, did he have to get fired today? Andrew was distraught, listening to the news about Qwertec every hour on the hour and texting Jamie at five-minute intervals, urging him to come home. Anyone would think he was the one who'd lost his job.

Trouble was, after weeks and weeks of working hard to secure a meeting, he'd finally arranged to hook up with the Iranian tonight. He knew it was his one window of opportunity. If he let it pass, it wouldn't happen. And it had to happen. If he didn't get to shag the Iranian, he'd explode, or implode, or go insane and open fire in a packed McDonald's.

Andrew had been the first person he'd called from his desk after his exit interview with Maguire.

'I told him what I thought of him and his rotten job,' Jamie had said, his breath catching in his throat. 'You should have seen the fucker's face!'

'I'd love to have been a fly on that wall,' said Andrew, and the two of them had laughed.

The truth was, though, that to his shame, Jamie hadn't opened his mouth. Although he'd been internally rehearsing a speech about the corrupt corporate system in which people were just flung aside in the name of capital gain, when it came to it he'd just sat nodding, like one of those dogs you saw on the dashboards of sad people's cars, while Maguire had insulted him, then outlined the details of the redundancy package. Afterwards he'd let himself out of the bastard's office without a word.

'You would have been so proud of me,' he had told Andrew. 'I stuck it to the man.'

'I *am* proud of you,' said Andrew, as the screen on Jamie's mobile lit up with a text.

It was from the Iranian.

Still on 4 tonite? 8, my plce. I wanna fck u hrd.

Jamie's stomach flipped. He'd started talking to the Iranian on Gaydar about a month ago, having come across his incredible profile and sent a private message. The Iranian's photographs showed the kind of guy you only saw in South American porn movies, square-jawed, unshaven, brown-skinned and incredibly buff, with a set of beautifully pumped-up pecs that were lightly covered with black hair. He was beefcake *cum laude*.

'And to show you how proud I am, I'm taking you to dinner at Chapter One tonight,' said Andrew. 'I'll make a reservation for eight o'clock, okay?'

'Chapter One? Don't you think that's a bit expensive?' Jamie said, to buy himself time.

He'd had a choice. A quiet, perfectly lovely dinner with Andrew, followed by some light cuddling before Andrew turned over, switched off the light and went to sleep on his side of the bed. Or mad, passionate, uncomplicated sex with a man who looked like a young Javier Bardem with the body of Daniel Craig, and was probably available for one night only. 'No strings,' the Iranian had insisted. Jamie knew this meant a once-only offer, which was fine by him. That was all he desperately needed. He'd not had sex, with Andrew or anyone else, for nine months and twenty-two days. And counting.

Jamie had eyed the screensaver of his computer, a picture of a topless Hugh Jackman, pouring a bucket of water over his perfectly toned body, and his loins responded with an urgent swell.

His phone had lit up again. The Iranian had sent him a picture message of his crotch, the tumescent outline of his dick clear beneath the white fabric of his underpants. Waiting 4 u, the accompanying text said.

'You know what?' he'd said to Andrew, suppressing a surge of guilt that threatened to steer him off the Iranian's course. 'Let's do dinner tomorrow night. I'm going for a drink with Lisa and a few of the others from work. We need to drown our sorrows.'

'You're right. Go for a drink with the gang,' said Andrew. 'I'll text you later to see if you've changed your mind.'

'There's no need. It'll probably be a late one.'

'And remember, everything will turn out just fine … I love you, Jamie.'

'I love you too,' Jamie had said, feeling a mixture of crushing shame and intense horniness.

Since then he'd been getting alternate texts from Andrew and the Iranian, his guilt at putting Andrew off turning to heart-pounding hunger as he texted filthy messages back to the Iranian.

A picture of what he assumed was the Iranian's hairy, perfectly globular arse appeared in his inbox as Katherine returned from the toilet where she'd spent the past half-hour. Her eyes were red-rimmed, her makeup streaked and the bun at the back of her neck was coming apart. Obviously she'd been crying.

It served Miss Ice Queen right. Jamie couldn't understand why Martin had invited her here in the first place. Didn't he know she'd been plotting against them all along?

Martin shoved up in the seat to let her sit down, his face a picture of concern. 'Are you all right? Can I get you anything?' he said.

Katherine shook her head and flashed one of her fake tight smiles. 'No, I'm fine, honestly,' she said.

There was silence. Then Martin raised his glass for another of his toasts. 'To freedom from the chains of Qwertec!'

'I'd napalm those offices if I could get my hands on the stuff,' said Jamie, not bothering to raise his glass.

'Napalm?' said Lisa. 'What's that?

'Vietnam,' Jamie said. 'Dissolves all organic matter. Little Vietnamese girl running for her life in black and white? Ring any bells?'

Lisa dipped her head and blushed, and Jamie felt a twinge of regret. Andrew was forever telling him to watch his tongue, that one of these days it would land him in boiling oil, never mind hot water. 'Sorry,' he said. 'I'm just a bit wound up.'

'That's okay,' said Lisa, giving him a little smile. She was always ready to forgive, which he found comforting and annoying in equal measure.

'Anyway, I'd bomb the place if I got half the chance,' said Jamie. 'Reduce it to rubble with Maguire inside. And all his memos.' Jamie knew he should be upset that Maguire had chosen him among the plebs to be dumped from the job, but he wasn't in the slightest. He hadn't a clue what the hell he was going to do once he was officially unemployed, but if he never had to be cooped up in a battery cubicle, staring at a computer screen again, he'd die happy.

'I've just realised,' said Lisa. 'After February, I'll never get another memo from Maguire.'

'Now that's something worth celebrating,' said Jamie.

'Memo to self,' said Martin, doing his impression of the old bastard. 'Must shave ears.'

'Oh, and his nose,' said Lisa. 'It was like a forest!'

'I'd say there are children leaving trails of breadcrumbs up those nostrils,' said Jamie. 'Poor things.'

'It's my birthday today,' Katherine blurted. 'I'm thirty-six.'

For a nanosecond, Jamie felt sorry for her. Even if they'd known it was her birthday, nobody in the office would have bought her a card or wished her happy returns – bar Lisa, who couldn't help being nice to everyone – because she was such a ball-busting bitch.

'Oh, you poor thing,' said Lisa, right on cue. 'Why didn't you tell us?'

'I don't know,' said Katherine. 'It didn't seem important, with everything else that's happened.'

'Not important?' said Martin. 'I'm ordering a bottle of champagne. We're going to have a proper celebration!'

Jamie didn't think he could stomach champagne on top of the six gassy bottles of Coors Light he'd already consumed, not to mention the shot of tequila they'd done while Katherine was in the bog. And he had good reason not to get too pissed.

His phone bleeped again with another picture message, this time of the Iranian licking his swollen lips, a madly sexy gleam in his eye. He looked dangerous, like he'd be an animal in bed. He was all of Jamie's fantasies come true in one hunk of man. Champagne or no champagne, he'd be able to perform for that.

8. What about Alice?

There was no champagne to be had in the pub, only a bottle of sparkling wine that wasn't even chilled. Still, Martin insisted on everyone singing 'Happy Birthday' as they raised their glasses. Even the two men at the bar joined in.

Katherine was filled with an almost itchy embarrassment at their faltering voices in the gloom of the pub, every eye trained in her direction, but at the same time she felt a small rush of pleasure. She couldn't have said why.

When the song died down, the barman switched on an ancient television that perched precariously on a bracket above the bar, possibly in an effort to discourage any more singing.

As Martin stood and toasted her birthday, and no more Maguire once again, her eye was drawn to a little white piece of shirt-tail that was sticking out of the top of his fly. For some reason, she found it so comical she laughed.

'What's funny?' Martin asked, but he was smiling at her.

'Nothing,' said Katherine, clamping a hand over her mouth. 'I'm a little tipsy, that's all.'

'Who isn't?' asked Jamie.

Katherine found herself on the verge of giggling again. It was like being on an emotional rollercoaster. One minute she was sitting on the edge of a filthy toilet, bawling her eyes out, the next she could barely contain her mirth. Biting her lip, she told herself to calm down. One more drink was her limit. What was it, four o'clock in the afternoon? She'd already had four.

'It's statistically proven,' Martin said, nearly knocking the table over as he fell back into his seat, 'that people who work together see each other for more time than they do their own families.'

'My poor children,' Lisa groaned into her wine. 'I'd better go home.'

Martin raised his glass. 'Here's to staying in touch after we leave,' he said, his words running into each other. 'Let's prove the bastards wrong.'

'Prove who wrong about what?' said Katherine. She was feeling a little less shaky now, although the piece of shirt-tail was still poking out of Martin's fly, threatening to throw her off balance again.

'We could a form book club and meet up regularly,' said Lisa. 'I read about other redundant people doing that in the Oprah magazine.'

'Book clubs are so last century, it's not funny,' said Jamie. 'I don't care what Oprah says.'

'A film club, then,' said Martin. 'What about watching films in each other's houses? We could choose our favourites.'

'The Redundancy Film Club,' said Lisa. Her black fringe looked lopsided.

'The Forced Redundancy Film Club,' said Martin, his glass still raised. 'Since we have no choice in the matter.' He turned to Katherine. 'Are you in?'

To her surprise, Katherine found herself tempted to say yes. But it was too much of a commitment, considering she'd have to get another job and would probably have to work more than ever. And she couldn't imagine herself visiting their houses, or having them over to hers. She was their boss, she reminded herself. She had nothing in common with any of them.

'I don't know,' she said. 'I'm not sure it sounds like my kind of thing.'

'Why not?' said Martin. 'Doesn't everyone like movies?'

'There are so many,' said Lisa. ' *Grease* . . . *Titanic* . . . *The Sound of Music* . . .'

'Ah, Jesus, no way. I'm not sitting through any of that bollocks,' said Martin. 'We'll watch quality films only. Classics.'

'But *The Sound of Music* is a classic.'

'Yeah, a classic piece of shit.'

The way he said it, his tone, set Katherine's teeth on edge and she remembered him at that dinner with the Japanese, mopping up the remainder of his sauce with the extra round of bread he'd ordered. 'You guys should definitely go for it,' she said. 'But count me out.'

Lisa hiccuped. 'Ah, come on,' she said, 'It wouldn't be right without you.'

'I'll second that,' said Martin, looking at her directly. 'Can we have a show of hands?' He and Lisa put theirs in the air.

'There,' said Martin. 'Now you have to be in the club. It's you … you know … ' He was slurring again.

'Unanimous,' said Jamie. 'And it's not.'

Over Martin's shoulder, the flickering TV screen drew Katherine's eye. A scene of turmoil was playing out on Sky News, with people crying and wobbly camera angles. Along the bottom of the screen a strip of text announced there had been a suicide bombing at a market in Afghanistan. A close-up of an anguished woman in a black headscarf showed the exact expression that Katherine had seen on Alice Little's face earlier that day.

Before he had left, Katherine had a vague memory of her father once telling her, 'There's always someone worse off than you, Kit Kat,' and he was right. When Alice had blurted out that her mother had just died, Katherine had reeled as if she'd been belted with a blunt instrument. She had felt an urge to walk away quickly, but this had been followed by an impulse to go to Alice and hug her. But that was unthinkable for all sorts of reasons. So, instead she'd stood beside Alice's desk and said, 'I'm sorry.' There was nothing else to say.

Alice had stood up abruptly, banging her knee off the desk. 'I have to go to the hospice,' she said. 'They need me to sign some papers.'

'I'll go with you,' Katherine said, without thinking. Who else was there to go with Alice to say goodbye to her dead mother? Katherine knew the father was dead too, the office had signed a sympathy card last January. She'd heard from Lisa that Alice was an only child, which wasn't surprising when you thought about it.

'No,' Alice said. 'That won't be necessary.'

'Are you sure? I can drive you.'

'No, but thank you for offering.'

Alice buttoned her coat up to the neck and Katherine watched her walk down the corridor, head bowed, hair drooping. Halfway to the lift, she turned and called, 'Will you tell Mr Maguire I had to go?'

Katherine pictured Alice now, standing beside her silent mother's hospice bed, the yellow butterfly bobby pin still in her hair. 'I'll join the club if Alice can join too,' she said.

'Alice?' said Jamie. 'You're kidding, right?'

'I've never been more serious.'

Martin shook his head. 'I think I'd prefer to watch *The Sound of Music*,' he said. 'Every month.'

'Alice's mother died this morning.'

'I heard,' said Lisa. 'The poor thing. Maybe we *should* invite her.'

'Listen to yourselves,' said Martin. 'This is Alice we're talking about. She hasn't even lost her job. It's supposed to be the Forced Redundancy Film Club, remember?'

'Have it your way,' said Katherine. 'You don't include Alice, you don't get me.'

Martin looked from Katherine to Jamie and Lisa and back again. 'Okay,' he said. 'Alice is in.'

'There isn't a snowball's chance in hell Alice is going to want in anyway,' said Jamie. 'Emily Dickinson wouldn't have a patch on that recluse.'

'Leave Alice to me,' said Katherine. She was beginning to feel a little more grounded, as if she had just taken on a project.

'So, we're all agreed?' said Lisa. 'Alice and Katherine are on board, and we're going ahead?'

'I'm only going along for the ride,' said Jamie. 'I'm jumping ship the minute it gets boring.'

'Fair enough,' said Martin, looking at Katherine rather than Jamie. 'So, you're definitely in?

'Yes,' Katherine said. 'I'm in.'

The inaugural meeting, it was decided, would be in Martin's apartment at the end of February, after the redundancies had been enforced. He was eager to be the first and said he knew exactly which film he was going to show.

'It's a surprise,' he laughed, after downing his pint. 'But I think you'll all like it. Even Alice No-mates.'

It was probably the billionth sequel to *Star Wars*, Katherine thought. Or, worse, one of those *American Pie* movies. She could just imagine him loving that kind of terrible trash.

February

Casablanca

Michael Curtiz, 1942

'I think this is the beginning
of a beautiful friendship.'

9. An Awkward Beginning

Martin's flat was and wasn't what Katherine had thought it would be. Built before apartment developments in the city centre had become stacked shoeboxes, it was a nicely proportioned first-floor space, divided into three fairly generous rooms. The carpet was mushroom, every wall was magnolia and the only form of decorative art was a framed poster for *Pulp Fiction* above a *faux*-marble fireplace. A shelving unit in the alcove held at least five hundred DVDs and there were further stacks in random piles around the place.

The main thing that stood out to Katherine when she first stepped into the apartment, however, was that it didn't smell of cigarettes. She had expected the place to reek.

There was a stupidly awkward moment when it was unclear whether they should kiss each other hello on the cheek or shake hands, which Martin broke by saying, 'Will I take your jacket?'

'Thanks,' said Katherine, shucking it off her shoulders. Without it, her arms, in their short, puffed sleeves, felt naked.

'You're looking good,' said Martin.

She'd spent an hour choosing what to wear before coming out and had eventually settled on an olive green Chanel-style suit she'd bought in a vintage shop in London's Notting Hill last summer, with a Christian Dior neck-tied blouse. Now she thought she looked too formal.

She handed over the wine she'd chosen from Barry's collection. 'It's a New Zealand shiraz. I don't know if it's any good.'

'Thanks very much,' said Martin, glancing at the bottle's label. He had clearly made an effort to dress up for the occasion too, although there was a small reddish stain – ketchup? baked beans? – on the front of his otherwise pristine white shirt. And his permanent five o'clock shadow was now more like seven o'clock, snaking down his neck.

When she'd first met him, she'd thought he'd be vaguely handsome if he lost maybe twenty pounds. He had big ears and a dimpled chin that jutted out like a shelf under full lips, but the rest of his face was well structured, with a Roman nose and strong, dark, copper-coloured eyebrows that peaked over intelligent blue eyes. In the intervening time all his oddly assembled features appeared to have blended together into one undistinguished mass behind an ever-present half-beard and a dishevelled head of muddy-ginger curls.

'Lisa's here,' he said. 'We're waiting for Jamie and Alice.' His breath smelt of Listerine.

'I hope Alice comes,' said Katherine. 'She didn't sound too enthusiastic when I talked to her this afternoon.'

The door buzzer went. 'That might be her now,' Martin said. 'Go on through. Lisa's having a fag on the terrace.'

The 'terrace' was a tiny metal-framed balcony off the living room that at a push might hold four people standing up. It looked down on the Liffey, which had risen so high with all the rain of the past few days that it sounded like rapids flowing by.

'Hi, Lisa,' Katherine said, standing by the half-open glass door, out of the way of the smoke.

'Oh, Katherine, you're here.' Lisa smiled, blowing a blue cloud into the chill February air. 'Wow, I love the blouse. It's very *Mad Men*.' Lisa was wearing a polo-necked sweater that was the same black as her hair and a pair of shapeless black trousers. Draped across the mass of her chest was a necklace made of chunks of turquoise plastic. Not for the first time, Katherine imagined taking Lisa shopping. She could do with losing a few pounds, but she still had a good hourglass shape that would be far better off accentuated with plunging collars, tucked waists, and less of the cheap jewellery. The ebony bob would have to go as well. She was too old for it.

'How do you like being a stay-at-home mum?' Katherine asked.

'It's weird,' said Lisa. 'I wake up every morning in a panic, thinking I have to be somewhere, and then I remember I don't. The day stretches out in front of me.'

Katherine knew what she meant. It was less than a month since those terrible final hours in the office, and already her days seemed eternally long, filled with a kind of bewildered nothingness.

At first she was gung-ho, carefully updating her CV and sending it to every company she could think might employ her, calling every contact she had in the computer and consulting businesses to let them know she was back on the market. She put her name down with every agency and scoured the Internet for job opportunities each morning, sending her CV off for those too. When all that was done, she used her new-found free time to catch up on all the things she had left hanging at home.

She cleaned the house from top to bottom, rearranging furniture and changing the location of pictures on the walls. She went into the attic and put some shape on the mess up there, sorting out the tangles of Christmas decorations dumped back in cardboard boxes once the season was over. She found photographs from various holidays she'd taken with the girls back in college days, and Barry in their first years together, and took them downstairs, carefully sorting them out into chronological albums. Then she got to work on the garden shed, throwing out piles of junk Barry had amassed in the two and a half years they'd had the house, even though they'd been in the house less than a year. She weeded and dug the garden beds, getting them ready for spring. She took every non-perishable food item out of the kitchen cupboards and put it all back in again in a new, easy-to-find order. There seemed to be no end of jobs to get her teeth into, until one morning two weeks in she woke up and discovered she had absolutely nothing to do.

Trying not to give in to blind panic, she sat at the breakfast table with her cup of tea and took long, deep breaths. Then, when she felt calmer, she called Marissa.

'What do you actually do with your days once you're on top of the housework?' she asked.

Marissa laughed. 'What do you mean, once I'm on top of it? I'm never on top of it. I'm always chasing my own tail.'

'I've done everything. The house is spotless and there's nothing else to do.'

'Well,' said Marissa, her voice going up a semi-tone at the end of the word, 'when you have children, it's different.'

Katherine had tried to get all three girls together for lunch a few times since finishing work, but either Marissa couldn't make it and Jean could, or Olive couldn't and Marissa could. In the end she'd met them separately, and on each occasion they had brought at least one of their children, which didn't leave much room for talk about threatened panic attacks.

At each lunch, Olive, Jean and Marissa had complained about not having any time for themselves because of their kids, but at the same time they seemed to be saying their children were the best thing that had ever happened to them.

Katherine sensed they all talked behind her back about her concentrating on her career instead of starting a family. Olive, she believed, blamed Barry. She'd never said it directly, but was always making digs at him for supposedly forcing Katherine around to his point of view, the nature of which was never explained. Jean was given to saying things like, 'poor Katherine,' every now and then, while smiling indulgently at her pudgy, red-faced little George. Only Marissa voiced her disapproval in so many words.

'Don't come crying to me when find yourself in your forties and desperate to get pregnant,' she said, to which Katherine replied, 'There are some women, believe it or not, who don't actually want children. It is possible.'

She could tell Marissa didn't believe she was one of them. She wasn't sure she believed it herself. There were times when she looked at the girls' toddlers with curiosity, or at infants being pushed in buggies along the street, wondering what it would be like to have a child; what it would be like to be a mother. But she never felt broody or heard the clock ticking. Barry's philosophical rejection of parenthood, his belief that there were too many children in the world as it was, suited her in a way: it allowed her not to confront the sheer enormity of motherhood head on. Still, there was part of her that wondered whether she'd change her mind and start producing babies if Barry got over his philosophical rejection of marriage ('It turns women into chattels') and they tied the knot. She had a few more years in her yet.

She hung up, shaking her head at Marissa's advice to get a facial to take her mind of things.

'A little pampering, that's what's needed at times like these,' she'd insisted. It didn't seem to strike Marissa that facials were a luxury Katherine couldn't afford.

And then the empty day stretched out in front of her.

'I find I've plenty to do with my days,' Katherine said now, smiling at Lisa, who stubbed her cigarette out on the terrace with the toe of her shoe. 'I never realised I had so much to catch up on.'

'You and me both,' said Martin, arriving with Jamie in tow. 'I've hardly had time to fart since starting back at the garage.'

Jamie had shaved off his goatee and was now wearing a moustache. On someone else it would have looked ridiculous, but it made him even more impossibly square-jawed and handsome. Lisa was always saying, 'what a waste!' which Katherine thought was kind of insulting to gay people, even if it was true about Jamie.

He was deeply involved in sending a text message and Alice was following him, clutching her bag with both hands. Katherine was struck by the fact that, apart from at Alice's mother's funeral, she had never seen her outside the office. Although she was wearing her standard outfit – blue cardigan, white blouse and grey A-line skirt – she looked a little less uniform. Maybe it was the traffic-light red lipstick.

'The first rule of Film Club is we don't talk about the recession,' Martin said, straightening up mismatched bowls of nachos and dips on the coffee table. 'The second rule of Film Club is we don't talk about the bloody recession.'

'What recession?' said Jamie, plonking himself on one of Martin's black leatherette armchairs.

'Sit anywhere you like,' Martin said to Katherine. 'I'll get you a glass of vino. Red or white?'

'Red, please,' she said, hoping he'd uncork the wine she'd brought. It was one of Barry's best bottles. She made a beeline for the other armchair, not wanting to be squeezed up beside anyone on the two-seater couch.

'So, what are we watching?' asked Jamie.

'*Casablanca*,' said Martin, setting down some wine glasses. 'The one and only.'

Jamie filled his glass to the brim with Katherine's shiraz. 'High romance and Nazi uniforms, my favourite combination,' he said, kicking his shoes off.

'You're in a good mood,' Lisa told him.

'I am, aren't I? It's a whole new me.'

'I've never seen the attraction,' said Katherine. 'Of *Casablanca*, I mean.'

'Have you ever actually sat down and watched it from beginning to end?' asked Martin.

'Of course I have. Maybe it's Humphrey Bogart. He doesn't do anything for me. It's those rubbery lips and sticky-out ears. He's sort of ugly.'

'But in a good way,' said Lisa. 'There's something more to him than looks. He's got great screen presence. Don't you think so?' This question was aimed squarely at Alice, who was sitting on a corner of the couch, holding her handbag on her lap.

'I don't know,' she said. 'I've never seen any of his films.'

'Well, you're in for a major treat,' said Martin, sitting down at the other end of the couch with a bottle of beer. 'Apart from *The Maltese Falcon*, this is Bogey at his best by a long shot.'

'I love him in *African Queen*,' said Lisa. 'I remember watching it one Sunday afternoon by the fire with Patrick, before the kids came along. It was unbelievably romantic. And I adore anything with Katherine Hepburn in it. She's probably my favourite actress of all time. Apart from Meryl Streep. And Kate Winslet … Oh, and –'

'For the love of Jesus, somebody press play,' said Jamie.

10. House and Home

To her surprise, Katherine found herself lost in *Casablanca* almost as soon as the overture began. Although its opening was violent, there was something comfortingly staged about the film. And she was wrong about Humphrey Bogart. In his white dinner jacket and dickie bow, holding a cigarette between his thumb and forefinger, he was incredibly watchable. You forgot all about rubbery lips and sticky-out ears.

She tried to remember the last time she'd seen it. Maybe it was early on, when she'd first been going out with Barry and they'd liked to watch old movies together on Friday nights in Katherine's little flat. They'd go to the video shop on Capel Street, get a bottle of wine from the off-licence downstairs and a takeaway from the Chinese next door. Without exception, Barry ordered sweet and sour pork with egg fried rice. He was a creature of habit.

Katherine could picture him still, sitting on the red sofa,

hunched over his plate and digging into his food, talking in fast bursts between bites while whatever film they had rented played on the TV. He'd had thick short-back-and-sides blond hair back then – it bleached almost snow white in the height of summer – and he was beginning to put on muscle, working out at the university gym at six thirty every morning. He was ambitious: the money was in management consultancy he'd told her, and that was where he was going the minute he finished college.

When he'd first asked Katherine out, she couldn't believe it: just about every other girl in first-year BComm had had her eye on him. He was one of the crowd right at the centre of the students' union bar, laughing uproariously at jokes only they were in on, the girls drinking vodka and Diet Coke, the boys slapping each other on the back.

Katherine had been in college for six months before he had taken any notice of her, although she had spotted him early on, steadily charting his course through shoals of freshers, sure of who he was and why he was there. On their first date he told her she had style and and he thought they looked good together and Katherine found herself blushing with gratification. With Barry she was one of the crowd laughing in the centre of the bar. Becoming his girlfriend had conferred a new social status on her, something she didn't even know she'd craved before she got it.

Suddenly she had friends. Marissa, Jean and Olive were going out with Barry's best mates, Spencer, Will and Sean, and overnight Katherine was one of 'the girls'. Unlike Barry or his friends, she had had to struggle to get to university and scrimped to stay there, but they didn't seem to notice or care. After a while, she began to feel as good as they were.

Barry helped her move into the flat over the off-licence at the beginning of her second year, and after that he stayed with her almost every night, going home to his mum's only for Sunday dinner. It was a hovel, really, that flat, in a grimy part of town, but Katherine ripped up the old, stained carpets and spent days layering whitewash on the floorboards. She spotted an overstuffed red sofa that she knew would look perfect on the expanse of white floor and Barry paid for it in one go, ripping out a cheque and insisting she take it. In the months that followed she filled the walls and shelves with the paintings and trinkets she rummaged for in the secondhand shops on Capel Street.

That flat. Katherine felt such a stab of nostalgia when she thought about it. More often than not there was no hot water and there were damp stains on the bathroom walls, but life had seemed so much simpler there. The rent was minuscule compared to what they were shelling out in mortgage payments today; there had been only college and Barry to think about; and their whole future had seemed mapped out without a crossroads in sight.

'You can't help wondering what happened to Ilsa and her husband,' said Lisa, dabbing her eyes as the end credits for *Casablanca* rolled. 'Did they get to America? Or did the Nazis track them down?'

'It was made in 1942,' said Martin, cracking open another beer from his six-pack on the floor. 'That's three years before the war was over. Think about it. Nobody knew if the Nazis were going to win or not.'

'I don't care about all that.' Lisa sighed. 'It's a love story, not a stupid war film.'

'I really wanted Rick to go off with Ilsa at the end,' said Katherine. 'It seems all wrong that she stays with her husband.' She was feeling a bit merry after too much wine and was keeping herself in check. She didn't want to slur.

'But the problems of two little people don't amount to a hill of beans in this crazy world,' said Martin, in his best Humphrey Bogart voice, and Katherine let out a loud guffaw.

Jamie turned to her, alarmed, as if he thought she were cracked in the head.

'The song is so beautiful,' said Lisa. '"As Time Goes By." Patrick and I used to have a song like that when we were first going out. What was it again?'

'I didn't like him,' said Alice. Everyone turned to her.

'Who?' asked Martin.

'Rick.'

'Do you know?' said Lisa, swirling the wine in her glass. 'For the life of me, I can't remember what our song was.'

'He has no morals,' Alice continued. 'He's selfish.'

Katherine's cheeks felt a prickly red from the heat of the fire. 'He's only putting on an act of being selfish,' she said. 'Inside he's got a heart of gold.'

'But he lets that man get arrested at the beginning. And he knows he'll probably be killed. And he keeps those papers he gave him.'

'What the hell?' said Martin. 'You've completely missed the point. The guy who got arrested was hardly St Francis of Assisi.'

Alice put her glass down on the coffee table. 'I don't think I missed the point,' she said. 'You don't know whose side Rick is on, even at the end when he goes off with that awful police captain.'

'I know!' said Lisa. 'It was 'How Deep Is Your Love' by the Bee Gees ...'

'*Saturday Night Fever,*' said Martin. 'Probably one of the most underrated films of all time.'

'It was on the radio in the taxi when he left me home after our first date, and we sang along,' said Lisa. 'I bet Patrick doesn't even remember ...'

'I think he's gay,' said Jamie.

Lisa gave a high-pitched giggle. 'Patrick might be a lot of things, but he's certainly not gay.'

Jamie shot her a poker-faced look. 'I'm talking about Rick,' he said.

'Yeah, right,' said Martin. 'You think everyone's gay.'

'No, listen,' said Jamie. 'When Ilsa first comes into Rick's Café, Captain Renault says that if he was a woman he would be in love with Rick. And Rick ends up walking into the sunset with the captain, rather than Ilsa, like they were a match made in homo heaven. Bet the captain's on top.'

'I think Ilsa's the selfish one,' Katherine said, with a yawn. She felt like taking off her shoes and curling her feet up under her, but she'd seen the beginning of a hole in the toe of her tights when she'd put them on earlier and she worried now that it might be gaping. 'She's the one who wants everything her way,' she added.

Martin gave a gruff laugh and popped the cap on another beer. 'Having her big affair with Rick and then dumping him like a hot potato,' he said.

'But she was afraid that if she told him the truth about her husband, he would have stayed and the Nazis would have arrested him,' said Lisa. 'She was doing it for the right reasons.'

'There is no right reason to be all over someone like a rash and not tell them you're with someone else,' Martin replied.

Katherine felt his eyes on her and shifted uncomfortably in her chair.

11. A Kiss Is Just a Kiss

Looking back, Katherine still couldn't say what had come over her. She had never been unfaithful to Barry – the very idea had never even crossed her mind. But at the Christmas party, when she'd found herself alone with Martin in that hotel corridor, laughing uncontrollably at some stupid joke of his, he had taken her face in his hands, put his lips to hers and she hadn't fought it. She'd pressed her body to his, as if it were something she'd do at the drop of a hat, not even caring about the heavy taste of cigarettes in his mouth.

Somewhere in the middle of it, though, she'd become aware of his stubble rubbing against her chin – Barry *never* had stubble – and had woken up to what she was doing. She'd pulled away. 'I'm sorry, I can't.'

'Why not?' Martin said. 'We're both grown-ups.' He had a big, sloppy grin on his face and was slurring his words.

Katherine had felt a stab of anger towards him. She hadn't asked for that or given any hint that she was interested in him. She smoothed down her skirt, which had ridden up her thighs a little. 'Yes,' she said, with a stiff smile. 'We're both grown-ups.' And although her legs had faltered, she'd walked away.

'Where are you off to?' he'd called after her. 'Ah, come on … Come back.' But he hadn't followed her, and she hadn't turned around.

The following Monday he'd come up to her in the canteen, put his tray on her table and said, 'Jamie told me you have a boyfriend. Is that true?'

'Yes, it is. Why?'

'Why didn't you tell me?'

'You didn't give me a chance,' said Katherine.

'I don't regret it,' he said. 'Kissing you.'

'Well, I do.'

She hadn't been able to get the taste of smoke out of her mouth. It had lingered all weekend, and when Barry had woken her up for Sunday-morning sex, she'd worried that he'd taste it off her.

Martin had turned to go, but then swung back. 'I don't believe you,' he said.

'Look, I'm sorry if you mistook my being friendly for something else,' Katherine replied. 'We were both very drunk.'

'I still don't believe you,' said Martin, fixing his stare on her.

Katherine had folded her arms. 'I don't care whether you

believe me or not. But one thing's for sure. It won't happen again.'

'Fair enough,' said Martin, folding his arms too and not moving from his spot. He had looked as if he was mocking her, which had made her hackles rise.

'You took advantage of me,' she said. 'And since we have to work on the same team together, I suggest we don't have this conversation again. It could make things very awkward.'

'Don't worry,' he said, picking up his tray. 'I won't make things awkward for you.'

She had felt a pang of regret as he'd walked away. He hadn't done anything wrong, really, and maybe there had been no need to be so mean to him. But he had to get the message. Nothing was ever going to happen between them.

That had been more than a year ago, and Martin had been true to his word. He'd never mentioned it again, hardly ever talking to her beyond the boundaries of business. Although sometimes she caught him looking at her in a way that made her glad she'd put him off as she had.

His voice was teetering on the verge of a shout now as he leaned in from the terrace doors while holding a lit cigarette outside, still going on about Rick and Ilsa. 'They never have sex,' he said, 'but there's animal lust between them.'

'And her husband only kisses her on the cheek,' added Jamie. 'No wonder she's gagging for it.'

Katherine yawned again and stood up. 'I don't know about the rest of you,' she said, 'but I'm absolutely exhausted.'

'What's your hurry?' asked Martin. 'The night is still young.'

He was patently drunk.

'We can share a taxi,' Alice said to Katherine, standing up too. She was still clutching her handbag.

'Great,' said Katherine, although sharing a cab with Alice across the city was not an appealing prospect.

'Who's next?' Lisa said. 'And what film are we going to watch?'

Nobody put their hand up.

'What about Katherine?' Jamie said, as Martin glumly flopped back on to the couch and opened himself another beer. 'We can get to see the big new fancy house.'

'It's not that big. It's in a terrace,' Katherine said, feeling inexplicably defensive, as if the home she'd put so much loving care into was something to be ashamed of.

'In Ranelagh,' said Jamie. 'Dublin's answer to Beverly Hills.'

'I'm dying to see what you've done to the place,' said Lisa, clapping her hands together.

'It's nothing fancy. Just a plain, ordinary house.'

'Yeah, right,' said Jamie. 'And the Pope is heterosexual.'

12. The Fundamental Things Apply

In the taxi on the way home, Alice became unusually talkative. She was full of how luminous Ingrid Bergman had looked in the movie, what a nice flat Martin had, how she had drunk too much wine . . . though Katherine hadn't seen her drink anything other than 7-Up all evening.

Then, as instantly as she had lit up, Alice became silent and turned to look out of the rain-speckled window. 'I wanted to thank you,' she said, 'for coming to the funeral.'

'I was glad to be there,' Katherine said.

'No one else from the office came.'

'Mr Maguire was there,' Katherine reminded her.

He had bolted the minute the Presbyterian service ended, leaving Katherine to go to the graveyard alone. She would have left with him, but outside the church Alice had given her a tearful smile and Katherine had understood how much her presence meant to her. She had surrendered herself to staying until the very end.

A huddle of mismatched mourners in anoraks had dotted the graveside. They'd looked like they read the obituaries for the latest funeral to attend. Katherine had thought of her own mother, living only a few hours' flight away in Valencia, but at the same time so far distant she might as well have been on another planet.

What would Mum's funeral be like? Would there be tearful goodbyes and long-awaited words of love on her deathbed? Or would she just pass away as she did everything else – in her own time, in her own way, with no particular need to contact her children?

After the vicar had said his final prayers, a bent, blue-rinsed old woman, wearing an improbable Barbie-pink coat and matching hat, had followed Alice in throwing a handful of clay on to the coffin. Then the few mourners had walked away in silence, like extras in a video for 'Eleanor Rigby'. There hadn't been a lunch organised or even coffee in the vicarage afterwards.

'They don't really like me,' said Alice, as the taxi drove on. 'I don't think they wanted me there tonight.'

'Of course they did. They wouldn't have asked you to join the club if they didn't like you.'

'You're different,' Alice said. 'You understand.'

Uneasy as it made her feel, Katherine knew what Alice was referring to: their equal lack of popularity at Qwertec. But she hadn't been unpopular in the way Alice was. The people at work didn't like Katherine for no other reason than that she was a strong manager who set the bar high. Alice was more like an untouchable. There was something off-putting about her. A kind of loneliness you wanted to steer well clear of, as if it threatened contagion.

Katherine was getting out of the taxi first, so she dug into her bag and found she had only a twenty-euro note to give to Alice to pay for her part of the journey. She handed it over, hoping she might get some change.

'Thank you,' said Alice, putting the money into her own bag and snapping it closed. 'See you next month.'

As Katherine took off her shoes in the hallway, she thought of how things had changed. A month ago, twenty euro would have seemed like small change. Now she was worrying about spending it on a taxi.

'Is that you, babes?' Barry called down from the bedroom.

'Who else would it be?' Katherine sighed, mounting the stairs.

He was sitting up in bed in the awful maroon pyjamas he'd bought with the Marks & Spencer's gift voucher his mother had given him for Christmas, a book balanced on his chest. It was Lord Sugar's autobiography. She had a brief vision of Barry, stiff-collared in *The Apprentice* boardroom, fighting tooth and nail for his place in the final, and it comforted her a little. With Barry she was safe. He was a man who survived at all costs.

'How was your night?' Barry said, without looking up from his book.

'So-so. We watched *Casablanca*. Martin got a bit obnoxious. He drinks too much, I think.'

'Arsehole,' said Barry, even though he'd never met Martin.

The twenty-euro note came into Katherine's head again. She sat down on the edge of the bed. 'Barry,' she said, 'the mortgage payment is due on Monday.'

'Is it?'

'I don't know how I'm going to pay my half.'

'You've got the redundancy money, babes.'

'One month's salary. That's hardly going to set the world alight. And they haven't made a decision on my statutory redundancy yet.'

Barry shut the book and gave her a questioning look, then lay down. He opened his arms. 'Come here,' he said.

Katherine stretched across the bed and laid her face on his chest. It felt sturdy, like a rock.

'I've never seen you like this,' Barry said, his arm around her, fingers stroking her shoulder. 'So needy.'

'I'm scared, Barry,' said Katherine. The admission made her heart beat hard. 'It's not only the mortgage, it's the bills. You know how much it all adds up to. And, right now, I've no way of contributing.'

'Babes, you of all people should know it's not worth being scared over money – sure, that's the first sign you're losing the game. Money comes, it goes, it comes again. You have to just roll with it. Can't you pay your share of the mortgage with your credit card this time?'

'But how will I pay off my credit-card bill?'

'Look, just stop worrying, will you?' he said, taking his arm from underneath her and shifting over. Then he stroked her hair. 'Everything's going to be fine, babes, I know it.'

She snuggled further into him. 'Maybe you're right,' she said, feeling a tiny glimmer of hope.

'Of course I'm right! Trust me, I'm a management consultant.' Barry let out a loud guffaw, and with it, the ray of hope Katherine had felt was replaced by a hardening of the dread that had lodged in her belly since the day she'd lost her job.

They lay in silence for a few minutes. 'Barry?' Katherine said eventually. 'We might have to pool our resources for a while. You know, just until I'm back on my feet.'

There was no reply.

'Barry?' Katherine repeated, lifting her head.

He was fast asleep, snoring lightly, his mouth half open.

Katherine unwound herself from underneath his arm and went into the en-suite to clean her teeth.

The vibration of the electric toothbrush in her mouth was familiar, but when she caught her reflection in the gilt-framed mirror above the washbasin, her eyes looked like those of a frightened animal.

13. You Must Remember This

Alice did not believe in ghosts. The shadow standing in the bay window of the bedroom on the first floor was a figment of her imagination.

Leave me alone, she said inwardly, peering through the window of the taxi at the unmoving shape behind the net curtain. It wasn't the first time she'd noticed it.

'That'll be twelve euros,' the taxi driver said, bringing her back to her senses.

Alice opened her bag and saw Katherine's blue twenty-euro note. Alice never usually had a reason to get taxis. She had entirely overestimated what it would cost. She'd fix Katherine up next time.

The house was bitterly cold when she let herself in. She switched on the hall lamp with its energy-saving bulb and a dim pool of jaundiced light emerged. Mrs Silver had advised her to leave the heating and the television on when she was out, during the winter at least. 'It would make the place more welcoming,' she insisted. But that was wasteful, and weren't the environmentalists always saying you shouldn't even leave your television in standby mode?

Alice went into the kitchen and filled the kettle for her hot-water bottle. She'd go up and turn on the Calor-gas heater she'd brought into her room after Mother had gone into the hospice, get it nice and warm and snuggle up with her book. If she still wasn't into it after another fifty pages, she'd discard it and start another tomorrow.

Above her head a floorboard creaked. Alice stood still with the kettle in her hand and listened for it to happen again. Nothing. It was an old house, full of creaks and groans at night. Best not to let her imagination run away with her.

She'd watched an episode of that television show with Mrs Silver last week, the one where people wandered around an abandoned house in the dark searching for ghostly presences, their eyes lit by infrared cameras so that they looked like hunted animals. That was why she was thinking like this. Every time they heard the slightest noise, the people on the show screamed as if the devil himself had just appeared, and Mrs Silver giggled into her cocoa.

'I don't know why you're laughing,' Alice had said. 'It gives me the creeps.'

'It's only make-believe, dear,' Mrs Silver replied, as the TV people had huddled together in fear. 'Don't they look funny?'

Only make-believe. Mother wasn't back to haunt her. She was gone and Alice was alone.

Everything had happened much faster than the doctors had predicted. They'd given her a year, eighteen months at the outside, but within four months she had failed so much that Alice was coming home from work to basins of vomit, wet sheets and bitter tears rolling down an emaciated face that bore hardly any resemblance to that of the woman she'd known.

When the district nurse had first suggested the hospice, Alice had been adamant that Mother should be allowed the dignity to stay in her own home. But the only way that could happen was if Alice took a leave of absence from work. She was fully aware that major cuts were coming in a few months and of how they would play out. Mr Maguire had been pointing out this or that person, saying they would be off the payroll when the time came. If she took any protracted amount of time off, he'd get rid of her too, she knew it. Only by staying close to him, being his eyes and ears, making sure his every single *i* was dotted and *t* crossed, could she be almost certain she would still have a job by the end of the year.

So she had gone to see the people in the hospice and they couldn't have been more understanding. And Mother, whom she expected to object to the betrayal of being cast off, had seemed relieved when the time came to leave the house.

'Take care of my owls,' she had told Alice, as two male nurses supported her down the garden path towards the waiting ambulance. She'd thought she would be coming back.

Alice had gone every evening to see her and twice a day at weekends, taking her nightdresses and underwear home to wash, holding her hand through hours of silence, every so often punctuated with a murmur for water or a sob of pain when the morphine ran low. Mother, who had been taciturn with Alice at the best of times in the full of her health, had become as speechless as a statue in her final decline. Every evening before she had left the side of the bed, Alice would kiss her papery cheek and say, 'I love you.' But Mother had never whispered it back.

Now that she was gone, there was no washing of nighties and underwear to be done. No visits to the hospice, no talking with the doctors about the best course of action, no sitting and stroking what was left of Mother's snow-white hair. The only thing that punctuated the free time was going over the back garden wall to bring Mrs Silver her dinner every evening, a duty Alice had taken up when Mother had left off after she'd become ill.

As Alice screwed on the lid of her hot-water bottle, pushing the sides together to get all the air out, the clock on the mantelpiece rang out. It was midnight. In her mind's eye she pictured Mother's collection of owls on every surface of the sitting room, their glass eyes all staring intently ahead. Each had its own place, the favourite, a handcarved and painted wooden owl wearing little wire-framed spectacles, at the centre of a row on top of the television, a gift from some nameless Brownie the year Mother had become Brown Owl.

At the turn of the stair, she thought she heard something from Mother's bedroom at the front of the house, a kind of shuffling noise.

'Don't be ridiculous,' she told herself aloud. 'There's no one there.'

She didn't want to go into that room, had hardly been inside it since Mother had left, but Alice knew she wouldn't be able to sleep unless she made sure she was alone in the house. It was that stupid television programme.

Turning the door handle, she took a deep breath and pushed it open, its hinges whining with age. She realised her heart was beating heavily against her ribs as she fumbled for the light switch.

The room was empty and still, and all of Mother's things were exactly as she had left them, the dusty pink eiderdown on the bed, the dressmaker's doll unclothed in the corner. Alice was turning to leave when something caught her eye. On the dressing-table with its chipped mirror and white lace doilies, the silver-framed photograph of her parents, which had stood there all her life, was lying face down. She couldn't remember it being in that position before.

A shiver made its way down her spine as Alice lifted the photograph up and put it back in place. It had been taken on the Isle of Man during their honeymoon. Her father, looking at something to his left, appeared distant, as if he wasn't fully present in the moment. Mother, with her head leaning on his shoulder, seemed happier than Alice ever remembered seeing her in real life. Her hair was thick and glossy under a hat with a peacock feather, and on her full mouth she wore dark lipstick, her teeth flashing white in a big, happy smile, with no hint of what lay underneath the surface.

Alice switched off the light and closed the door behind her. She went into her own room, undressed quickly and decided against turning on the gas heater. She got into her cold bed, pushing her hot-water bottle down under the sheets with her feet. After trying to read for a while, but getting nowhere, she gave up and lay back to think.

Even though she had felt as out of place as she'd expected she would, she had enjoyed the night. Lisa and Katherine had been friendly, and Martin, to whom she had never spoken properly before, was attentive, topping up her a glass whenever it ran low. He'd made her a white wine spritzer, as well as Lisa – wine mixed with 7-Up. It had tasted quite nice and gone straight to her head.

The best thing about the evening, though, was Ingrid Bergman. Of course Alice had heard of *Casablanca*, but it had never sounded like her cup of tea. She wasn't big on either romances or war films. As she imagined it would be, *Casablanca* was full of all sorts of passionate speeches and big moral contradictions, but as the film unfolded, she had realised she was watching something of great beauty, like a painting or a Ming vase. Ingrid Bergman was wonderful; the close-ups of her face were sad, yet her eyes glowed. Her loneliness was obvious and the shock she showed at the end of the film, when Humphrey Bogart made her leave without him, was so real that Alice was living the scene with her.

As Alice turned off the bedside lamp, she thought she heard a small scraping sound coming from the corner where the wardrobe stood. She kept her eyes wide open in the darkness, listening for it again, but there was nothing. She had probably imagined it.

'Goodnight, Mother,' she whispered before closing her eyes, as she had done every night since her mother's death.

She fell into a deep sleep almost immediately and began dreaming the dream. The one she'd been having ever since she'd searched for the adoption agency online.

Mother came softly into the room wearing her floor-length cotton nightie, her thin hair tightly wound in curlers, and sat on the end of Alice's bed. 'I know what you're thinking of doing,' she whispered.

Alice lifted her head from the pillow. 'I promised you I wouldn't,' she said, her tongue thick with sleep.

'I'm your mother. Always remember that.'

'I will.' Alice sighed and lay down again. 'I will.'

14. The Usual Suspects

The red numerals on the digital clock-radio beside the bed showed 02:04 as Jamie struggled to open his eyes. Saeed was snoring loudly beside him, one leg thrown on top of his over the duvet. Jamie moved it carefully aside and inched out of bed, willing his eyes to adjust to the darkness so he could see where his clothes were strewn.

His underpants were beneath the quilt somewhere, so he decided to pull on his jeans without them. The last thing he wanted to do was stir Saeed. He'd wanted to leave the minute they were finished earlier on, but Saeed had held him hard and insisted he stay. After a brief struggle, he'd nodded off, tired after the intensity of the sex.

And now Jamie remembered. They'd been in the throes of fucking earlier on when Saeed had slapped him. Not on the arse, which he regularly did, but on the face. No, *across* the face. Hard.

'What the fuck did you do that for?' Jamie cried.

'What?' Saeed said. 'What I do?'

'You hit me, you pervert.'

'Come here,' Saeed said, pulling Jamie's face into his damp chest. 'You like it. I know you do. Silly boy.'

'I didn't,' Jamie said, his voice muffled by Saeed's mound of chest hair, but he began to wonder if he actually had.

'You want to come?' Saeed murmured. 'It's your turn.'

He reached down and Jamie breathed in sharply, leaning back with his eyes closed. 'Yes,' he whispered. Andrew's face flashed across his mind, smiling without a care in the world. Jamie willed the vision away, and concentrated on the sensation that was spreading through his body.

In the flesh, Saeed looked even more like a porn star than he did on his Gaydar profile. When Jamie had met him that first night, he had been so overcome with lust, he couldn't speak. The two of them had just gone at each other like they were in a wrestling match where the objective was to get each other's clothes off and make each other come as quickly as possible. Lying with Saeed afterwards, Jamie had felt like crying with relief. The release after so long without sex was powerful. But that had been the only emotion involved.

So when Saeed said, 'This is one-time thing only,' Jamie had nodded, got up, put his clothes back on and kissed the Iranian goodbye for ever.

So much for that. The next day, when Saeed had texted and asked if they could meet again, it hadn't taken Jamie long to make up his mind. And since then they'd been shagging at Saeed's place two or three times a week, always in the afternoons.

Tonight had been an exception to the rule. Saeed had texted while they were all watching *Casablanca*, and Jamie had agreed to go to his place afterwards. He texted Andrew to say they were having a great night at Martin's and not to wait up.

He had found it hard to concentrate on the rest of the film and could hardly wait for the conversation that followed to end. It was wrong lying to Andrew, but the truth was that they'd never been getting on better. Since Saeed had come into the picture, it was like all their unspoken problems had been ironed out. It was a win-win situation.

Saeed was snoring now, short little snorts that came so quickly together he didn't seem to be breathing out. Jamie looked at him for a moment, felt a stirring in his groin, then back at the clock. Although he'd told him not to wait up, he knew Andrew wouldn't sleep until he got home. It was best to leave while Saeed was out for the count.

He closed the bedroom door behind him quietly and tiptoed through the flat.

Outside Saeed's building, it was a different world. The city's clubs had all just closed and drunk people were milling about everywhere, shouting, singing, hanging out of each other like it was Mardi Gras rather than a miserable wet February night. A guy was standing in the doorway of the shop next door, pissing and shouting a string of obscenities to no one in particular.

Jamie reached into his pocket to see if he had enough money for a taxi and found only a two-euro coin. He headed towards the ATM.

At least there was no queue, although a guy was sitting on the wet pavement beside it with a grubby paper cup. 'Spare change, man?' he said, pulling the hood of his coat tight.

Jamie took the two-euro coin out of his pocket and dropped it into the cup. 'Sorry,' he said. 'That's all I've got.'

He keyed his pin code into the machine and concentrated hard on what he was doing so the man wouldn't bother him further.

Across the road a group of lads were grabbing their crotches, wolf-whistling at some girls walking by. There were three of them, all wearing tracksuit bottoms and T-shirts although it was still raining.

'Hey, you,' one called. 'Get me some fuckin' money, will ya?'

It took Jamie a moment to realise the guy was talking to him. He willed the cash machine to go faster.

'Hey, faggot,' the lad shouted. 'I'm talking to you.'

Jamie pulled the twenty-euro note from the mouth of machine, shoved it into his pocket and began to walk quickly away. With horror he realised the three young men were crossing the road to follow him.

'We're talking to you, queer boy,' one called. Jamie quickened his pace. He'd seen an *Oprah* show about situations like this where an expert said the best thing to do was just run, but for some reason his legs wouldn't do it.

'What's wrong, faggot? You a liddle scaredy-cat?'

Jamie stopped in his tracks and turned. 'Fuck you,' he said.

'What did you say?' asked the largest of the three. His face was slick with rain and Jamie could see veins pulsing in his tattooed neck.

'I said, fuck you.' Jamie repeated. He couldn't think of

anything else, and his tongue seemed to be swelling in his mouth, trying to prevent any more words getting out.

The three were on him in no seconds flat, punching and kicking without caring where their fists or feet landed. Jamie felt his lip burst open with the second fist that caught his face. He bent over, trying to get his breath, but another kick took his legs from under him. He whimpered, a pathetic, weak sound he had never heard himself make before.

'Dirty . . . fucking . . . queer . . .' the big guy said, aiming a kick to his side with each word.

'No,' Jamie moaned, as he tried to shield himself. 'Please.'

'Leave him alone,' a man's voice said.

His assailants laughed, and another kick landed in Jamie's stomach.

'Is this your boyfriend?' one of the guys asked, the one who had called him from across the street in the first place. 'Fuckin' queer.'

'I said leave him alone,' the man said again. Doubled over on the pavement, Jamie saw that he was wearing a mismatched pair of trainers, one gaping open to show dirty bare skin. It was the man from beside the bank machine.

'Fuck off home, if you know what's good for you,' one of his attackers said to him, then sniggered. 'Or have you no home to go to?'

The kicking stopped. Jamie lifted his head to see his three attackers advance on the homeless guy.

'Are you sure you want to do this?' the guy said to them, his voice calm and measured. 'I have a lot of friends with no homes to go to. You wouldn't want to show your face around here again.'

The runty guy, who had said nothing so far, guffawed, but the big one grabbed him by the shoulder and said something Jamie couldn't make out. Then the three walked off.

'Faggot!' one called, and as quickly as they had set upon him, they disappeared into the night.

'Are you all right?' the man asked.

'I think so,' Jamie said, trying to pull himself up off the ground.

'Here.' The man offered him his hand. He smelt of wet clothes that had been left in a laundry basket too long. 'Don't mind them,' he said. 'They're just scangers.'

'Thanks,' Jamie said, touching his lip. It pricked, as if a wasp had driven its sting into the soft flesh.

'No worries,' the man said. His eyes met Jamie's and there was a flicker of unspoken recognition, the silent mutual exchange of gay men on the street.

Jamie couldn't figure out how people nowadays could identify him. No one had ever called him queer when he was growing up. It had never been a problem for him, like it had been for other people. People like David Flannery.

The memory of David caused his throat to catch. He didn't want to cry. Not now, on the street like this.

What had changed? Was there a big fucking arrow in the sky pointing at him, following him around with the word 'gay' emblazoned on it?

The lights at the junction to George's Street turned green and a taxi appeared. Jamie put up his hand and, miraculously, it slowed down. 'Where to?' the driver asked, not looking in his mirror.

Right now the only place he wanted to be was with Andrew, to feel his soft kisses and whispers of comfort. But Jamie smelt of sex. He usually took a shower at Saeed's. Tonight, in his haste to get out, he'd totally forgotten.

Anyway, he didn't deserve Andrew's kisses. Every kiss Jamie had shared with Saeed had been an act of betrayal.

He gave the taxi driver his mother's address and sat back, holding his side, where a sharp ache had started up.

Maybe the beating had been punishment. Maybe it was the wake-up call he needed.

15. A Case of Do or Die

Lisa had been putting off telling Sofia for weeks. After the redundancies were announced, Patrick had told her to give the au pair notice, that if Lisa was going to be at home with the children from now on, there was no need for an au pair. They couldn't afford it, for starters.

But it was easier said than done. The children loved Sofia and she was good with them, always able to step in and calm them down when they got over-excited. She had come a month before Lisa had gone back to work after her maternity leave with Aaron and had settled in instantly, as if she had always been part of the family. The eldest of nine siblings, she was no stranger to small children.

Lisa had given her *Getting Down With Bringing Up Kids*, but Sofia said, 'It is in English and I do not read English very well.'

Lisa tried to order it in Ukrainian online, but there didn't seem to be a translation, so she set about imparting the knowledge she had gained from reading it.

'Mm,' Sofia would say, smiling and nodding as Lisa told her about 'The Security Code', which was central to Dr Karen Schuster's theory that children thrived on routine, fixed and unchanging. Every chapter in *Getting Down With Bringing Up Kids* sprang from this idea and, accordingly, Lisa had posted on the kitchen wall each of the children's Security Codes, typed on an A4 piece of paper, breaking their days down into half-hour segments.

'I understand, yes,' Sofia had said, at the beginning, when Lisa had walked her through each routine, but after that she hadn't seemed to bother with it. If Lisa veered from the routine, chaos ensued, but Sofia seemed able to keep the boys happy with mere nods. Maybe it was that, at eighteen, Sofia was little more than a child herself and could still talk their language, a skill Lisa felt she herself had long forgotten.

She was a little hung-over from the Film Club meeting the night before, probably exacerbated by smoking. It had been a lovely night, though, and the film such a great choice. When she came to think about it, showing *Casablanca* was so in keeping with Martin. He wasn't unlike Bogart in the film, gruffly witty and nonchalant with sadness lurking inside him. Lisa was sure of it.

She'd smoked three cigarettes. Up till now, two was her limit. It was dangerous to be in the company of smokers: they led you down a road on which it was not very easy to do a U-turn.

She switched on the kettle and put a plate of yesterday's croissants into the microwave to soften them up. A nice breakfast would make it easier to let Sofia go.

Before he'd left for work, Patrick had said, 'Tell her today, okay? Or else I'm going to have to do it.'

'I wish you would,' Lisa said. 'I'm dreading it.'

Patrick looked at his watch. 'Shit,' he said. 'I'm going to be at least half an hour late. Bloody Germans and their meetings at the crack of dawn.'

'Your tie's a bit wonky,' Lisa said, reaching out to straighten it.

Patrick sighed and gave her a smile as she fiddled with the knot, but he looked harried. Last night when they'd been woken by Aaron's crying, he'd jumped out of bed and said something about the alarm clock being broken. He'd thought he'd slept in for work.

Lisa patted his tie down and handed him his briefcase. 'I'll tell Sofia today, I promise,' she said, strengthening her resolve.

'You know it'll be easier coming from you. You two are as thick as thieves.'

'That's the problem,' Lisa said. She handed him the packed lunch Sofia had made last night, as part of the new economy drive, and kissed his smoothly shaven cheek. The scent of his aftershave gave her a pleasurable little jolt and she imagined pulling his shirt off and leading him back to the bedroom, the way she had once or twice before the children were born, before being on time for work had become so important to them both.

'Don't forget to pick up my suit from the dry-cleaner's, will you?' he said, kissing her back before turning to Theo and Ben. 'Now, you two, be good boys for Mummy today, won't you?'

'Daddy goes to work,' Theo told Ben, his mouth overspilling with Rice Krispies.

'Say bye-bye,' Lisa said, and Ben lifted his little hand to wave.

'Bye-bye, Daddy.'

Upstairs she heard the shower start, the signal that Sofia would soon be down and the dreaded conversation would have to take place. She'd better get Aaron up first. He'd finally nodded off at seven this morning. If she left him much longer, his routine would be even more messed up and she'd get no sleep again tonight.

When she came down, with a groggy Aaron in her arms, Sofia was sitting between Theo and Ben, her silver-blonde hair wrapped in a turban of olive green towel, her usually pale cheeks red from the heat of the shower.

'Good morning,' she said, looking up at Lisa a little warily.

She knows, thought Lisa, but somehow this made telling her even harder. She popped the microwave open and brought the plate of croissants to the table with a pot of coffee. 'Sofia,' she said. 'We have to talk.'

The words came out in a tumble of back-to-front sentences, Sofia's lashless eyes growing larger and larger as Lisa tried to explain but got it all wrong. 'I'm sorry,' she said eventually. 'I wish things were different.'

Sofia leaned across the table. 'It is okay,' she said, resting her hand on Lisa's. 'Don't worry.'

Tears began to leak out of the corners of Lisa's eyes. Aaron in his baby chair, Theo and Ben, with their bowls of cereal, were quietly looking at her, like a rapt audience at the theatre.

'I will just go to dry my hair,' said Sofia, standing up. She walked quickly out of the kitchen.

Lisa took one of Aaron's bibs, which had been left on the

table, and dabbed her eyes with it. 'Are you finished?' she said to Theo and Ben, who were still sitting silently, Rice Krispies floating in the milk left in their plastic bowls.

She took the bowls to load them into the dishwasher and was bending over trying to wedge them in the packed bottom tray when she felt a sharp kick to her ankle. 'I hate you, Mummy,' said Theo. He was wearing his slippers, but it still hurt. The kick had taken all his force.

'Theo!' she cried. 'What have I told you about kicking?'

As Theo ran off, Ben echoed, 'I hate you, Mummy.'

Where had they learned the word 'hate'? Lisa wondered, rubbing her ankle. She only ever told them she loved them.

Aaron began to whimper. He was hungry. His Security Code said he should have been fed an hour ago. And it was Potty Time for Ben, and Dressing Ourselves Time for Theo.

What was she going to do without Sofia?

A shriek of of pain came from under the table – Ben's pain. Theo ran out to the playroom.

'Did you hit your brother?' Lisa called after him, but he didn't answer.

Ben, red-faced and bawling, came out from under the table, his arms held up to be lifted. 'Theo hit Ben!' he wailed, as Aaron's whimper turned into an all out roar for food.

Maybe it wouldn't hurt to stick them in front of a DVD while she fed Aaron. Just this once. Although there was nothing in *Getting Down With Bringing Up Kids* about television time.

16. What Can I Do You For?

Brady's Motors was down a little side-street off Newmarket Square, a part of the city Katherine had never been to before. She parked on the street because its yard was bumper to bumper with cars in various states of repair. The ground in between was dotted with potholes full of black water, rainbows of oil floating on their surfaces.

'The weather's been so bad, we've hardly had a chance to work on anything,' said Martin, leading her through a small garage that held two half-stripped cars sitting side by side. In one corner there was a stained, rust-coloured armchair, a mug of tea on its arm. The wall above it was festooned with a calendar featuring a half-naked girl holding her huge breasts out to the camera and various cuttings from the sports pages of tabloids.

Careful to avoid the oil slick on the floor as she followed Martin between the two cars, Katherine pulled her Louis Vuitton coat around her. 'If this isn't a good time, I can call again,' she said.

'It's as good a time as any,' Martin replied. In his overalls he looked smaller somehow, kind of boyish. He pointed to a metal staircase that led up to a small office built on scaffolding above the garage, its interior almost hidden by twisted venetian blinds.

When they got inside he took a cloth from the pocket of his overalls and wiped the brown leather seat of a swivel chair at the desk. Katherine sat down on the edge, hoping there wasn't any grease on it.

'So, what can I do you for?' said Martin.

'There's something wrong with my car's engine,' said Katherine. 'It makes a weird sound when I go from second to third gear.'

'The BMW Z8. A lovely car, that is.'

Katherine nodded. Men always knew its specifics in a way that women didn't, or couldn't be bothered to. She liked that about it. 'The garage that sold it to me has gone out of business,' she said. 'And I need to get it in proper working order before I . . . decide what to do with it. I was hoping you might be able to help me.'

Martin, leaning against the office desk, said nothing for a

moment and she realised he was looking at her with sympathy, his forehead knitted. Hot shame made its way up her neck, threatening to break out into a full blush.

'Well, can you?' she asked in a vexed effort to stop the spread. 'Help me?'

Martin straightened. 'If you decide to sell it, you know you won't get half what you would have got for it this time last year?'

'Yes,' said Katherine, pulling her right-hand glove tight. She'd looked up different dealers online to see what they were selling last year's Z8s for and, minus what she still owed the bank for the car, she figured she could get enough to cover her part of the mortgage for two months. If she sold it privately, she'd make a little more.

'It's a real shame,' said Martin, with a shake of his head. 'I always thought that car suited you.'

'It's only a car,' said Katherine, although she had agonised over getting rid of it. But it wasn't as if she had a choice.

'So, do you reckon selling it's your best option?' Martin asked.

Katherine's throat tightened. She hated feeling so exposed. 'Look, I just need to know what's wrong with it and how much it will cost to repair. Can you do that for me?'

Martin smiled. 'All right, all right, calm down,' he said.

'I *am* calm,' Katherine said, although she was struggling not to stand up and run back down the metal staircase.

Martin gave her a wide smile, but his eyebrows were still knitted. 'I'll give it a full service,' he said, 'and you only need to worry about the cost of any parts it needs. And I might be able to get a fair price for it, if you leave it with me.'

'You'd be able to do that? Really?'

'What are friends for?'

Friends . . . She'd accepted his friend request on Facebook last week after it had been sitting in her request box for ages, and with Film Club, she'd accepted she wasn't his boss any more.

But actual *friends*? Katherine felt uneasy about it, even if she could use a friend right now.

'And sure, while I'm at it, why don't I take a look around to see if we can find a little runabout to replace it with?' Martin continued. 'You can't be doing without wheels.'

'That's very kind of you, Martin,' she said, with a firm smile, 'but there's no need to go to that trouble.'

'It's no trouble, honestly.'

Again Katherine had the disquieting feeling that he was pitying her.

'Any luck on the jobs front, by the way?' he asked.

'There's a few leads,' she lied, not quite able to hold his gaze. 'One of them looks quite promising.'

'Is it in IT?'

'Yes,' Katherine replied, as she grappled to think of her next move.

Mercifully, heavy footsteps were clanking up the metal staircase, interrupting the interrogation.

'It's my father,' Martin mouthed, before the tiny doorway was filled with a large-framed man wearing a hound's-tooth jacket over his overalls, his big nose so mottled and red it was hard to take in anything else about him.

'What do we have here?' he said, and gave a phlegmy cough. A waft of alcohol filled the air.

'Katherine,' said Martin, 'this is my father, Tom.'

'Hello, Mr Brady,' said Katherine, taking her glove off and reaching her hand out to shake his.

'Well, look at you now,' said Martin's father, gazing at her approvingly. He teetered to the side a little and let go of her hand to balance himself on the desk.

'You all right, Dad?' Martin asked.

'I'm fine. Don't be clucking round me like a mother hen.' He turned back to Katherine. 'Very pleased to meet you. We were beginning to think our lad was one of those queer fellas.'

'Dad, for Chrissake . . .' said Martin.

'It's not like that,' Katherine interjected quickly. 'I used to work with Martin.'

Martin's father harrumphed and lowered himself into the seat Katherine had just vacated. 'I'd say it was a real pleasure working with you, love,' he said.

'Dad!' said Martin, his face reddening. 'Have some manners, will you?'

The older man burst into a fit of coughing, his breathing jagged, shoulders heaving.

'Maybe you should go home and lie down,' said Martin. 'You're not looking the best.'

'Lie down?' said his father, his coughing fit over as abruptly as it had begun. 'Sure, I've a full day's work to put in here. I can hardly rely on the likes of you to do it, can I?'

Martin looked at Katherine in silent apology, rubbing his grease-stained fingers on the belly of his overalls.

'Waster,' the man muttered, under his breath.

Now it was her turn to feel sorry for Martin, but instead she felt a wave of indignation on his behalf. 'Mr Brady,' she began, and instantly felt Martin stiffen beside her.

'You can call me Tom, love,' said Martin's father, leering at her, his legs set wide apart in his chair.

Katherine cleared her throat and glanced at Martin for a split second. He was visibly cringing. 'Mr Brady,' she repeated. 'Tom … I've asked Martin to fix my car. I wouldn't entrust it to anyone else.'

'Is it that BMW parked outside the gates?' he asked.

Katherine nodded, her eyes flickering towards Martin again.

'She's a fine thing,' said Martin's father, with another leer. 'There's nothing as beautiful as the engine on a clean BMW.'

'Which is why I'm so delighted that Martin has agreed to look after it for me.' Katherine coolly met his gaze. 'Qwertec's loss is clearly your gain, Mr Brady.'

For a moment Martin's father looked confused, like he'd been wrong-footed but didn't know how. Katherine took a breath and flashed her best bright smile, holding out her hand. 'A pleasure to meet you,' she said, indicating in the nicest possible way that they were done.

'And you,' said Mr Brady, getting unsteadily to his feet.

As he shuffled down the metal staircase, visibly chastened, Martin gazed at Katherine in wonderment.

'I don't know if I've ever seen anyone manage to pull the rug out from under him like that before,' he said, once the older man was out of earshot.

'I didn't do anything,' Katherine replied.

'No, really,' he insisted. 'You can come back and do that again any time.'

Katherine gave a soft laugh.

'Sorry about the old man,' said Martin. 'In half an hour he won't even remember going on like that to you.'

'No,' Katherine replied, as emphatically as she could. 'You have nothing to be sorry for. And thanks, by the way.'

'For what?' said Martin.

'For your help. It means a lot to me.'

'Well, if you need anything, I'm always here.'

'Thanks,' Katherine said again, and for the first time since she'd lost her job, she felt something approaching relief.

March

Breakfast at Tiffany's

Blake Edwards, 1961

'We belong to nobody, and nobody belongs to us.
We don't even belong to each other.'

7. A Tour of Katherine's House

Martin wished Katherine would sit down. From the moment they'd arrived she'd done nothing but fuss, going in and out of that 'galley kitchen', adding to the already huge collection of dips and things to stick into them, making sure everyone had their drinks topped up, saying, 'Now, what have I forgotten?' and disappearing again. The rest of them were standing around the white-carpeted sitting room, talking in hushed tones, as if they were in a funeral parlour.

The house, he had to admit, was done up to perfection, and slap-bang in the heart of Ranelagh, the place where everyone had wanted to live when the going was good.

When Jamie finally arrived, last and late as per usual, Katherine eagerly said, 'Shall I give you all the guided tour?' For a moment you could imagine what she'd looked like as a little blonde-headed girl.

'I thought you'd never ask,' Jamie said, taking Lisa's arm. He showed only the smallest trace of the attack, a vague swelling that gave his mouth a slightly lopsided look. According to Lisa, who had breathlessly told the story when she arrived, one side of his face had ballooned so badly, he had looked like the Elephant Man. She said Jamie had told her he didn't want them going on about it, but Martin felt he had to say something.

'Sorry to hear about what happened to you, man,' he said. 'Bastards should be locked up.'

Jamie's eyes welled, and Lisa put an arm around his shoulders. But he lifted his chin and said, 'These things happen all the time. I'm over it.'

'Of course you are,' said Lisa. 'But if you need to talk about it . . .'

'I don't, okay? When's this guided tour going to start?'

'This way,' Katherine said, leading them out of the sitting room and down the wide hall, past a row of paintings that looked as if they'd come from a modern-art museum. She was wearing a plain black dress that went down to just above her knees, gathered in with a black belt at the waist. On her, it looked like high fashion.

Five minutes into the tour, Martin began to wish he hadn't left his beer on the sitting-room mantelpiece. Guiding the group from the ground floor up the stairs, Katherine pointed out this fitting or that piece of furniture while Lisa oohed and aahed in awe.

Jamie asked questions about the age of every antique, complimenting Katherine's ability to 'fuse Queen Anne dressers with Bauhaus chairs', while Alice hung around in the background, peering out from underneath her hair.

Martin noticed that the boyfriend's name wasn't mentioned once as Katherine led them from room to room, and Lisa pointed out what she called 'the wow factor' that had been incorporated into each: wallpaper printed with massive sunflowers in one, a big blue picture of a swimming-pool, identified by Jamie as 'a Hockney print', in another.

Katherine showed it all off, smiling brightly, but Martin was sure he had picked up some tension beneath the surface. She kept squeezing her hands, the way she had that day when she'd come to the garage to ask if he'd take a look at her car, and her eyes darted, like they were engaged in some sort of covert operation.

Martin made all the right sounds, with Lisa and Jamie, but his mind was on the cold beer, warming in the heat of the fire, waiting for him in the sitting room. He couldn't see the attraction of owning so much stuff. When everyone else was clambering on to the property ladder, he had continued renting his flat, which he was glad about now. If Katherine and What'shisname had spent on this house anything like the sum it would have been valued at two years ago, they were in big trouble. Now it was probably worth half what they paid for it, so they were either saddled with struggling to pay it off for the rest of their lives, or the banks would be stepping in soon. And what good were Hockney prints and designer chairs when you had no home to put them in?

All Martin had to do was pay his rent and bills, buy food and have enough left over for a few pints every now and then. The work at the garage would more than suffice, even if it had its ups and downs. And there was no more Maguire looking at his watch if Martin was so much as a minute late. He had his father to deal with, though.

For the first while after he'd come out of the hospital six months ago, Dad had declared himself a teetotaller. The doctors had insisted he couldn't drink any more and he was taking them seriously. But, gradually, as anyone could have predicted, he had slipped into having the odd glass of wine with a meal, then to drinking just one or two cans in the evenings, watching Sky News. Before you knew it, he was going down to Dinty's again at opening time, just for one pint. Then it was back to the pub for lunch, washed down with a couple more Guinnesses, and his drinking day continued as if there had never been a break. If anything, it was getting worse.

'We found it in a junkyard in Tuscany,' Katherine was saying, her fingers brushing against a stone sink that looked like a horse trough and was fixed to the wall of what she called 'the master en suite'.

'It looks so old!' Lisa said, her hands clasped together at her chin. 'I mean, like antique old.'

'It's medieval,' said Katherine. 'At least, that's what the dealer told us. But you never know with Italians.'

Martin found it about as interesting as watching paint dry, but he did his best to look attentive. To tell the truth he was keener on eyeing Katherine than the furniture and fittings in her fancy house. So much so that he'd barely been able to look her way since he'd arrived, as if his eyes would betray him. Not that she'd thrown too many glances *his* way either.

It was there, wasn't it? That unspoken thing. He couldn't be imagining it. He'd felt it the last time they'd met too. Not that trusting his instincts had done him any favours at the Christmas party, mind you. He'd listened to the hippie-dippy wisdom of his sister, Nell.

She had once told him that if you felt someone in a room was thinking about you, they were. Everyone had this kind of energy that picked up on other people's energies, or something like that.

'If you feel it, you should act on it,' Nell told him, so at that fucked-up Christmas party he now wished he'd never been at, he'd stupidly followed her advice.

Well into the night, Katherine had stumbled with him out of the function room into the corridor that led to the toilets, honking with laughter at his impressions of Maguire, who was half passed out at his table with the drink. Her face was so close to his, her wine-stained lips glistening, her eyes sparkling, and it had seemed like the most natural thing in the world to kiss her.

Big mistake that had turned out to be. Nell's bloody 'energies' had turned out to be a figment of his imagination.

Since then Katherine had been professional to the core, engaging with him on work matters clearly and concisely, but she had never talked to him about anything other than his job, never once met his eye, and he had never heard her laugh again. If he had known she had a boyfriend, he wouldn't have gone near her in the first place. He wouldn't have got his hopes up.

But then again, maybe he would. He had loved Jennifer; he still loved her in a way. But he had never experienced the kind of feeling with her that he'd had when he'd kissed Katherine. It had been like getting lost and not giving a fuck if you ever found your way back.

18. Faking It to Make It

Breakfast at Tiffany's turned out to be one of Lisa's favourite films of all time too. No surprises there. Alice said she had never seen it – had she ever seen any film? – and Jamie went on a bit about the original book and how different it was from the movie, which had got rid of the gay undertones. No surprises there either.

'What gay undertones?' Katherine asked.

'In Truman Capote's original book the George Peppard character is a closet gay,' Martin explained. 'There is no love story between him and Holly Golightly. They're just friends.'

'But *Breakfast at Tiffany's* would be nothing without the love story,' said Lisa. 'It's the heart and soul of the film. They're two drifters off to see the world . . .' She was looking a bit the worse for wear. Her hair was greasy and there was a wound on her left cheek, like somebody had dug their nails into it. Lisa didn't mention it and Martin didn't ask. Neither did anyone else.

Katherine gathered herself up as if she was going to make a speech, patting the parting of her scraped-back hair as she began, 'I think Holly Golightly is a great character. Her life is pure chaos and she has hardly any money, but she's always got great style and she's brave. She's out there, taking care of herself.'

Martin helped himself to another glass of shiraz. He'd made his way steadily through the six-pack of beers in the fridge. 'She's a fake,' he said. 'Even her name is made up.'

'She's faking it to make it,' said Katherine. 'There's nothing wrong with that.'

'I love that she's faking it but you get to see how vulnerable she is underneath,' said Lisa. 'That's what gives the film its heart.'

'What does it mean when a man gives her fifty dollars for the powder room?' Alice asked, making her first contribution to the conversation.

'In the book she's a hooker,' Jamie said. 'Fifty dollars for the powder room is the nearest they could get to Audrey Hepburn turning tricks.'

'George Peppard is a prostitute too,' said Lisa. 'Well, not George Peppard himself but his character.'

'Is he?' said Alice, incredulously. She was turning over the *Breakfast at Tiffany's* DVD box, studying its content as if it might reveal some hidden secret. A set of rainbow-coloured plastic bangles clacked against each other on her wrist.

'Too right he is,' said Jamie. 'He's being paid by the old glamourpuss in the turban for sex, even though there isn't a hint of between-the-sheets action to be seen. She's his sugar-mummy.'

'I hate the way that woman is demonised,' said Lisa. 'And she's not old. She's about my age.'

'She's fabulous,' said Jamie. 'Just like the wicked queen in *Snow White*.'

'And, as usual, the man gets it all on his own terms,' Lisa went on, her cheeks reddening. 'She has to be humiliated and made feel crap about herself just because she has the nerve to say what she really wants.' She turned to Martin. 'Do you have any fags? I'd love to have just one.'

'I wouldn't mind one too,' said Jamie.

Katherine cleared her throat and gave a kind of fixed smile. 'I've put an ashtray on the table outside on the deck,' she said, standing up to clear some empty plates from the coffee-table.

'Jesus, it would freeze the balls off a brass monkey out there tonight,' said Martin, pulling a lighter from his pocket.

'There's a patio heater,' said Katherine, her back to the room. 'Just press the red button and it comes on automatically.'

She left for the kitchen and Jamie made a Miss High and Mighty face behind her back.

The back garden was a bit of a wind-trap, so Martin lit his cigarette with his head inside the french windows, then handed it out to Jamie so that he could light his from the tip. 'Still pretending to be a smoker then,' he said.

'Yep,' said Jamie, exhaling a mouthful of smoke. 'I'm traumatised and I need a crutch.'

'I know,' said Lisa, taking Martin's cigarette to light hers. 'It takes ages to get over something like that. The body may recover, but psychologically you were invaded during that assault. It's like your mind has been raped.'

Jamie coughed out another mouthful of smoke. 'Oh, it's not that,' he said. 'I'm booked to go away with Andrew tomorrow. For a spa break. In a hotel in the middle of nowhere.'

'God, you're so blessed,' said Lisa. 'I can't remember the last time myself and Patrick had a weekend together.'

'You can go in my place any time,' said Jamie. 'A spa weekend is my idea of hell. But Andrew's been going on and on about it ever since "the incident" and eventually I had to give in.'

Martin took a deep drag. 'You have my sympathies, mate,' he said, exhaling. Spa breaks had been one of Jennifer's pet projects. He couldn't count the weekends he had been forced to hang around hotels in towelling robes, sipping herbal tea after having his face plastered with products by women who described what they were doing as if they were explaining neurosurgery to a toddler. Wasted weekends, as it turned out.

Lisa was surveying the orange tip of her cigarette. 'You're lucky that Andrew takes care of you so well,' she said.

'I know,' Jamie agreed. 'I just wish we weren't missing Lady Gaga night at the George on Saturday. They've got all the best drag impersonators coming in from London.'

'Nice to see you've got your priorities right,' said Martin.

'It's just that there'll be nothing to do. Just me and Andrew having breakfast in a hotel restaurant, lunch in the same hotel restaurant and dinner in the same hotel restaurant. The spa treatments are the only entertainment on offer.'

'You can make your own entertainment,' said Lisa.

'Nudge, nudge, wink, wink,' added Martin.

'I think I'd prefer Lady Gaga,' said Jamie, his chin tilted towards the stars in the clear night sky.

Martin flicked the butt of his cigarette on to the gravel beneath the garden decking. 'Let's go in,' he said, 'I'm freezing me bollocks off out here.'

When they arrived back into the sitting room, Katherine and Alice were watching the DVD extras. Some talking head was being interviewed about the theme song, 'Moon River', winning the Best Song Oscar in 1961.

'When Audrey Hepburn sings it, with her little guitar, she's like a child,' Katherine was saying. 'You get to see a different side to her.'

'It's such a sad song,' said Alice. She closed her eyes as an orchestral snippet of 'Moon River' was played, and Audrey Hepburn stood outside Tiffany's eating her take-out breakfast.

'I don't think it's sad,' said Lisa, sitting down. 'It's a very happy song. It's like a nursery rhyme.'

'It sounds sad to me,' said Alice. 'I think the film is really sad too.'

Jamie threw his eyes up to heaven. 'It's a comedy, sweetie,' he said. 'If that's not too alien a concept to grasp.'

'But the girl in it is all alone. Nobody understands her.'

'George Peppard understands her,' said Katherine. 'And he loves her.'

'No, he doesn't,' said Alice. She was fiddling with the plastic bangles on her arm.

'Of course he does,' said Lisa. 'They go off together in the end, don't they?'

'He just wants her to be the same as everyone else,' said Alice, her expression unyielding. 'But she can't. She'll never be normal.'

This was the most Martin had ever heard Alice say, and although he had felt moved at the end of the film, when Holly ended up in the guy's arms, he had to admit she had a point. You couldn't see Holly Golightly married with kids, living in the 'burbs.

On the TV screen a clip from the final scene of the film was playing, Holly searching in the alleyway for the cat, rain bucketing down on her face.

'I've never understood why she threw the cat out of the taxi,' said Katherine. 'It seems so out of character.'

'The cat *is* her,' said Martin. 'When she finds it at the end, we're supposed to believe she's finding herself.'

Katherine looked impressed. 'I never really thought about it like that,' she said, and Martin experienced a pleasurable thrill of pride.

'Right, time for me to go,' said Lisa, gathering herself together. 'The babysitter wants to get home early and the kids will be up at seven in the morning, jumping on top of me.'

'It's Saturday morning,' said Jamie. 'Can't your husband get up with them?'

'He's got a golf tournament in Kilkenny. He's there now, staying overnight so he can get a good sleep beforehand.'

'And that's supposed to be fair?'

'Golf is the only thing he has to help him unwind. Seriously, you can't imagine the pressure he's under at work. They've let go half the staff. He's doing the jobs of three people.'

'What's that big scrape on your face?' Alice asked.

Lisa's hand flew to her cheek. 'Theo did it,' she said, and added, 'it was an accident.'

'It looks irritated,' said Katherine. 'I've got some Savlon, if you want to put some on before you go.'

'Don't be silly,' said Lisa, emitting a little laugh. 'It's only a little scratch.'

'Kids,' said Jamie, putting his coat on. 'Can't live with 'em, can't shoot 'em.'

'Before everyone goes, we still have to decide who's showing the movie next month,' said Martin.

'I'd be happy to do the honours,' said Jamie.

'So would I,' said Alice. She was focused on the carpet.

Jamie raised an eyebrow, exchanging a look with Lisa. 'If you're sure,' he said. 'I can do it the following month. And then Lisa, if that's okay with everyone.'

'Good,' said Alice, lifting her head. She looked relieved.

Jamie, Lisa and Alice all lived on the same route, while Martin's flat was on the other side of the city. The dispatcher said he would have to wait half an hour for another taxi, so he found himself standing in the hall alone with Katherine, waving goodnight as Alice put her umbrella up for the ten-foot walk in the rain to the front gate while Jamie and Lisa linked arms.

19. Waiting Round the Bend

'That was a good evening,' Martin said. In the warm glow of the hallway lamp, the tiny yellow flecks in Katherine's eyes made them look amber instead of green. For a moment there was a comfortable silence between them, but the second the taxi pulled away, the atmosphere went cold.

'Barry will be home any minute,' Katherine said, closing the front door.

'One more for the road?' said Martin.

'I think I've probably had enough for tonight.'

'Ah, c'mon. One more won't hurt.'

Katherine gave him an uncertain look. 'I suppose not.'

Martin put his coat down on a chair. Katherine picked it up and hung it on the hall stand, brushing the back of it with her long white hand. Her nails were painted pale pink.

'I think I have a buyer for your car,' he said, when they were sitting down again on the couch. 'He's willing to pay eighteen K.'

Katherine reached out to poke the embers in the fireplace. 'I was hoping for twenty two. It's only a year old.'

'I reckon eighteen is the best you'll get.'

There was silence until Katherine said, 'I suppose I'll have to take it. It's not like I've much choice.'

'I'll set it up, so. Give your man a call tomorrow.'

Katherine turned back from the fire and gave him a resigned smile. 'Thanks for organising it, Martin.'

'You're welcome,' said Martin, and a warm glow that was definitely not alcohol-related settled in his stomach.

The room descended into silence once more, which Katherine eventually interrupted. 'I hope you liked my choice of film,' she said. 'It's hardly a favourite with *Star Wars* fans, I'd imagine.'

'Neither is *Casablanca*,' Martin replied. 'But I'm a *Star Wars* fan with eclectic taste.'

Katherine gave a soft laugh, the light from the fireplace flickering on her face. She turned to him again and opened her mouth to say something, but then she bit her bottom lip.

'It's a good film,' said Martin, rushing to fill the gap. 'Although I'd never have put that guy with Holly Golightly at the end. They're like chalk and cheese.'

Katherine leaned over to poke at the embers of the fire once more. 'I think they're the perfect match,' she said. 'She's all over the place, he's very grounded. They cancel out each other's flaws.'

'Ah,' said Martin. 'So it's a practical arrangement. Not a romance after all.'

Katherine stayed gazing into the fireplace. 'Of course it's a romance,' she said. 'But can't romance be about people who actually suit each other rather than high drama all the time, like in *Casablanca*?'

Martin didn't know what he thought. When he was first with Jennifer, she'd often say, 'We're perfect for each other. We were meant to be together.' But for all their complementary characteristics, there had always been plenty of high drama. He'd never quite believed it when Jennifer said they were meant to be together, but when she'd left for the last time, he'd begged her to come back, crying, 'But we were meant to be together!' And he'd really believed it.

'I just can't see the likes of Holly Golightly settling down happy ever after with that kind of bloke,' he said, putting the memory out of his head. 'I can't imagine her tied to the kitchen sink in suburbia.'

'But what if that's what she wants?' asked Katherine. 'Not being tied to the kitchen sink but … you know … an ordinary life with a husband and kids. Someone to love her for who she is … Security.'

'*Security?*' Martin spluttered. 'That would be like a dirty word to Holly Golightly.'

'It's like you weren't watching the same film,' Katherine said, reaching for her wineglass. 'Security is exactly what she's looking for.'

'But what about that line she says at the end, about being put in a cage?'

'Well, maybe she's looking for security but, at the same time, doesn't know what she wants,' said Katherine. She swirled the wine that was left in her glass. 'Maybe she's confused.'

'So the guy kisses her in the rain at the end and suddenly she's not confused? Very convenient.'

Katherine pushed his foot with hers. 'Bloody hell!' She laughed. 'You're right, it's a practical arrangement. You've taken all the romance out of it.'

'I'd never have taken you for such a romantic,' Martin said. He was feeling it again, that damned energy.

'And I'd never have taken you for the practical type,' Katherine retorted, draining her glass.

From the hall came the sound of the front door opening.

Katherine stood up. 'That'll be Barry,' she said, all business now.

Barry walked into the room and she went over to kiss him on the lips.

'Who's this?' Barry asked, pulling away.

'Oh, sorry,' said Katherine. 'This is Martin. From Film Club. Martin, this is Barry.'

Barry's handshake was like a vice. He was a bit taller than Martin, and built like a brick shithouse, all pumped-up beneath his white shirt and loosened tie. The only non-gladiator thing about him was his hair, which was just a collection of thin blond wisps trying to masquerade as a thatch.

'The famous Martin,' Barry said, flashing a porcelain-white smile, his grip tightening.

'I was just leaving,' said Martin. 'Work in the morning and all that.'

Barry turned to Katherine. 'Where's the rest of them? I thought there was a whole crowd of you.'

'They've all gone home,' said Katherine. 'Martin's waiting for his taxi.'

'Plenty of cabs on the street,' Barry said. 'It's not rush-hour yet.'

Martin cleared his throat. 'Barry's right,' he said. 'I can get a cab outside.'

'Are you sure?' Katherine asked. 'It's pouring out there.'

'Absolutely. A little bit of rain never hurt anyone.'

Katherine hesitated, then said, 'I'll leave you to the door, then.'

'Just a minute, mate,' said Barry. 'I hope you haven't been behaving like you did at your last Film Club thingy.'

'Barry . . .' Katherine protested.

Barry put his hand up to her as if to brook no argument. 'No offence,' he said, his slate-grey eyes firmly on Martin, the porcelain smile still in place, 'but I don't want you getting drunk and obnoxious at your little meetings, okay? It's not right, mate. It's out of order.'

Martin turned to Katherine in confusion. She was wringing her hands again, looking at the floor. 'I don't know what you're talking about,' he said, meeting Barry's eye again.

'As I said, man, no offence,' Barry said. 'I'm just looking out for my girlfriend.'

'I don't understand,' Martin said to Katherine. 'What did you tell him?'

Katherine bit her lip. 'I'm sorry,' she said.

Martin shook his head in disbelief. 'I should go. I'll get a taxi outside.'

'See ya,' said Barry, picking up the TV remote control.

Katherine followed Martin out into the hall. 'I'm sorry about that,' she said. 'He's a bit pissed. He's been out with the lads.'

'You said I was drunk and obnoxious?' Martin said, pulling on his coat.

'I didn't use those words,' said Katherine.

'Well, at least now I know what you really think of me. For a minute there, I thought we were going to be friends.'

'We *are* friends,' said Katherine.

'I don't think so,' said Martin. The rain was bucketing down, monsoon-style, but he ploughed out into the street without caring. All he wanted to do was get away from her.

20. Other Bridges to Cross

When Alice went in to check on Mrs Silver before letting herself into her own house, she found the old lady wide awake and watching one of her *CSI* shows.

'You wouldn't believe this one,' Mrs Silver said, her hair glowing like a blue halo in the light behind her chair. 'It's about a murderer who strangles cleaning ladies with the cords of their own Hoovers.'

'I've done it!' Alice said.

'Pardon, dear?'

'I've invited them. They're coming to my house for the next Film Club meeting, this time next month.'

Mrs Silver turned the television down with her remote control. 'That's good news,' she said. 'I'm so glad.'

'I don't know,' said Alice. 'Maybe it was a mistake. They don't like me very much.'

'Nonsense. What's not to like? Your meeting will be a great success, I have no doubt of it.'

Mrs Silver meant well, but sometimes Alice wondered if she was fully compos mentis. Today, for instance, when Alice had brought in two lamb chops and some mashed potato for her dinner, earlier than usual, Mrs Silver had impressed on her the importance of having 100-watt bulbs in all her light fittings. 'You want to see where you're going on these dark nights,' she'd insisted. 'You don't want to trip up and kill yourself. Your body might not be discovered for ages.'

She watched too many of those crime-scene programmes. And sometimes it seemed the old woman couldn't distinguish between herself and Alice, that she thought Alice was simply a younger Mrs Silver. She was forever warning Alice not to make the same mistakes as she did, although what those mistakes were was never discussed.

'You must make strudel,' said Mrs Silver, her magnified brown eyes lighting up behind the thick lenses of her spectacles. 'Oh, and rugelach! I haven't made those for ages. I'll help you.'

'I invited them because of what you said to me earlier,' said Alice. 'About people getting to know the real you by seeing where you come from.'

'That's right. It's the best way to show people who you are.'

Alice sighed and sat down. 'That's the problem,' she said. 'I don't really know where I come from.'

'Don't be silly, dear. You come from next door.'

'But when you think about it, that's not true.'

Alice wasn't sure how much Mrs Silver knew. She had never discussed being adopted with her, and Mother had hardly been the most revealing of individuals.

'Mother didn't want me to look for my birth mother,' she said, and waited for Mrs Silver's reaction.

The old woman looked at the television screen. The ad break was over and CSI Miami was back on. Alice sensed she wanted to turn the volume back up.

'I'm sure that's not true,' Mrs Silver said eventually.

'She never said so out loud, but she let me know in other ways,' Alice said.

'What other ways?'

'It's hard to explain. She was always telling me that she was my real mother. Not anyone else.'

'Maybe she was worried that you might love your birth mother more, if you found her.'

'I'll never love anyone more than I loved Mother,' Alice said.

Mrs Silver leaned forward and put her tiny wrinkled hand with its magenta-painted nails on Alice's. 'Of course not, dear,' she said. 'I know you miss her very much.'

'But I can't stop thinking about my birth mother,' Alice said. 'Since Mother died, it's all I've been able to think about.'

'You must find her, then,' said Mrs Silver.

'Mother wouldn't like it.'

'I lost my mother, you know. A long, long time ago. My father, too, and my two beautiful sisters. I was taken here and I never saw them again. Having your family is the most important thing.'

'Yes,' said Alice. 'You're right. I'm so sorry.' It was unthinking to go on about her birth mother. Mrs Silver had lost her entire family in Germany during the war. Alice was vague on how she'd been rescued from the Nazis and ended up in Ireland – she'd always been afraid to draw her on the subject – but she knew she'd ended up here alone at ten years of age.

'So, you will look for your mother?' Mrs Silver asked.

Alice shook her head. 'What if she's dead? Or if she wants nothing to do with me?'

'You will cross those bridges when you come to them. There are other bridges to cross first.'

'I don't know where to start,' said Alice, even though she had looked up the website for the Irish adoption agency on her computer at work.

'We must contact the relevant authorities,' said Mrs Silver, lifting her remote control. 'Tomorrow we will sit down and write a letter requesting a meeting. That's the first bridge to cross.'

'You'll help me?'

'Of course I will, dear. Of course I will. Now, if you'll excuse me . . .' Mrs Silver turned the volume back up on *CSI*.

Alice crossed the garden wall and dug into her bag, searching for her front-door key.

The search for her mother would begin tomorrow. She couldn't quite believe it.

As she turned the key in its lock, she thought she heard a door slam inside the house.

21. Two Drifters

The journey, which, according to the computer in Andrew's 4x4, was supposed to take an hour and a half, ended up taking the guts of three hours. What was the use of satnavs and cars that went from zero to eighty miles per hour in no seconds flat when the traffic was so bad coming out of the city that you invariably got where you were going as fast as a rustbucket on wheels?

Luckily Jamie's mother had sent them off with a Tupperware box of sandwiches when they'd popped around to see her earlier. Now that Andrew had got him on the road, there was no stopping until they got to the hotel, not even for a drive-in McDonald's on that shitty little roundabout outside Athlone.

'You want one?' Jamie asked him, opening the lid.

'I'll pass this time,' Andrew said. 'We can get something to eat when we arrive. Maybe have a few cocktails.'

'*If* we arrive,' Jamie said. He took out a sandwich and lifted the two slices of white bread apart to see what was between them, but couldn't make out exactly what it was. His mother had called them 'surf 'n' turf sambos', and there was a definite smell of salmon paste. Maybe the little brown pieces mixed in with it were bits of mince.

He took a tentative bite and switched on the radio. It didn't taste too bad.

On Newstalk 106, which Andrew always listened to, they were going on about the number of jobs lost at a microchip manufacturing plant in Galway, which was the last thing anybody in their right mind wanted to hear about now – or at any time, for that matter. Shoving the rest of his sandwich into his mouth, Jamie pressed the automatic channel searcher. It landed on Jazz FM where some crooner was singing 'Moon River'.

'Andy Williams,' said Andrew. 'I love this song.'

'Only you would know that,' said Jamie, taking a bite from the other half of his sandwich.

'My mother had *Andy Williams's Greatest Hits* when I was a kid. I used to play it all the time.'

They listened to the song in silence, Jamie thinking back to the scene from *Breakfast at Tiffany's* with Audrey Hepburn singing it on the fire escape outside her apartment window. It was the only non-camp part of the movie. The rest of it was just one big gayfest, without the shagging. If Truman Capote had been allowed to write the screenplay, it wouldn't have had every shred of sex extricated from it.

'Story of my life,' Jamie had said to Lisa, in the taxi on the way home from Katherine's, and she'd laughed.

'You wish,' she replied, completely misunderstanding what he had been trying to say. Like all heterosexuals she believed all gay men had fantastically abundant sex lives.

Jamie reached out and switched off the radio. 'I'm sick of that bloody song,' he said. 'It's like music you'd hear shopping in Lidl.'

'They don't play music in Lidl. It's part of their policy.'

'My point exactly.'

Andrew heaved a sigh and shook his head. 'You could at least try to get into the spirit of this weekend,' he said. 'You really need a break, you know. What happened to you was terrible. People get really depressed after violence like that.'

'Oh, God,' Jamie said. 'I wish you'd stop going on about it.'

'You're in total denial, you know. And I understand. I know how sensitive you are. But you have to take care of yourself.'

'I *am* taking care of myself. I promise.'

Being in denial was the only way forward. Otherwise Jamie wouldn't be able to walk down the street without the fear that some other psycho mob might notice the big gay arrow in the sky pointing directly at him. People got killed in gaybashing attacks. It was a common occurrence.

He hadn't mentioned it to Saeed when he'd called him to say their fling was over. He'd just said the time had come to move on and that he wished him all the best.

'Don't be silly,' Saeed said. 'Come later. I have a thing for you. A little present.'

'No,' said Jamie. 'It's finished. I don't want to see you any more.'

'You will come. At ten, when I am finished with work.'

'No,' Jamie repeated. 'Goodbye, Saeed.' And he hung up.

It seemed better to do it that way. Cut and dried. When temptation reared its sexy head, as he knew it would, Jamie vowed to think back to the moment in the middle of the assault when he'd heard the gay homeless guy speak. He'd had a deep, resonant voice, not unlike that of God in a Charlton Heston movie. 'Leave him alone,' it had said, and Jamie heard the message loud and clear: he was to leave the Iranian alone and stop being unfaithful to the man who loved him. He was being rescued, being given a second chance.

The hotel was an odd mixture of super-modern concrete and steel architecture fused to an old cream-painted ice house. Andrew had booked a suite; champagne and chocolates were waiting for them with a welcoming message from the manager. One wall was made of glass and looked out to a still, wood-lined river, on which a pair of swans glided by without a care in the world. The sky was swollen with purple-grey clouds that touched the tips of the pine trees on the river's far side.

'Isn't this beautiful?' Andrew said, coming up behind Jamie and putting his arms around him. 'All we have to do is relax and enjoy ourselves from here on in.'

'Don't you have any case work to do?' Jamie asked. Usually Andrew went everywhere with an armful of client files.

'I don't,' said Andrew. 'This weekend is for you. No, it's for us. If there's one thing the assault has taught me, it's that I need to pay more attention to you and stop focusing on my clients so much.'

'But your clients need you,' said Jamie. And they did. Even though the influx of immigrants had tailed off with the recession, the queue of asylum seekers seeking Andrew's legal aid was still endless. It was a pain in the arse when he had to work Saturdays, or take phone calls in the middle of the night, like he was their therapist or something, but Jamie liked the fact that Andrew cared about his clients so much. His support was unwavering.

'You need me,' said Andrew. 'We need each other. We're the most important people in each other's lives.'

'I know,' said Jamie, and leaned back into Andrew's arms.

Andrew kissed his neck. 'I want to be with you all the time,' he murmured.

Jamie thought he could feel Andrew's dick against his arse cheek – hard.

'Come to bed,' Andrew murmured.

'Listen to you, mister.' Jamie smiled, turning to unbutton Andrew's shirt. 'Sounds like today's my lucky day.'

They fell on to the bed, struggling to take each other's clothes off.

'Careful!' Jamie laughed as Andrew fumbled at the zipper on his jeans. 'We don't want any nasty accidents.'

By the time they were naked under the covers, Andrew's dick was flaccid again.

Jamie massaged it with his right hand while they kissed, but he knew the moment was over. Andrew was kissing him back, but there was no response.

After another minute, Andrew pulled away. 'I'm sorry, honey. I'm a bit tired.'

'It's been a long drive,' Jamie said. 'You should have a nap.'

'I love you,' Andrew said, leaning in to kiss him lightly. 'You know that, don't you?'

'Yes,' Jamie replied, kissing him back and stroking his forehead.

Instead of retreating to one side of the bed, Andrew fell asleep, spooned against Jamie's back with his arms wrapped tightly around him, his head nuzzling Jamie's neck. Jamie almost nodded off too, surrendering his frustration to the secure warmth of Andrew's body, but the room, as hotel rooms were apt to be, was overheated and soon the bed's luxury cotton sheets began to feel clammy.

Jamie lifted his head out of the covers and tried to take a lungful of air, but couldn't breathe properly. He pulled himself out of Andrew's grip.

'What?' Andrew said.

'Nothing, honey. Go back to sleep.'

Andrew grunted and turned on to his other side. Jamie lay on his back, staring at the ceiling. It was painted a pristine white, like the rest of the suite. Not a crack, not an undulation, not a single mark to interrupt its wall-to-wall blankness.

Later they'd get up and go down to dinner, showered, shaved and dressed in their best pressed jeans and shirts, a perfectly turned-out gay couple. The gays who had it all – style, good looks, great taste and endless fantastic sex. When they got back to their room they'd repeat a version of what had just taken place. And so on into infinity. And beyond.

The trouble was, Jamie couldn't talk about it. And neither could Andrew. It was sitting there between them like an elephant that had grown too complacent in the room.

Jamie prided himself on being someone who wasn't afraid to say what was what, but every time he vowed to raise the subject of sex with Andrew, or the lack thereof, his nerve failed him. He was afraid that if he brought it up, it might spell the beginning of the end.

With Saeed there was no need for talk. It was just great sex with no strings attached and it made Jamie feel sane again. With Andrew the strings were everywhere. Their lives were bound together, their emotions completely entangled. Yet while Jamie couldn't imagine his life without Andrew, neither could he imagine it stretching out before him without sex. Something would have to give.

Jamie shifted on to his side and bunched the pillow under his head.

If you thought about it in a certain light, having it off with Saeed might be a way of saving his relationship with Andrew. Not all the time, like before. Just every now and then. Often enough to tide him over.

But how fucked up was that?

Jamie twisted back on to his other side to face Andrew. When he was asleep, Andrew looked vulnerable, as if some terrible thing could happen to him and he wouldn't be able to defend himself. Jamie experienced a surge of love for him that also felt like sorrow.

Cheating on someone wasn't love, was it? No matter how you tried to justify it.

22. Chocolate Biscuits and Sympathy

The old man buying the box of Coco Pops smiled at Lisa sympathetically, which was more than she could say for the girl behind the till, who looked at her like something she'd found on the sole of her shoe.

With her right hand she awkwardly lifted groceries out of the trolley while Theo screeched and tried to pull away from her left. If she let go, he'd run off and cause chaos in the aisles.

Sitting in the trolley's babyseat, Aaron wailed to be picked up again, fat tears rolling down his red cheeks. But she had only one pair of hands. Thank God Ben was happy to be left in the crèche.

'Here, let me help you,' the old man said, taking one of the bags Lisa had thrown on the checkout, which was beginning to pile up. He was neatly done up in a shirt, tie and suit jacket, this thin, white hair scraped into a precise comb-over across the dome of his head. Dapper, thought Lisa. Maybe he's gay.

'I'm fine, honestly,' she said.

'You've got your hands full.' The man smiled. 'It's no bother at all.'

Lisa wondered who he was buying the Coco Pops for. Himself, most likely. Probably lonely. Getting himself a little treat.

She was reaching into the trolley to pull out a bag of potatoes when Theo's teeth bit painfully into the soft flesh at the base of her thumb, causing tears to spring into her eyes. She let go of him. Theo stood for a moment, looking at her, challenging her, and then ran.

'I'm sorry,' she said to the man. 'Could you?' She nodded at Aaron, who was still bawling his eyes out.

'Of course,' the man said, and the girl behind the till rolled her eyes. As Lisa set off in pursuit of Theo, Aaron's cries became hysterical.

She found Theo in the biscuit aisle trying to open a packet of chocolate Digestives with his teeth. His auburn curls – nobody knew where they'd come from – looked wild. 'No, Theo,' she said. 'You're not having those. We have perfectly good biscuits already.'

'I want them!' Theo cried. His voice had tipped over into that high-pitched, nasal whine before the storm.

'Okay,' Lisa said. 'Just this time. But you have to wait to eat them later. In the car.'

'Now! NOW!'

Lisa sighed, opened the packet and gave him one. 'Now will you be a good boy and let Mummy do the shopping?' she asked, but he didn't answer. He was licking the chocolate off the biscuit.

When she got back to the till, Aaron was smiling at the old man, batting his beautiful long eyelashes and gurgling.

'My oldest was like this lad,' the man said, touching Theo's shoulder. 'Wild as a hare. But he calmed down eventually.'

The thing about Theo was that he had been the perfect baby. From three months old he had slept through the night, only cried a little when he was hungry and needed to be changed, and generally was the soul of placidity, perched in his Bumbo Baby Sitter, watching the world go by.

Lisa put it down to *The Contented Little Baby Book*, which she had followed to the letter, never missing a moment of his routine, blacking out the windows in his room and keeping the house as quiet as a library when he went down. But The Contented Little Baby Book never said a word about contented little babies who turned into little toddlers who threw blue-face tantrums three, four, five times a day. Or unmanageable little toddlers who turned into five-year-olds who hated their mothers.

Since she had stopped working and Sofia had left, he had grown to hate her so much that there was never an instant of happy communication, never a cuddle, never a moment's peace, except when he was sleeping, which was difficult enough to achieve in its own right. And the kicking, scratching and biting never stopped.

After the incident where he'd made her face bleed by pinching it so hard, she'd cut his nails every third day to keep them down to the very stubs. Last month he'd broken the skin on her arm with a bite, hanging on, dog-like, while she'd screamed and tried to push him away. Lately he'd taken to running at her when she least suspected it and headbutting her in the leg. Her thighs were covered with bruises.

Why did he hate her? She couldn't think what she'd done, or was doing, to make him so full of rage. If anything she'd been softer with him than the other two, more focused on his every whim. If it weren't for the fact that he expressed blind adoration of Patrick so regularly, she would have thought there was something wrong with him developmentally.

'Sometimes boys are like that,' Patrick assured her. 'He'll grow out of it.' Patrick seemed to think that as Lisa had been raised in a house of girls she was clueless about mothering the opposite sex. But surely children were children. If a child was acting up, did it matter which sex it was? No. Lisa was doing something wrong, she knew it. She just had to work out what it was.

The worst of it was that now Ben was beginning to copy Theo, not only in words but in actions too. Lovely, sensitive Ben, whom she'd thought would never harm a fly, had kicked her in the shin the other day as she was taking some peas out of the freezer. Granted, it had hardly hurt, but give him a few years and his kicks would be as painful as Theo's. And Aaron would be following suit.

'It was a pleasure,' said the old man, when she thanked him. As he walked off she felt the urge to tip him. But she was being stupid. How insulting would that have been?

She gave Theo another biscuit to get him into his car seat, and although Aaron was whining at being put down again, he'd be asleep in a couple of minutes, once she got the engine running.

She had to pick Ben up from the crèche, then Patrick's suit from the dry-cleaner's. She kept forgetting to do that.

In the back, Aaron let out a squeal of pain and began wailing again.

'Did you hit your little brother?' Lisa said, turning as best she could to Theo.

'No,' said Theo. But he was smiling.

Turning on the indicator to pull out, Lisa pulled down her sun visor and caught her reflection in its mirror. The sight of her eyes so tightly framed in the small rectangle gave her a claustrophobic feeling. She imagined unclipping her seatbelt, opening the door and just walking away between the rows of cars, towards the mountains that hovered majestically in the distance.

23. Rainbow's End

The girl in the temping agency hadn't sounded too enthusiastic, but Katherine wasn't going to let that put her off. 'The position might be permanent if they find the right person,' she'd said. 'It's filing and basic office duties. A bit lower than your league, but it's the only even vaguely suitable thing we have on the books.'

'A job is a job is a job,' said Katherine to herself. Considering none of her contacts had come back with even a sniff of work, this was the only step she could take forward. At least she wasn't standing still.

Rainbow Recycling was situated beneath the railway tracks, at the end of a narrow alley on the industrial northern outreaches of the city. Two men in green boiler-suits leaned against stacked bales of compressed paper, smoking and silently watching Katherine as she picked her way across the uneven concrete yard in her Miu Miu heels, narrowly avoiding a reddish brown lump of dog shit. She'd dressed up Holly Golightly-style for her first day. It was maybe a bit much but she wanted to make a good impression.

The centre of operations consisted of two grey Portakabins jammed together, with uneven steps going up to a door at one end, flanked by rusty metal banisters on either side. Katherine took a deep breath and walked up them, opening the door into a small, neat office with wood-effect linoleum on the floor and two desks facing each other from opposite corners.

'I'm Katherine Casey,' she said, holding out her hand to the woman who sat behind one of the desks. Her bleached hair was thin and wispy, receding at the front. 'I'm from the agency. For the temporary job?'

Without taking Katherine's hand, the woman shouted over her shoulder. 'Gus! Get out here!'

Gus appeared in the doorway behind her, completely filling it with his girth. 'What do you want now?' he said, before noticing Katherine. Like the woman behind the desk, he gave her a once-over, then asked, 'She from the agency?'

'Yeah,' the woman said. 'Another.'

'That's your desk over there,' Gus said. 'Jacinta here will show you the ropes.' He was breathing heavily as if he'd just lifted a set of weights.

Jacinta took a clipboard from a hook on the wall and flicked through the sheaf of papers attached to it before handing it to him. 'There's a consignment from DCC. You'll need to sort through it,' she said, looking at Katherine from the corner of her eye.

Gus took the clipboard and ambled out of the front door of the Portakabin, barely squeezing through. Katherine hung her coat on the back of the chair behind her desk and sat down. 'So, where will I start?' she asked.

Jacinta didn't reply. She leaned back against her desk with her arms folded, still appraising Katherine. On her fingers she wore an assortment of heavy gold rings.'You can start by taking that hoity-toity expression off your face,' she said, standing up and going over to a grey metal filling cabinet in the corner beside Katherine's desk. 'I've seen more like you in the last few months, with your airs and graces, than I've seen flies take to shite, and I know what you're thinking.'

'What am I thinking?' Katherine asked.

'You're thinking you're too good for the likes of this. You're thinking you'll bear it until something better comes along because you need the money for your big-shot mortgage.'

'That's not true! I'm here to do my my best.'

'Yeah?' said Jacinta. 'Well, do your best with this.' She tapped the filing cabinet. 'I want you to put all the files in here in alphabetical order, and make sure the right documents are in the right folders before you do. I haven't got time to be training you in the routine around here when you'll be gone before the day is out.'

The woman in the agency had said 'filing and basic office duties', but still Katherine's heart sank. From heading a strategic sales team that covered the whole of Ireland and the UK at one of the world's leading computer companies to arranging files in a horrible, damp, smelly Portakabin – it was a humiliation she'd never imagined suffering. Jacinta was right: Katherine did think she was too good for it.

But she heard her father's voice telling her to grin and bear it, to do her best. 'Wait and see. It'll all come out right in the end,' he would say, if Katherine was upset when she was little.

'What are you waiting for?' Jacinta said. 'A bus?'

The filing cabinet turned out to be an unsalvageable mess. The files it contained were almost impossible to quantify, roughly stuffed with odds and ends, receipts, invoices and pieces of paper with illegible sentences scrawled on them. Several times, Katherine asked Jacinta if she was filing the right receipt with the right invoice, or what one of those pieces of paper meant, but Jacinta barely lifted her head away from her computer. She seemed to be involved in something amusing, given the snorts she made every now and then before spurts of enthusiastic typing.

'You'll work it out,' was all she eventually said.

Throughout the morning Gus came and went, huffing and puffing all the time, but never turning his sweaty red face in Katherine's direction. The two men in the yard came in for a cup of tea at eleven, and drank it sitting around Jacinta's desk, no one saying anything at all.

Katherine asked for directions to the bathroom and found herself in a murky little cubicle where bleach battled with the stench of stale urine. She hovered over the cigarette-burned toilet seat, afraid to let her skin touch it, holding her pencil skirt up as far as it would go and counting the hours until her first day would be finished.

At lunchtime a man with a tray of sandwiches called into the office and Katherine chose a chicken and stuffing roll. She ate in silence at her desk, trying not to look at Jacinta, who had bought an egg sandwich and was chewing with her mouth open.

'Had enough yet?' Jacinta asked, after a while, a glistening yellow piece of egg stuck to her chin.

'Yes,' said Katherine. 'That was delicious.'

Jacinta gave a hollow laugh. 'You're some tulip all right.'

Katherine met her eyes. She knew exactly what was going on. Jacinta was marking her territory. It didn't matter who Katherine was, or where she had come from. This woman was going to make her life hell if she stayed.

Katherine went back to the filing. At ten euro an hour, if she lasted until five o'clock, she would make eighty euro, and that would go towards next week's food shopping. She wouldn't have to dip into what she'd got for the car just yet. Martin had sent her the cheque without a note.

Eighty euro. Was it worth the humiliation? Would it really make the slightest difference when push came to shove?

She was on her knees searching through the contents of the

bottom drawer of the filing cabinet when Jacinta came in from the back office with a pile of bulging folders in her arms and dumped them on Katherine's desk. 'Here,' she said. 'These need to be sorted.'

'How do you mean, "sorted"?' Katherine asked.

'Make sure they're up to date. Make sure the invoices and receipts are in the right sequence.'

Katherine looked at the folders, which had spilled half their contents into an amorphous mess when Jacinta had flung them on to the desk. Eighty euro? All the money in the world wouldn't recompense her for trying to please Jacinta, who was going to treat her like a dog no matter what she did.

'All right, you win,' Katherine said.

'What do you mean by that?' Jacinta replied. The smile that had curled the side of her mouth was gone.

'You're right,' said Katherine. 'I *am* better than this. No, forget that. I'm better than you. At least I wouldn't kick somebody who was down.'

'Get off the stage, for fuck's sake. You haven't all day to be standing around here complaining.' Jacinta turned on her heel and went back to her desk.

Katherine grabbed her coat and headed for the door.

'Where do you think you're going?' said Jacinta. Her voice was faltering now. 'The agency told me you had no other work.'

'I'm going home,' said Katherine. 'This isn't for me.'

'You won't be paid at all unless you stay for the required hours today,' Jacinta said. 'It's company policy.'

'Well, you can shove that company policy where the sun doesn't shine,' said Katherine. 'Because I'm out of here. No amount of shit pay is worth this.'

Jacinta's eyebrows shot up. 'But what about the filing? You haven't even made a dent in it.'

Katherine hoisted her bag on her shoulder. 'You know what?' she said. 'You can shove the filing up there beside your company policy. And when you've finished that, why don't you give yourself a break and get something done with that hair?'

As she walked, head up, along the alley and away from Rainbow Recycling, a large yellowish splodge dropped on to her left shoulder. She looked up at the sky for any more birds hovering to take aim.

'Go for it!' she called to a passing seagull.

It wasn't as if things could get any worse.

April

The Wizard of Oz
Victor Fleming, 1939

'A heart is not judged by how much you love;
but by how much you are loved by others.'

24. The White Envelope

Katherine wished she hadn't arrived so early. From the kitchen she heard the crash of crockery landing on the floor, then Alice apparently arguing with someone. Katherine wondered if she should go in and help but, on second thoughts, decided to leave her to it. Alice was so nervous that helping would probably do more harm than good.

She shivered and shifted in her chair. All around her the eyes of a multitude of miniature owls stared at her in the murky light of the room. It had the aura of a museum and the same kind of old smell, as if nothing had been moved from its place in years. In itself the electric fire, with its plastic coal and painted flames, was worthy of a museum and gave off hardly any heat.

She had spent the afternoon surrounded by little girls at her sister's house, all dressed as Disney princesses for Kitty's seventh birthday. Her niece was the Little Mermaid and there had been three Belles, two Cinderellas and a lone Snow White. In the cramped environs of Lucy's council flat, they'd been pretty loud princesses, and their increasingly sticky fingers had left all sorts of stains on their dresses. There should have been baby wipes on hand, but the whole thing was chaos, except for the bit at the end when they'd all settled down for the story Kitty had begged Katherine to read to them. As she'd looked around at the roomful of big eyes, she was reminded of sitting on her father's knee, looking up at him as he read to her.

Afterwards Lucy had insisted that her boyfriend give Katherine a lift to Alice's house, which was why she was there so early. For the entire journey he had talked about the weather, the only subject they had in common, in his heavy Brazilian accent. After a while Katherine had run out of descriptions for rain, so she had looked at it through the passenger window instead.

She couldn't understand what her sister saw in Paolo. He was five foot high, covered with hair from neck to toe and spoke hardly any English. What in God's name did they talk about?

Nonetheless Lucy's girls seemed to adore him. Eleven-year-old Laura, as sleek and copper headed as he was heavy-set and dark, was nearly as tall as him and acted as if he was her brother, chatting away to him about *Glee* and *iCarly*, although he said little in reply. Kitty hung on to Paolo like a pet monkey, crawling over him as he sat on Lucy's sofa, rarely opening his mouth.

To Lucy he seemed to be a kind of fixture or fitting, shoved up so she could eat dinner in front of the television or sent to wash the dishes when the meal was finished.

'He should at least make an effort to learn a little English,' Katherine told her sister. 'How long has he been here now?'

'Four years,' said Lucy. 'And why? He's getting by fine without it.'

'He might be able to get some work. You know. Earn a living?'

'Oh, come off it. You can't get a job. What chance does he have?'

It had stung, but it was true. It had been three weeks since the day she had spent temping for Rainbow Recycling. Since then she'd applied for sixteen jobs, from shop assistant to call-centre operator and anything she could find in between, but hadn't been offered a single interview. Some of them hadn't bothered to let her know she wasn't being considered.

The last rejection letter she'd received, from a home-shopping catalogue company that was looking for an operations manager, had told her she was over-qualified for the position. Another, from an IT corporate, had said she'd be better to streamline her qualifications into the consulting sector.

But the consulting sector didn't want to know. Every morning she got up and looked for jobs online, sending her CV out as often as she could. For the rest of the day she sat in the house, while Barry was out at work, surrounded by expensive things she had bought with so much care and love but that seemed utterly worthless now.

A wardrobe full of designer labels, a spare room lined with shelves for shoes, handbags and other accessories: what did it all mean? If she took them into the second-hand designer shop on Clarendon Street, she wouldn't make enough to cover next month's bills, never mind recoup the vast amount they had originally cost.

She wandered from room to room in her dressing-gown and wondered how it had all ended like this. When she'd left college and started in consulting, she had understood that this was the right way forward, the way to make herself secure. Everyone was in on the deal, everyone believed in its promise. She worked hard, and money began to roll in, more money than she had ever thought she'd earn, and she wasn't even halfway up the ladder. She could spend what she wanted. She had earned it. She would always earn it.

She looked at the art on the walls, fingered the ornaments selected to enhance every corner; she lay on her form-fitting, memory-foam mattress and stared up at the chandelier she had brought back from Morocco and painstakingly reassembled so that it could fit this room, and tried to force herself to believe it was all over. The good times were gone. Finished. Kaput. The promise had been empty. It would not be made good on.

But that couldn't be right, could it? There was still a part of her that didn't believe it, and as long as that part of her was alive, she would be able to go on. The moment it died, panic would take over – she'd hurtle over the edge of the cliff into terrifying darkness.

And then the letter had come. The pristine white rectangular envelope had lain face down on the hall floor that morning like a new promise – but it had turned out to be the straw that broke the camel's back.

She was being turned down for statutory redundancy for her ten years at Henderson: 'We regret to inform you that the decision has been reached because there was a break of service of over eleven months between your tenures at Henderson Consulting and Qwertec Solutions,' the letter said, with calm formality.

The year's leave of absence had seemed the perfect idea, a space for Katherine to supervise the building of the extension and renovations to the main house, a time for her to gather herself before the next phase of her career.

Her redundancy money from Qwertec, along with what she'd got for the car, had paid her share of the mortgage for the past two months. For all other expenses she had relied on the paltry savings in her Credit Union account, but that was a road fast winding towards its end.

Over the past few days Katherine had called her mother's mobile a few times, but she couldn't get through. An automated quick-talking Spanish voice came on the line, presumably telling her that the number was unavailable.

'I wish she'd at least answer my texts when she goes down to the village,' Katherine had told Lucy. 'There's some signal in the main square.'

'She's not texting you back because she knows you're going to ask for a loan,' Lucy said.

'I was thinking more about asking her to ask Liam for a loan.'

Lucy snorted. 'That skinflint wouldn't give up half a sandwich if a child was dying of starvation in front of him.'

It was true. Their stepfather had made a fortune on the property market and had been savvy enough to cash in and get out while the going was good. But he didn't like sharing his wealth with anyone.

'I don't know why you won't ask Barry to pay the mortgage until you get work,' Lucy said. 'He certainly earns enough.'

Katherine took the letter and its envelope from the table and tore them in two. Lucy was right. They'd shelled out all their savings and cashed in their shares to pay off half the value of the house as a deposit when they'd bought it. Barry could afford the remaining mortgage for a few months.

25. Poor Judy

'Oh, *The Wizard of Oz*!' said Lisa. 'I loved it when I was a kid!' She was sitting in Mother's chair, fingering the doily Alice had put on its scuffed, upholstered arm.

'I don't think I've ever watched the whole thing through,' said Katherine. 'I kind of lose interest in it once Judy Garland sings "Over The Rainbow".'

'Looks like today's your lucky day,' said Martin.

There was something 'off' about him, Alice thought. From the farthest corner of the sofa, where he had sat down with his six-pack of beer, he was speaking a bit too loudly, like an actor in a play.

'Uh, what's with the owls?' said Jamie, picking up one of the ceramic miniatures on the mantelpiece and putting it down facing in the wrong direction.

Alice resisted the urge to turn it into its proper position. 'My mother was a Brown Owl with the Brownies,' she said. 'They were all presents from girls in her pack. She collected them.'

'Creepy,' said Jamie. Lisa glared at him. 'But in a good way.'

'So why *The Wizard of Oz*?' Katherine asked. 'I didn't know we could choose children's films.'

'We can show any film we like, remember?' said Martin. 'That's the original rule.'

'Except *The Sound of Music*,' Katherine shot back. 'I seem to remember you making that very clear.'

'That's right,' Martin said, his arms folded.

'I watched *The Wizard of Oz* with my mother when I was a little girl,' Alice said. 'At Christmas.'

There was something wrong with Katherine too. She didn't seem comfortable. Alice wondered if it had something to do with the house. Or maybe she'd chosen the wrong wine. She'd bought six bottles of merlot on the advice of a man in the supermarket. The label on the bottle said it was 'structured and velvety, with raspberry and blueberry flavours enhanced by spicy notes'. It had certainly sounded lovely.

'I don't think I'd let the boys see *The Wizard of Oz* yet,' said Lisa. 'They're far too young for the Wicked Witch of the West. All those old children's films have really scary stuff in them, even the Disney ones. I think they believed it was good to frighten kids. But anyone writing about child psychology nowadays says that's totally wrong.'

'So you keep saying,' said Jamie. 'The cut on your face healed well, by the way.'

Lisa went back to fingering the doily on her chair. 'It was only a scratch,' she said.

Alice offered around a plate of egg sandwiches cut into quarters. Mrs Silver had said to make them in case the dips weren't enough – and a good thing too. Martin took two and devoured them in nearly one bite. Then he took two more and held them in a napkin on his lap.

'Are we going to watch the film or not?' he said, opening another can.

Jamie's phone bleeped and he took it out of his pocket. 'I may have to leave early,' he said, reading his text message.

'I wish you'd turn that phone off for once,' said Lisa. 'It's very distracting.'

'I'll turn mine off if you turn yours off.'

'But I have to have mine on for the babysitter, in case there's any problem.'

Jamie's eyes flashed. 'And my life is less important than yours because I don't have children?'

Lisa was sitting up, wagging her finger. 'That's not what I said, Jamie, and you know it.'

'Girls, girls, calm down,' said Martin, his face lighting with a smile for the first time that evening.

'Yes,' added Katherine. 'Why don't we just watch the film?'

Alice pressed play on the DVD and, after the credits, Dorothy's face filled the television screen. She looked the picture of innocence, so perfect and untouched.

'Poor Judy,' Jamie said. 'How pear-shaped it all went.'

'But she was beautiful,' said Alice, gazing at the screen. 'Like an angel.' Jamie found fault with everything, she thought. He imagined he was funny, but he wasn't. Not at all.

'That's one of the mad things about *The Wizard of Oz*,' said Martin. 'She looks so perfect, but she was already ruined.'

Alice wished they'd be quiet. Nobody had carried on the conversation like this once the movie had started at their houses.

'Ruined?' said Katherine. 'Don't you think that's a little over the top?'

'No,' said Martin. 'I don't. She was addled with drugs most of the time on the set. They gave her downers to sleep, uppers to work, and other stuff to keep her weight down.'

'There's all sorts of gossip about the Munchkins getting drunk on set and pinching her arse,' said Jamie. 'Kinky little fuckers.'

'Do you mind not using that kind of language?' said Alice.

'As long as I'm allowed use that kind of language back in Kansas, Your Holiness.'

Katherine swallowed a bite of her sandwich. 'I think you can feel this incredible loneliness from Judy Garland,' she said. 'There was always something very isolated about her, like she was on one side of a window looking at the world going by on the other.'

'That's because of all the fighting that went on between her mother and father,' said Jamie. 'He was gay, you know.'

Martin took a swig of his beer. 'Here we go,' he said.

'And while we're at it,' added Jamie, 'the Lion is, like, totally queer, with the big hair-do he gets before seeing the wizard and the way he gives the Tin Man the eye.'

'You can't say that,' said Alice. 'It's a children's film.' She was beginning to wish she hadn't chosen it. They were pulling it apart, divesting it of its magic with all their talk of drug addiction, perverted Munchkins and homosexuality. And it hadn't even properly begun.

'Seemingly, I'm not allowed say anything at all,' said Jamie. 'Maybe I should just leave.'

'Please stay,' said Alice, quickly. What would the others think if he stormed off?

26. The Adoption Agency

Alice's visit to the adoption agency, accompanied by Mrs Silver, had been about as useful as Dorothy's visit to the wizard. Alice had looked forward to it with mounting anticipation as the day drew nearer, thinking it was going to provide all the answers to her questions. Instead it had proved to be a dead end.

'I'm afraid these things take time,' Mrs Babcock – she had told Alice to call her Miriam – said, putting on a pair of glasses attached to a gold chain that hung around her neck. 'It isn't simply a case of giving you a telephone number and sending you on your way.'

'But you do have my details on file?' Alice asked again.

'There are procedures, paperwork to be filled out and permissions to be sought – that kind of thing.'

'I was born on the tenth of June 1973. So you would probably have the name of my mother and her address at the time filed under that date. Or under my adoptive parents' name – Little.'

'We also advise counselling for you and your birth mother, should she wish to meet you. This should take place before anything is arranged.'

'I see,' said Alice. 'How long does that take?'

'I wouldn't like to say. It all depends on whether the birth parent is willing to meet. Assuming the birth parent is still with us.'

'Still with us?'

'Alive, Miss Little.'

Mrs Babcock opened a drawer in the side of her desk and extracted a large red book. 'Now,' she said, licking the ends of her fingers delicately as she turned its pages, 'let's make an appointment for you to go through your file. Yes. I have a date. How does the first of June sound? At twelve thirty.'

Alice's face fell. 'But that's over two months away,' she said.

Mrs Babcock shut the book and gave a tight smile. 'We'll see you then,' she said.

Alice stood up to leave, but Mrs Silver, who had said nothing since they'd sat down, reached out and put a hand on hers, motioning for her to be still.

'Miriam,' Mrs Silver said. 'Can I ask you a question?'

'Are you related to Miss Little?' she asked.

'Not exactly, dear. But my question is a simple one. Is Miss Little legally allowed access to her file?'

'Her file is the property of this agency. If that's what you mean.'

'Oh, I'm sure it is. But isn't there something called the Freedom of Information Act, which entitles Miss Little to see the contents of that file?'

'Of course there is. We're not denying Miss Little access to her file. I have set up an appointment for her to come and view it on Monday, the first of June.'

'But we're here now, Miriam. And there's no time like the present, is there, dear?'

'I'm afraid that's out of the question. We're extremely busy. No. You'll just have to come back on the appointed date.'

Miriam Babcock stared icily at Alice and drummed her rust-coloured fingernails – the exact same shade as her tight-set hair – once on her desk.

'I'm wondering,' Mrs Silver said, after a moment, 'if Miss Little were to send you a solicitor's letter, would that speed the process up?'

Mrs Babcock's hand went to take off her glasses again. 'I don't think there's any need for that,' she said.

'Neither do I,' said Mrs Silver. 'But would a solicitor's letter help?'

'Help? I don't really know.'

'Perhaps your supervisor will have more information for us on the matter. Would you be a dear and get him for us? Or her?'

'We don't like to get into legal exchanges,' Mrs Babcock said. 'It's not our policy.'

'I understand,' said Mrs Silver, her tone like that of a mother soothing a baby. 'So would it be possible for Miss Little to see her file today? Or at least by the end of this week?'

Coming out from behind her desk, Mrs Babcock gave Mrs Silver a withering look. 'Wait here one moment,' she said, and exited the office, closing the door with a sharp click.

'How do you know about Freedom of Information Acts and all that kind of thing?' Alice whispered, once she was sure the woman was out of earshot.

Mrs Silver's eyes twinkled and she tapped the side of her nose. 'I heard about it on that television show with the judge on it. You know, the one with the very cross woman with brown hair. She's Jewish, I think.'

'*Judge Judy*?' Alice said.

'That's right. I thought it was worth a try. Miriam isn't very helpful, is she?'

'No,' Alice agreed, as Mrs Babcock swept back into the room.

'Mr Holmes will see you in the basement,' she said. 'It's down the hall, the last doorway on your left.'

'Thank you, Mrs Babcock,' Alice said.

'Thank you, Miriam.' Mrs Silver smiled. 'You've been a great help.'

Mr Holmes was an elderly man who looked as if he lived in the dusty basement. Bent and bespectacled, he spoke in disjointed sentences that went off at tangents.

'Yes, let's see,' he said, walking down an aisle of floor-to-ceiling shelves containing box files. 'It's very . . . Alice Little, you said? . . . inconvenient.'

Alice stood by the entrance to the stacks, saying nothing. Mrs Silver took her hand.

'L,' Mr. Holmes went on, laboriously climbing up a small ladder attached to the shelves. 'Most . . . Little, yes, Alice . . . inconvenient . . . Ah, yes, here we are . . .'

He brought a box file to the big table and opened it, taking out a slim green folder. 'I'm afraid you can only see one part . . .'

He opened the folder, and as he did so, Mrs Silver let go of Alice's hand. 'You will have to apply to the relevant authorities,' he said, sliding the green folder, which contained one flimsy page, across the table. 'Very cold for this time of year.'

Mrs Silver bent down suddenly, her blue-rinsed head bobbing about at the foot of the table, 'I seem to have dropped my glasses,' she said.

'I'll help you,' Alice said, bending down too, but Mrs Silver gave her a sharp 'No.'

'I'll leave you,' Mr Holmes said, taking the rest of the box file with him.

'It's my birth certificate,' Alice told Mrs Silver, poring over the piece of paper he'd left behind. 'But it doesn't give my mother's name or my father's. It only says the date of birth and where I was born. The Earlsfort Nursing Home.'

'It's short form,' said Mrs Silver, out of breath from her exertions under the table. 'Your long-form birth certificate would have more details.'

'But Mrs Babacock said I needed special permission to see taht because I was adopted.'

'Here,' said Mrs Silver, and handed Alice an envelope that looked as if it had been crumpled and smoothed out again. 'This slipped out when Mr Holmes opened the file. He didn't notice.'

The envelope was addressed in blue ink to the adoption agency in a tight, neat hand. The same handwriting took up less than a quarter of the lined page inside, addressed Ballydehob, Co. Cork, and dated, 15 June 1973.

> *To whom it may concern*
> *Please take care of my little girl. She is windy and gets uncomfortable if you lie her down directly after her bottle. She is very sensitive. Please be gentle with her.*
> *Yours faithfully,*
> *C*

'C,' said Mrs Silver. 'That must be her initial.'

'How would she know to say that I'm sensitive?' said Alice, looking at the dates on the birth certificate and the letter. 'She barely had me more than a few days.'

'Mothers know things about their children from the moment they're born, dear. It's the way these things are.'

A click-click of heels came from the hallway and Alice quickly pushed the letter into her bag just before Mrs Babcock put her head around the door. 'I expect you saw what you came to see,' she said.

'Not exactly, Miriam,' said Mrs Silver. 'There's a whole box of other paperwork that Mr Holmes took away.'

'You will have to apply to the parish to see any other files.'

'What about my long-form birth certificate?' asked Alice.

'Unfortunately we can't give you that. It is up to us to protect the identity of your mother, in case she should choose not to meet you.'

'That doesn't seem very fair,' said Mrs Silver.

'It depends on how you look at it,' Mrs Babcock replied, with a wan smile.

'So, how do I apply to see the rest of my file?' said Alice.

'Come back to my office and I'll give you the relevant forms. The next thing, of course, is for us to contact your mother to see if she is amenable to meeting you.'

27. No Place Like Home

'I've never really got the ending,' said Jamie, as the swelling orchestra brought the *The Wizard of Oz* to a close. 'Why would anyone in their right mind want to go back to black-and-white Kansas when they could stay in Oz?'

'There's no place like home,' said Katherine. 'Even if the alternative is more colourful.'

'Oh, come on! In Oz, she's a hero. At home nobody gives her the time of day. Her life in Kansas sucks.'

Martin took his beer can away from his mouth. 'Her quest is to go home. If she didn't get there in the end, it wouldn't be Hollywood, would it?'

Alice felt she had better contribute something. The film had been her choice, after all. 'I don't like it that Oz isn't a real place,' she said.

'Well, duh,' said Jamie. 'It's a movie.'

'No, what I mean is that in the original books Dorothy went back to Oz lots of times. But in the film it's only in a dream.'

Lisa sipped her wine. 'So, really, she never leaves home at all.'

'When you put it that way, yes,' said Martin. 'Although I don't think the film is about staying at home or getting back home.'

Alice frowned at Martin and noticed that everyone else was waiting for him to speak too. 'What do you mean?' she asked.

'I read somewhere that it's about religion. The two witches are the battle between good and evil, and Dorothy, in the middle, is searching for God.'

'The yellow brick road is her life path,' said Katherine, sitting up.

Martin sat up too. 'The Scarecrow, the Tin Man and the Lion are her own brain, her own heart, her own courage.'

'Is the Wizard God?' said Lisa.

'Nope,' said Martin. 'To find God, you don't have to go any further than your own backyard.'

'Somebody shoot me,' said Jamie. 'Is this Sunday School or a film club?'

Alice had never thought about the The Wizard of Oz as a religious parable. For her, it was about escape into fantasy rather than a reflection of the real world. At seven years old, she had watched it with Mother and Father on Christmas Day, an exception to the rule: although Christmas was a celebration of the birth of Our Lord Jesus Christ and not a day for sitting in front of the box, Mother had said they could watch it. As long as the television was turned off immediately afterwards.

All three of them sat down after dinner, Mother and Father in their chairs by the fire, Alice alone on the couch. Mother had talked all the way through the film, sipping the one sherry she allowed herself and reliving her memories of watching it in Belfast with her own mother. Alice had never seen her so animated before, but she'd wished she would be quiet.

In the moments when Mother wasn't speaking, the film had sucked Alice in until she'd thought she was part of the story, not just witnessing it. But then Mother would say something to Father, like 'Look at Judy Garland, Daddy. It's hard to believe she's dead and in the ground. God rest her soul and grant her eternal exile from the hell fires.'

Father would murmur in agreement and Alice would be wrenched back to her place on the hard couch with the acrid smell of boiled Brussels sprouts wafting in from the kitchen.

When the film was over, Mother had arranged the chairs in the room so that they could be used as makeshift pews, and they had prayed that they would be worthy to witness the second coming of the Lord Jesus Christ on Judgment Day.

'What about the sinners?' Alice asked. 'Shouldn't we pray for them?'

'Yes,' said Mother. 'We must pray for them most of all, that they will bow to the will of our one true God, whose only Son's blood was shed for them.'

When they were done praying for the sinners, Alice was sent to bed. From her window, she watched Dolores Egan, from the house across the road, skate up and down her front drive in darkness, wearing the new boot-skates she'd asked Santa for and obviously received. Alice had asked for boot-skates too, but received instead a new coat and shoes, which she knew she should be grateful for.

Dolores waved up at her and Alice tentatively waved back. Mother didn't like the Egans. They were Catholic, and the only thing worse than Catholics, she said, were pagans.

'When I was a little girl,' Alice said to the Film Club gathering, 'I used to stand in my bedroom and click my heels together and say, "There's no place like home. There's no place like home." And I really believed it could work.'

'But you *were* home,' said Jamie. 'You were in your bedroom.'

Alice was taken aback. She had never thought of it like that. 'I suppose I was,' she said, frowning.

Jamie smiled at her. There was a first time for everything, she thought.

28. An Apology

Martin was dying for a smoke. But since Barry had mentioned that Katherine had said he drank too much, he felt as though she was watching his every move and, despite himself, he didn't want to make a wrong one.

So what if he liked a drink or two? It was just a social thing, the same as it was for her, so who was she to judge? He'd counted the glasses of wine she had consumed so far tonight and the current tally was four. Martin congratulated himself. He had drunk the same number of cans.

He tried to catch Lisa's eye. It would be better if she suggested going for a smoke. But she was still on about the next-door neighbour who was babysitting for her.

'She does! She looks like Margaret Thatcher!' she was saying. 'Patrick says she's her doppelganger.'

'I could think of worse lookalike babysitters,' said Jamie. 'Myra Hindley . . . Eva Braun . . .'

Lisa shivered. 'I want to get home before Patrick's Lions Club auction is over,' she said. 'He'd go crazy if he knew I'd asked her to mind the boys. He can't stand Mrs Doherty.'

'You should rub it in his face,' said Jamie. 'Serves him right for letting you down at the last minute like that.'

'An auction for cholera sufferers in Haiti is a lot more important than Film Club,' Lisa replied.

Jamie smirked. 'Why do I get the impression that those are Patrick's words, not yours?'

Martin couldn't take it any longer. 'Do you want to come out for a smoke?' he asked Lisa, steadfastly avoiding Katherine's eye.

'I promised myself I wouldn't,' Lisa said. 'I have to be strong.'

'Fair enough,' Martin said, standing up. 'Will I go out the back?' he asked Alice.

'The door is locked. I'll have to let you out.'

Alice followed him into the kitchen and from the pocket of

her cardigan extracted a bunch of keys. 'You're the first,' she said.

'The first what?'

'The first person ever to smoke in the back garden. My mother disapproved of cigarettes.'

'She's not the only one,' Martin said, and then, realising he had spoken of Alice's mother in the present tense, corrected himself. 'Sorry. She wasn't the only one.'

Alice gave him one of her pale little smiles as she turned the key in the back door. 'It's all right,' she said. 'Sometimes I think Mother is still here. Watching everything. It's like that when someone dies, you know. Someone you love.'

'I'm sure it is,' Martin said gently, stepping past her into the dark garden. As he lit his cigarette and inhaled deeply, the idea of Alice's mother disapprovingly looking on made him shudder. There was a creepy feeling about the place, even the garden. All the dusty owls in the dark sitting room were like a crowd of flying monkeys, waiting to attack. Or the stuffed animals in Bates Motel.

He was halfway through his cigarette when Katherine's head appeared out of the back door.

'Hello,' he said. 'You're the last person I expected to see out here.'

'I wanted a breath of fresh air,' she said.

'Plenty of that to go around.'

They stood in strained silence, Martin trying to hold what was left of his cigarette as far out of range as possible, Katherine looking up at the inky black sky, her hands held together at her waist.

'I wanted to apologise,' she said, after a while. 'The way Barry put it … what I said about your drinking. It wasn't like that.'

'Then what was it like?'

'I just told him you got drunk when we were watching *Casablanca*, that's all.'

'That's all?' Martin knew his voice sounded like a petulant teenager's, but he couldn't stop himself.

'Well, I said that sometimes I think you drink too much,' said Katherine. She wasn't looking at him.

'Everyone drinks too much,' said Martin. 'You're hardly a teetotaller.'

'That's true, but …'

'But what?'

'Oh, I don't know. Look, I didn't mean to hurt you, Martin. I'm sorry if I did.'

At the word 'hurt', Martin realised that that was exactly what she'd done. She'd hurt him.

'It's all right,' he said, stubbing out the butt of his cigarette against the wall of the house. 'I'm a big boy. I can take it.'

'So we're friends again?'

'Friends,' said Martin.

Without warning, she reached out to give him a hug. His head nearly bumped into hers and she gave a quiet laugh. 'Sorry,' she said again.

Her body was warm against his and she smelt of lavender.

29. Like a Light Switch

Lisa hoped Mrs Doherty wouldn't smell the smoke on her breath. She'd bummed one cigarette from Martin just before she'd left, a reward, she felt, for having to go early. The rest of them didn't have responsibilities like she did.

Why shouldn't she have one little cigarette now and then? It wasn't a sin, and the odd one probably wasn't doing her any harm.

She smoked quickly in the little alleyway that ran down the side of the end house on the street, where she was sure nobody would catch her, unless your man from number forty-seven came out to bring his dog for a crap. Judging by the state of the alleyway, this was where it did its business regularly.

Mrs Doherty had been surprisingly amenable when Lisa asked her to babysit, even though they'd had a distant relationship at best ever since Lisa and Patrick had moved into the cul-de-sac five years ago. The very first time they'd met, Mrs Doherty had delivered what Lisa thought was a backhanded compliment about Theo. 'What a lovely baby,' she'd said. 'Any idea what has him crying so much?' And that was before Aaron was born. Aaron, who bawled all night, every night.

Things had remained perfectly civil between them, but Lisa had always felt judged by the older woman, and was conscious of how she behaved with the kids if she knew Mrs Doherty was within earshot, or on curtain alert. And if her supposedly helpful comments were anything to go by, often delivered over the garden wall that was all too low for Lisa's liking, she felt sure Mrs Doherty thought her mothering skills to be wanting.

Patrick had nicknamed her the Wicked Witch of the West, which was a bit of a coincidence, she thought, given the night that was in it.

Wicked Witch or not, when Lisa, in her desperation to get out, had asked her to mind the boys for a few hours, Mrs Doherty had smiled and said, 'Just let me get my knitting.' Lisa could have thrown her arms around her and kissed her. Patrick's last-minute refusal to mind the boys had left her in a state.

She understood that he was head of the committee, and that the meeting was for a charity auction. But, let's face it, they weren't polishing their haloes when they went to the pub afterwards. And Patrick didn't seem to understand that Film Club was her only outlet, the only thing that got her away from the children. As soon as his car had pulled away, she had knocked on Mrs Doherty's front door.

'I'll be back in three hours, before Aaron needs his night feed,' she'd promised. 'The other two won't wake up until he does.' She'd written down her mobile number in case anything went wrong.

After finishing the cigarette, which wasn't half as enjoyable as she'd imagined it would be, Lisa let herself in to find Mrs Doherty fast asleep with her knitting on her lap, the volume on the television turned low. She gave her neighbour a gentle nudge.

'I must have nodded off,' Mrs Doherty said, stretching her arms out wide. 'How was your evening?'

'Great, thanks. How was yours?' Lisa said. 'I hope they weren't too much trouble.'

'There wasn't a peep out of them. As good as gold.'

'Thank you so much for doing this, Mrs Doherty,' Lisa said. 'I won't impose on you again.'

'My name is Nora,' said Mrs Doherty. 'And there's no difference between watching television in my living room and watching it in yours.'

The moment the door closed behind Mrs Doherty – Nora – and Lisa was alone in the hall, Ben started crying. Lisa darted into the downstairs bathroom to wash the bitter aftertaste of smoke out of her mouth before going up to him. He might wake Theo and Aaron if she didn't get upstairs quickly, but Patrick would be home any minute now. She couldn't risk him smelling cigarettes on her breath.

When she walked into the boys' bedroom, Ben was standing up in his cot, rubbing his eyes with his fists. Theo was fast asleep, his quilt thrown aside, one leg dangling off the side of his bed. She went over and pulled the quilt over him, gently pushing his leg underneath it. His hair was damp on his forehead with sleep sweat and one hand was lying open on the pillow behind his head, its fingers pulsing every now and then. Her heart surged with love for him, as it often did when she watched him sleep. When he was dead to the world like this, he was like the baby he had once been. It made her remember who he really was.

Ben, only half awake, really, was easy to settle again, but in the box room next door, Aaron would be awake and bawling for his feed any time now.

Ben was just beginning to snore lightly, his button nose a little blocked with the cold he had picked up at the crèche, when Patrick came into the room and put his arms around her waist. She stopped stroking Ben's hair and leaned back into Patrick's chest, her head under his chin. He was exactly ten inches taller than her and she fitted into his shape perfectly.

'You're the best mother in the world, do you know that?' Patrick whispered.

'I don't think so,' said Lisa.

Patrick turned her around to face him. 'You are. Those kids want for nothing.'

'Theo hit a little girl in the playground today. He really hurt her.'

'Did he?' Patrick kissed her earlobe. She could feel against her lower back that he was hard and leaned into him. 'He's a wild one, that boy.'

'That's what the old man said.'

'What old man?'

'Just some man in the supermarket ages ago. Never mind.'

Patrick kissed her nose. 'C'mon to bed,' he said.

'How did the meeting go?'

'It was good. I'd say we'll make a fair bit at the auction.' He put his lips to hers, his tongue gently probing her mouth.

When he kissed her like that, in the first moment their lips met when he wanted sex, she always instantly turned on to it. He could flip her like a light switch.

'We watched *The Wizard of Oz* tonight,' Lisa said, as his hands began to massage her bum. 'It was weird seeing it after all these years.'

'Was it?' Patrick mumbled, pushing her towards their bedroom.

'I'd forgotten how freaky the Wicked Witch is.'

'You're my wicked witch,' said Patrick, unzipping his trousers.

He was so urgent tonight he was pushing her skirt up, pulling at her panties within seconds of landing on the bed. She found she was ready for him and let out a low sigh as the tip of his penis touched her.

'Stop,' she whispered. 'Get a condom.' But he was already deep inside her.

His tongue pushed into her mouth and she pulled him as close into her as she could, struggling to be part of his flesh, for him to be part of hers, the soft hairs on his shoulders sending shots of electricity through her fingers.

As the rhythm of their bodies together escalated, Lisa murmured urgently, 'Don't come inside me,' and Patrick nodded, his face red, his mouth open and then he let out the cry he always did before he ejaculated: 'Oh, God! Jesus!'

As he nestled his head in her shoulder, getting his breath back, Lisa internally calculated. It was just over two weeks since she'd had her period. They couldn't afford to be having sex without protection, but at least she was in the safety zone.

In the next room, Aaron started bawling for his feed.

30. Locked-in Syndrome

When Jamie woke up, Saeed was gone. The clock read 10:30, which meant he had already left for the daytime shift. Jamie closed his eyes again and stretched his legs into Saeed's side of the bed. He could sleep for a while longer. After all, he was hardly in a rush to get anywhere.

The whole thing had started up again completely by accident. Andrew had been away on a law conference in Scotland a few weeks ago and Jamie had gone to Lisa's that Saturday night for dinner accompanied by more than a few glasses of wine. On the way home he'd asked the cab to stop at Dragon where he knew he'd get a few more drinks – it closed late.

He'd just ordered a bottle of Coors Light when he caught sight of Saeed standing at the foot of the stairs to the smoking area, his biceps bulging from a tight white T-shirt, one thumb hooked into his belt buckle.

Saeed noticed him at exactly the same time and raised his beer bottle in salute.

The rest was a bit of a blur.

Jamie had resisted at first, saying he had to go home. But the pull was too strong. He could practically feel the testosterone pounding through his bloodstream when Saeed pushed him against the wall of the dance-floor and kissed him, stubble grating against his chin. When Saeed had grabbed him by the arm and pulled him towards the exit, he'd followed, like a zombie desperate for flesh.

Jamie snuggled up, taking in the spicy smell of Saeed from the pillow next to him. He'd told Andrew he was staying at his mother's last night, because it was near Alice's house, and the morning's most pressing appointment back at the apartment was *The Jeremy Kyle Show*.

Andrew thought *Jeremy Kyle* made for depressing viewing, but Jamie understood the attraction. For all the thousands of people who were not working, who were sitting on couches letting their lives tick by and doing nothing of real merit, it was like a salve to watch Jeremy Kyle lay into his guests. The people who turned up on the show were invariably the worst specimens of humanity. You could veg out in judgement of them all day long, now that Life TV was showing repeats every half-hour until five.

Not that Jamie was letting his life tick by. He was just waiting.

'For what?' Andrew asked. 'Godot?'

'Very funny, Mr Culture Section of the *Sunday Times*. I'm waiting for the right thing to come along.'

'Things don't just come along, Jamie. You have to go out and get them.'

'I know that. But I don't know what to go out and get, so I'm waiting for the right idea.'

The redundancy package would keep him going for another twelve months, with Andrew paying the rent and bills. That was plenty of time.

Jamie had no intention of joining queues of people lining up to be interviewed for scantily available jobs. His plan was to 'get a new skill set', as Andrew called it. He had no idea yet what that skill set should be.

The only trouble with *Jeremy Kyle* was that it was so repetitive. How many men in tracksuits reacting to DNA-tests that revealed whether or not they were the fathers of children born to women with bad teeth could a person watch? Over the past few weeks, Jamie had been inviting Saeed over to his and Andrew's place for alternative entertainment. It was fun while they were shagging, and great not having to move off the couch to get it, but every time Saeed left, Jamie had cleaned the house from top to bottom. He didn't like the way Saeed fingered everything, like he wanted to leave his mark. And when Andrew had come home in the evenings, Jamie could hardly look at him.

'Maybe we shouldn't do it here any more,' Jamie had said one afternoon, after they had done it in nearly every room, bar the broom cupboard. 'We'd be safer at your place.'

'Always my place, my place, my place,' Saeed had complained, snuggling up to Jamie on the sofa. 'This is better.'

'You want us to get caught, is that it?'

'Maybe. Then I can have you for myself.'

'I told you, that's not going to happen.'

'I know,' Saeed had said. He had licked Jamie's neck. 'No strings attached.'

'You should go,' Jamie had said.

'In a minute,' Saeed had grunted, undoing the top button of Jamie's jeans. 'In a minute.'

Jamie's eyes snapped open. Somewhere in Saeed's flat he could hear the special ringtone he'd put on his phone for Andrew, 'I Had The Time Of My Life' from *Dirty Dancing*. He jumped out of bed and went for the door.

It refused to budge. Jamie pulled at it with all his might, and then in frustration pushed his shoulder against it, as if it might open outwards.

The only window in the room looked out on to a narrow, rubbish-infested alley four floors down, but there was no fire escape. Outside the bedroom door, his mobile stopped ringing. Andrew was probably leaving a voicemail. For a moment Jamie had an urge to shout, 'Help!' As if Andrew might hear him.

Saeed had kept on about wanting to keep Jamie to himself last night, saying, 'I want to see you when I come home from work, waiting here for me.' He must have been planning it. He'd taken Jamie's phone out of the room and locked the door behind him, leaving him without any means of escape.

If someone came into the alley below the window, he could shout to them. But what good would that do? They'd have to break down two doors to get to him, or call the police. And what would that lead to?

Jamie slumped on the bed. He had no choice. He'd just have to wait until Saeed got home from work at four.

A minute later, he realised he needed to pee, badly. Where was he supposed to go? Could he pull a chair over and stand on it to piss out of the window? He looked around for a chair and saw in the corner, beside the rickety chest of drawers, three empty litre-sized plastic water bottles. On top of the chest of drawers lay a tray covered with a tea-towel.

Saeed had carefully set the whole thing up. Jamie lifted the tea-towel off the tray and, sure enough, there was a sandwich, wrapped in cling-film, a small bottle of water and a glass. Rations for the day.

He sighed, lifted one of the plastic bottles and unzipped his jeans. As he was pissing he remembered reading a novel about a man who had prepared a soundproof living space with double-locked doors in the cellar of his house, then kidnapped a girl and kept her in it. Was Saeed thinking along the same lines? Was this part of a longer-term plan?

At least he could have left a magazine or a book. He'd thought of food and limited toilet arrangements, but he hadn't considered entertainment. One thing was clear: this signalled the absolute end for himself and Saeed. Once he was set free, Jamie would never see the crazy Iranian bastard again. And he'd stay faithful to Andrew, even if it killed him.

He ate half of the sandwich and got back into bed. What else was there to do but try to sleep? He dreamed he was on the yellow brick road, walking and walking for mile upon mile. He kept expecting to bump into the Scarecrow, but there wasn't a soul to be seen anywhere, just the road winding endlessly into the distance, surrounded by rolling green hills. He came to a fork, with a sign that said, 'This Way', so he followed its arrow to the left. As far as his eye could see, the road stretched towards the horizon. And then, abruptly, it ended, the yellow bricks stopping at the edge of a cliff that looked down into pitch darkness.

Just as he was about to jump into the abyss, Jamie woke up with a jolt, caked in sweat. He was bursting to go to the loo again and had to fill a second bottle. Then he ate the other half of the sandwich and lay down.

He was pacing the room, beginning to worry about his increasing need for a shit, when the key eventually turned in the lock.

'What the fuck did you do that for?' Jamie shouted, launching himself at Saeed when he walked in.

Saeed held him away with one hand. 'I came back early,' he said. 'I was horny.'

'Horny? You're a fucking lunatic!'

Saeed pushed Jamie hard in the chest so he fell backwards on to the bed. 'Shut up,' he said, and popped open the buttons on his jeans to reveal a hard-on pushing against his boxers.

As Saeed leaned over to kiss him, Jamie realised he was hard too. 'This is so fucked up,' he said.

'Shut up,' Saeed said again.

One last time couldn't hurt, could it? After that, it was curtains for the whole crazy, warped thing.

31. Interest Only

Katherine opened the oven door to check the chicken. It was beginning to look dark brown and shrivelled. Barry had promised he'd be back for dinner at seven, but it was ten past eight now and there was still no sign of him. He wasn't answering his mobile either.

Her resolve to talk to him about his taking over the bills for a while seemed to have shrivelled with the chicken. She'd called Lucy earlier for a little support, but their conversation had only served to put her nerves further on edge.

'Isn't that what your bloody boyfriend's for?' Lucy had said. 'Taking care of you?'

'I could say the same to you,' Katherine had snapped. Although Lucy was two years younger, she talked to Katherine as if she was completely naïve. Lucy was bringing up two children by different fathers who had long since disappeared, and she treated Kathcrine as if *she* was the clueless one.

'I'm taking care of my boyfriend for now,' Lucy returned. 'He'll take care of me when the time comes.'

'I'll believe that when I see it,' said Katherine.

'Okay, I'm hanging up now.'

'Don't go.'

'Look, all I'm saying is you've been with him for eighteen years. If he loves you and cares about you, he'll step up to the mark. You'd do it for him without blinking.'

Lucy had been right. Barry knew that whatever he needed

from Katherine, all he had to do was ask. So why was she finding it so hard to ask him for what she needed?

She turned the oven to its lowest setting and tried his mobile again. His voicemail activated immediately, which meant his phone was powered off. He was probably at some meeting and his battery had run out. That was most likely why he hadn't texted to explain his lateness.

She'd had two texts from Martin about a car he'd found for her. 'You'll be well able to afford it,' he'd texted back, after she'd said she didn't know if a buying a car was possible right now. 'It's for half nothing.'

'Maybe,' Katherine texted in return, trying to sound noncommittal, but when he didn't reply, she worried that she'd pissed him off with her lack of enthusiasm. But what could she do? There was next to nothing left in the bank and her credit card was maxed out. And she'd told him not to go and find her a car anyway.

She was just about to take the chicken out of the oven when she heard Barry's key in the door. She patted the front of her hair into place and waited.

'Sorry, babes,' Barry said, loosening his tie as he came into the kitchen. 'I got stuck on a conference call to Dubai.' He looked as if he'd just had a workout, all flushed and pumped up.

'I'm not sure if the dinner is edible any more,' Katherine said. In anticipation of what she had to ask him, she felt she didn't have the right to be annoyed, even though she had told him before he'd left that morning that she was doing his favourite Jamie Oliver roast chicken. That they'd have a special night in.

'I had a McDonald's earlier,' he said. 'I'm not hungry, really. Any wine uncorked?'

Katherine poured him a glass of the Montepulciano she'd picked from his collection, bought on their holiday in Tuscany three years ago.

'Barry,' she said, steeling herself. 'We need to talk.'

He sighed and sat down at the breakfast bar. 'I know,' he said, which Katherine took as a positive signal.

'It's not going to be like this for ever,' she began. 'I'm sending out CVs every day. I'll get something eventually.'

Barry took a mouthful of wine. 'That's what I keep telling you,' he said.

'But in the meantime, we have to work something else out.'

'You're right,' he said. 'I've been thinking about it too.'

Katherine felt a wave of relief. 'You've still got savings. And you're earning enough to pay the mortgage for a few months and get by.'

Barry swirled the wine left in his glass and sniffed it. 'The Montepulciano?' he said. 'I was keeping it for a rainy day.'

'It'll only be for a short while, until I get back on my feet.'

'Listen, Katherine,' Barry said, putting his glass down. 'This isn't working.'

'What do you mean? What isn't working?'

'It used to be fun. We used to have a laugh together, remember?'

'Of course,' Katherine said. 'It's not always going to be this way.'

'It used to be about you and me. But now it's all about you.' He took another mouthful from his glass and waved his free hand, taking in the room. 'No. It's all about this.'

'That's not true. I – we—'

'When's the last time we had a conversation about something other than how you're going to afford paying for this house?'

Katherine's stomach gave a little lurch, like a rumble on the Richter scale. 'I don't understand,' she said. 'What are you trying to say?'

'I wasn't on a conference call earlier. I was driving around, trying to get up the courage to tell you.'

'Tell me what?'

'I don't want to live like this any more. I'm moving back to my mum's house.'

Katherine grabbed the edge of the breakfast counter to hold herself steady.

He was leaving her?

'We can rent the house out until things get better and we can sell it for something like it's actually worth,' Barry went on.

'Rent the house out?' she heard herself say.

'I talked to the bank manager and he says we can switch to interest only for the next two years. The estate agent said we should get one and a half grand in rent per month, which should just about cover the mortgage we've got out on it.'

'But that would mean I'd have to move out too.'

'That's right.'

'I have nowhere else to go.'

'What's happened to you, Katherine? You were never the type who put blocks in the way before. This is a solution. You can't afford the mortgage. Renting the house out will pay it off for now. Think of it that way.'

Tears began to leak out of the corners of her eyes, hot and wet. 'Don't do this, Barry,' she said, her throat constricting. 'Please.'

She had been with him since she was eighteen. The thought of life without him didn't seem credible.

'I need some time to work it out,' said Barry.

'We can work it out together. I know we can. Please.'

'Christ ... Stop saying "please", will you? When did you get so needy?'

'But ...' said Katherine. She looked at him through her tears. In his more romantic moments, Barry had always called her his 'little waif', and she would picture the Little Match Girl outside the window of the warm, cosy house being suddenly let in instead of freezing to death outside. She couldn't remember the last time he'd called her that. And in the story, the Little Match Girl only imagined she had been in the house while she froze to death anyway.

Barry stood up and put his two big hands on her shoulders, holding her firmly to face him. 'Look at you,' he said. 'You've changed so much.'

'No, I haven't. I'm still the same.'

'You used to be a trouper. You used to be the first one out of the starting gate.'

'I still am. This is only temporary.'

'You used to be like me.'

Katherine's breath caught in her throat. 'Don't,' she said, shaking her head. 'I would never have done something like this to you.'

'And here we go again,' said Barry, with a loud sigh, pulling his arms away. 'God, I can't stand the way you've started whingeing like this.'

When Katherine said nothing, he put his hands back on her shoulders. 'Look,' he said. 'It's only a break. Until we get some perspective.'

Katherine put her forehead on the rock of his chest and closed her eyes.

'I'll call you, okay?'

'Okay,' Katherine heard herself say. Her voice sounded far away.

And then she was left standing alone in the kitchen of what used to be the home she shared with her partner.

May

Edward Scissorhands

Tim Burton, 1990

'The light concealing cream goes on first.
Then you blend, and blend, and blend.
Blending is the secret.'

32. The Yellow Cinquecento

The little car sat in the driveway, its mustard-yellow paintwork reflecting in puddles from the sudden downpour.

'I know it's not much,' Martin said, surveying it through the sitting room's bay window, 'but it's a good runabout and it's very easy on petrol.'

Katherine didn't reply. She knew she should be annoyed, but his enthusiasm was swamping her misgivings.

'You'll get at least a year out of it, and it should be cheap to insure.'

'I told you not to do this,' she said eventually.

'But I picked it up for half nothing. The guy practically handed it to me.'

'I don't care what you got it for, you shouldn't have bought it.'

No matter what the car cost, Katherine couldn't afford it and she couldn't bear being put in the position of having to say so.

'It's a present,' Martin said, as if he had read her mind. 'And it's taxed for the next six months, so you only have insurance to pay, which you can do monthly.'

Katherine shook her head. 'I can't accept it,' she said. 'It's too much.'

'It's nothing.' Martin smiled, jangling the keys in front of her. 'I got it through the garage so it's not coming out of my pocket.'

Katherine gazed out of the window at the little yellow car. It looked so grubby and vulnerable in the driveway where her BMW and Barry's Merc used to gleam side by side. It was shocking how quickly life could change. The two cars were gone. Contracts had been signed, the date was set and four tenants, three guys and a girl, were due to move into the house at the end of the month. Barry had said he'd manage them, be the landlord, as it were.

'I can't take a car from you,' Katherine said.

'It's a done deal,' Martin said, holding the keys out.

He'd called over out of the blue with the car. Katherine knew he had the best intentions, but it felt like accepting charity. Then there was the fact that the thing wouldn't last twenty-four hours parked outside Lucy's flat, which was to be Katherine's home for the foreseeable future: cars were burned out there on a nightly basis.

And she didn't relish being pitied either. It was like being flung into the past. After her father had gone and they had had nothing, people used to look at her in a way that said, 'God help you, child,' but for all their charitable thoughts she had still become an untouchable.

'Why don't we take it for a test drive?' Martin said. 'You can get the feel of it.'

'This isn't a good time,' Katherine said. 'Maybe another day.'

Martin's face fell. 'You're turning your nose up at it, aren't you?' he said.

'No,' Katherine protested. How was she supposed to explain to him that she was burning with shame, rather than feeling above it? It was just the latest episode in what felt like an omnibus edition of her inevitable humiliation, which had obviously been waiting around the corner since the day she'd decided to make good for herself.

'Martin, it was so kind of you to get it for me. I really appreciate the gesture,' she managed. 'It's just—'

'That's not how it sounds to me.' Martin interrupted, a little like an upset child.

Katherine felt suddenly sorry. She wasn't doing anyone any good by wallowing in self-pity, and she had to learn to project a more positive attitude. Wasn't that what Barry had said when he was packing his bags? Instead of always finding the bad, she should search for the good in things.

'Oh, go on, then,' she said. 'What harm can it do to take it for a spin?'

Martin gave her a wide grin. 'Where would you like to go?' he asked.

'Here, hand them over.' Katherine smiled back, gesturing to the keys. 'We'll go down to Ranelagh Park and back.'

It drove as she'd expected it to drive. A sewing-machine on wheels, the whole car shuddering if she went above forty. But she was determined not to show any dismay and instead commented on the positive aspects, like how easy it was to park, because it was so small, and its cute cassette player.

'I saw one like that on *Antiques Roadshow*,' Martin said. 'It was worth a bloody fortune.'

Katherine started giggling as she tried to manage the gear stick, which was as stiff as a girder.

'Try the wipers,' Martin said. 'They're state-of-the-art.'

Katherine switched them on and they juddered across the windscreen, coming to a halt. She laughed when they juddered back. 'They had wipers like these in the last Bond car, didn't they?' she said, and Martin guffawed.

As the little car wove its way through the traffic, Katherine began to feel oddly elated. If she got it on the open road, it would probably break down within five miles, but as she moved up and down the gears with the clunky clutch, the tiny yellow Cinquecento felt bizarrely as if it would take her anywhere she wanted to go.

She protested a little more when Martin insisted she drive him back to the garage, then take the car home, but decided she'd accept the gift with good grace. After all, that was how it was intended, and she did, as Martin put it, need a set of wheels, no matter what kind of chassis was sitting on top.

'See you tomorrow night,' Martin said, leaning back into the car after he got out.

'Tomorrow night?'

'At Jamie's. For Film Club.'

'Oh, yes,' Katherine said, the merriment she'd felt driving the car instantly deflating. 'See you then.' She'd totally forgotten, and now that he'd reminded her she felt a stab of dread at the thought of facing them all, having to smile and chat and pretend that her life hadn't fallen apart at the seams.

33. Neat Little Packages

Andrew wouldn't stop hovering. Spraying Windowlene on the glass coffee-table one more time. Lining up the bottles in the wine rack, labels to the top. He was getting more OCD by the day.

'It's not like you're going to be here watching them judge your slovenly habits,' Jamie said. 'What time is your dinner anyway?'

'Not till eight thirty,' said Andrew. 'But I can cancel if you want me here to help.'

'Andrew. We've been through this already.'

'I don't know why you don't want me around your new friends. I'm not that scary.'

'I *told* you. It's not that I don't want you around them, I just want this night for myself.'

If Andrew had had his way, he and Jamie would have been joined at the hip 24/7 since day one of their relationship. Andrew didn't seem to need a life of his own: he was perfectly happy doing everything as one half of a couple. Without any work, Jamie was feeling more and more claustrophobic. There seemed to be fewer and fewer outlets for him to do his own thing without Andrew right by his side.

Andrew sprayed some furniture polish on the cleared-off mantelpiece and began to wipe. 'I'll just stay for twenty minutes after they arrive and then I'll go.'

'I knew I should have done this at my mother's. It's my Film Club with my friends, remember?'

'And have her sitting there all night, subjecting them to twenty questions and then twenty more? I don't think so.'

'It would be better than having you tiptoeing around, cleaning up messes they haven't even made yet,' Jamie said, taking the furniture polish out of Andrew's hand.

Andrew pushed back the hair that flopped over his forehead and stuck his bottom lip out in a mock sulk. He was beginning to age, Jamie thought. He'd be forty-one in three weeks and it was starting to show.

When they'd first met, Jamie had thought Andrew looked too young, even though he was eight years his senior. With his lemony fringe constantly getting in his eyes, the acne scars on his chin, his tank-tops and wire-framed glasses, he had a kind of preppy adolescent air that Jamie had never gone for before. That they had ended up together was a complete accident, a drunken one-night stand that had turned into a date that had turned into a seven-year relationship.

It was the longest Jamie had been with anybody. The three torturous years he'd spent with Simon during his early twenties seemed fleeting in comparison, even though they'd been the worst time of his life.

Andrew was everything Simon was not – in a word, sane. He was also loyal, dependable, affectionate and solvent: all the things people looked for in a partner. If he pictured his life without him, Jamie felt cast adrift.

Andrew gave the free-standing unit that divided the kitchen from the living room another wipe. They'd been first in line when Ikea had opened in Ireland to get it, along with every other piece of furniture in the place, the entire interior chosen by Jamie from a display for medium-sized apartments. Not that he liked it that much. Ikea suited Andrew better, he thought. Its form-fitting, production-line economy went well with his need to have everything in his life boxed up into neat little packages.

'*Edward Scissorhands*,' Andrew said, picking up the DVD box from the top of the television cabinet so he could dust. 'It's a bit on the romantic side for you, isn't it?'

'It's got an unhappy ending,' said Jamie. 'A bit of realism.'

'Realism? It's a film about a guy with scissors for fingers.'

'Whatever. Look, they'll be here any minute.'

'I hate being left out,' said Andrew. 'I like being part of your life.'

Jamie gritted his teeth and went into the hall. 'You *are* part of my life,' he said, coming back in with Andrew's coat. 'But not tonight. Now, get out of here. Pronto.'

'I'll be back,' said Andrew, doing a bad imitation of Arnold Schwarzenegger in *The Terminator*. He kissed Jamie on the tip of the nose. 'Don't do anything I wouldn't do.'

'That leaves me far too much leeway,' Jamie said, turning him around and pushing him towards the door. 'Did anyone ever tell you you have a great arse?'

'You did,' said Andrew.

'And don't forget it, Mr Man.'

Somewhere in the bedroom, Jamie's mobile bleeped a message alert.

'That's probably Lisa,' he said, as Andrew pulled on his coat.

It was more likely Saeed. He'd texted at least twenty times already today, although when the first message had come through, Jamie had replied ':-(', their signal for 'this is not a good time'.

'Who's texting you?' Andrew had asked earlier.

Jamie had stretched out on the couch and reached for the remote control. 'It's the man of my dreams.' The best line of defence was to tell some semblance of the truth and pretend it was a joke.

'Coming on his white horse to take you off my hands, I hope.'
The phone had bleeped again.

'Actually, who is it?' said Andrew. 'It's beginning to get annoying.'

'Actually, it's none of your business,' Jamie had snapped, but then he'd relented. 'It's my mother,' he'd lied. 'She's giving me her recipe for Thai green curry chips for tonight. Like I'd serve that travesty.'

As it turned out, when he located his phone in the bedroom after Andrew had left, this text *was* from Lisa.

'Can't make it tonite. Totally wrecked,' it said.

Jamie called her straight back. 'That's no excuse,' he said. 'Get your arse over here this instant.'

'Seriously,' Lisa said. 'I can hardly keep my eyes open.'

'*Pleeeeease*,' Jamie begged. 'Don't leave me alone with them. Have a can of Red Bull or something. You'll be fine.'

'I'll see,' Lisa said. 'But start without me one way or the other.'

34. Alice Digs a Hole

Alice was wearing one of those big flowers Sarah Jessica Parker had worn in *Sex and the City*, a floppy pink thing, pulling the collar of her navy cardigan to the side with its weight. 'Are the others here?' she asked, looking around the empty room.

'Yeah, they're hiding behind the couch,' Jamie replied, and when Alice's eyebrows shot up in alarm, he added, 'They're on their way. Have a seat. Glass of wine?'

'No, thanks,' said Alice. 'Water will be fine.'

'Ah, go on, throw caution to the wind.'

'Do you have any 7-Up?'

'I think so. I'll just go and see.'

In the kitchen, Jamie texted Lisa: *hurry up 4 gods sake*. Martin had called to say he was running a half-hour late, and there was no sign of Katherine.

When Jamie returned to the living room, Alice was sitting on the very edge of the couch, chewing her lip. She gave a little cough as he set a glass of flat 7-Up, from a bottle that had been in the fridge for aeons, in front of her.

'Lovely day today, wasn't it?' he said.

'Beautiful,' said Alice.

Outside, a car alarm went off in the distance.

'So, how have you been?' Jamie asked.

'Fine, thanks.'

'Old Maguire treating you well?'

'Yes.'

Jamie heaved a sigh. 'Jesus, Alice, give me a break. I'm doing all the work here.'

'Pardon?'

'This is a conversation, yeah? Participate!'

'Oh, sorry. I . . . Well . . . I don't think Mr Maguire looks very well. He's lost a lot of weight.'

'He always had that big red face. Secret drinker, I'd say.'

'I'm worried about him.'

'No need to worry about Maguire. He wouldn't think twice about you.'

Alice cleared her throat again and looked down at her slip-on loafers. 'What film are you showing?' she asked.

'*Edward Scissorhands*. Do you know it?'

Alice brightened. 'Oh, yes. I saw it in the cinema a long time ago. I remember thinking he reminded me of myself when I was small.'

'Who?'

'Edward Scissorhands.'

'The resemblance is uncanny.'

'He wanted to fit in but they all hated him.'

Jamie stood up. 'Let me freshen that up,' he said, holding

his hand out for her 7-Up glass. When he came back with some sparkling water – no 7-Up left – she was still sitting on the edge of her seat, staring into the middle distance.

'I didn't mean to make you uncomfortable,' she said, her voice barely audible.

'You didn't,' Jamie lied.

She faced him. 'I never say the right thing. It always comes out wrong.'

What had he done to bring this on? Why was she suddenly confiding in him? 'Don't be so hard on yourself,' Jamie said, trying to give her a reassuring smile. 'I wonder where Katherine is. You haven't heard from her, have you?'

'Do you ever feel like that?' asked Alice. 'Like you don't fit in?'

'Never.'

'I was just wondering, because you're gay.'

Jamie couldn't believe his ears. 'What?' he managed.

'I mean you're not . . . not the norm.'

'Not the *norm*?' Jamie spluttered. 'If I didn't know different, I'd say you're being homophobic.'

Alice spilled some water down her chin as she jerked her glass away from her mouth. 'No!' she said. 'I didn't mean it like that.'

'How did you mean it, then?

'What I'm saying is, you're not like other people. Gay people are . . . well . . . different.'

Jamie lifted the remote control, switched on the television and internally began to count to ten as his mother had advised him to do when he was losing his temper. 'I'd stop digging that hole, if I were you,' he said.

Jamie had been twelve when he'd first heard the word 'gay'. He was sitting cross-legged on the floor in front of the *The Late Late Show*, his pyjamas on and his hair still wet from the Saturday bath, and a priest in a collar was being interviewed. The presenter had asked the priest if he was 'a homosexual'.

Jamie's ears had pricked up.

The priest had looked taken aback. 'Yes,' he said eventually, 'I am.'

'I'm scarlet for him,' said Jamie's oldest sister Jean, and the other girls giggled.

'I don't know.' Da had sighed, throwing a briquette on the fire. 'What's the world coming to?'

'Let him without sin cast the first stone,' said Ma.

Jamie had studied the priest on the screen. He had dark hair, parted to the side and slightly pockmarked skin, his forehead creased with a worried frown. Jamie didn't know what 'homosexual' meant, but he was fascinated.

The next day he'd asked Raymo, who was a year younger – born so soon after Jamie they could have been twins, his mother sometimes said – but he knew everything there was to know.

'It means you're gay,' Raymo said, making his wrist go limp and sticking his hip out.

'What's "gay"?'

'You'll know soon enough.'

As it had turned out, Raymo was right on the money.

Within weeks of starting at St Audeon's secondary school for boys Jamie had known that gay was bent. It was a faggot, a shirtlifter, a fairy, a pansy, a poofter, a steamer, a queer, a shit-stabber, a bum bandit, a fudge packer, a mincer, and it was at the very bottom of the food chain. If you wore white socks, you were gay. If you liked Kylie, you were gay. If you were good at art or music, you were gay.

And once you were branded gay, you became a universal object of derision.

You were also gay if you enjoyed lying naked with David Flannery, your bodies close together under the covers of his bed while Mrs Flannery thought you were doing your maths homework together.

By the end of first year David Flannery was branded gay (he

walked like a girl) and became the universal object of derision at St Audeon's. Jamie never tormented him like the others, but he never spoke to him again.

Throughout his years at St Audeon's, nobody so much as suspected that Jamie was gay, and David Flannery never said anything to anyone. But Jamie still remembered the way David had looked at him, like he was worse than any of the guys who had done the bullying. Like he was the worst thing imaginable.

Alice apologised several times before the others arrived, and although Jamie told her to stop worrying, inside he was fuming. She couldn't have revealed her feelings more glaringly if she was wearing a T-shirt that said: 'I hate fags.'

And, no, he wasn't overreacting.

35. What Everyone Is Searching For

Lisa had texted Jamie to start the movie without her, but when she arrived, they were all waiting. 'You should have gone ahead,' she said. 'At this rate we'll be here half the night.'

'It's not a long film,' said Jamie, handing her a glass of wine. 'Drink this. You look like you need it.'

'Oh, God, no.' Lisa flopped down between Alice and Martin, who were at either end of the sofa. 'Just get me a glass of water.'

'It's *Edward Scissorhands* tonight,' said Martin, impatient as usual to get going.

'I don't think I've seen it,' said Lisa. 'Is Johnny Depp in it?'

'Isn't Johnny Depp in everything Tim Burton directs?' said Jamie. 'That's a real love story.'

'The thing I remember most about *Edward Scissorhands* is Winona Ryder dancing around in the snow,' said Katherine. She was dolled up to the nines in a 1950s floral print cocktail dress, her hair in a chignon and a string of pearls around her neck, softly catching the light. She looked on top of the world, smiling for all she was worth although, as far as Lisa knew, she hadn't found a job yet.

'It was ice,' said Martin. 'From the ice sculpture of an angel he was making for her.'

'It's a fairytale, like *Beauty and the Beast*,' Alice said. She seemed more and more comfortable and vocal as the meetings went on, which was nice, Lisa thought. She used to feel sorry for Alice back at Qwertec where she'd hardly had the nerve to open her mouth.

Martin nodded in agreement, but then shook his head. 'If it's a fairytale, it's *Pinocchio*,' he said. 'Edward wants to be a real boy, just like Pinocchio did.'

He had trimmed his wispy red beard and cut his hair back, which was an improvement, Lisa felt. But he was definitely putting on more weight.

'Oh, yes,' said Alice. 'I see what you mean. Maybe it's influenced by a lot of different fairytales.'

'I don't want to be a pain, but I need to be out of here by half ten,' said Lisa. 'I've got the Wicked Witch from next door in again, so I have to be home before Patrick discovers her. Maybe we should watch the film.'

She found it hard to concentrate on *Edward Scissorhands*, fighting off waves of tiredness. She didn't know why she'd let Jamie convince her to come. Since they'd let Sofia go, Lisa found herself getting more and more exhausted. The boys never let up, and the housework was just as relentless.

For all its fairytale allusions, the film left her feeling down. All the scenes between the mother and Edward made her want to cry. Nothing the woman did could save the boy with no hands. No amount of unconditional love could prepare him for the awfulness of the real world.

'He was so vulnerable, it would break your heart,' she said, when the final credits were rolling.

'But you want to grab him by the shoulders and shake him,' said Katherine. 'Tell him to cop on.'

Jamie held his chin between his thumb and forefinger. 'It's a very complex film,' he said. 'On one level it's telling you that fitting in is the most important thing but on the other that it's the worst fate imaginable.'

'Did you rehearse that?' asked Martin.

Jamie looked insulted, then relaxed into a wide smile. 'Endlessly,' he said.

'I think he's like a lost little boy,' said Alice. 'An orphan nobody loves.'

'But the mother who takes him in loves him,' said Lisa. 'I think that's plain.'

'It's more complicated that that,' Alice replied, and Lisa got the feeling she was being cut off.

'Did anyone else think he was like the Tin Man in *The Wizard of Oz*?' asked Katherine.

Martin nodded enthusiastically. 'There's loads of *Wizard of Oz* references,' he said. 'Like, in a way, all the characters are missing something. The same as the Tin Man or the Lion or the Scarecrow.'

'Edward's missing his hands,' said Lisa. 'Who else is missing what?'

'What Edward is really missing is a father,' said Martin. 'He's missing a family.'

'Did you rehearse that?' Jamie asked.

Martin laughed and reached for another beer. 'No, it's off the top of my head. I swear.'

'I hate it that he ends up alone,' said Katherine. 'It's too sad.'

'But he has to,' said Martin. 'Or we'd never get the moral of the story.'

'What *is* the moral of the story?' Lisa said, her mouth

stretching into a wide yawn. If she didn't get up and go home, she might fall asleep here and now.

'When Edward realises Kim loves him, all the bad stuff he feels about not being perfect falls away. He learns to love himself.'

'But they don't end up together,' said Katherine. 'He winds up all alone in that castle.'

'That depends on how you look at it,' said Martin. 'He finds happiness.'

Katherine fingered the string of pearls around her neck. 'I'd still settle for the life he had before they drove him out of town, no matter how messed up it was,' she said.

36. The Gay Glass Ceiling

'Leave that and come to bed,' said Andrew. 'I'll do it in the morning.'

'If you insist,' said Jamie, closing the dishwasher. 'There's still some wine left in the fridge, if you want some.'

Andrew opened the frosted-glass cabinet above the sink to get a glass. 'How was it tonight?' he asked. 'Your movie go down a storm?'

'I think they all liked it. Although Martin went on one of his anorak rants at the end. Seemingly, Tim Burton is a very overrated director.'

'I like all Tim Burton's stuff,' Andrew said, opening the fridge to take out a half-drunk bottle of white. 'Especially *Pirates of the Caribbean*.'

'That's not Tim Burton, you eejit!'

'No? How about *Pirates of the Caribbean: Dead Man's Chest*?'

Jamie gave him a push. 'Now you're just messing with my head.'

'That's a boyfriend's prerogative,' said Andrew, filling his glass. 'Shall I pour you a nightcap?

'Yes, please,' said Jamie. 'Anyway, *Edward Scissorhands* was better than having to sit through *The Wizard of Oz* in Weirdsville, surrounded by a million ceramic owls. Alice is such a freak! She was wearing one of those SJP flowers tonight.'

'Hilarious.'

'Yeah, not so funny, as it turns out. She's also a total homophobe.'

'Most people have a bit of it, if you dig deep enough.'

'She apologised about fifty times before she left, insisting she didn't mean what she'd said. The sad thing is, she believes that's true.'

'What did she say?'

'Homosexuality is not the norm.'

'Who wants to be the norm?' Andrew said. He put his arms around Jamie and hugged him close. 'I like being different. It's one of the good things about being gay.'

Jamie pulled away. 'Being gay hasn't done you any good,' he said.

'Well, I wouldn't have met you if I wasn't a big girl's blouse.'

'What about that gay glass ceiling at work you're always complaining about? Or how the other guys in the practice treat you like you're some sort of lightweight?'

Andrew took his wine over to the sofa. 'Come and sit down,' he said, patting the cushion beside him. 'I want to talk to you.'

'You do more for those asylum seekers than any of the other straight layabouts in that practice. For God's sake, you even take your clients out for drinks because you think they need to make new friends!'

Andrew sighed. 'Can we change the record?' he said.

Jamie opened the dishwasher again and started putting glasses into it. 'All I'm saying is, I hate it when you go on like that, about it being great to be different. In the real world we all know that's not true.'

'Okay, honey. Whatever you say.'

Sometimes Andrew annoyed him out of the blue. They'd be

having a perfectly fine time together, but then he'd say something that got on Jamie's nerves so much, he wouldn't be able to stop himself hitting out. Not that it was Andrew's fault. He didn't mean to be annoying. He just was. Sometimes.

'Come and sit down,' Andrew said again, and when Jamie relented, he added, 'Do you want to hear about my evening?'

'With dull-as-dishwater Dylan?' Jamie said, letting Andrew put an arm around him. 'Do I have to?' All Andrew's gay friends were nerdy and political, but Dylan was nerdy to the power of nerdiness.

'It was very interesting, as it happens. He went off on one of his rants.'

'Did you shoot him? Please say you did.'

'He was on about gay marriage. How the government should introduce equal marriage for gay couples instead of civil partnerships.'

'As riveting as ever,' said Jamie. 'Did he say anything that was actually interesting?'

Andrew was quiet for a minute. 'I've been thinking,' he said eventually. 'We've been together . . . what? Six years.'

'Seven on the fourteenth of July.'

'We should think about doing it, you know.'

'Doing what?'

'Getting whatever they call it – civilly partnershipped.'

'Is this like a proposal?' Jamie laughed, but inside he tensed.

'Do you want it to be?'

37. Bird on a Pink Fur Toilet Lid

When Martin got home there was a message on his answering machine from his mother. Come hell or high water, she would not call him on his mobile. Having read horror stories in the

Reader's Digest about the radiowaves cellphones emitted, she didn't want to add to Martin's chances of brain-fry.

'Hello, Martin, this is your mother,' her telephone voice said. 'I'm calling about your father. I don't want to alarm you but he's behaving very strangely and your sisters are not answering their telephones either. So, if you get this message, can you please ring me back at six-five-four-two-oh-one-two.'

She always left the home number at the end of a message, as if Martin wouldn't remember it.

He called back immediately and his mother answered after one ring. 'Hello, six-five-four-two-oh-one-two,' she enunciated slowly, reminding him of the mother in *Edward Scissorhands*, always so softly exacting about the details of etiquette.

When Martin identified himself, his mother gasped, 'Oh, Martin, thank God it's you. I'm at my wit's end.'

'What's going on?' he said.

'It's your father. He's lying on the bathroom floor talking about birdwatching. He keeps repeating himself.'

'He's plastered, that's all. He spent half the day holding up the bar at Dinty's.'

'He's never been like this before. I can't lift him up.'

'It's late, Mam. Put a blanket over him and let him sleep it off.'

'But the way he's going on . . . I'm worried, Martin. He's never been like this before,' she repeated.

'Okay.' Martin sighed. 'I'll get a taxi and be there in half an hour.'

He was half locked himself and had been looking forward to a few more cans and a couple of smokes before bed, but what choice did he have? Nobody ever warned you about what happened as your parents aged. How your life got sucked back into theirs.

The taxi took half an hour to arrive, and when it did, he recognised the driver as the man who had brought him home from Katherine's the night her boyfriend had said she'd told him that Martin drank too much.

He called his mother again to say he was running late, but she didn't answer. She was probably upstairs in the bathroom with his father, the only phone in the house, with its old-fashioned dial, glued to the spot on the hall table where it had sat for longer than Martin had been alive.

As the taxi made its way through town, Martin started thinking about Katherine again. She hadn't even mentioned the Cinquecento tonight. Sitting there, looking so expensive and uptight, she had hardly said a word to him at all, except about the movie, which in Martin's opinion had not been a great choice. People called *Edward Scissorhands* a classic but, as far as he was concerned, it was flawed, like all Tim Burton's films.

She'd looked beautiful, though . . .

Shit. When was he going to accept that he wasn't even a blip on Katherine's radar? She'd wrinkled her nose when he'd brought over the car, like it had had a bad smell. And yet, when she'd eventually agreed to take it out for a run, his heart had actually leaped with joy, a puppy thrilled with even the slightest crumb from her table.

It was a waste of time. Katherine had made it clear, had said it out loud way back after the Christmas party: the last thing she wanted was him. All this time later, here he was, still hoping she'd fancy him back.

Pathetic. That was what Jennifer had called him when he'd begged her to come home that night, tears running down his face as he'd stood in the rain outside her parents' house. And she'd been right.

As Martin let himself in through the front door, his mother appeared at the top of the stairs. 'He's up here,' she called. 'I don't know what to do with him.'

'What's *he* doing here?' his father asked, when Martin came to the bathroom door. He was propped up against the side of the bath, his head hanging down and his mouth hanging open. One leg of his grey trousers revealed a dark stain and the room reeked of a mixture of booze and piss.

'Maybe we should call an ambulance,' his mother said.

'C'mon, Dad. We'll get you into bed,' Martin said. He got on his hunkers and put his hands under his father's armpits.

'Careful,' his father hissed. 'Don't disturb it.'

'Disturb what?'

'The little bird. The blue tit.'

'He keeps going on about it,' Martin's mother said. 'No matter what I say, he insists it's there.'

'Where?' Martin said.

'On the toilet, you eejit,' his father barked. 'Are you blind as well as stupid?'

Martin's mother stood framed by the bathroom door, with round, frightened eyes. 'I hope he isn't having one of his turns,' she said.

Martin looked at his father, who was staring at a point somewhere on the pink fur-covered toilet lid, then back at his mother. 'Maybe we should let the bird out,' he said. 'It's probably scared shitless.'

His mother's jaw dropped and she gaped at Martin as if he might be drunk out of his mind too, but then it dawned on her what he was doing.

'Careful, for fuck's sake,' his father repeated, as Martin climbed over him to get to the bathroom window. He pushed the line of Radox shower-gel bottles to the side of the sill as gently as he could and placed the roll of toilet paper, covered with a yellow knitted doll, in the washbasin so he could get to the window's handle.

'Now, Dad, you give the bird a nudge to go out,' he said.

'I can't,' his father said. 'I'm not able to move.'

'You do it, Mam,' Martin said.

She gave him a dubious look, then advanced to the toilet seat on tippy-toes. 'Shoo,' she said, to the imaginary blue tit. 'Off with you now.'

'Don't frighten it!' his father hissed. 'Stupid woman!'

'It's gone, Dad,' Martin said, after a moment, and closed the window. 'Now let's get you out of here.'

It was like hauling a heavy sack of coal, but eventually, between them, Martin and his mother got him out of his wet trousers and into bed.

'I don't need your help,' his father mumbled, as Martin pulled off his socks. 'You're nothing but a waster.'

Downstairs, his mother made a pot of tea and put some ginger-nut biscuits on a plate. 'Thanks for coming over,' she said, pouring Martin a cup. 'I don't know what I would have done without you.'

'We'll bring him to the doctor in the morning,' Martin said. 'It's better to let him sleep now. I'll stay the night too.'

'You're a good son,' his mother said. 'Thank you.'

He watched as she put a half-teaspoon of milk into her cup, no more, no less, trying to keep her hand steady.

'You don't have any beer in the house, do you?' he asked.

38. We Must Go to the Mountain

'I'm afraid she doesn't want to meet you.' Over the phone, Mrs Babcock's voice had a receding quality, as if she was shutting doors as she spoke. Which, in effect, was exactly what she was doing.

'But I don't understand,' Alice said. 'Did she say why?'

'As I told you, it is not incumbent on a mother to give a reason.'

'But did she? Did she say anything, give any indication at all?'

'I'm afraid that our communication with your mother is

strictly confidential. What I suggest is that you come in and meet our counsellor to talk about putting this behind you for the time being. It's not the end of the process.'

The process. It sounded so clinical, so divorced from the disappointment of discovering your mother didn't want you. Not back then, not now.

'Would you like to make an appointment?' Mrs Babcock asked.

Alice pictured her taking her big red book out of the drawer in her desk and opening it to search for an appropriate date. 'I don't think so,' she said.

'We highly recommend it.'

'No,' said Alice. 'Thank you, Mrs Babcock. Goodbye.'

'Miriam,' said Mrs Babcock. 'I said you should call me Miriam.'

'Miriam,' Alice repeated.

She was just about to hang up when Mrs Babcock said, 'She may come around in time. We find that this is often the case when the birth mother is first contacted. There is a lot of fear. A lot of guilt.'

'I understand, thank you.'

'I don't want to give you false hope, but leave it for six months to a year and we'll try again. She may be in a better frame of mind by then.'

'Six months to a year?' Mrs Silver exclaimed, when Alice told her. 'You've not seen your mother in thirty-eight years and still you must wait?'

'Mrs Babock says it happens a lot. The mother is often very frightened of meeting the child she gave away.'

Mrs Silver pointed her remote control at the television and switched it off. 'I remember my mother's face when she had to say goodbye,' she said. 'She was smiling and telling me that everything would be all right, that we would be together once more very, very soon. But there were tears dripping from her chin. She knew she would never see me again. Your mother has the chance to see you, the beautiful girl she lost so long ago. She should take it with both arms open.'

'But I can't force her to meet me. I don't even know where she is.'

'The letter!' Mrs Silver said. 'Do you still have it?'

'Yes. It's here in my bag.' Alice took out the envelope. She'd kept it with her since Mrs Silver had found it, poring over it at night as if its handwriting could connect her to her mother.

'The fifteenth of June 1973, Ballydehob, County Cork,' Mrs Silver said, reading closely with her spectacles pushed high on her nose. 'That's where we must start.'

'Start what?'

'How does the saying go? If the mountain will not come to Muhammad, then Muhammad must go to the mountain. That is what we must do, Alice. We must go to the mountain.'

39. A Sixteen? That Couldn't Be Right

Nothing in any of the books told you about how to shop for clothes with three children in tow. Crammed into the dressing room with Lisa, Ben and Aaron were screaming their heads off, both wanting to be picked up from the double buggy she'd just about edged in. Theo was wedged into the gap between the bottom of the dressing-room door and the floor, struggling to get out and lunging to bite her hand whenever she reached down to drag him back in.

'Just give Mummy a minute,' she said, pulling the black-and-white top she'd chosen from the clearance rack over her head. It was a sixteen, but that was the only bargain size they had. She could take it in at the sides if it was too loose.

The trip to TK Maxx had been spur-of-the-moment. If Katherine could arrive at Film Club last night looking like a million dollars despite her financial difficulties, then Lisa could at least start making an effort too. As Dr Phil said, if you projected positivity to the outside world, it had a positive effect on your whole life.

For the last week she hadn't had the energy to clean the house, so the place was going to rack and ruin around her, and the boys seemed to be getting worse with every passing day. Patrick, running to and from work, seemed oblivious to her exhaustion, and she didn't want to nag in the way her mother had constantly gone on at her father.

Patrick had whispered goodbye to her when he'd got up at the crack of dawn this morning to get his flight to Cologne, where he had a meeting, but she had pretended to be asleep.

She had decided to go on the shopping trip after Theo had climbed up on the sofa and head-butted her. She had thought at first that he was going to give her a kiss. He hurt his forehead because it cracked against her chin, which led to a fit of hysterics that quickly spread to the other two. Getting out of the house was the only thing she could think to do. Though she was seriously wondering why she'd thought a trip to the shopping centre would offer any solutions.

She pulled the top down and looked at herself in the mirror. A sixteen? That couldn't be right. It felt too tight around the chest, and the way it was gathered under the arms made her gut protrude as if she was pregnant.

Lisa's stomach plummeted.

She couldn't be, could she?

'I want out!' Theo shouted, pulling himself free of the spot under the door. 'Out!'

The sickness that hadn't quite amounted to anything but hadn't quite gone away . . . The constant overwhelming waves of tiredness . . .

'*Muuuuummy!*' Ben cried over Aaron's wail. '*Muuuuummy!*'

The craving she'd had after she'd got home from Film Club last night, for Häagen-Daz frozen yoghurt.

'*Muuuuuummy!*'

'OUT!' Theo shouted.

'Give Mummy a minute,' she said automatically, pulling the top off and reaching for the stained sweatshirt she had put on that morning.

'OUT!' Theo screamed again, and ran at her, digging his nails into her wrist with all his might.

'Ouch!' Lisa cried. She pulled her hand away and then, hardly knowing what she was doing, slapped him across the face.

The dressing room went silent, the youngest two stunned into open-mouthed muteness. Theo seemed to shrink in front of her.

'I'm sorry, honey,' she said, reaching out for him. 'I didn't mean to.'

Theo pushed her hand away, his eyes fixed on hers, his stare venomous.

In the buggy, Aaron started whimpering again.

'*Muuuuuuummy!*' Ben cried.

Lisa leaned against the dressing room's flimsy partition wall, closed her eyes and began to sob.

40. Does Anyone Own a Name?

'Look, Auntie Katherine, it's Princess Aurora.'

Kitty handed over a drawing of Disney's Sleeping Beauty, which Paolo had printed from the computer for her to colour in. Her long hair was bright yellow, Kitty's enthusiastic crayon marks wandering far beyond the lines.

'I did it for you because you look like Sleeping Beauty,' Kitty said. 'Your hair is the same colour as hers.'

'It's really lovely, thank you.' Katherine smiled with as much gusto as she could muster, and put the drawing down on the nest of tables beside the couch.

'I'll do another,' Kitty said. 'A better one.'

'She is a very good artist, no?' Paolo said, and Katherine gave another smile, nodding in agreement. When would they all to go to bed so she could pull out the bed-settee and get some sleep? All she wanted to do was close her eyes.

'Kitty never stops making drawings for you,' Lucy said. 'I have a stack of them in the kitchen drawer so high.'

'You never gave them to me.'

'We did, remember? A picture of fairies putting on a fashion show.'

'Oh, yes,' said Katherine, remembering Lucy admonishing her for saying she'd hang it in the living room and not doing so.

Katherine was too tired to argue now. It was typical of Lucy to insist that she come and live here until she got a place of her own and then waste no opportunity to tell her how neglectful she'd been.

Lucy had signed on for unemployment benefit the day after she'd failed her Leaving Cert and never signed off. She hadn't the first clue how demanding a career was. How there was little space for anything else.

'It's time for bed now, girls,' Lucy said, and Katherine heaved an internal sigh of relief.

'But I want to stay up with Auntie Katherine,' Kitty said.

'Absolutely not,' said Lucy. 'It's far too late.' She turned to Laura. 'Will you make sure she brushes her teeth properly?'

Laura carefully put a marker in the page of her Harry Potter book, which she had told Katherine with great pride that she was reading for the sixth time, and took Kitty's hand.

'Night night, Kit Kat,' said Lucy, giving Kitty a kiss and a hug.

The name felt like a stab to Katherine's chest, but she tried not to show it as the girls took it in turn to kiss her goodnight, Kitty hugging her tightly and saying, 'I love you, Auntie Katherine.'

'When did you start calling Kitty that?' she asked Lucy, when she was sure the girls were out of hearing.

'Calling her what?'

'Kit Kat.'

'I don't know. Why?'

'It was Dad's name for me,' Katherine said.

'For God's sake. You don't own the name. It's anyone's to use.'

'But Dad used it, not anyone else.'

'Right,' said Lucy, slapping the arms of her chair with the heels of her hands and standing up. 'I'm going to bed.'

'Don't just walk away like that.'

'You know what, Katherine? You need to build a bridge and get over it. What happened happened. We can't go back and change it. We have to move on.'

Katherine looked around the cramped room, with its row of knickers drying on the radiator and every other space cluttered with pointless junk. 'This is moving on?' she said.

'At least I didn't shut down,' Lucy said. 'At least I didn't run away.' She stood there for a moment, her fists balled at her sides. Then she stalked off down the hall to her bedroom.

Paulo sat through the exchange, saying nothing. After the bedroom door slammed, he turned to Katherine and smiled. 'It's a good name,' he said softly. 'Kit Kat.' And then he followed Lucy to their bedroom.

After she'd slipped under the duvet that was kept beneath the bed-settee, Katherine listened to their muffled voices from Lucy's room, deep in a conversation she couldn't make out. They went silent after a while and Katherine pulled the duvet over her head, afraid she might hear them having sex. The flat's walls were paper thin.

She closed her eyes and into her mind came a picture of

Edward Scissorhands, his eyebrows arched in permanent distress, alone in the bedroom of the house he'd been adopted into, not knowing where to put himself, how to get comfortable.

At his mother's house, Barry would be lying on the bottom bunk underneath his old Action Man duvet. The thought made her miss him desperately.

She turned over on to her side, trying to get comfortable. The truth was, Barry probably wasn't thinking about her now.

When she looked back on it, she couldn't believe her own stupidity. She had spent years thinking she was doing the right thing. Her and Barry moving up the ladder. Her and Barry buying the big house, the fancy cars, the paintings, the furniture . . . Coming home from their two holidays a year, posting pictures on Facebook of the fabulous time they'd been having together in places she wouldn't have dreamed of as a child …

But it had all turned out to be a sham, not the perfect life she'd told herself it was. And there was no one to blame but herself because she'd believed in it.

But, in a way, hadn't it been perfect? Katherine's whole world had been mapped out with the promise of life with Barry. Without it she had absolutely nothing, and she had absolutely no one to share it with. She pined for the double bed they had once shared, with Barry's arms around her and the certainty that she would wake up beside him the next morning.

She heard a thud, and lifted the duvet to listen. A soft giggle – Lucy's – and a smothered laugh from Paolo.

Katherine pulled the duvet over her head again, afraid this time that they might hear the sound she was making. A long, low moan that came up from the pit of her stomach, like the cry of a wounded dog.

June

Thelma & Louise
Ridley Scott, 1991

'Well, we're not in the middle of nowhere,
but we can see it from here.'

41. Drowning by Numbers

'Just throw your coat anywhere,' Lisa panted. She was pitching brightly coloured toys into a plastic storage box, reaching under the sofa to retrieve a purple Barney doll that sang a disconsolate 'I love you, you love me . . .' when she eventually got hold of it.

A cat stood on a sofa arm and stretched languorously before inching its jet-black paws out to Lisa's back to lever its way to the floor.

Katherine chose not to throw her coat anywhere. It was one of the few precious pieces she'd kept after selling the rest of her collection to the second-hand designer shop, a Prada. 'Can I do anything?' she asked.

'You could pour yourself a glass of wine,' said Lisa, picking up a plastic cup and dabbing at a sticky dried-in juice stain it had left on the coffee-table with a piece of kitchen paper. 'It's in the kitchen. Glasses in the cupboard above the sink.'

Katherine made her way into the kitchen, stopping to hang her coat on the end of the banisters. There was a sense of barely held-at-bay chaos about the house. Things were shoved out of the way behind cushions, hastily kicked under carpets. The kitchen had been cleaned, there wasn't a dish in the sink or a crumb on the counter, but when Katherine finally found the wineglasses in the last press she opened, they had greasy fingermarks on them. She began wiping them away with a tea-towel that smelt vaguely musty.

The kitchen was part of an extension with large, plate-glass doors that looked out on to a decked patio lined with box hedges

171

that had grown out in parts and were bald in others. A little blue bicycle with stabilisers lay on its side. A square wooden table and three chairs stood at odd angles, their untreated surfaces mottled with rain stains.

'I keep meaning to trim those hedges,' Lisa said, coming into the kitchen behind her. 'I just never seem to get the time.'

'It's a beautiful garden,' said Katherine.

Lisa gave an empty laugh. 'It used to be,' she said. 'Once upon a time.'

Her roots were a good inch long, a nondescript mousy grey, one side of her black bob shoved haphazardly behind an ear. The ample chest of her uniform black polo-neck sweater was encrusted with a yellowish substance.

'You don't mind if I leave you alone for a few minutes?' Lisa said. 'I haven't had time to change yet and look at the state of me.'

'Go for it.' Katherine smiled and handed Lisa a glass of wine. 'Take that with you.'

'If anyone arrives, tell them I'll be down in a minute.'

While she waited, Katherine found a half-used kitchen roll in the cupboard under the sink and began polishing a few more wine glasses. She was way too early, but there would have been no point in going back to Lucy's after she'd eventually got out of the unemployment office, then coming all the way across the city again.

Her visit to the dole office had taken much longer than she'd expected. The receptionist had hardly looked at her when she'd told him she wanted to sign on for jobseeker's allowance. 'Take a ticket and wait for booths one to four,' he'd said, pointing loosely in the direction of a bank of black plastic seats that seemed to be fully occupied.

Katherine's ticket was numbered 126 and the digital counter on the wall said 97, which meant there were almost thirty people in the queue before her. She spotted a seat in the back row, between a woman in a grey sweatsuit, her black hair tied up at the top of her head with a Dayglo green scrunchie, and a man in a suit and tie who seemed to be doing his best to look as if he was just passing through. The rest of the place, she realized, after she had been sitting down for a few minutes, was divided into those two camps: people in suits studying their phones, as if they were the most interesting thing in the world, and others in tracksuits complaining loudly although no one was listening. Katherine was wondering where she fitted into the mix when she spotted a lone woman, sitting on the edge of her seat in the first row, in a buttoned up powder-blue duffel coat. She looked like Dorothy alone in the haunted forest.

'Fuckin' queues,' the girl beside her said, eyeing Katherine's bracelet. 'It's always the bleedin' same.'

'Yes, I'd say it is,' Katherine replied, with a tight smile, wishing she had brought a book or at least one of Lucy's celebrity magazines. While she was waiting for a bus earlier she had gone into a newsagent and fingered *In Style*, the monthly fashion Bible she could no longer afford. She hadn't realised before that moment how not having money put the small things you had once taken for granted at the furthest reach.

The queue moved at a snail's pace, the girl beside her commenting on the inconvenience she was being put to every time the digital counter on the wall flipped to another number. After an hour and fifteen minutes of studiously ignoring her and everyone else, Katherine found herself sitting at booth number one in front of a woman with the biggest Afro she had ever seen.

'Fresh claim?' the woman said.

'I suppose so,' Katherine replied.

The woman looked up. 'Make your mind up. I haven't got all day.'

'Yes,' said Katherine. 'It's a fresh claim.'

'Take these forms. Fill in the blue one and the pink one. The yellow one is for your information. Take a ticket, and when you've completed them, bring them to booths five to eight.'

Katherine's new ticket said 56. The digital counter on the wall beside booths five to eight said 22.

It was another forty-five minutes before she was seen again, at booth seven. At least the guy who took her forms had a friendly smile. He studied them for a moment, said, 'Wait here,' and disappeared for another ten minutes.

When he came back he pushed the blue form towards her. 'It says here that you're renting out a property,' he said.

'Yes,' Katherine replied. 'I had to move out because I couldn't afford the mortgage.'

'Rent is counted as income, I'm afraid.'

Her heart plummeted. If she was turned down for Social Welfare, she'd have no money to live on at all. 'But I have nothing,' she said. 'I'm completely broke.'

'I've spoken to my supervisor,' the guy replied. 'It might be a problem.'

'But I've been paying PRSI for years. I should be entitled to some sort of Social Welfare.'

The guy smiled at her again, but this time his smile seemed more jaded than friendly. Tapping at his keyboard, he said, 'I'm making an appointment for you to come back next Wednesday at three o'clock. We'll let you know then whether or not you've been approved.'

42. The Wild One in Chintz

Saeed, as per usual, was late. Forty minutes late at the last check. Normally Jamie's threshold for waiting on anyone was twenty minutes tops, but he wanted to get this meeting out of the way and Saeed, as if he knew what was coming, had put him off four times already.

Why coffee? he'd replied earlier, when Jamie had texted to confirm. *There r bttr things we can do ;-)*

We need 2 tlk, Jamie texted back, and at last Saeed agreed to come after his shift at work.

Usually they met behind securely closed doors, so Jamie had chosen a café a bit out of town on the bus route to Lisa's. He could get there for Film Club once his work here was done. The chances of anyone recognising him were few.

Still, sitting in a corner at the back amid the rattle and hiss of an ancient coffee machine, he worried that someone who knew Andrew or, even worse, Andrew himself might walk in. He was being paranoid, but you never could tell in Dublin. It was a small city and you were always bumping into someone you knew.

While he waited, he passed the time updating his Twitter profile on the new iPhone Andrew had bought him for his birthday. He'd taken him to dinner at L'Écrivain on Saturday and handed him the iPhone in a ribbon-wrapped box.

When he'd opened it, the surprise had caused Jamie almost to burst into tears, and for the first time since Andrew had made his roundabout proposal, he felt he'd been right to say yes. He had leaned over the table and, feeling a weird sense of urgency, said, 'I really love you.'

'I love you back,' said Andrew, his eyes shining in the candlelight, and relief had flooded through Jamie's body. Why was he feeling like this, he'd questioned himself, still on the verge of tears. He hoped it wasn't more anxiety about the street attack. He'd thought he was well over that by now.

Wondering what the Forced Redundancy Film Club is watching tonight? #greatmovies,' he tweeted, although he knew perfectly well it was *Thelma & Louise*. Lisa had phoned him in a flap last week about whether she should show that or *Pride and Prejudice*.

'If I have to watch Keira Knightley pouting at Mr Darcy for an hour and a half, I'll end up doing a *Thelma & Louise* off the nearest cliff,' he'd said.

'But *Thelma & Louise* might be a bit much,' Lisa replied. 'At least there's no rape scene in *Pride and Prejudice* and no one commits suicide at the end.'

'Trust me, *Pride and Prejudice* would have been a much better film if someone *had* committed suicide. Preferably at the beginning.'

The little bell on the steamed-up door of the café rang and Saeed walked in, looking put-upon. He was wearing one of those studded leather biker jackets that had gone out with the dodo and a pair of jeans decorated down the front with seriously dodgy bleach patterns, but he looked like a Middle Eastern Marlon Brando walking into a scene from *The Wild One* – if *The Wild One* had been set in a coffee shop with chintz curtains and middle-aged women nattering above a stereo playing *The Best of Simply Red*.

'Here,' Jamie called, standing up and beckoning Saeed over. Already he was getting the stirring down below, the one that made him give up all his good intentions.

'Nice place,' Saeed said. He pulled a chair out, its feet scraping against the tiled floor, and sat down with his legs spread apart.

'Coffee?' Jamie asked, trying to catch the waitress's eye.

'I suppose.'

'They do great cup cakes.'

Saeed pulled open his leather jacket and patted his rock-hard stomach. 'I don't eat cakes,' he said, with a leer. 'They make you fat like a pig.'

Jamie had eaten two while he was waiting. He could always burn the calories off at the gym when he started working out again. He hadn't cancelled his membership yet, so he could get back on the treadmill any time he wanted to.

'I wanted to talk to you,' he began.

'I know. You told me.'

'Well, the thing is—'

'Come home with me,' Saeed interrupted. 'This is not a good coffee shop.'

'The thing is, Andrew has asked me to marry him.'

Saeed snorted. 'This is what the gays do in this country, they marry?'

'Yes – well, we get civil partnerships.'

'In my country, that would never happen.'

'I know,' said Jamie, 'but Ireland is different. It's easier to be gay here.'

'That's what you always say, but I don't think so. It is the same as everywhere else.'

'Anyway, you and I can't see each other any more.'

'Why?' Saeed said. The little nodule of calcium above the bridge of his nose disappeared into a frown. 'It doesn't make no difference.'

'Of course it does. I'm marrying Andrew. I can't walk up the aisle with a fuck buddy on the side.'

'You always say this "fuck buddy" thing. I am not a fuck buddy.'

Jamie picked up his iPhone and put it into his pocket. 'Look. We had a great time together. But it couldn't go on forever. It's time to say goodbye. You can't text me any more or call. You should delete my number.'

'No,' Saeed said, his fist curled on the table before him. 'I will not delete your number. I love you.'

It was Jamie's turn to snort. 'Are you out of your mind?' he said. 'This isn't love.'

Saeed leaned in so his face was very close to Jamie's. 'Yes, it is,' he said, his voice low.

There was an unmistakable hum of threat in the air.

'Look,' said Jamie, pacing out the words, 'I'm sorry if you feel that way. I don't.'

'Yes, you do,' said Saeed. The corners of his mouth were turned up, but it didn't look like a smile.

'No, I don't,' said Jamie. 'You can take my word for it.'

'What if I go to Andrew and tell him about us?'

Jamie's pulse quickened. 'You wouldn't,' he said. 'Would you?'

'Yes,' said Saeed, sitting back and spreading his legs again. 'I would.'

'What could you possibly gain by doing that?'

'Come home with me now,' Saeed said. 'Or I will tell him.'

'But that's blackmail.'

Saeed pushed himself away from the table and stood up. 'Let's go,' he said.

'No,' said Jamie, trying internally to count to ten.

'Then I tell Andrew everything.'

Jamie got to six. 'Do whatever the fuck you want!' he snapped. 'I'm not giving in to blackmail.'

'Okay,' said Saeed, zipping up his leather jacket. 'I will.'

Jamie watched him leave the coffee shop, willing his heart to slow down. It was better to call his bluff. Saeed was a pussy underneath the macho Iranian façade. He'd never tell Andrew. Not in a million years.

43. Pride and Procrastination

Downstairs the doorbell rang, and Lisa listened to Katherine's heels clicking on the hall tiles as she went to answer it. From the sound of the voices, Alice and Martin had arrived together. Lisa had been irritated that Katherine had come so early, but now she was glad she was here to let them in. She didn't think she could face anyone just yet.

In the dim curtained-off light of the box room, she sat on the edge of the empty single bed, still holding the glass of wine Katherine had given her, and watched Aaron sleep through the bars of his cot. A new tooth had been pushing up for the past couple of days and she'd given him Calpol to ease the pain, so he'd probably stay out for the count for a few more hours. He looked so peaceful and the room was so quiet, she felt like lying down and nodding off to sleep beside him.

She should have cancelled Film Club, as she had been threatening to do all week, but somehow she believed that if she broke tonight's arrangement, there would be no going back.

Getting Patrick's mother to agree to take Theo and Ben for the night had been like extracting blood from a stone. She had hummed and hawed over it for ages, not committing to anything until Lisa had told Patrick to intervene, knowing that anything the beloved son asked for would be granted. It had done the trick and the boys had been so excited going off with Patrick earlier on, Theo's backpack stuffed with Lego he never used and Ben carrying his favourite teddy by the leg. It broke Lisa's heart to think that Patrick's mother didn't want them, that she was minding them on sufferance.

Lisa's mother would have been only too glad to take them, would have jumped at the chance, but unlike Lisa's sister-in-law, Tessa, who seemed to leave her children with Mum day in, day out, Lisa and Patrick didn't have the luxury of living a stone's throw from her.

And, anyway, there was no way her mother would ever stick to the boys' routines. Lisa had been brought up in a world where everything down to whether or not she might go to school in the morning was at her mother's whim. At least Patrick's mother could be trusted to get the boys to bed on time and not allow them run around like headless chickens into the night.

Aaron gave a little grunt and turned his head to the side, his soother slipping from his mouth. She loved watching him sleep. She loved watching them all sleep.

During Theo's first year, she and Patrick had often stood watching him in his cot after he had nodded off. It had felt so connected, like they were a little unit separate from the world in the darkness, her head on Patrick's shoulder, his arm around her. Theo was their own little miracle, a fully functioning human being they had created together. Her mind went back to the slap in the dressing room of TK Maxx and she flinched. How had it come to that?

In the chest of drawers in her bedroom across the hall, the pregnancy testing kit was waiting. She had bought it the day she'd gone shopping and discovered a size sixteen didn't fit, fully intending to use it the moment she got home. But in the bathroom, prising off its packaging, she found couldn't go through with it. She'd stuffed it under the bras and pants in her underwear drawer and told herself she'd do it tomorrow.

That had been four weeks ago, and although she hadn't had her period since then and the morning sickness hadn't abated, she told herself that until she did the test she couldn't really be sure she was pregnant.

No matter where she was, though, the picture of the kit, sitting beneath her underwear, stayed in her mind, always there, always waiting for her.

She went to the bathroom and poured the wine down the plughole. Downstairs the doorbell rang again and Katherine let Jamie in.

'Where's Lisa?' she heard him ask, but didn't catch Katherine's muffled reply.

Hearing his feet on the stairs, Lisa prepared herself to smile and do what she had to do.

44. On the Edge of a Cliff

'It's completely dated,' said Martin. 'Look at their clothes, the soundtrack … Geena Davis's hair, for fuck's sake.'

'Okay, I agree the beginning might seem a bit eighties,' said Katherine, 'but as the film goes on they lose the makeup and big hair. They end up looking like they could be from any time.'

Lisa tried to catch Jamie's eye, but he was lost in a world of his own. Sitting between Martin and Katherine, Alice followed their argument with turns of her head, as if she was at a tennis match.

'Well, the feminist thing has dated,' said Martin. 'It's hard to believe anyone ever thought it was groundbreaking.'

'But it *is* groundbreaking,' said Katherine. 'It *is* a feminist film.'

'A feminist film directed by a man.'

'It doesn't matter that a man directed it. What it's saying is that women are always being trapped in little boxes by men. Having to be nice little wives or good little girlfriends. Thelma and Louise break free of that. They don't need to please men to be happy.'

'I don't understand why they drove off the cliff,' Alice interjected, leaning forward on the couch. 'It makes no sense.' She had come proffering a bunch of flowers, red carnations from the Spar on the corner, which Lisa had found oddly touching.

'They have to die at the end because they're very naughty girls,' said Jamie.

'That's what I mean!' said Martin. 'How does punishing them for being bad girls make it a feminist film?'

'Because when they drive over the cliff, they're taking control of their own lives,' said Katherine. 'They're saying, "Fuck you," to all the men who want them to give themselves up.'

Before tonight, what Lisa had loved about the film was that, no matter how many times you watched it, you were left feeling as free as Thelma and Louise, that you could get away with things you'd never dreamed of doing, that the world was full of possibility. You could drive into the distance, leaving behind all the stuff that tied you down, all that mundane rule-following.

But this time was different. Looking at the film with that

pregnancy kit waiting in her underwear drawer, she saw two women running for their lives and being set back every time they thought things were going their way. They were two little mice trying to dodge traps, but ending up in the biggest trap there was: a car on the edge of a cliff with nowhere to go but forward.

Why couldn't they get to Mexico? What would have been so wrong in letting them have their freedom? What *Thelma & Louise* told you was that there is no point in dreaming of escape because there is no such thing.

Lisa turned to Katherine. 'I think you're wrong,' she said. 'They don't take control of their own lives. They drive off the cliff because they have no other choice.'

'They could have chosen to go back,' said Alice. 'The detective was a nice man. He might have helped them.'

'Helped them pick out curtains for their cells on Death Row, more like,' said Jamie. When he'd arrived earlier, he'd run upstairs to Lisa and told her about his affair, the words spilling out in a torrent of too much information.

'I wish I'd never met the son-of-a-bitch,' he'd said, when he'd finished. 'Can you believe it? He's trying to blackmail me into having sex with him.'

Lisa knew she was supposed to make reassuring sounds and be firmly on Jamie's side, and she'd done her best, but she couldn't help feeling that Jamie had made his own bed to lie in. Andrew was an attentive, loving boyfriend who saw only the good in Jamie. Other partners might not have been so patient.

And what did Jamie think? That he could sleep around behind Andrew's back with impunity?

For a minute, Lisa had hoped he'd ask how she was, so she could unburden herself too. But then she'd realised that if she said anything there'd be no avoiding the pregnancy test. Jamie would leave her with no choice.

Instead she'd said, 'We'd better go down. They'll be wondering what we're at up here.'

Jamie had groaned. 'One affair is enough for me. Although, if you were up for it, I'd do my best.'

Martin was arguing with Katherine about *Thelma & Louise* again. 'It's like a cartoon western,' he said. 'The women are the good guys and the men are bad.'

'Let it go,' said Jamie. 'Have another beer or ten.'

Lisa gave Jamie a warning look. It was hard to gauge where Martin's drinking might take him. Mostly he was perfectly fine, funny and amiable, but sometimes his mood would turn sour in an instant and he'd lash out. There was no point in pushing him.

'Like Thelma's stupid husband,' said Martin, his voice going up a notch. 'Or the guy in the truck they blow up. That's completely—' The ringing of a mobile phone interrupted his flow. He looked confused for a second, then reached down to pull his out of his pocket. 'Shit,' he said, looking at the screen. 'I have to take this.'

'I've got two words,' Jamie said, when Martin had left the room. 'Brad and Pitt. Why is no one discussing the most important thing in *Thelma & Louise*?'

Lisa found herself smiling for the first time tonight. Jamie had a point. 'No matter how many times you watch it, you can't help hoping he won't steal their money,' she said.

'It was a bit embarrassing, though, wasn't it?' Alice said. 'The way he was jumping around the place with his top off in the hotel room. People don't really go on like that in real life.'

'Jumping around with his top off made him a star,' said Jamie. 'There's nothing embarrassing about that.'

Martin came back into the room and stood by the door, silent.

'What's wrong?' Katherine asked. His face had drained of all colour.

'I have to go to the hospital,' he said. 'It's my father. He's had a stroke.'

'Oh, Martin! I'm so sorry,' Lisa cried. She stood up and went over to him, but wasn't sure what to do next.

Katherine was standing up too. 'Which hospital is he in?' she asked. 'I'll take you.'

'I can drive,' Martin said. 'It's only down the road.'

'You're in no fit state,' Katherine said. 'St James's, is it?'

45. Calm Before the Storm

Left behind with Lisa and Jamie, Alice felt awkward and fidgety. The atmosphere in the room had plummeted, as if somebody had let the air out of a balloon.

'Poor Martin,' Lisa said, looking at the television screen, which played the same bit of the *Thelma & Louise* theme over and over again. 'I hope it's only a mild stroke.'

'"I'd say it was massive,' said Jamie. 'Martin once told me his old man's a complete dipsomaniac. Like father like son, I'd say.'

'Jamie!' said Lisa. 'That's so disrespectful! And I don't think heavy drinking leads to strokes. Does it?'

'I should go,' said Alice. 'I have an early start in the morning.' She didn't feel comfortable with the turn the conversation had taken.

'Those were the days.' Jamie sighed. 'When we had early starts.'

Lisa gave a wry laugh. 'Speak for yourself,' she said. 'I'm up at the crack of dawn every morning.'

'How are things going in that kip, anyway?' Jamie asked Alice. 'Maguire still the worse for wear?'

'He's been off work a lot lately,' Alice replied, putting her bag down again.

'No change there, then.'

'It's different from before. It's like he disappears into thin air.'

It was very difficult without him, everybody looking to Alice for decisions on things, blaming her for not getting back to them with Mr Maguire's responses to their emails. But how could she respond? She wasn't the decision-maker. He was.

Jamie poured himself and Lisa another glass of wine. 'I've a supremely juicy piece of gossip,' he said.

'Jamie …' Lisa said, in a cautionary tone, but she had tipped her head closer to his, all agog.

'Guess whose boyfriend just dumped her like yesterday's leftovers?'

Lisa frowned at Alice, biting her lip, before turning back to Jamie. 'Go on,' she said 'Tell us.'

'Katherine!' Jamie exclaimed. 'I met Ciara Kelly who used to work in Accounts, who heard it from some guy in Marketing, who golfs with Barry's brother. Barry gave Katherine the old heave-ho and she's gone to live with her sister.'

'That can't be true,' said Lisa. 'She never said a word.'

'Why would Little Miss Perfect tell us anything? She wants the world to believe she has it all sewn up.'

Alice lifted her handbag. 'She might have wanted to keep it private,' she said. 'I don't think it's fair talking about her behind her back like this.'

'Fair schmair,' said Jamie, a big, cat-like grin plastered across his face.

Alice didn't return it.

The early start Alice had alluded to, which Jamie had assumed was just another day at work, was not that at all. Instead she had taken the day off and booked seats for herself and Mrs Silver on the train to Cork. From there it was a two-and-a-half-hour bus journey to Ballydehob, the little town Alice's birth mother had put as her address in the note she left. That had been thirty-eight years ago, so Alice didn't expect to find much, but Mrs Silver had high hopes for the journey.

'An investigation must always begin somewhere, dear,' she said. 'And Ballydehob is as good a place as any. In these small towns everybody knows everybody else's business. There's bound to be someone who remembers your mother, or knows what happened to her.'

Those words, 'someone who knows what happened to her', remained on Alice's mind.

What had happened to her? Sitting in the front seat on the top deck of the bus that was driving her home from Lisa's house, Alice told herself one of many stories about C. In this one, she went to England on the boat after her baby was taken away. There she trained to be a nurse and met a man who loved her and helped her put her broken heart behind her. She was there now, still patrolling the silent night wards of a hospital, wondering about her lost little girl.

Sometimes Alice tried to imagine more exciting lives for her mother. Watching *Thelma & Louise*, she pictured her first like Louise, glamorous and rebellious, not able to settle down to the life that was prescribed for her in stifling Ballydehob. Then her imaginary mother became Thelma, running blindly away from some terrible thing that had happened to her.

But those mothers felt too much like fiction. Ascribing to C a simple life – a nurse in England, a farmer's wife in Cork – brought her closer, made her more tangible, even if she was still little more than a figment of the imagination.

Since she'd made the decision to go to Ballydehob with Mrs Silver, the house had become almost unnaturally quiet. All its creaks and groans seemed to have dried up and disappeared. Maybe it was the good weather, or maybe Mother had finally accepted Alice was moving on with her life and departed.

Whether Mother was there or not, Alice still tried to keep the peace, whispering little reassurances into the silence every now and then, saying good night to her at the end of the day, as she always had. Sometimes now she missed the idea of Mother's presence, lurking in dark corners, watching her every move. At least when she'd been there it was like company.

Getting off the bus, Alice walked around the corner into her road, searching in her bag for her housekeys. It wasn't until she was standing in front of the house that she saw every light in every window was lit, blazing out into the darkness.

'Mother …' she whispered, advancing towards the front door. Maybe the silence had been the calm before the storm.

46. What Colour Are My Eyes?

Patrick sat down heavily on his side of the bed. 'I know you're awake,' he said.

For a second Lisa considered continuing the pretence, then turned towards him and mumbled, 'What time is it?'

'Did you hit Theo?' he asked.

Lisa jerked her head up. 'What?'

'You heard me, Lisa. Did you or did you not hit Theo?'

'Did he tell you?'

'No, he told my mother. She called earlier on, in the middle of my meeting.'

'Oh, God,' Lisa said. She lay down again and put a hand over her eyes.

'I thought we were going to bring up our children without slapping them,' said Patrick.

'We are,' said Lisa, cringing inside. 'It was an accident. I'm sorry.'

'Hitting a child is never accidental. I can't believe you did it.'

'It just sort of happened, before I knew what I was doing.'

Lisa knelt up and put her arms around Patrick from behind. 'It'll never happen again, I promise.'

He shrugged her away. 'Why did you do it?'

'It was like an unconscious reaction. He bit me again, really hard.'

'He's a tiny child, Lisa. A little bite from him compared to a slap from you is nothing.'

Lisa reached over to switch on the bedside light. 'Look,' she said, rolling up her pyjama sleeve to show the map of welts on her arm. 'Are you telling me that's nothing?'

'You need to be firmer with him. But slapping him is out of the question.'

'He's going to school in September. What's he going to be like with other children if he's like this with me? He's always hitting Ben too, and lately he's started on Aaron.'

'School will sort him out. He needs to be with more kids his own age.'

'He needs help, Patrick. He needs to see a child psychologist.'

Patrick sighed heavily and put his head into his hands. 'He's five years of age, Lisa. He's not going to a shrink.'

'There's something wrong with him.'

'No, there isn't. He's a normal boy, not something out of one of your self-help books.'

'That's easy for you to say,' said Lisa. 'You're the only one he's not aggressive with.'

Patrick lifted his head. 'Maybe that's because I know how to handle him properly.'

'Handle him? You're never here long enough to see him do anything wrong!'

'It always comes down to this. It's my fault because I can't be here all the time. What am I supposed to do? Quit?'

'It's like I'm doing this all on my own, Patrick. And I can't cope.'

'How did our mothers cope? How did their mothers cope? You just have to get on with it. We all do. That's the way life is.'

Lisa felt close to tears. 'But what if I end up hitting him again?'

Patrick lay back on the pillows and closed his eyes. 'You won't,' he said.

'I'm so ashamed. I honestly didn't mean to do it.'

Patrick turned towards her and reached out to stroke her hair. 'I know it's hard,' he said. 'It's hard for both of us right now. But it won't be for ever. The boys will grow up and you won't remember any of this. You'll look back and laugh about how cute they were. That's what my mother does.'

Lisa found it hard to believe Patrick's mother laughed about anything, much less the children she had once ruled with an iron fist.

Just before she nodded off on her side of the bed, she asked, 'Patrick, what colour are my eyes?'

'What sort of a question is that?' Patrick answered, his voice groggy.

'It was in the film we watched earlier on. *Thelma & Louise*.'

'Blue. They're blue.'

'Yes,' she said. 'They are.'

The pregnancy testing kit sat in her underwear drawer, waiting. 'Patrick,' she whispered. 'Please hold me.'

47. Around the Corner

The hospital waiting room was devoid of windows. Around its unadorned olive green walls an assortment of grey and red plastic chairs sat disconsolately under harsh fluorescent lights, three of them occupied by members of a family huddled together and murmuring. They were here with a girl who had been brought in with a brain haemorrhage an hour ago.

Martin, his mother and sister had been in the intensive-care ward with his father for the past half-hour. Because she wasn't a family member, Katherine hadn't been allowed beyond the nurses' station. Not that she wanted to go in. She wasn't here to intrude on the family. She wasn't sure what to do with herself, really, whether to stay or go.

She'd made sure Martin had got to the hospital in one piece, had gone through the ordeal of meeting his mother and sister, Nell – the other sister, Mary, was on her way home from Spain – and faced the same enquiring looks as when she'd met his father in the garage. She'd sat with them while they waited for the doctors to be finished examining him.

Now that Martin was back at the bedside, she thought she should go home, but somehow couldn't bring herself to leave. It didn't seem right, like abandoning him in his hour of need, even though he had his family around him.

Across the room, the older woman in the little group had begun to sob. Her husband glanced at Katherine and she smiled at him. He looked utterly lost. 'I'm going down to the coffee machine,' she said. 'Can I get you something?'

His wife dabbed at her eyes. 'It's our girl, Chrissie,' she said. 'They say she's only got a fifty-fifty chance of making it.'

'You should concentrate on the fifty per cent that *will* make it,' said Katherine. 'That's a big percentage.'

'She was fine this afternoon,' the woman said. 'Going on about the part she has in the Musical Society. Laughing about how she's playing a woman twice her age. And now she might be taken away from us, in the blink of an eye.'

'You never know what's around the corner,' the man said, and Katherine nodded because it was true.

Too true.

Their mother had been smoking in the kitchen when Katherine and Lucy had arrived home from school all those years ago.

'How was school?' Mum asked and Katherine bit her bottom lip. She'd been sent up to Mother Perpetua's office for being disruptive in class. Her best friend, Eileen, had leaned over and whispered that their teacher, Miss Wilson, looked like a smelly old donkey and Katherine had burst into a fit of uncontrollable giggles. She was so hysterical, she almost wet herself.

In the kitchen, as her mother stubbed out her cigarette in an overloaded ashtray, Katherine decided against saying anything about the incident. She'd tell Daddy when he got home and they'd have a good laugh together about it. Miss Wilson *did* look like a donkey!

'Sister Aloysius said I was the best in the class at art,' Lucy said, taking her schoolbag off her back. 'She put my drawing on the wall.'

'That's good,' Mum said, and instantly Katherine knew something was wrong. Her mother's voice sounded choked, her face was white and her hand, as she lit another cigarette, was trembling.

'Is everything okay, Mum?' Katherine asked, watching her mother intently. She hadn't put on any makeup today and her eyes were puffy.

'Daddy's had to go away for a while,' her mother said.

'When will he be back?' asked Lucy.

'I don't know.'

'Where is he?' Katherine said. Her stomach churned in the way it did when she felt like she was going to throw up.

'I told you. He's gone for a while.'

'But where?'

Her mother fixed her eyes on Katherine and ran her free hand through her hair. 'Not now, Katherine, okay?' she said. 'I'll explain later.'

Panic rose in Katherine's throat. 'Please, Mum,' she begged. 'Where is he?' She was aware of Lucy standing behind her, looking dumbly on.

Slowly her mother got to her feet and moved to the sink, taking a drag of her cigarette as she went. She stood there, looking out of the window, saying nothing. Then she turned around with wet eyes.

'He's in love with someone else,' she said. 'He's gone to live with her.'

A nurse came into the waiting room and beckoned the family of the brain-haemorrhage girl to come with her. Katherine shook herself and stood up. She'd get herself a cup of coffee, and if Martin hadn't come back before she was finished, she'd text him and tell him she'd had to go. He'd understand. It was two in the morning, after all.

She was putting coins into the coffee machine when she saw him coming towards her, shoulders slumped and head bent. His father was gone: it was written all over the way he walked.

'How are things?' she asked tentatively, as he came nearer.

'It's over,' Martin said. 'They've switched off the machines.' He had his arms wrapped around himself.

'I'm sorry,' she said.

'I kept hoping he'd wake up,' Martin said, as they sat down in the empty café area. 'That he'd say something to me.'

'What did you want him to say?'

'I don't know. Something. Anything.'

'Sometimes it's too hard for people to say goodbye,' Katherine said.

'I didn't want to hear him say goodbye.'

'What then?'

'That he loved me, maybe. That he wasn't ashamed of me.'

Katherine watched him as he stared, glassy-eyed, into mid-space and her heart went out to him. 'People have very strange ways of showing their love,' she said, and reached over to put her hand on his.

48. Ploughing in, Regardless

'The best place to start is the local pub,' said Mrs Silver, studying the book she'd bought at the station, *The Lonely Planet Guide to Ireland*. Even though it was a warm day, she was wearing an orange tweed jacket, brown leather gloves and a white woolly hat that made the blue-rinsed strands of her hair look luminous against her forehead. 'It says here that Ballydehob's pubs are some of the friendliest in the world. That bodes well.'

They didn't really need the guidebook. Ballydehob was a town on one street, a hill dotted with pastel-painted shopfronts – a health-food store, a post office, a hairdresser – their windows glinting in the midday sun. Alice was reminded of the town in *Edward Scissorhands*.

'"Ballydehob is home to several famous artists, writers, sculptors and craft workers,"' Mrs Silver read. 'I must say, it's not what I expected at all.'

A young woman in a tie-dyed T-shirt, her head thick with rust-coloured dreadlocks, walked by on the other side of the street, wheeling a toddler in a buggy, its mouth covered with a jammy substance. 'Excuse me!' Mrs Silver called. 'Could you tell us which is the best drinking establishment in town?'

The woman crossed the road. 'Best pub?' she asked, and when Mrs Silver nodded, she pointed towards a little brown-fronted bar on the opposite corner. 'Everyone who visits here goes to Carroll's,' she said. 'It's an institution.'

Alice followed Mrs Silver across the road, wondering whether it had been a good idea to come here. The adoption agency wouldn't like it one little bit.

Mrs Silver was becoming more and more interfering where Alice was concerned. Letting herself into the house and turning on all the lights like that. Taking Alice by the hand into each and every room to show her the place wasn't haunted. She'd meant well, but it was a little too much. Alice wasn't like her: she needed to take her time with things, not plough into them regardless.

The bar was just a small room with a tiled floor. All the tables and chairs were different from each other, lending the place a cluttered, homely look, and every available wall space had a poster or framed picture on it, the most imposing being a portrait of a half-naked man that seemed to fit in perfectly and be out of place at the same time. Behind the bar an old woman with short grey hair, was polishing glasses.

'Hello,' she said, the o of her greeting rising in a sing-song Cork accent. 'What can I get for you?'

Alice followed Mrs Silver's lead and sat up on one of the high stools at the bar. 'I'd like a 7-Up,' she said.

'And I'll have some of your Guinness,' Mrs Silver said.

Silently the woman took a glass and put it under the Guinness tap, pulling the handle so it began to fill with black liquid. She filled it three-quarters of the way, held it up to look at its contents in the light, then put it to rest on the counter. Alice wondered how many times she had carried out that ritual. It was probably second nature to her.

'You're not from around here, are you?' the barwoman said.

'No,' Alice replied. 'We're from Dublin. We're here for the day.'

'We don't get many day visitors from Dublin,' the woman said, taking Mrs Silver's now settled Guinness from the counter to fill it up to the brim. 'But you're welcome here anyway.' She put the glass with its creamy top in front of Mrs Silver, who lifted it, closed her eyes and took a sip.

'Germans say they are the best beer producers in the world,' she said, licking her lips. 'But they can't make anything like this.'

'Oh, we've plenty of Germans hereabouts,' the barwoman said. 'And they all like their Guinness.'

'Actually, we're here on a little investigation,' Mrs Silver said, cutting to the chase. 'We're looking for someone who used to live in the area. A woman, possibly in her mid-fifties or early sixties.'

'What's her name?'

'We don't know,' said Alice. 'We have her first initial. C.'

The woman put down the glass she was polishing and rubbed

her hands on the side of her housecoat. She smiled wryly. 'This is a big township,' she said. 'It could be anyone.'

It was a wild-goose chase. How had they expected to come all the way down here and find someone just based on an initial?

The front door of the pub opened, letting a shaft of sunlight into its dark interior and silhouetting the large frame of a woman.

'Afternoon, Mary,' she said to the barwoman, closing the door firmly behind her. 'I've brought over your post.'

'Meena,' said the barwoman. 'You might be able to help these people. They're looking for someone who used to live in the village.' To Alice and Mrs Silver she added, 'Meena's been postmistress for the last thirty years. She knows everyone around these parts.'

Alice recounted the only information she had: the initial, that the woman had lived here in 1973, was probably in her mid- to late fifties or early sixties now.

'That's not much to go on,' said the postmistress, folding her arms. She wore a cross-over apron and her black hair, tied in a bun, was scattered with iron-grey strands. 'Why are you looking for her, do you mind me asking?'

Alice opened her mouth to speak, but Mrs Silver put a hand on her shoulder and said, 'I'm afraid that is confidential information. I'm sorry.'

The postmistress and the barwoman exchanged a glance.

The postmistress sniffed. 'I'm afraid we can't be of help at all then,' she said.

Alice wondered why Mrs Silver was being so unforthcoming, then realised she was right to be circumspect. It was a rural place, after all. An *Edward Scissorhands* town, where secrets were probably best left buried.

'We have a letter,' Mrs Silver said. 'We could show you the envelope it came in, but not the letter itself.'

Alice dug in her handbag and brought forth the envelope.

The postmistress craned her neck a little to get a glance at the letter as Alice took it out and put it back in her bag.

'I'm sorry,' Alice said. 'It's confidential.'

Shrugging, the postmistress took the envelope and held it close to her face in the pub's murky light.

'Let me see, Meena,' said the barwoman, holding her gnarled hand out.

The postmistress smiled to herself and passed the letter over. 'I'm sorry,' she said. 'I've never seen that handwriting before.'

July

Cinema Paradiso

Giuseppe Tornatore, 1988

'Life isn't like the movies. Life is much harder.'

49. Lions and Tigers and Bears

'Why are we stopped?' Kitty said, leaning as far forward as her seatbelt would let her.

Katherine turned the ignition and pumped the accelerator hard. 'I don't know,' she said. 'I can't get the bloody thing started.'

'You said a bad word,' said Kitty. 'Bloody.'

The man stuck behind her in a silver Mercedes jammed on his horn and Katherine glared at him in her rear-view mirror. She wanted to flip him the finger, but having the girls in the back seat forced her to keep her cool.

'It's a very old car,' Laura explained, to her little sister. 'Sometimes they break down.'

Katherine tried turning the key again, but the engine, which had been turning over like a wheezing old man when she'd tried before, had given up the ghost. She felt like hammering the steering wheel with her fists, screaming at the top of her lungs, 'Why? Why can nothing go right for me?' She took a deep breath and rolled down her window to let in some air.

The Merc jerked out from behind and its driver paused to flash her a dirty look.

'What?' Katherine shouted at him, as he darted away. 'It's not my fault!'

In her rear-view mirror she noticed the girls exchange a look. Then, in the Merc's place, another car behind her began to honk its horn, and the one behind that too.

'You should switch on your hazard lights, Auntie Katherine,' Laura said, 'so the other cars will know that we've broken down.'

How did Laura know these things? Sometimes it was as if she was the adult and Katherine was seven years old, like Kitty. Katherine searched on the dashboard for the hazard-light switch and eventually found it hidden to the bottom left of the steering wheel. She switched it on and unhooked her seatbelt, trying to think what to do next.

'I'm hungry,' said Kitty.

'You can't be,' said Katherine. 'You had breakfast less than an hour ago.'

'But I *am*.'

'Okay, take out one thing each from your lunchboxes. Just one.'

Paolo had packed them last night, with a ham sandwich, an apple, a bag of crisps and a Penguin bar each. Kitty, who couldn't get enough chocolate and didn't know the meaning of waiting for good things, unwrapped the Penguin.

'I'm not hungry,' said Laura.

'Okay,' said Katherine, forcing herself to breathe in through her nose and out through her mouth. 'Just Kitty, then.'

A large dollop of rain landed on the windscreen, hastily followed by a deluge and Katherine quickly rolled her window up. She couldn't even bring the girls for a simple trip to the zoo without the gods conspiring against her to bring it all to a miserable halt.

The whole thing had been Lucy's idea. She'd said it would help Katherine to get to know the girls better. Katherine would normally have been stung by this remark. She knew such comments were barbed and intended to make her feel at fault, but the more time she spent living with Lucy, the less guilt-ridden she felt.

Through the rear-view mirror she watched Kitty concentrate intently on eating her Penguin. Laura looked disconsolately out of the window at the rain. The sisters were as different from each other as chalk and cheese – Laura with her carefully plaited copper braids and the purple pinafore she'd laid out last night in preparation for today's trip; Kitty's blonde mass of ringlets, inherited directly from Lucy, and her haphazardly thrown together shorts and Little Mermaid T-shirt. It was hard to believe the girls had the same mother, given they had different fathers.

'What are we going to do?' Laura asked, turning from the window, her pale, high forehead creased with worry.

'We'll sort something out,' Katherine said. 'Let's just wait until the rain stops.'

The truth was that if she had never accepted this old banger from Martin, she wouldn't be in this situation now. She flipped open her phone, hoping her credit would last for one more call, and dialled his number.

'Katherine!' His voice was on the line after less than one ring.

'The car is broken down and we're stuck in the middle of a lane of traffic and I don't know what to do,' she said.

'Have you turned your hazard lights on?'

'Of course.'

'Try turning the key and pumping the accelerator to feed fuel to the engine.'

'I tried that. It's completely dead.'

'Where are you?'

'In the middle of Rathmines, outside the library.'

'Okay, I'm coming to get you. I'll be twenty minutes, max.'

It took him less than fifteen and by the time he arrived the rain had gone and patches of clear blue sky were poking out between dissipating clouds. Katherine got out of the car and stood beside him as he poked around at the engine, his head beneath the mustard-yellow bonnet.

'How have you been?' she asked, her irritation calming down while he worked. She hadn't seen him since his father's funeral, and even there she hadn't seen much of him because so many people had been lining up to give their condolences.

'Managing,' said Martin, screwing off the radiator cap. 'It's quiet in the garage without him.'

'It was a big funeral. A lot of people liked him.'

Martin lifted his head out of the engine. 'That's the thing about my father,' he said. 'He was a lovely guy to everyone he met, whether he was sober or not, but drunk at home he was an arsehole.'

'He drank a lot?'

'All day every day for most of his adult life,' said Martin. He held a piece of the engine in his hand. 'Your alternator is banjaxed. I'll have to tow it back to the garage and get a replacement.'

Katherine's shoulders slumped. What could you expect with an old banger? Worse, with a cursed woman driving an old banger?

'Where were you off to?' asked Martin.

'I was bringing my nieces to the zoo. We can get a bus, I suppose.'

'No. Let me drive you. We'll push the car into that loading bay and leave the hazard lights on till I come back with the tow-truck.'

'Are you sure? I'm interrupting your day.'

'It's my pleasure,' said Martin, and when Katherine looked dubious he added, 'Honestly.'

Ensconced in the back of his car, Laura looked relieved while Kitty chattered about all the animals she was going to see. 'There's a big safari bit with lions and tigers ...'

'And bears, oh, my!' Martin chorused. Both the girls broke into giggles.

'That's from *The Wizard of Oz*,' Laura informed Kitty. 'Remember?'

'"Lions and tigers and bears, oh, my!"' Kitty shouted.

'"Lions and tigers and bears, oh, my!"' Martin and Laura chorused.

Katherine found herself laughing and joined in with the the refrain.

'There's a train, you know,' Martin told Kitty, when the mirth had calmed down. 'It takes you all around the zoo and you can get off when you want to see anything, like the seals being fed or the chimpanzees' tea party.'

'Oh! Can we go on the train, Auntie Katherine?' Kitty cried. 'Can we?'

'We'll see,' said Katherine. Because of her years paying PRSI she was entitled to six months of jobseekers allowance. It had finally come through yesterday, but she'd given most of it to Lucy for food and rent. The train might cost extra.

As they pulled up outside the zoo, Katherine said, 'Thank you for this, Martin. You've been a great help.'

'Can Martin come with us?' Kitty asked.

'No, Kitty. Martin has to go back to work.'

'Well,' said Martin, 'I *am* my own boss now. I can come and go as I please.'

'So, you can come?' said Kitty, as Laura glared at her.

'I suppose so. If it's all right with Auntie Katherine.'

'Please?' Kitty begged. 'Can he?'

50. Look, a Butterfly!

The little one, Kitty, had the same olive-green eyes as Katherine, the same little bump on the tip of her nose. She never stopped moving, climbing up railings, dashing towards the next new animal to be seen, pulling Katherine by the hand to the monkey's tree, asking Martin for a piggyback and wanting to jump down again the minute she was on his shoulders. The older girl, Laura, was kind of sulky and obviously didn't want him around.

'This was supposed to be a day with our auntie,' she told

him, when Kitty and Katherine were out of earshot watching the seals being fed. 'Just the three of us.'

'I'm sorry,' said Martin. 'I didn't know that.'

'Mum said Auntie Katherine needed to get out and have a bit of fun. So we said we'd take her to the zoo.'

'That was very nice of you.'

'Are you going to stay with us for the whole day?'

'Not the whole day,' said Martin. 'Just for an hour. I'll have to get back to tow your auntie's car.'

They stood beside each other quietly for a couple of minutes, Laura's hands shoved into the pockets of her pinafore, watching Katherine lift Kitty up so she could see the seals better. The sun had come out at last, and in its light, the white of Katherine's plain shirt was blinding. It was tucked into a pair of form-fitting faded blue jeans, their bottoms rolled up over low-rise cowboy boots. Her hair was tied back into a ponytail the colour of butter.

She turned and smiled at Martin, shielding her eyes with her hand.

'You don't look like her last boyfriend,' said Laura.

'Her last boyfriend?'

'Barry. He had muscles and he was bald here.' She pointed to the front of her own head to illustrate. 'Mum says Auntie Katherine is far better off without him.'

Katherine had put Kitty down and was walking towards them, holding her hand.

'Are you saying that your auntie Katherine and Barry have split up?' Martin said.

'Yes,' said Laura. 'She lives with us now.'

'Laura! Laura!' Kitty called. 'Come and look at the seals. One of them ate four whole fishes. Auntie Katherine says he'll explode if he eats any more!' She made the sound of an explosion and went running back to the railing that looked over the seal enclosure, dragging Laura with her.

'Why didn't you tell me?' said Martin.

'Tell you what?' said Katherine.

'That you and Barry had split up.'

Katherine met his eye briefly before turning back to watch the girls. 'We haven't exactly split up,' she said. 'We're on a break.'

'Since when?'

'About two months ago. We've rented the house out and he's back home in his parents' place.'

'I can't believe it,' said Martin. 'You've kept this to yourself for two whole months?'

'No, I haven't. Just because I didn't tell you it doesn't mean I didn't tell anyone else. My family knows. My friends know.'

'And I'm not your friend?'

Katherine hesitated. 'Look, I'm sorry I didn't tell you. I just didn't find the right time, that's all.'

Kitty came running back, with Laura in tow. 'Can we get ice cream? Please?'

'No,' said Katherine. 'We haven't eaten our lunch yet. Let's go and sit on that bench under the tree and have a little picnic.'

As they walked towards the tree, Martin hung back a little and lit a cigarette, watching her, flanked by the two little girls, Kitty skipping and Laura strolling to Katherine's pace. She was single now. Free …

'That's disgusting!' Kitty said, when he caught up with them. 'Smoking is yuck.'

'And it gives you lung cancer, and you die a horrible death,' said Laura.

'You're a little ray of sunshine, aren't you?' Martin said, and he squashed the cigarette out on the inside rim of the bin beside the wooden bench.

'So, what happened with you and Barry?' he asked Katherine, when they were sitting down, sharing the packed lunches she had taken out of Laura's backpack.

'It's complicated,' she replied.

'What's complicated?' asked Laura, frowning.

'Life,' Katherine said. 'But don't you worry your little head about it. Here, share my Penguin with Kitty.'

'Maybe it's not,' said Martin. 'Complicated, I mean. Maybe life is simple.'

Katherine reached out to touch Kitty's hair. 'It used to be,' she said. 'I think that's why Barry left. Because it wasn't simple any more.'

'Look, Auntie Katherine,' said Kitty. 'A butterfly.'

A red butterfly with black-edged wings hovered in a little circle over their heads, then fluttered away. A little further on, on another bench, a little girl said, 'Look, a butterfly!'

'Where to next?' Katherine said, snapping the lid of her plastic lunchbox closed.

'I want to see the lions and tigers and bears,' said Kitty.

'Me too,' said Laura.

'Me three,' said Martin, and Kitty slipped her hand into his without even looking up at him.

Katherine brushed some crumbs from her jeans as she stood up. 'To the jungle, then,' she said.

'"Lions and tigers and bears, oh, my!"' said Kitty, and all four set off towards a little humpback bridge and the winding brick road beyond it that led to the Plains enclosure.

51. Upstairs Downstairs

The hotel manager, whose tie looked as if it was choking him, said, 'Take some time to browse through our brochure. I just have to step away for a moment.'

The cover of the brochure he had pushed across the Queen Anne coffee-table featured a photograph of an ecstatic white-veiled bride and her handsome, stoic groom taken beside the ornamental maze in the hotel's pristine gardens.

'They should really have a version of this with two grooms or two brides on the cover,' said Andrew, turning it over.

'Oh, for pity's sake,' said Jamie. 'You can't expect the whole world to change overnight to accommodate something that's only just been introduced.'

'If they want our custom and our money, they should cater to our needs. Christ knows, this place is expensive enough.'

It was the third venue they had been to see that month. Andrew had unilaterally rechristened Saturdays 'wedding-planning days', and he had a list of possible hotels the length of his arm. His list of requirements was twice as long.

'It says here that you can book the whole hotel and provide your guests with spa treatments the day after the wedding,' said Andrew. 'There are thirty-four en-suite rooms.'

'You seem to be forgetting that one of us is unemployed,' said Jamie. 'Booking entire hotels might be a bit on the extravagant side.'

'We're keeping our options open, that's all. We can't plan the perfect wedding if we don't know what's out there.'

A waitress arrived and put two blue Wedgwood cups and saucers in front of them, with a pot of coffee and a tiered stand of crustless sandwiches and cubic iced cakes. 'Is there anything else I can get you, sirs?' she said, with an almost imperceptible curtsy.

'What *is* this?' Jamie hissed as she walked away. '*Upstairs Downstairs*?'

'More *Downton Abbey*,' said Andrew, picking up one of the iced cakes and examining it. 'They pay attention to detail here.'

'It's all a bit old people's home, if you ask me. Cucumber sandwiches and "Clair de Lune". I'd say people have actually died in these chairs.'

Andrew took a sip of his tea, the cup clinking on the saucer as he replaced it. 'You always find something to complain about. The last place was too modern, the place before too gaudy.'

'I think we should have a small ceremony, with preferably just the two of us involved. I don't know why we have to go singing it from the rooftop of some overpriced hotel hanging on to the Celtic Tiger by its fingernails.'

'Because I want to sing it from the rooftops. I'm marrying the man I love. I've got the legal right to do it at last. I want to celebrate with a big party for all our family and friends.'

'It's not marriage, though, is it? It's civil partnership, which isn't the same thing.'

'When did you become so politically engaged? Usually you glaze over at the mere mention of gay rights.'

Jamie picked up his teacup and put it down again. 'I'm just saying it's not marriage, that's all.'

'It's the same commitment,' said Andrew, as the hotel manager made his way towards them. 'We make the same vows, "till death do us part".'

'So, have you had a chance to look at our brochure?' the manager said, pulling up a seat and putting a large leather-bound book on the coffee-table. 'Our pricing depends on the time of year you wish to have your reception, and the menu you choose.'

'How many can the function room accommodate?' said Andrew.

'We can seat two hundred and the capacity for guests invited to the evening celebrations expands to two hundred and fifty.'

As if he was seriously considering having a reception for two hundred in a hotel from an era when the homes of the landed gentry had met the seventies, Andrew took out his little red notebook and jotted down this information. He looked so earnest, it was kind of heartbreaking.

Jamie wanted to share the enthusiasm, to throw himself into the excitement of it, but he couldn't. Part of him was absolutely sure he wanted to go through with the whole thing, to have his future with Andrew decided for once and for all, but another part wanted to bolt every time Andrew mentioned a hotel, photographer or florist. The more plans Andrew put into motion, the more real the wedding became.

As if to bear this out, Andrew said to the manager, 'If we were to make a provisional booking, how much would the deposit be?'

'We require a non-refundable deposit of twenty per cent and payment of the full amount a month in advance,' said the manager, opening his book. 'When were you looking at having your ceremony?'

'I was thinking a Saturday in April next year. A spring wedding.' Andrew beamed at Jamie. 'What do you think?'

Jamie cleared his throat as he watched the manager flip through the book to see if any April dates were free. He didn't want to fight with Andrew over the cost of the place in front of the manager, so he said nothing, smiled vaguely and shrugged.

'You're in luck,' said the manager. 'We have no bookings for April yet.'

'Great!' said Andrew, touching Jamie's knee for a millisecond. 'We'll have to talk about it once we get some quotes from you, but we're very interested.'

'Hmm,' said Jamie.

'How many guests will you inviting to the reception?' the manager asked, writing in his book.

Andrew asked for quotes for 100 and 150 and the manager promised to email the figures by Monday.

'This is our first,' said the manager, closing the book.

'Your first what?' asked Andrew.

'Our first gay wedding.'

'Congratulations,' Jamie deadpanned. 'You must be thrilled.'

The manager put his hand to his mouth and gave a polite cough. 'Absolutely,' he said. 'But in the interests of being up front from the start, there are a few things I need to make clear before we go any further.'

Andrew lifted his head out of his notebook and pushed his glasses up on his nose. 'Such as?' he asked, his forehead knitted.

'Well, I suppose the best way to put it is that Farmfield House has had a long history in the local community.'

'And?' said Jamie, narrowing his eyes.

'We like to adhere to certain values. It's important for the people in the area.'

'I don't understand,' said Andrew, taking off his glasses and rubbing the bridge of his nose. 'What exactly are you trying to say?'

The manager straightened his tie. 'Our mission is to give you the very highest quality service,' he said. 'We simply ask that you and your guests respect the history of Farmfield House while enjoying your day with us.'

'As opposed to having an orgy?' said Jamie, standing up. 'Come on, Andrew. We're going.'

'I'm sorry," said the manager said, suddenly flustered. 'I didn't mean to upset you.'

'You didn't?' said Jamie and turned back to give the man a piece of his mind.

In the car, as they wound their way down the tree-lined drive that led away from Farmfield House, Andrew said, 'I don't know why you had to be so confrontational. There are better ways of educating straight people about being gay.'

'That man was beyond education. He had the emotional intelligence of a housefly.'

'Perhaps so, but did you have to tell him that to his face?'

'Believe me, I could have said a lot more. I only held back because you were there.'

They sat in silence for a good fifteen minutes as Andrew negotiated his way on to the M50 towards Dublin. As they were approaching the Red Cow Junction, he said, 'I have to go into work this afternoon to meet a new client.'

'But you never meet clients on Saturdays,' Jamie said. 'I thought we could go to the pictures. They're showing *Meet Me In St. Louis* at the Screen. The one where Judy looks anorexic.'

'Sorry, honey. It's just that this guy sounded particularly desperate. He's gay and he's really frightened that he might be deported back to Iran.'

52. Rose Cottage

The house was surrounded by rose bushes. Its pillarbox-red door and little white wooden-framed windows peeped out between heavy profusions of pink and yellow and red flowers blooming on thick, thorny stems. Like a cottage in a fairytale.

Alice stood on the opposite side of the road and looked at it, glancing left and right every now and then to see if anyone was near. This was her third visit to Ballydehob since Mrs Silver had told her what she'd found out.

'Your mother's name is Celia Deasy,' Mrs Silver had said, after sitting Alice down in her kitchen one day two weeks ago and pouring two cups of tea. 'She lives on Church Road, about a half-mile from Ballydehob. The house is called Rose Cottage.'

Alice could hardly believe her ears. 'How do you know all this?' she asked, her heart pounding.

'I have my ways,' said Mrs Silver, touching the side of her nose with one finger.

'But how?' Alice persisted. 'The barwoman didn't know anything. The postmistress didn't. Nobody we asked in the village had a clue.'

'That postmistress,' said Mrs Silver, stirring her tea and tapping the spoon off the rim of the cup, 'She was lying when she said she knew nothing. I've seen that look before.'

'Pardon?' Alice said, trying to catch up.

'Tony Soprano,' said Mrs Silver. 'He always has that shifty look in his eye when he's telling a lie. I've seen it in every episode.'

'So, how did you … What did you …?'

'It was very simple,' said Mrs Silver, and Alice heard a hint of pride in her voice. 'I called her at the post office and I offered her the only thing that people like Tony Soprano are interested in. Money. In return for information.'

Alice's mouth dropped open. 'How much?' she asked.

'That doesn't matter, dear. What matters is she told me who your mother is. Now you can go to see her.'

Still struggling to digest this information, Alice went through every detail of Mrs Silver's dealings with the postmistress again. When there were no more questions to ask, she took a moment, then asked Mrs Silver if she'd come with her to Ballydehob again.

'Oh, no,' Mrs Silver, said, with a firm shake of her head. 'This time you must go alone.'

Twice since then Alice had gone as far as Rose Cottage, stood outside it for a little while, then walked back to the village to get the bus to the railway station and home.

In the days leading up to each journey there, she told herself she'd have the courage to go up and knock on the door, that she'd make herself do it come what may, but by the time she got there she'd find herself paralysed on the roadside, unable even to approach the front gate.

She'd met the counsellor at the adoption agency, who had given her much the same advice as Mrs Babcock had, that she'd have to wait until her mother contacted her to go any further towards a meeting. The counsellor encouraged her to discuss her feelings about being adopted, but Alice was unable to share anything other than the most prosaic information. By the end of the session, the counsellor seemed impatient for her to go, which was understandable, considering they had sat opposite each other in near silence for the best part of an hour.

What if Celia never agreed to meet and Alice never got to talk to her? There she was, living in her rose-covered cottage, only a few feet away. All Alice had to do was go up and knock on the door.

'Hello, can I help you?' Alice was so lost in her thoughts she hadn't noticed a woman in a floral summer dress emerge on to the doorstep. Her arms were folded.

Alice tried to speak, but nothing would come out. The woman was painfully thin, her straight, slate-grey hair pulled tightly back from her high-cheekboned face. Her mouth, pursed and enquiring, did not look friendly. She was neither Thelma nor Louise.

'Are you lost?' the woman asked, when Alice failed to reply.

'No,' said Alice, trying to think on her feet. 'I was just admiring your roses.'

The woman's face relaxed a little, but she didn't smile. 'They're desperately in need of pruning,' she said. 'I keep meaning to do it, but I don't know where the time goes, these days.'

'They're beautiful,' said Alice.

'You're not from around here,' the woman said. 'From the accent, I'd say you were a Dubliner.'

'Yes,' said Alice. 'I'm just here for the day. I came on the bus.'

'A fair way to come just for a day.'

Alice couldn't think of an answer so she just stood there silently, taking her mother in. She was much smaller than Alice had pictured her, all bones and angles, her sharp elbows sticking out by her sides. There were cross-hatches of deep lines around her eyes that made her look older than Alice imagined she was, but her neck was not that of an older woman. It rose from her collarbone, long and swan-like, holding up a sharply defined chin. Her mouth, stretched thinly across her face, was just like the one Alice saw in the mirror every day.

'Where are my manners?' the woman said, as Alice stood there mutely staring. 'You must be thirsty standing out in the midday sun like this. Come in and have a glass of water.'

Alice followed her through the front door into a little sitting room that echoed the rose profusion of the garden. The wallpaper was printed with oversized blue flowers, the curtains had red roses running through them and the furniture and cushions were upholstered in rose prints.

'Sit down,' said the woman, coming in from the kitchen behind the sitting room with the water. 'Take the weight off your feet for a few minutes.'

Alice did as she was told, but found herself unable to speak again until the woman – Celia – introduced herself and asked her name.

'I'm Alice,' she replied. 'Alice Little.'

'Nice to meet you, Alice. So, tell me, what brings you all the way to Ballydehob for the day?'

'Oh, I just thought it would be nice to get out of the city. I've never been to this part of the country.'

Celia gave a thin smile and began coughing. 'But I've seen you before, haven't I?' she said, when she'd cleared her throat.

'No. I don't think so.'

'Of course I have. I've seen you outside, standing across the road and looking at the house a few times.'

Alice felt a prickly heat advance up her neck. 'I just wanted to see where you live,' she said.

Birdsong outside the open window pierced the silence that fell. Alice stared hard at the blue rose-printed carpet under her feet, her teeth clenched, then looked back up at her mother.

Celia's voice wavered. 'Who are you?' she said. 'Why are you really here?'

Alice squirmed in her chair with discomfort. The words she had rehearsed throughout every train and bus journey had deserted her and she couldn't think what to say. She put her water glass down and took a deep breath, her throat constricting. 'I'm your daughter.'

Celia did not move a muscle. She sat opposite Alice, her chin held high and her mouth closed in a tight line.

'Say something,' said Alice. 'Please.'

Celia's voice was cold. 'When the agency told me you were looking for me, I knew it would be only a matter of time before you came. Then the postmistress told me someone was snooping around . . .'

'Why don't you want to see me?'

'Because it's too late. Because nobody knows about you. I told *no one*.' Celia stood up and put out her hand for Alice's water glass. 'You should leave,' she said. 'You've seen me and now it's done with.'

'But don't you want to know anything about me?'

'No,' said Celia, without blinking. 'I don't.'

'You owe me an explanation at least. Why did you give me up?'

'I don't owe you anything. I gave you to a good family and you were better off. Go home to that family now. Go home to where you belong.'

'But they're gone. Both my parents are dead.'

Celia went quiet again. A gold carriage clock ticked on the mantelpiece as she stood with her hands clasped together at her waist, her eyes focused on some point beyond Alice's shoulder. Then she met Alice's gaze. 'I can't replace your parents,' she said. 'It's too late.'

'Please?' Alice said. 'Just talk to me for a little while.'

Celia closed her eyes. 'You should go,' she said. 'You'll miss your bus.'

With a shaking hand, Alice took a piece of paper out of her bag and a pen. 'I'll leave you my number in case you ever want to contact me,' she said.

'That won't be necessary.'

'Please, take it,' Alice said, pushing the folded-up paper into her mother's hand.

She stumbled out of the front door and down the garden path, then set off on the road back to the village. Every fibre of her being wanted to turn back to her mother's house, but it was useless. Instead she kept on walking away, numb with shock, her eyes glazed.

53. A Ton of Bricks

Typically, Theo was the soul of good behaviour now that she'd finally made a decision to talk to Dr Fairlie. The one time Lisa hoped he'd act up, he was calm and even a bit chatty with the GP, telling him about the new toy car his daddy had bought for him and how, in September, he was going to the big school.

'So, what can I do for you today, Mrs Fingleton?' Dr Fairlie said, after handing Theo an orange glucose lollipop from the jar he kept on his desk. He had been her doctor since her early twenties and probably knew her more intimately than most, yet from the moment she'd got married he'd addressed her formally as Mrs Fingleton. He was at most a couple of years older than her, but his whole air, with his greying temples and frameless spectacles, was that of someone vastly her senior.

Lisa looked at Theo, who was concentrating on peeling the plastic wrapper off his lollipop, then back at the doctor. She didn't want to talk about Theo as if he wasn't in the room. All the books said it was disturbing for children to hear themselves being spoken of negatively in the third person.

'It's a bit awkward,' she said, indicating Theo with a sideways glance. 'Could we have a chat in private?'

Dr Fairlie paged one of the nurses on Reception. When she came in, he asked her to take Theo out to the play area in the waiting room. 'We've got a brand new garage for cars with a tow-truck and emergency lights,' he told Theo, as the nurse led him from the room.

'Has it got a hammer?' Theo asked.

The nurse, a slight Chinese girl with kind eyes, said, 'I'm not sure. Why don't we go see?'

'What seems to be the problem?' Dr Fairlie asked, when they were alone.

'It's Theo,' Lisa said. 'He's become very violent towards me.'

'In what way?'

Lisa rolled up the left sleeve of her blouse where a brand new set of toothmarks overlaid the welts from scrapes he had given her yesterday. Dr Fairlie held her arm and examined it for a moment. 'How long has this being going on?' he asked.

'He attacks me every day, and most of it is unprovoked. It's not when I tell him to do something or not to do something. It comes out of the blue. I always think I'll be ready for it, but he catches me unawares. I can't tell you how long it's been. It seems like he's always hated me.'

'Hate is a very strong word, Mrs Fingleton. I've seen this kind of thing in a few children and usually it's quite simple to sort out.'

Lisa felt a vague flutter of hope. 'How?' she asked.

'Well, I'm not the right man for the job. Theo will have to see a clinical child psychologist. I know a very good woman I can refer you to.'

'That's what I was afraid you were going to say,' said Lisa. 'My husband is totally against it.'

The doctor gave her one of his considered smiles. 'I'm sure he'll come around, Mrs Fingleton. It's not such a big deal, these days.'

'I wish I could be as certain of that as you are.'

Dr Fairlie sat back in his chair, pulling a pen out of the breast pocket of his white coat. 'I'll contact Dr Sheila Harvey at Crumlin Children's Hospital and ask for the nearest appointment,' he said. 'In the meantime I can prescribe something to keep you calm while all this is going on. I can see you're quite overwrought about the situation, which doesn't do any good.'

'Oh, I can't take medication,' said Lisa.

'Why not?' Dr Fairlie asked. 'From my records I don't see that you're on anything else.'

'I think I'm pregnant,' said Lisa.

It was the first time she'd said the words out loud. You were expected to be flooded with relief at the moment of unburdening yourself like this, but she felt more panicked than she ever had. And nauseous. She put both hands on her knees and tried to take a deep breath.

'How far gone might you be?' said the doctor.

'Three months,' Lisa said. 'Possibly. I haven't told my husband.'

'Three months and you haven't come in for a check-up?'

'Eh, no, no, I haven't,' she said. 'Oh, God, I'm going to be sick.'

Later, in the reception area, Lisa tried to concentrate on playing with Theo while she waited for the doctor to call her back in. Mercifully there were no other children in the play area, which took up a small corner of the room away from the circle of sofas in the main waiting section.

'This is where the broken-down car goes,' she said, kneeling on the playmat and putting a little red car on the back of a metal pick-up truck.

'No, Mummy, *noooooo*! That's wrong!' Theo snatched the car off the back of the truck and flung it across the room. Lisa shrugged apologetically at the Chinese nurse in Reception; she gave her a kind smile before answering her phone.

'Well, where does it go?' she said to Theo.

'You don't know. Mummies don't know about cars.'

'You could show me.'

Theo went running to get the car he had thrown, and when he came back, Lisa leaned down and said, 'Show Mummy where the car goes when it's broken down.'

Theo drove the little red car on the playmat towards the pick-up truck and then, without warning, picked up the truck and whacked Lisa on the forehead with it.

'Ow!' Lisa cried, her forehead stinging from the belt of hard metal. 'Bold boy!'

She looked up and saw that everyone in the waiting room was focused on her and Theo, including Dr Fairlie, who was standing beside the reception desk, stroking his chin.

'Mrs Fingleton, can you come with me?' he said.

She followed him, like a child being led to the headmaster's office for punishment.

'Are you feeling better?' he asked, pulling out a seat for her.

'Yes,' Lisa said. 'It was the morning sickness, that's all.'

'Well, Mrs Fingleton . . . Lisa . . . your calculations are almost right. You are approximately ten weeks pregnant.'

'Oh, Jesus,' Lisa said, the news hitting her like a ton of bricks even though it was no surprise.

'I'm going to set you up for an appointment with Dr O'Neill, your usual obstetrician at Holles Street. And I've set up an appointment for Theo to see Dr Harvey at Crumlin Children's Hospital in three weeks' time. I suggest you go home and sit down with your husband to tell him that you're both having another baby, and that your son is in need of real help.'

54. The Italian Job

Just as Martin was about to press play on the DVD, Jamie excused himself for the toilet again and, sitting on the edge of the bath, pulled out his iPhone. He'd tried Saeed countless times already today, but the prick wasn't answering. Jamie couldn't even get through to his voicemail.

'Answer, you fucker,' he mouthed into the phone, as Saeed's

number continued to ring out. It might just be a coincidence that Andrew's new client was a gay Iranian, but how many gay Iranians were there in Dublin? At least if he got through he'd find out one way or the other. But what would he do then? If Saeed *was* Andrew's client, how was Jamie going to head him off at the pass?

When Andrew had come home on Saturday evening, Jamie had asked, as casually as he could, 'How did your meeting go, honey?'

'What's this?' said Andrew. 'You're taking a sudden interest in my work?'

'Well, why not? I've got nothing else to think about here by myself all day, have I?'

Andrew laughed and went to the kitchen to pour himself a glass of wine. 'Honestly, I won't bore you with the details,' he said.

Jamie fidgeted with the strap of his watch. 'What was the Iranian like?' he tried.

'Fine. He's got good English, which is a help. Usually you have to have a translator and it makes things awkward.'

So far so Saeed, Jamie thought. Trying to sound casual, he asked, 'Does he have a job?'

'In a restaurant, yeah. But it's under the table. He came here on a student visa.'

'What restaurant?' Jamie asked, almost forgetting his feigned off-handedness.

Andrew took a mouthful of wine. 'Jesus, Jamie. What is this, *Mastermind*? Usually you're the one going on about *me* being obsessed with the clients.'

'I'm just interested, that's all.'

'Actually, he asked me about you too. Well, he asked me if I had a boyfriend. I think he has the hots for me.'

'Yeah, right,' Jamie said, rolling his eyes. 'As if.' He resolved not to ask any more questions. He couldn't afford for Andrew to become suspicious.

But later, during an ad break on *American Idol*, Andrew brought the subject up again. 'He's bloody good-looking, that guy,' Andrew said.

'Ryan Seacrest?' Jamie asked, incredulous. 'I've seen more lifelike Ken dolls.'

'No, silly,' Andrew said, laughing. 'I'm talking about my Iranian client. Saeed.'

Jamie pressed the red end-call button on the screen of his phone and cursed. Although every second Iranian man was named Saeed – Saeed himself had three uncles called Saeed – this Saeed's appearance in Andrew's offices seemed far too close a coincidence. Yet Jamie still held on to the hope that this was exactly what it was – a coincidence.

From the hall, Martin called, 'Hurry up, for fuck's sake, Jamie! We're waiting.'

'Coming,' said Jamie, and flushed the toilet to give the impression that he'd used it.

Back in Martin's beige-painted sitting room they were all lined up on the sofa and armchairs, facing the television.

'Shove up,' Jamie said to Lisa, who had put on so much weight lately that she was taking up half of the couch. She shifted to the left to make room for him, practically squeezing the life out of Alice, who was on her other side.

'Ladies and gentleman, I give you *Cinema Paradiso*,' said Martin. 'The best movie about movies ever made.'

'Is it a foreign film?' asked Alice. 'I don't really like subtitles.'

The film was one of those Italian jobs where everybody shouted at each other, waving their hands maniacally in the air and pointing their fingers, but the subtitles read as if they were having polite conversations. Even though everyone else seemed entranced by it, Jamie couldn't concentrate.

If Saeed really was Andrew's new client, it was only a matter of time before he spilled the beans, and that would be the end of it all. Andrew would never forgive him. Their seven years together would be down the drain and Jamie would be out in the cold.

'The smallest things make them happy,' Katherine said, interrupting his worrying. On the screen a crowd had gathered to watch a film that was being projected on to the wall of the town square. The old projectionist, Alfredo, was showing it because nobody could afford a ticket to the cinema.

'I know,' Martin agreed. 'They're like little children at the pictures for the first time.'

'I like that the little boy's nickname is Toto,' said Alice. She turned to Martin. 'Do you think that's a reference to *The Wizard of Oz*?'

'Could be,' said Martin. 'Although I'm not sure if *The Wizard of Oz* was big in Sicily.'

They watched the rest of the film in silence and, despite himself, Jamie found his throat going dry at the end, when all the kissing scenes the village priest had censored from films over the years were played. Lisa was weeping openly, and even Alice, who to Jamie's mind registered emotion like a robot on Xanax, was dabbing her eyes with a balled-up hanky she'd taken out of her cardigan sleeve.

'I kept hoping he'd meet the girl again,' said Katherine, once they had reverentially watched the credits, 'but it would have seemed unrealistic if he had, I suppose.'

'The whole thing was unrealistic,' said Jamie. 'People don't go on like that, except in Italian movies.'

'Well, it's a film about films, so why shouldn't it be like the films it's talking about?' said Martin.

'You've lost me there,' said Jamie. 'Why don't you have another drink?'

'No, what I mean is it's not *meant* to be real. It's a movie about movies.'

Jamie sighed loudly. 'So you keep saying,' he said.

'Jesus,' Martin said. 'Sorry for breathing.'

'That's okay,' Jamie replied. In the silence that ensued he became aware that everyone else in the room was exchanging glances.

'I thought it was very realistic,' Lisa pitched in. It was the first thing she'd said all night.

'Oh, *come on*,' Jamie countered. Now he felt pissed off with them all. He felt pissed off with the whole world. 'Who in their right mind would stand outside a girl's window night after night for months on end, waiting for her to say she'll go out with him?'

'It's meant to be a fairytale, I think,' said Alice. 'Alfredo tells Toto the story of the soldier who waited for the princess for a hundred nights, and then Toto does the same thing. He waits for the girl.'

'But the soldier gave up on night ninety-nine,' said Martin.

'Yeah,' said Jamie. 'What a waste.'

'The princess didn't love him,' said Katherine. 'If she did, she would never have left him waiting outside her window like that.'

Martin cracked open a beer. 'He does meet the girl when he's grown-up at the end, you know. In the Director's Cut.'

'Were they still in love?' asked Lisa. 'I hope so.'

'That's for me to know and you to find out,' Martin replied, with a wink. He was smiling his bleary smile, the one he got after four beers. Two more, thought Jamie, and he'll be slurring his words, talking utter bollocks.

55. Exit Maguire

With Lisa and Martin out smoking on the terrace and Jamie having disappeared to the bathroom again, Alice and Katherine were left alone in the sitting room.

'Something's wrong with Jamie,' Katherine said, once Jamie was out of earshot. 'He's like a demon tonight.'

'Is he?' Alice said, sounding genuinely surprised. 'He's always like that with me.' Then she went quiet, fiddling with her heavily laden charm bracelet, which jangled every time she moved her hand. The pieces on it – a little house, a horse, a tiny crescent moon – had a cheap gold sheen.

'How are things in work?' Katherine asked, to fill the silence.

'Awful,' said Alice, adding nothing else.

'It can't be that bad,' Katherine said. 'At least you have a job.'

Alice bit the knuckle of her forefinger. 'I'm not sure whether to tell you,' she said. 'I've been told to keep it top secret.'

'Tell me what?' Katherine asked, her interest piqued.

'Mr Maguire has been diagnosed with a brain tumour.'

'Oh, my God,' said Katherine, shaking her head in disbelief. 'That's awful.'

Since the day he'd shafted her, Katherine had felt nothing but anger towards Maguire. Sometimes she held him responsible for it all – losing Barry, the house, everything – but now she imagined him sick and frightened, and the resentment melted away. Maguire couldn't cope with anything left of field, anything he couldn't control or manipulate.

'Is it serious?' she asked, knowing that brain tumours were always serious.

'They caught it early,' said Alice, 'not like with my mother. He might have a good chance.'

'Thank God,' said Katherine, and she really meant it.

'He's had to take early retirement,' Alice continued.

'I'm not surprised,' said Katherine. 'Although it can't be that early. What age is he? Sixty?'

'The trouble is, there's no one to replace him,' said Alice, her charm bracelet rattling.

'No, I don't imagine there is,' said Katherine. Her mind momentarily wandered back to *Cinema Paradiso* and the people watching the film projected on the wall of the village square, carelessly happy in the magical moment. In some ways, working at Qwertec seemed like a lifetime ago.

'Since he left the European deal has come to a standstill,' Alice went on. 'People are worried there's going to be more redundancies.'

Katherine was wrenched back into the present. 'But I thought the deal went through last March?'

'There were delays, but Mr Maguire said he had everything in hand. Now he's gone, it looks as if the whole thing might fall through.'

'What about the new guy Maguire promoted instead of me?'

'Oh, no. Not him. He didn't last at all.'

Lisa and Martin came in from the terrace, bringing a waft of smoky air with them. 'That's my one and only,' Lisa was saying, pulling the door behind her. 'I shouldn't be smoking at all. I promised the doctor.'

'The doctor?' said Katherine, still turning over in her mind what Alice had told her. 'Is everything okay?'

'Just a little indigestion, that's all.' Lisa dragged her eyes away from Katherine's. Then she changed the subject. 'I could watch that film all over again. It was so good. Alfredo was such a great character.'

Katherine could have pursued her line of questioning, but Lisa's expression clearly told her not to go there. 'I loved it too,' she said instead. 'I think it's the best movie we've seen so far.'

'*Casablanca* was my favourite,' said Alice, and Katherine's memory was jogged.

'Did anyone notice that Alfredo had the poster for it on the wall of his projection booth?' she asked.

'You noticed,' said Martin.

Jamie, who had been in the bathroom for another inordinate amount of time, popped his head in the door. 'It's time for me to go,' he said. 'I'll let myself out.'

Martin stood up, veering a little to one side, and said, 'Are you all right, mate?' He'd had far too much to drink, Katherine thought. He was getting messy.

'I'm perfectly fine,' said Jamie. 'I'll see you all next month.'

Lisa gave him a worried smile. 'Call me?'

'Sure,' said Jamie. He had an odd look in his eyes, like fear.

'What's up with him?' Katherine asked Lisa, when he had gone.

Lisa shrugged. 'I don't know,' she said, and Katherine had the feeling she was withholding something. She was going to pursue it further when Lisa changed the subject back to the film.

'Wasn't Alfredo lovely, though?' she said. 'He's like the perfect father. The one every child needs.'

56. The Great Escape

When Katherine was twenty-one, her father had written to tell her he was moving to Australia. He'd asked if he could see her before he left.

Katherine had drafted her reply carefully, telling him that she wished him the best but couldn't meet him. She'd finished the letter by saying it would be better if they had no contact in the future, that she didn't want him in her life.

Watching the ageing Alfredo in *Cinema Paradiso*, she tried to imagine what her father would look like now. He was sixty, probably still ruggedly handsome, maybe white-haired, and tanned from the Australian sun. He had respected Katherine's request by never trying to contact her. Lucy hadn't heard from him either.

He had come home just once after he'd left, when they were children, on Christmas Day of that year. He'd arrived bearing gifts but stayed only for half an hour. Her mother had refused to wait in the room and Katherine had sat by the empty fire grate with her present, two Enid Blyton *Secret Seven* books, which she felt were too young for her because she was eleven now.

She'd squirmed inside as Lucy crawled all over their father

on the couch. Then, as abruptly as he'd appeared, he'd stood up and said he had to leave.

'Please don't go, Daddy,' Lucy had begged, but he'd ruffled her curls and said, 'Don't worry, Lulu. I'll see you soon.'

'Happy Christmas, Kit Kat,' he had said to Katherine, and although she, too, had wanted to beg him to stay, she'd said nothing.

After that, it was as if he had never existed. Most days, when Katherine and Lucy came home from school, their mother was in bed, the house was cold and the curtains were closed. Sometimes there was no food in the cupboards or coal to light a fire.

One day in school, Eileen put her hand up and went to the top of the class to whisper something to Miss Hamilton. The next morning Eileen was sitting beside Lorna Clancy.

'You smell bad,' Eileen said, when Katherine asked her why she'd moved seats.

Katherine was filled with a cringing shame she had never felt before. She'd bathed both herself and Lucy on Saturday night with a sinkful of lukewarm water, but it mustn't have been enough. She sniffed at the cardigan of her uniform and tried to remember the last time it had been washed.

After that Eileen and Lorna whispered together in the playground whenever Katherine passed by and burst into loud giggles.

Lucy got into trouble for kicking her teacher, Sister Aloysius, in the shin and Katherine was called into the headmistress's office, alongside her.

'I understand that there are difficulties at home, Katherine,' Mother Perpetua said, 'but this kind of behaviour is out of the question.' It was if Katherine had kicked Sister Aloysius.

On the way home Lucy had sulked and dragged her feet. Fuming, Katherine had picked up her own pace and left her sister slouching behind, but then she had thought of Daddy, and how Lucy was missing him as much as she was.

She had stopped and waited without turning, putting out her hand. When Lucy caught up, she took it and, hand in hand they made their way up the street.

'Don't do it again, Lucy,' Mum said, in a cracked voice when Katherine told her what had happened, and Lucy had promised she wouldn't. Then Katherine had pulled the curtains over because the light was hurting Mum's eyes. She'd brought Lucy downstairs, where she could keep an eye on her while making dinner. Oxtail soup from a packet, with bread and cheese.

For a long time Katherine had waited for her father to come back, even for another visit. But he never did.

The day before Katherine's twelfth birthday, Mother Perpetua told her about the scholarship exams for a place at St Columkille's, a boarding school for girls in Tipperary. It was known to be the best in the country.

'You're an ideal candidate, Katherine,' Mother Perpetua said.

Katherine had seen it for what it could be: an escape from the misery and shame her father had left behind. In the lead-up to the exam, she worked harder than she had at anything before, studying late into the night and then getting up for school every morning. It was as if her life depended on it.

She got a full scholarship.

The day she left home for St Columkille's, her mother took her to the bus station. 'It's like you're all grown-up,' she said, reaching out to fiddle with Katherine's scarf. 'How did that happen all of a sudden?'

Katherine had fixed her scarf back into place. 'We all have to grow up some time, Mum,' she said. She couldn't look at Lucy, who stood beside their mother, quietly crying.

Before she got on to the bus, she steeled herself and leaned down to kiss Lucy's cheek. 'Don't worry, Lulu,' she whispered, using their father's nickname for her. 'I'll be home very soon.'

'Who'll mind me?' said Lucy, her breath catching between each word.

'Mum will, of course. Won't you, Mum?' Katherine looked at her mother beseechingly.

'Of course I will,' said their mother, taking Lucy's hand. But her smile was weary and Katherine knew she wanted to be back in her darkened bedroom.

As the bus drove away, Katherine had watched her little sister get smaller and smaller through the back window. She had known that, although she might return for weekends and holidays, she would never really come home again. She had known that, just like their father, she was abandoning Lucy.

57. Martin Pops the Question

Carrying his beer, Martin followed Katherine out to the hall when she went to get her mobile phone to call a taxi. He stumbled over the corner of the coffee-table on the way.

'What's your rush?' he asked. 'I thought you liked the film.'

'It's late,' Katherine replied, buttoning her jacket. 'I'm tired.'

'Ah, stay a while,' said Martin. 'You know you want to.'

Katherine stopped searching for the taxi number in her phone and looked at him. His eyes were glazed. He'd been drinking solidly since he'd arrived, probably even before that. 'No, Martin, I have to go,' she said.

'Will you go out for dinner with me?' he asked, the words pouring out over each other with no gaps in between.

From the moment at the zoo when he'd found out about Barry, Katherine had known this question was coming. The girls had gone on about him all the way home, Laura saying, 'Martin is in love with you,' pitching Kitty into fits of giggles.

'You're in lo-ove! You're in lo-ove!' Kitty teased, and Katherine had assured them she most certainly was not.

Up until this moment she hadn't known how she would respond if he asked her out, but now she did.

'I'm sorry, Martin, but I don't think that's such a good idea.'

'Why? Why not?' he said, like a scolded child.

'Why don't you ask me when you're sober?' said Katherine.

'What exactly is that supposed to mean?' he asked. 'So what if I've had a couple of beers watching a film with my friends?'

'But it's not a couple of beers, is it? It's never a couple of beers. And it's not just that. It's the *way* you drink.'

Martin looked gobsmacked, but Katherine was on a roll. 'Keep it up, Martin, and you're headed the same way as your dad.' It was out before she knew it and she regretted it the same instant.

The effect it had on Martin was visible. He crumpled. Then, after a moment, he pulled himself together and shot back, 'You think you're so fucking perfect, don't you?'

Katherine reeled. 'I don't,' she said, sounding petulant, she thought.

'You do. And you know what? You're nothing special, Katherine. No job, no house. And, worse, your boyfriend dumped you and you couldn't even tell your friends.'

Katherine grabbed his arm. 'Don't,' she said.

'Don't what?' Martin replied, his blazing eyes boring into hers. 'Don't tell the truth?'

'And you wonder why I won't go out with you?' she said, hardening her voice.

Martin lifted his beer. 'Not any more,' he said, and drank it down.

August

When Harry Met Sally

Rob Reiner, 1989

'You realise, of course, that
we could never be friends.'

58. Family Values

'But why do you have to go so far away?' Kitty asked. She was sitting at the table, her chin in her hands, bottom lip out.

'Auntie Katherine *told* you,' said Laura. 'She has a job interview.'

'But when are you coming back?' said Kitty.

'I'll be home before you know it,' said Katherine, putting her makeup bag into her onboard case. 'And I'll bring you back something nice.'

Kitty didn't look convinced, but the promise of a gift at least made her bottom lip go in again.

Zipping up her case, Katherine marvelled at the synchronicity of it all. If she had not joined the Film Club, insisting that Alice be part of it, she would never have been in the loop and she wouldn't now be going to Chicago to interview for Maguire's job. The morning after she'd seen *Cinema Paradiso* at Martin's, she had taken a deep breath and dialled Alice's extension at Qwertec.

'I'm the perfect replacement for Maguire,' she told Alice. 'I know every little thing about that European deal, inside and out. I could take up where he left off without blinking.'

'I see,' Alice replied, although her voice was tinged with doubt. 'I'm not sure how I can help you, though.'

'You could talk to Geoffrey Ryan in Headquarters and put my case forward. He'll listen to you.'

'Why would he listen to me? He probably doesn't even remember who I am.'

'You were Maguire's right hand. You know more about who

the perfect person for the job is than anyone. And if they're as desperate as you say they are for a replacement, they'll value your input.'

While Alice went quiet at the other end of the phone, Katherine held her breath. She needed Alice in her corner. It was her last chance.

'I'm not sure if it'll do any good,' Alice said eventually, 'but I'll make the call.'

If Katherine had been beside Alice, she would have thrown her arms around her. 'Oh, thank you, Alice!' she said. 'Just tell him that no one else is better placed to take the job, okay? And make sure he knows how much work I put in on the European deal.'

'Okay,' said Alice. 'I'll do my best.' And she hung up.

The next day, the American office called Katherine to arrange an interview and flights to Chicago. Geoffrey Ryan wanted to meet her in person.

'If I were you, I wouldn't start counting my chickens,' Lucy said, when Katherine told her she'd move back to her own house if everything worked out.

Kitty looked up from her drawing. 'Are you going back to live in your own house?' she asked.

'I hope so,' said Katherine. 'If I get my job back.'

'I don't want you to go!' Kitty cried. 'You only just came.'

'I wouldn't be going for a while yet,' said Katherine. 'And my house isn't very far away, remember?'

'But I don't like it there. I always have to be good and not touch anything.'

'You're being silly,' Laura said, glaring at Kitty, but her own chin was wobbling as if she might burst into tears at any moment. 'You didn't think Auntie Katherine was going to stay for ever, did you?'

'I want her to stay for ever!'

'It's okay, Kit Kat,' said Paolo. 'Don't cry.'

'It's not fair,' said Kitty. 'I want Auntie Katherine to be in our family.'

'But she is in our family, silly,' said Laura. 'She's Mummy's sister, remember?'

Kitty shook her head vigorously. 'If she goes away, it'll be the same like it was before. Auntie Katherine will always be busy. She won't be in our family any more.'

Katherine met her sister's eyes, expecting hardness, but instead she looked as if she was going to cry too. She felt a surge of shared sadness, then anger. What had Lucy been saying about her to the kids?

'Christ,' she said, zipping her case shut. 'I can't take this right now.'

'Take what?' Lucy asked, giving her a doleful look.

'*This*. You making me feel guilty for having my own life.'

Lucy stiffened. 'Paolo,' she said. 'Take the girls out, please.'

'Where to?' asked Paolo.

'I don't know. Bring them to McDonald's or something. Just go.'

'Yay!' said Kitty, instantly forgetting her tears. 'McDonald's!'

When they were gone, Lucy sat back down at the table and, staring squarely at Katherine, said, 'I resent that you think I make you feel guilty.'

'But you do,' said Katherine. In the time it had taken the girls to get ready for McDonald's, her stomach had grown queasier and queasier. She'd started this confrontation, but now it was taking all her courage to stay with it. There were things that had never been said between them. Things that were always just beneath the surface.

'You've been making me feel guilty since the day I went to St Columkille's,' Katherine went on, bracing herself for Lucy's reply.

Lucy's jaw dropped. 'You didn't just go away to school,' she said. 'You disappeared into thin air.'

'I came back, didn't I? For weekends and holidays. I was there for three months every summer, for God's sake.'

'You were there, but you weren't, really. You froze us out, Mum and me.'

'That's not true!' Katherine said. 'I did my best. You know I did.'

'Whatever you say.' Lucy sighed. 'You have your memories. I have mine.'

For some reason an image came into Katherine's mind of the two of them when they were very small, making dresses for a broken Sindy doll out of toilet paper, drawing buttons and belts on them with marker pen. She shook it out of her head. 'We all have to take responsibility for ourselves,' she said. 'It's hard, Lucy, but that's life.'

Lucy's mouth opened and shut. Then she fixed Katherine with a bitter stare. 'You're right,' she said. 'We all have to take responsibility for ourselves. But that doesn't give us an excuse to walk out on other people.'

'That's not what I did,' Katherine said, her stomach churning.

Lucy stood up and noisily gathered cups from the kitchen table. 'Yes, it is,' she said. 'And if you can't admit it, there's no point talking about it.'

Katherine felt a flare of rage towards her sister. 'So, unless I say it's my fault you made such a fuck-up of your life, there's no point in talking about it, is there?'

Lucy stopped what she was doing and turned on Katherine. 'I'm not the one who made a fuck-up of my life!' she said. 'I mightn't have a big-shot house in swanky fucking Ranelagh, but at least I'm happy.'

'What's that supposed to mean?'

Lucy heaved another sigh. 'Look, Katherine,' she said. 'Go to America. Get your job back. Move home. I don't care any more what you do. It's your life.'

Katherine grabbed her case. 'Yes,' she said, and walked to the door. 'It is my life. And I don't have to make excuses for it, to you or anyone.'

59. Out of Sight, Out of Mind

As had become her habit over the past few weeks on coming home from work, Alice sat on Mother's chair in the sitting room with the curtains closed, the glassy eyes of the owl collection all staring fixedly through the gloom. Sometimes she would stay there for hours, saying nothing. Other times she'd talk to Mother.

'You were right,' she'd say into the emptiness. 'I never should have looked for her.'

She would listen out for some noise – a floorboard moan, the clank of an element in the attic water tank – as if this might constitute Mother's agreement. But the house was deathly quiet and all Alice could hear was her own breathing.

Tonight she had been sitting in Mother's chair for about half an hour when she decided to close herself into the room under the stairs and see if that elicited some response. She hadn't been in there since she was fourteen, and although it seemed much smaller, the space was less claustrophobic. She imagined the slide and click of the bolt on the outside of the door and Mother's voice saying, 'I don't want to hear a peep out of you, madam. Not a peep. Do you hear me?'

Out of sight was out of mind, was what Mother had said. Although she had picked Alice out of all the little babies to be adopted, sometimes she didn't want to hear ungodly illegitimate little girls, who didn't have the right to say anything at all or to be here.

It was pitch black under the stairs and still smelt of shoe polish and old carpet. She waited, as she had so many times, for her eyes to adjust to the darkness and softly hummed the notes of the song she used to sing to herself back then to keep the fear away. It came from one of Father's records, a collection of folk ballads, but she still didn't know its name.

Sometimes she would be left under the stairs for so long that she'd fall asleep, waiting for the click and slide of the bolt to signal that she could come out. A cheese sandwich and a glass of milk would be waiting on the table in the kitchen for her. Mother would be in the sitting room with Father, the sound of canned laughter from the television drifting out.

Alice would eat the sandwich as quickly as she could, drink the milk, then tiptoe out through the hall and up the stairs to her bedroom.

With her knees up against her chest, Alice whispered Mother's name into the darkness under the stairs and listened hard. But still there was nothing. Even the old Electrolux fridge in the kitchen, which often rattled and shuddered, was completely silent.

'I'm sorry, Mother,' Alice said. 'Please forgive me.'

As if she had said some magic word, she heard a door whine slowly open somewhere in the house. Alice shut her eyes and held her breath, her heart beating fast. Don't be frightened, she told herself. This is what you wanted.

The sound of soft footsteps got louder as they came into the hall. They stopped with a floorboard creak just outside the door of the under-stairs room. There was a moment of silence so complete, it seemed as if the world had stopped turning – and then Alice's stomach plummeted.

Mother was going to lock her in. If that happened, she'd never get out. She'd die in here.

Letting out a cry so high-pitched it pierced her own skull, Alice launched herself at the door and pushed it open with all her might. 'No! Mother! No!'

'Mein Gott!' Mrs Silver shouted, and fell back against the wall, gripping her chest.

Alice, blinded by the light, shielded her eyes with her hand. 'It was you?'

'My poor heart! Why did you do that?'

'I thought you were Mother,' Alice said. 'I thought you were going to lock me in again.'

Mrs Silver, still breathing heavily, digested this information. 'Your mother locked you under the stairs?' she asked.

'A long time ago,' Alice said. 'When she found it hard to cope with me.'

'Oh, but Alice, that's awful. You must have been terrified.'

Alice's heartbeat was beginning to slow to its regular pace. 'At first,' she said, 'but I got used to it.'

'What age were you when it began?'

'I was three or four. It was before I went to school.'

'Awful . . .' Mrs Silver repeated, shaking her head slowly. 'You poor little thing.'

Alice gave an involuntary smile. She hadn't thought of herself as a little thing for a long time.

'You will come next door with me now, out of this dark house, for a cup of tea,' said Mrs Silver. 'It's not right that you come home at night and sit under the stairs alone. Not right.'

Later, as they sat at Mrs Silver's white-cloth-covered kitchen table, over tea and Marietta biscuits, the old woman put her wrinkled, liver-spotted hand with its diamond wedding ring over Alice's. 'Sometimes we have to accept terrible things. If we don't accept them, and make peace with them, where will we be?'

'I wanted my real mother so much,' said Alice. 'It hurts to know that she doesn't want me.'

Mrs Silver filled Alice's cup again from the blue china teapot. 'When I was a little girl, I used to imagine that my mother might come and find me,' she said, adding a drop of milk. 'But she was gone for ever, and my father and sister were gone too. After the war, when it came out about what happened to the Jews in Germany – all over the Irish newspapers, with those terrible photographs of the camps – I imagined the horrible ways they could have died. For many years I blamed myself for not staying and dying with them. Then I met my Sammy. He said that I was a child when it happened, that staying with them was not my decision to make. He taught me to accept and to live looking forward, instead of back. And this is what you must do, Alice. Your mother, the one who brought you up, is dead and she is never coming back, no matter how much you want her to. What she did to you was terrible, but who knows what things were in her mind at the time? You must accept what happened and look forward. And you must accept that the mother who brought you into the world, for whatever reasons of her own, cannot have you in her life.'

'But she's all I have,' said Alice.

'No,' said Mrs Silver, putting her cup firmly on its saucer. 'That is not true. You have your new young friends. And you have me. I will not desert you.'

Mrs Silver meant well and Alice felt an enormous swell of gratitude to her. But now that she had seen Celia in the flesh, she couldn't get the picture of her, surrounded by the halo of roses, out of her head. It was too soon to let go. She didn't even know how to.

60. Gone to Ground

For the first time in months, Jamie felt proud of himself. The interview had gone much better than he'd expected. The course tutors weren't in the least bit fazed that he didn't have a portfolio or much experience. They'd bought into Jamie's enthusiasm for the course without question.

He'd found out about it in a prospectus of two-year certificate courses at the McColgan Private College of Further Education that Andrew had left lying on the coffee-table the previous week. It wasn't the first brochure he had left around, as a not-so-subtle hint that Jamie should think of doing something with his life now that he was eight months out of a job, but it was the first that Jamie had picked up.

'I used to read the Habitat catalogue when I was growing up,' he told Andrew, after finding out details about the course. 'One of my mother's friends used to bring it over to the house for me every time there was a new one. Ma said she had ideas above her station, but she knew I loved looking at the furniture. Maybe that's what I was always meant to be. An interior designer.'

'You should apply,' Andrew said. 'A lot of people are acquiring new skills at the moment. It's the way to go.'

The application process couldn't have been smoother. Jamie filled out a form online, gave his bank details and was invited for interview. The course tutors who met him in the McColgan Private College of Further Education's minimalist, white-painted interview room – a woman in a powder blue trouser suit with blow-dried hair and a very handsome, craggy-cheeked man, who looked like Robert Redford in *Out of Africa* and met Jamie's eye with lingering regularity – told him about all the elements of the course: history of textiles, photography, environmental psychology, ergonomics (whatever that was) and, most intriguingly, field trips to see international architectural and design classics.

When they were finished, they asked Jamie a few questions about himself, his last job and his love of design, and Jamie told them how he had painstakingly and lovingly furnished his friend Andrew's flat. He never mentioned Ikea.

The woman gave an impressed nod and the man stood, holding out his impeccably manicured hand. 'Welcome on board,' he said, shaking Jamie's for a fraction of a second longer than was necessary. 'I think you have a natural flair for design and are making an important step towards a bright new future.'

'Thank you, Mr Fitzroy,' Jamie said. 'You won't regret it.'

'Call me Stephen.' Mr Fitzroy smiled, and Jamie felt a pleasurable pang.

Now, in the lift on the way up to the flat, Jamie tried to imagine what Stephen Fitzroy's chest hair might be like. If his eyebrows were anything to go by, it was probably a rug of white gold draped over a pair of nicely defined, pinnacled pecs, as his tight pink shirt had given away. As a rule, Jamie didn't consider men over forty-five as fantasy fodder but, it had to be said, Fitzroy was well preserved for a man for his age, which was probably fiftysomething-or-other.

'Would I?' Jamie queried aloud, as the lift reached the floor of the flat, but then he stopped himself. He'd only just narrowly avoided losing Andrew because of Saeed. Why would he go there again?

At least Saeed was a thing of the past, and none of the dire consequences Jamie had been imagining had come to pass. He hadn't returned any of Jamie's calls in the past month, and when Jamie eventually went looking for him at the restaurant, he was told Saeed had quit. There was no answer whenever Jamie tried the buzzer at his flat either, so it looked like he'd moved out and moved on. When quizzed gently about him, Andrew said Saeed had fallen off the face of the earth and was no longer in contact. 'Sometimes that happens,' he explained. 'They come looking for help, but when they realise the enormity of the task ahead, they go to ground.'

Andrew still wasn't back from work when Jamie let himself in, so he poured himself a glass of chardonnay and called his mother to tell her the big news.

'Are you really sure it's what you want to do, love?' she asked. 'Only it sounds very expensive to me.'

Jamie held his tongue. This was the woman who had forced him to apply for a position at the bank the moment he'd left school, insisting that it was 'a good, secure job that will set you up for life'. She wouldn't know creativity if it came up and introduced itself to her. 'Education doesn't come cheap these days, Ma,' he said. 'I have what's left of my redundancy money to pay for the course, and it will pay me back tenfold when I'm designing houses for rich bitches with more money than sense.'

'If you say so, love. Although your father says that kind of thing – interior design or whatever you call it – has gone down the tubes since the recession.'

'Where did he read that? Page three of the *Sun*?'

'We're just worried about you. You have a lot of expenses coming up, with the wedding and all. Maybe you should look for a proper job.'

'I wish everyone would stop calling it a wedding,' said Jamie. 'It's a civil partnership, okay?'

His parents had greeted Andrew's announcement over Sunday dinner as if their only daughter had told them she was marrying a doctor and planned to give them six healthy grandchildren born wearing 'I Heart Grandma & Grandpa' T-shirts. His brothers and sisters were even more excited, already arranging his stag, even though April was still a provisional date for the ceremony.

Jamie was grateful that his family accepted him the way he was and embraced Andrew as one of their own. But sometimes it was too much. He didn't see them acting like that with any of the other in-laws. It was like they were overcompensating.

'I'll call you tomorrow, Ma,' Jamie said, hearing Andrew's key in the front door. 'Love you.'

'Jamie? Are you home?' Andrew called from the hall.

'In here!' Jamie shouted back. He felt a surge of elation, imagining Andrew's delight at hearing his news about the course.

'I've had the longest day. I need a drink,' Andrew said, putting his briefcase down.

Jamie pecked him on the cheek and went into the kitchen. 'I

have your favourite chardonnay chilling in the fridge. Or would you like red?'

'I'll have the white, thanks. How did your interview go?'

'I got it!'

'They let you know already?'

'They were well impressed with me. They said I have a natural flair.'

Andrew put his arm around Jamie's shoulders, and squeezed. 'That's great, honey. I'm really happy for you.'

'Me too. I'm cooking a meal to celebrate.'

'Spag bol?' Andrew asked, as he sat down on the armchair and began to unlace his shoes. Jamie nodded. It was his special dish. Well, his only dish.

'Speaking of dinners,' Andrew said, 'you remember that Iranian client I had?'

Jamie stopped at the breakfast counter, his back to Andrew. 'Yes … I think so,' he said.

'He got back in contact. I've invited him to dinner on Friday week.'

Jamie spun around. 'Jesus, Andrew! No way. He's not coming here.'

'That's a bit over the top, don't you think? He's a good guy. He's gay and he needs to make new friends here. I don't know why you always have a problem with this.'

'They're clients, Andrew, not friends. You get too obsessed with them.'

'He needs a little help fitting in, that's all. Having him to dinner isn't going to do any harm.'

'Well, I won't be around,' Jamie said, realising he would have to be – if he couldn't speak to Saeed in the meantime.

Andrew sipped his wine. 'I don't see why you're making such a big fuss, honey,' he said. 'Seriously, Saeed is a really nice guy.'

61. Martin's Choice

Martin leaned back as far as he could on the wooden bench and closed his eyes, letting the heat of the August sun tingle on his skin. He'd been sitting there for half an hour, while tourists and summer students strolled around the grounds of Trinity College, pointing out its sights or heading towards the white marquee that had been erected in the furthest corner of the main campus grounds with the words 'MSF Volunteers Wanted' on a sign over its entrance.

At Trinity College there was a gentle sense of separation from the rush of life. Once you had walked through the darkness of its entrance arch and into the bright expanse of cobbles, courtyards and greens, all overlooked by quiet white-framed Georgian windows, you felt as if you were no longer in the heart of the city.

It was a space Martin needed and he'd made the unprecedented move of closing Brady's Motors for the day to take it. His father, who had spent practically every working hour of his life in the garage, bar that time in the hospital last year, was probably spinning in his grave, but about fifteen minutes after he'd arrived there that morning, Martin had felt that if he didn't get out of the place immediately, he might end up head-butting the wall.

He was still bristling from what Katherine had said. When he'd spoken to Nell about it, he had expected her to be on his side, as she had steadfastly been throughout their lives, especially when it came to anything about their father. But instead she'd said nothing for a minute, her eyes gently probing his. Then she'd opened her mouth and said, 'She might have a point, Martin.'

He couldn't believe what he was hearing. There Nell was, sitting at the bar with a dirty big glass of Guinness in front of her, telling *him* he drank like their dad. Talk about the pot calling the kettle black. 'For fuck's sake, Nell, I'm not dependent on the stuff like he was. I'm a social drinker, that's all.'

'I hate to say this, but that's like something Dad would have said.'

'So, you're telling me I'm an alcoholic?'

'I think you drink a lot and that it could become a problem for you.'

Martin looked at the dregs of the pint in front of him and then at her almost full glass. 'Why have you never said this to me before?' he asked.

'I've wanted to, but I haven't had the courage until now. I didn't want to hurt you.'

'I don't fucking believe this.' Martin got up to go out for a cigarette.

'Martin,' Nell said, when he returned, 'alcoholism is in our genes. I never drink without thinking of it. I'm always afraid I might end up just like Dad was, or like Uncle Jim or, even worse, Uncle Fred. I always worry about it.'

'You're far too bloody sensible to be a wino.'

'I think the only way for you to find out whether or not it's a problem for you is to give up the drink for a while. Go off it for a few months and see what it's like. If you reckon you don't have a problem after that, then go back on it. But at least give yourself a chance.'

Martin's pint had been on its last legs and he'd dearly wanted to go to the bar and order another, but Nell was watching every drop he drank. She took a small sip from her sanctimonious, barely touched glass, leaving a frothy moustache above her lips.

'Fuck this,' he'd said, and got up to order another. 'You want one?'

'No, I'm fine with this for now.'

While he'd waited at the bar for his Guinness to be poured, his ears had tuned into the background music playing on the bar's stereo: Jimmy Durante singing 'As Time Goes By'. It had made him want to hit something and weep at the same time.

When he'd sat down again, his sister had read his mind. 'So tell me about this Katherine,' she said. 'What's she like?'

'She's all right, yeah.'

'And you like her?'

'We're chalk and cheese. It's pointless.'

'Ah,' said Nell, with an understanding nod. 'She doesn't like you back. Not in the same way.'

'Maybe she'd like me back if I gave up the drink. There's something about the way she looks at me. It's not platonic, if you know what I mean.'

Nell took a cardboard coaster from the holder in the middle of the table and began tearing a corner off it. 'Don't do it for her,' she said.

'What do you mean?'

'Don't give up alcohol for her. If you're going to do it at all, do it for yourself.'

'I haven't even said I *am* giving up the drink,' Martin had protested.

Now on the Trinity College bench he tried to imagine his life without the booze. He didn't drink that much, did he? Over the past ten days, how much had he consumed? As he did the calculations in his head, a homeless guy wearing a floppy Mickey Mouse T-shirt and jeans caked with grime wandered past him. He looked about sixty, the same age as Uncle Fred. 'Any spare change?' he said.

Martin fumbled in his pocket, trying not to breathe in the acrid stench of stale alcohol wafting his way. 'Here you go,' he said, handing the man a tenner. 'Don't spend it all in the one shop.'

The guy, hardly believing his luck, shuffled off and Martin stood up.

He'd told Nell he was a social drinker, but most of his drinking had been done at home in front of the telly, watching DVDs by himself. He'd been drunk every night for the last ten nights in a row.

People were still coming and going from the marquee at the

back of the grounds with the MSF sign above it. Behind his back Martin heard the homeless guy saying to someone else, 'Any spare change?'

MSF stood for Médecins Sans Frontières, didn't it? Martin stood up, shook himself and walked towards the tent as if he'd fully intended to check it out from the moment he'd arrived on the grounds of Trinity College.

62. Halfway Out of the Frying Pan

Patrick was beginning to grey at the sides of his head. Lisa hadn't noticed it before, but the late-evening sunlight streaming through the bedroom window picked out hints of silver among the brown. He was sitting on his side of the bed, flicking through the TV channels and complaining about nothing good ever being on, like a sulky little boy.

She'd told him about the baby over dinner at their favourite Italian restaurant, the one they used to go to all the time before the children were born. 'Spring it on him in a public area,' Jamie had advised, when she'd eventually confided in him that she was pregnant but hadn't mustered up the courage to tell Patrick. 'That way, if he has a bad reaction to start with, he won't be able to shout.'

'He might be delighted, you never know,' Lisa had said, trying to convince herself that this was a possibility.

'I want to know what kind of man doesn't notice his wife is four months pregnant.'

'I never really show when I'm pregnant until the last two months and then I balloon.'

'Sweetie, I hate to be the bearer of bad news, but you ballooned kind of early this time around.'

Emma from number seven had said she'd babysit, promising on her mother's life not to cancel at the last moment, and Lisa waited until Patrick was home from work with a cold beer in his hand before telling him she was taking him out for a surprise dinner.

'But I have a Lions Club meeting, honey,' he said. 'It's a planning meeting for the Christmas fair, remember?'

'I called Bill and he said they could do without you just this once.'

Patrick didn't know how to delegate. His problem was he thought nobody could do the job as well as he could, which invariably meant he ended up shouldering most of the work, whether in his office or at the Lions Club. It was all taking its toll on him. He'd started falling asleep on the sofa at night, still in his shirt and tie, and in the mornings it was like he dragged himself into the shower and out to work, hardly able to speak he was so tired.

All through the meal, Patrick had been listless and distant. By the time dessert came, Lisa was toying with not telling him tonight after all. But she had to. It was now or never.

'Patrick,' she began, steeling herself. 'I've got something to tell you.'

His spoon had stopped halfway to his mouth. 'What is it?' he said.

'I'm pregnant.'

The spoon had hit his dessert dish with a clatter. 'Fucking hell. Are you sure?'

The woman at the next table had shot Lisa a dirty look and said something to her dinner partner behind her hand.

'I don't fucking believe it,' said Patrick, his voice going up another decibel.

Lisa had smiled apologetically to the next table. 'Calm down,' she told Patrick. 'People are listening.'

'I don't give a damn if they are or not.'

Lisa looked at her husband. He wore the expression of a man who'd just been told the world was about to end. 'How did you not notice?' she said. 'I'm four months gone.'

'I thought you were just putting on weight. I didn't want to say anything in case I upset you.'

'That makes two of us,' Lisa said ruefully.

Patrick was shaking his head. 'We can barely afford three children as it is. How are we going to manage a fourth?'

'We'll find a way. We'll have to.'

Patrick gave a strangled laugh. '*We*'ll find a way,' he said. 'Jesus Christ!'

'I'm not exactly over the moon about it either.'

'That's easy for you to say.'

'What's that supposed to mean?'

Patrick had put his two hands on the table as if he was trying to steady himself. 'It means I'm the one out working my balls off to earn the money to keep this family going. I'm the one who has to keep it all afloat.'

'I didn't get pregnant by myself, you know,' Lisa snapped, lowering her voice. 'There were two of us in it. And you were the one who didn't want to use a condom.'

Patrick gave an incredulous snort. 'So now it's my fault?'

'It's nobody's fault,' Lisa said, trying to force herself to calm down. 'It just is. Do you think I'm not sick at the thought of having to manage another child when I can hardly manage the three I already have?'

By the time they'd got home neither of them was speaking. They'd got into bed and Lisa had lain on the very edge of her side, too tired to cry. She'd wrapped her arms around herself, registering her now considerable bump. Jamie was right. How had Patrick not noticed?

After about ten minutes of silence, Patrick had moved to her side and put his arms around her from behind. 'I'm sorry,' he whispered into her ear. 'I reacted like an arsehole.'

'It's okay.'

'Turn around.'

Lisa turned to him and he rested his palm against the side of her face. 'It's just that I'm in shock,' he said. 'I didn't expect this. Another baby.'

'Neither did I.'

He gave her a soft kiss, his lips damp. 'You're right. We'll manage. We always do.'

Lisa put her head on his chest. 'You think so?' she said, looking at an old cobweb hanging from the corner of the ceiling that she had neither the energy nor the inclination to dust away.

The next morning, Patrick had been only half there, stressed and sulking, as if they hadn't had close, urgent sex last night before falling asleep in each other's arms. He'd barely grunted when she'd given him his coffee, so she'd thought it best not to mention the appointment letter that had arrived from Crumlin Children's Hospital for Theo to see the psychologist.

She could wait for a few days before hopping out of the frying pan and into that particular fire.

63. When Woody Met Doris

Katherine adjusted the drawing above the mantelpiece again and stood back, arms folded, to make sure it was hanging straight. She was still in two minds about giving it top billing in the sitting room, but picturing Kitty's face on seeing it hanging in pride of place, she decided she'd leave it there at least until Lucy, Paolo and the girls came for dinner next week. Kitty's latest interpretation of the Little Mermaid was so loose that only the brash red crayon marks that represented her hair gave it away, but in its new frame, surrounded by an expanse of pristine white, it had a certain abstract charm.

It replaced the Markey landscape Barry had loved, which was now hanging in an alcove in one of the spare bedrooms. Katherine had made lots of little adjustments like this since she'd moved back in, putting the paintings and prints up in different places, shifting the furniture, buying new wallpaper for the study, trying to build the house back into a home – into her home, rather than her and Barry's.

But she wasn't really sure about any of the decisions she'd made. Last week, on a night she couldn't sleep and was lying frustrated at the thought of the intensive day of work ahead, she'd got up and moved all the paintings back into their original spots. But the next day, when she got in after another twelve-hour shift, she'd started relocating them again.

Barry was still unreachable. She'd left messages on his voicemail saying he should come over so they could work out what to do about the house now that she was back there. Knowing Barry, he probably didn't want the hassle of it, but Katherine needed to have it sorted out before she could settle down again.

The doorbell rang, announcing the first Film Club arrival and Katherine adjusted the painting again before going out into the hall. It was Alice, wearing the little canary yellow A-line coat she had picked out when they'd had a few hours' shopping time before the meeting in Paris last week. She'd accessorised it with a matching yellow plastic hairband and the effect was surprisingly chic. Who would have known Alice had such good taste?

'Long time no see,' Katherine said, kissing her cheek and Alice gave a rueful grin.

'You'll be sick of me soon enough,' she said.

'Sick of the best assistant I ever had? I don't think so.'

Katherine was telling the truth. She'd always known that Maguire would have been lost without Alice, but in stepping into his shoes at Qwertec, she'd learned what that really meant. Alice was always two steps ahead. She never let a ball drop and she really liked her job, so there was no competitive edge to get in the way of a smooth working relationship.

Alice followed her into the kitchen. 'I got a call from Mr Maguire's wife,' she said.

'How's he doing?' asked Katherine.

'He's having radiotherapy and responding well.'

'That's great news,' Katherine said, although as long as there was a chance of Maguire getting better, she worried there was also a chance of her being pushed off the skyscraper again.

There was another knock at the door. Martin and Jamie were on the step, and Lisa was coming in the gate behind them. Her mouse-grey roots were now so long that it was as if her split ends had been dipped in an inch-deep pool of black dye. She'd gained even more weight.

Katherine wondered if Lisa was depressed. She'd never been one for dressing up, but until now she'd had some concern for her appearance.

She didn't meet Martin's eye. What he'd said to her the last time they'd seen each other still stung.

'How's everyone at Qwertec?' Jamie asked breezing past her into the hall and before Katherine could answer, added. 'Oh wait, I don't care.'

'Nothing's changed,' said Katherine, ignoring his sarcasm. 'It's still the same old office.'

'I bet they love having you back cracking the whip.'

'What are we watching?' Martin interrupted, shucking off his jacket.

He threw his eyes up to heaven as Katherine said, '*When Harry Met Sally*.'

'Meg Ryan,' he said, walking into the sitting room. 'Great.'

'I like what you've done with the furniture,' Lisa said, when everyone was sitting down. 'And that's a new painting, isn't it?'

'The Little Mermaid,' Jamie said. 'An abstract expressionist interpretation.'

Katherine laughed. 'I'm impressed,' she said. 'It's by my seven-year-old niece.'

'I'm a gay man. I can spot Ariel at fifty paces.'

'I'll pour some wine and we can watch the movie,' said Katherine. 'I got some beers in for you, Martin.'

'I'll just have a glass of water,' said Martin. 'Or some juice if you have it.'

They all turned to stare at him.

'What? I don't feel like drinking. Is that a crime?'

'I brought some orange juice,' said Alice. 'You can have some of that if you like.'

'Perfect,' said Martin. 'Now can we watch the film?'

In the kitchen, pouring his juice, Katherine wondered if he was not drinking tonight because of what she'd said to him last time. Whenever she thought about it, she felt hot shame. Her suggestion that he was becoming his father had not only been insensitive but plain mean.

When she came back into the sitting room, Martin was holding forth as the opening credits of the film played. 'When Woody Allen met Doris Day, more like,' he was saying, his hands gesturing every syllable.

'I love those old Rock Hudson and Doris Day movies,' said Lisa. 'They hardly ever show them on TV any more.'

Katherine handed him his juice. 'When Woody Allen met Doris Day?' she said. 'I don't get it.'

'*When Harry Met Sally* is essentially a film in which the guy from Woody Allen's films meets the girl from Doris Day's films,' he explained.

'I don't think Meg Ryan is anything like Doris Day,' said Lisa. 'She's too kooky.'

'Yeah,' Jamie agreed. 'Imagine old Doris faking an orgasm in public.'

'Think about it,' said Martin. 'Doris Day films are all about Rock Hudson trying to charm the pants of her but not getting anywhere. In *When Harry Met Sally*, Rock is replaced by Billy Crystal, playing it like Woody Allen in *Annie Hall*. But he's still trying to get into Meg's knickers. And she plays it like Doris until the bitter end.'

'I'm not sure,' said Katherine, who had watched *When Harry*

Met Sally more than any other DVD in her collection. 'When *Harry Met Sally* is about much more than a guy trying to get a girl into bed. It's about women being from Venus and men being from Mars.'

Martin nodded earnestly. 'Which is what all Doris Day films are about. And most of Woody Allen's films too.'

'You could say that about any romantic comedy,' Alice said, and Martin turned to her with an appreciative smile.

'Never a truer word was spoken,' he said.

'Unless it's a gay romantic comedy,' said Jamie, 'which would be all about men being from Mars and other men also being from Mars.'

64. Jamie Paves the Way

Katherine couldn't believe she'd forgotten how the final scene from *Casablanca* had been worked into the plot of *When Harry Met Sally*. When it came up in the conversation between Harry and Sally near the start of the movie, Martin met her eyes for a moment of mutual recognition.

The rest of the gang didn't notice the first time, but later on, when Harry and Sally were discussing the film in split-screen, both of them watching it late at night in their own beds, Jamie said, 'What's with *Casablanca*? It's all over this Film Club like a rash.'

'It seems ages since we watched it,' said Lisa. 'Like a lifetime ago.'

'It makes me want to watch it again,' said Katherine. She deliberately avoided Martin's eye as she said this.

'There's a lot of talking in this film and it's hard to concentrate when everyone else is talking,' said Alice.

'Get *her*,' said Jamie, nudging Lisa, but no one responded. All eyes were glued back on the TV screen.

Alice was right. And so was Martin. For much of the film, Billy Crystal and Meg Ryan had detailed conversations about the relationship between men and women, just like Woody Allen and Diane Keaton did in *Annie Hall*. Katherine had always loved *When Harry Met Sally* because its romance seemed very real. It was the conversations that gave the film its true-to-life quality, not the ending where Sally finally fell into Harry's arms. That bit was pure fantasy.

'It's like Carrie Bradshaw stole all her ideas from Sally Albright,' said Jamie, when the film was over. 'You know the bit with the four girlfriends having lunch, talking about dating after divorce? It was pure *Sex and the City*.'

'Complete with Carrie Fisher,' said Martin. 'Looking good as always.'

'I didn't recognise her without the Danish pastries,' said Katherine. She was feeling a little merry and warm-cheeked from the four glasses of wine she'd finished far too quickly. Martin, she noticed, had shaved his neck around the edges of his beard, giving his chin a nicely chiselled look.

'And the whole thing is set in New York,' said Jamie, warming to his *Sex and the City* comparison. 'And they talk about sex all the time. Meg's fake orgasm is so Samantha, it's a joke.'

'It's the only bit of the film I don't really get,' said Lisa. 'It's like they just put it in there for a laugh.'

'She does it to give Harry a wake-up call,' said Katherine. 'He thinks he knows it all, but really when it comes to women he knows nothing.'

'I've never faked an orgasm,' said Lisa. 'Not once in the twelve years Patrick and I have been together.'

'Jesus,' said Martin. 'Now *this* is turning into an episode of *Sex and the City*.'

'Seriously. I faked it a few times with boyfriends before I met Patrick. But I've never had to with him.'

'How about you, Alice?' said Jamie, flicking the rim of his

wine glass so it rang out like a boxing-match bell. 'Ever faked it?'

'That's none of your business,' said Katherine, jumping to Alice's defence. She was under no illusion that Jamie had warmed to her, but for some reason he increasingly had it in for Alice. He never gave her a break.

Martin put his hand on Jamie's shoulder. 'Give it a rest, man,' he said.

'It's all right,' said Alice. 'I don't mind.' She faced Jamie. 'I've never faked an orgasm because I've never been with anyone. Sexually, I mean.'

Jamie shifted awkwardly in his seat. 'TMI, sweetie,' he said. 'Too much information.'

'You asked,' said Alice. 'I'm only answering.'

'I couldn't imagine my life without sex,' said Lisa. She had a dreamy look on her face.

'You might be better off without it, missy,' Jamie said, 'considering your condition.'

So that's what it is, thought Katherine. Lisa's pregnant!

'You can't keep it a secret for ever,' Jamie added, as Lisa glared at him with burning cheeks. 'I'm just paving the way.'

'Paving the way for what?' said Alice.

'I'm pregnant,' said Lisa. 'I was going to tell you all before, but I've been waiting for the right moment.'

'Congratulations,' said Martin. 'Number four … wow.'

'When are you due?' Katherine asked. From the look of her, it was soon.

'The first of January,' Lisa said.

'A New Year's baby,' said Martin. 'You might end up making headlines.'

Lisa didn't reply, so to fill the gap, Katherine offered her babysitting services, even though she couldn't imagine being able to manage Lisa's brood. 'If you feel like you need a break before the baby comes,' she added.

'You can adopt them, if you like,' said Lisa. 'They'd go to you without blinking an eye.'

'That's the spirit.' Jamie laughed. 'You need to lighten up, girl.'

Alice rounded on him. 'I don't think that's funny,' she said, her eyes burning. 'Adoption is no laughing matter.'

Alice had sworn Katherine to secrecy when she'd told her the story of finding her birth mother. 'I'd prefer to keep it private,' she'd said, although Katherine assured her that such things happened all the time, that maybe it would be better for Alice to share it than keep it to herself.

'I have shared it,' Alice had said, closing the subject. 'With you.'

65. More News

'I've got some news too,' Jamie said, once Lisa's revelation had washed over everyone. 'I'm going back to college. To study interior design.'

'Congratulations, sweetie,' said Lisa, clearly relieved that the focus was off her. 'It's perfect for you.'

'I know! It's at the McColgan Private College of Further Education. Supposed to be the best place to study interior design in the country.'

'The McColgan Private College of Further Education?' said Alice. 'I read something about it in the newspaper yesterday. Is it in financial trouble?'

'How could it be starting new courses in September if it is?' asked Jamie. 'Jesus, Alice, you always have to find a way to put a damper on it, don't you? Everyone else here is happy for me.'

'I'm happy for you,' Alice insisted. 'I am, I swear. Maybe I was reading about some other college.'

'While we're at it,' Martin interrupted, 'I have some news of my own.'

Something about the way he said it gave Katherine the feeling she wasn't going to like what she was about to hear.

'I've volunteered overseas with Médecins Sans Frontières.'

'What?' Jamie hooted, forgetting his fracas with Alice. 'You're a doctor now?'

'They need project managers. I gave them my CV and they said I looked like a possible candidate. The first round of interviews is next week.'

'But don't Médecins Sans Frontières send you to wartorn countries?' asked Katherine. In the back of her mind, she remembered a story about some MSF volunteers being kidnapped in Chechnya.

'Mostly to places of conflict, yes,' said Martin, 'but to poverty-stricken countries too.'

'How long would you be gone?'

'A year to start with. But I haven't even done the interview yet. They might not take me.'

'What about the garage? Who's going to manage it?'

Martin gave her an odd look and Katherine realised she was asking too many questions.

'I'm going to sell it as a going concern and give the proceeds to my mother,' he said. 'I never really wanted to work in the place. And, let's face it, there's nothing keeping me here, is there?'

'That's great news, Martin. I hope you get the job,' said Lisa. She had started awkwardly pulling on her jacket and was trying to get up off her seat at the same time. 'I'm sorry to bow out so early, folks. I get tired so quickly. I don't remember being as bad when I was pregnant with the others.'

'I'll give you a lift,' said Martin, offering his hand to help her up. 'I promised to look in on my mother, so I have to pass by your place anyway.'

He was smiling so breezily that Katherine felt a pang of something like regret. She was sure she'd been right to put him off but now he'd moved on.

Katherine left them to the door and watched as they walked down the driveway, Martin putting his arm around Lisa and pulling her in close, her head coming to rest on his shoulder. He said something to her that made her crack up with loud laughter as they turned the corner beyond the gates. Katherine realised it was the first time she'd heard that sound from Lisa in months.

When everyone was gone and she had tidied the place up, Katherine still didn't feel like going to sleep. Instead she got into bed, puffed up the pillows and and turned on the TV. There was nothing on, so she decided to watch something she'd recorded on the digital box. She flicked through the films and found *Casablanca*, which she'd forgotten she'd recorded a few weeks ago.

What had Jamie said about *Casablanca*? It was all over their Film Club like a rash. Katherine smiled to herself and settled down to watch it.

But tonight, as the film unfolded in the darkness of her bedroom, it became more and more about the terrible privations of war instead of a broken romance. Katherine began to wonder if those kidnapped MSF volunteers in Chechnya had been released unharmed. War zones didn't have the same rules as other places. Innocent people who weren't supposed to be in the firing line died every day.

After *Casablanca*'s final scene had played out, Katherine flicked the TV off and slipped under the duvet, shivering as if it was a winter's night instead of balmy August. As she reached out to switch off the lamp, her phone, sitting on the bedside locker, vibrated and its screen lit up. She had left it upstairs on silent all evening, deliberately missing calls from the American office, which would just about be closing for the day now.

She sat up and pushed the phone's menu button. Instead of work, it had logged four missed calls from Barry. And one text message: *I need 2 see u. xxx*

September

To Kill a Mockingbird

Robert Mulligan, 1962

'You never really understand a person
until you consider things from his point of view . . .
Until you climb inside his skin and walk around in it.'

66. Giving Up Boo

It was hard to get used to the big red for-sale sign. It appeared larger than others Alice passed. Every time she arrived home from work and turned the corner from the bus stop, the shock of seeing it was fresh.

She put down her umbrella and shook the rain off it. 'Deceptively spacious mid-terrace property within walking distance of city centre,' the estate agent's description said. 'The property is in need of redecoration throughout, but many impressive original features are intact. It will appeal to a growing family's requirements or would be of equal interest to investors.'

Selling it had been Mrs Silver's idea. 'What do you want to be in such a big place for?' she said. 'It's not right for one small girl to have so many rooms.'

At first Alice couldn't even consider selling it. She had lived in it her whole life. She couldn't, wouldn't, imagine living anywhere else.

But the incident under the stairs had frightened her, and in its wake Mrs Silver's suggestion took root. In a strange twist, it was choosing the film for this month's club evening that had helped her to see things more clearly, and make the decision to put the house on the market.

To Kill a Mockingbird was her favourite book and film, an obvious choice for the club. Once upon a time she had imagined herself as a kind of Boo Radley, the freak of the neighbourhood. The story was told through the eyes of children, who were haunted by the spectre of Boo. That he turned out to be their saviour at the end didn't matter to Alice. As long as she could remember her terror at being locked under the stairs in her home, she would be a child haunted by the ghost of Mother. Her own personal Boo.

If she stayed cooped up in the house with Mother, she'd go mad.

Mrs Silver had summed it up when she said, with a finger pointing to her forehead, 'There is no such a thing as a ghost, dear. There is only what happens in the mind.' That was when she had suggested Alice sell the house.

After a month more of sitting alone in its dim rooms, filled with memories of Mother, good and bad, Alice went next door to deliver Mrs Silver's dinner, took a deep breath and said, 'I'm ready. I'm going to put the house on the market.'

'Good!' said Mrs Silver. 'Of course, you might not get as good money for it as before. Every day on the news I hear, "House prices falling. More people unemployed." When is it going to stop? You're lucky to have a job.'

'I've thought it all through,' Alice continued. 'I'll buy a smaller place nearby, maybe in that new apartment block on the canal. That way I'll be able to keep bringing you your dinner every day.'

'Oh, don't be silly, dear. I'll manage,' said Mrs Silver, but Alice registered a note of relief in her neighbour's voice.

'I'll miss being next door to you, though,' said Alice. For a long time Mrs Silver had been the only one looking out for her, and it was comforting to know she was only a stone's throw away.

Mrs Silver tutted. 'Are you moving to Australia?' she said. 'No, I didn't think so.'

From inside the house, the phone began to ring. Alice leaned her brolly against the porch wall, put her key in the door and turned it reluctantly. The phone hadn't rung once since Mother was dying and the hospice had called to say they had a place for her.

'Hello?' she said, but there was only silence. She imagined the sound of shallow breathing. 'Hello?'

The line went dead.

She put the receiver back in its cradle, her fingers trembling. Mrs Silver said only crazy people believed in ghosts. Had Alice imagined the phone ringing?

The hall was silent as a grave – the phone's shrill tone punctured it again.

Alice picked it up immediately and cried, 'Leave me alone!'

'Alice?' said a woman's voice. 'Is that you?'

It wasn't Mother's voice, but it was familiar. 'Yes, this is Alice. Who am I speaking to?' she said, trying to regain her composure.

'This is Celia. Celia Deasy . . . Your . . . We met in my house in Ballydehob.'

'Celia?' said Alice. Her voice – Celia's – sounded as if it was reaching out from a very long distance.

Celia coughed. 'I wasn't going to call,' she said. 'But . . . Well . . . I would like to see you. If you think you could come again.'

'Yes,' said Alice, without hesitating. 'I can come tomorrow.'

'I'm not in my house. I'm in Bantry Hospital. Do you know where that is?'

'I can find it. Why are you in hospital?'

'I'll explain everything tomorrow. I'm on St Theresa Ward.'

'St Theresa. Yes. I'll have to get a train and a bus . . . It will probably be the afternoon before I'm there.'

'Just come. And, please, if anyone asks who you are, a nurse or an orderly, say you're one of my old students. It's best that way.'

67. Pop Psychology

Dr Sheila Harvey had kind eyes. The rest of her was as starched and efficient as hospital corners, but every time her eyes met Lisa's, they seemed to be saying, 'I understand. I agree. I know what you're going through.'

For the most part, however, they were focused on Patrick, who wasn't giving an inch.

'Theo is five years of age, Mr Fingleton,' Dr Harvey said. 'He is no longer a toddler. The behaviour described at length by your wife and witnessed during our play session together was not a tantrum. It was aggression. And it was directed at Lisa. Don't you think that's interesting?'

Patrick shook his head, as if to stop anything the psychologist said lodging in his brain. 'Children always behave differently with their parents than they do with other people,' he countered.

'But Theo doesn't behave like that with you.'

For a moment Patrick was stumped. He looked at the doctor and then at Lisa. Then his eyes wandered to the glass partition behind which Theo was building a tower as tall as himself with giant Lego blocks. They were teetering to the side and Lisa willed them to stay upright. The mental image of them falling connected itself to the pain at the base of her thumb, where Theo had bitten her earlier during the play session. Patrick had been asked to observe them from a hidden spot.

'Maybe Theo's like that with Lisa and not me because he sees her more,' he said. 'It's always the ones we're closest to that we hurt the most.'

'It's interesting that you've come to that conclusion,' said Dr Harvey, and her eyes met Lisa's again. 'I know,' they said. 'I understand.'

'It's only a phase,' said Patrick. 'He'll grow out of it. All boys do.'

'Maybe,' said Dr Harvey, but she didn't sound convinced. She picked up a silver pen from her desk and held it horizontally under her bottom lip with the thumb and forefinger of each hand. 'I believe your son is presenting symptoms of a condition we call Oppositional Defiant Disorder, or ODD.'

Patrick snorted and pushed his chair back.

'Hear me out, Mr Fingleton,' Dr Harvey said, gesturing

for him to sit down. 'All children are oppositional from time to time, and you're right when you say it's normal behaviour. But the kind of behaviour we see in Theo is a normal part of development for toddlers and early adolescents. When it reaches into early childhood and is frequent, consistent and sustained, it becomes a serious concern.'

Lisa hadn't read about ODD in any of her books, but she could go online and type it into Google. She made a mental note to do so when she got home.

'In children with ODD we see an ongoing pattern of uncooperative, defiant and vindictive behaviour towards authority figures, sometimes towards one authority figure in particular. Theo's behaviour towards Lisa is one symptom. His inability to play without becoming angry and his expression of that anger with direct violence are others.'

'Symptoms,' said Patrick. 'You make it sound like he's sick.'

'ODD is a very treatable condition. There are some genetic markers for it, but for the majority of children it's a question of addressing their home situation. There may be some relationship issues between both of you and Theo that are adversely affecting him.'

'What are you saying?' said Patrick. 'That we're to blame?'

'It's not about blame. It's about finding the right way to deal with the problem. I think the next step should be individual evaluations. I would like to schedule separate meetings with you both to discuss your home life and to assess ways forward.'

'Separate?' said Lisa. 'Why can't we do it together?' It had taken all her effort to get Patrick here today with her. Getting him to come on his own would be impossible.

'Because with most couples, there are things they individually experience and feel that they aren't fully comfortable discussing in front of each other.'

Patrick said nothing as Dr Harvey's fingers tapped at her computer keyboard and she suggested possible dates for each of them to come in. Eventually he gave grunt of agreement for Friday of the following week at ten a.m.

Lisa gave an internal sigh of relief. Having Dr Harvey take the upper hand was so much easier than trying to force the situation herself.

'In the meantime, I want you to praise Theo's positive behaviour and give him little rewards for being good,' Dr Harvey said. 'When he's violent, Lisa, I want you to walk away from him without emotion. Take yourself out of the situation, and if he follows you, don't react. Don't make eye contact with him. Don't speak to him. He needs to differentiate between reactions to good behaviour and unacceptable behaviour.'

'At least she didn't put him on medication,' Lisa said, above Theo's cries, when they left Dr Harvey's office, although part of her wished the psychologist had prescribed a miracle cure-all pill.

'Theo!' Patrick shouted. 'Shut up.'

'I want the LEGO!' Theo screamed, dragging at Lisa's hand.

In the lift, Theo pummelled her thigh with his fists over and over again, screaming, 'I want the Lego! I want the Lego!' and when they got out on the ground floor he bolted for the glass front doors.

'This is bullshit,' Patrick said, running after him.

'I know,' said Lisa, when she caught up with them. 'We've done the right thing, though. At least now we can get to the bottom of it with Dr Harvey's help.'

'No, Lisa. This whole thing is bullshit. ODD? These doctors are always coming up with new labels in capital letters so they can treat normal children as if they're sick— Theo! Calm down, will you? I'm not buying into it. You can if you want, but I'm not coming back. And I don't want Theo coming back either.'

Lisa stopped walking and closed her eyes. She imagined the world around her receding into the distance until she was left completely alone in inky blackness, without any attachment holding her down.

Floating.

Patrick's voice came out of the dark: 'Lisa? Hurry up, will you? I have a meeting at two thirty.'

68. The Cost of Freedom

Early on in their relationship, Andrew had spelled it out for Jamie. He was talking about his ex, the dreaded Alex, who, for all his political correctness, had had it off with other guys left, right and centre.

'The trouble was he couldn't wait to tell me,' Andrew said. 'It was like he wanted me to be jealous, to prove that I loved him. I would have been better off not knowing anything.'

'I wouldn't want to know, either,' said Jamie. 'So, if you have one-night stands, don't tell me. Unless it's with George Clooney.'

Andrew had laughed as if Jamie was joking

When he'd finished laughing, he said, 'I want a monogamous relationship, Jamie.'

Now Jamie watched him passing the bowl of salad to Saeed, and felt an intense twinge of regret. Andrew was being so kind, so hospitable, so bloody nice … He hadn't the first clue what was going on.

'Would you like some dressing for that?' Andrew said, pointing at a bottle of Paul Newman's.

'No, thank you,' Saeed said. His eyes crept over the table and up into Jamie's face, like a pair of black spiders. 'In my country, we don't have this dressing. We have good oils.'

'The Irish diet is very boring,' agreed Andrew, too enthusiastically. 'I grew up eating potatoes and meat every day. We didn't know the meaning of flavour if it didn't come out of a salt cellar.'

'The flavours in Iran are many. It is one of the things I miss most. The food. And my family.'

'But didn't your family reject you for being gay?' asked Andrew.

'Yes, they did,' said Saeed. 'But this does not mean that I do not miss them. They will kill me if I go back to Iran. But they are still my family.'

Jamie reached for the wine bottle.

'Take it easy with that,' said Andrew, giving him a look that said, *Make an effort, please!* 'At this rate we'll drink the place dry before the main course.'

Jamie filled his glass to the brim. 'That's terrible about your family, Saeed,' he said, after taking a large gulp. 'I don't know how you could forgive them for being such complete and utter arseholes.'

Andrew blanched and eyed Jamie incredulously.

'They do what they think is right,' said Saeed, chewing his lettuce, it struck Jamie, like a cow chewed its cud.

Jamie put his glass down. 'But what they're doing is not right. It's insane.'

Saeed swallowed. 'They have their reasons. When I told them I was in love with a man they were angry because it is against Islam. That is why we had to run away.'

'You ran away with your lover?' said Andrew. 'You didn't mention him before.'

'He is gone now,' said Saeed, and his eyes locked on Jamie's. 'He died.'

'That's terrible,' said Andrew. 'I'm so sorry.'

'Excuse me,' said Jamie. He stood up to go to the bathroom, knocking over an empty water glass.

He locked himself in, took a deep breath and told himself he could get through this. But what would getting through it mean? What did Saeed want? Was some sort of gameplan in action?

Jamie should have known it from the beginning, from the moment Saeed had first slapped him during sex, that he was lock-me-up-and-throw-away-the-key, Glenn-Close-in-bunny-boiler-mode crazy.

He turned on the tap and splashed his face with water, looking at himself in the mirror. Should he be afraid of Saeed? Of what he might do? Was Andrew in danger now?

Andrew seemed safe as houses when Jamie went back to the table. He was sharing some joke with Saeed, both men laughing softly with their heads inclined towards each other.

Suddenly Jamie knew what the gameplan was. Saeed wanted *Andrew*. He wanted to steal him from under Jamie's nose, just to spite him.

'You bastard,' Jamie muttered, under his breath.

'What, honey?' asked Andrew, his elbow touching Saeed's on the table.

'I said, I'm famished,' said Jamie. 'Time for the main course, I think.'

With Andrew in the kitchen, still talking over the clatter of plates and serving spoons, Jamie leaned over the table to Saeed and said, in a low voice, 'I know what you're at, and don't think for one minute you're going to get away with it.'

'I don't know what you're talking about,' said Saeed.

'Andrew and I are getting married. That's the end of it. You need to fuck off and leave us alone.'

'That is not what I need.'

'What are you talking about? You freak.'

'I need a boyfriend. Someone who does not come and go when they please. Someone like Andrew.'

'Over my dead body.'

'If that is what you want.'

'What do you mean, if that's what I want? I want you out of my life. Out of our lives.'

'It's too late for that, I think. Andrew is helping me now. He's my friend.'

'I'll tell him about us,' said Jamie. 'He won't be so nice to you then.'

'You can if you want. But you will lose him. And then you will be alone, just like me.'

Andrew came in from the kitchen, carrying a plate piled high with steaming slices of roast beef. 'I think the meat's overdone,' he said, putting it in the centre of the table. 'I didn't time it right.'

'It smells very good,' said Saeed.

'I hope it tastes like it smells, then!' Andrew touched Saeed's shoulder as he said this and smiled. Not in the way an immigration lawyer would usually smile at a client, Jamie couldn't help but notice.

69. Welcome to Stepford

Although he hadn't asked her to, Nell had done some research and said this was the best meeting for Martin to attend. It was in a Methodist church hall, the kind they held Sunday-school classes in, and there wasn't one person under the age of fifty in the group. If ever there was something that might turn you back to drink, it was the assortment of silent people sitting in a circle around the pristine room. They all looked on the verge of suicide.

The leader tonight was a woman called Margaret. On the wall behind her was a sign, saying, 'This Too Shall Pass'.

'My name is Margaret and I'm an alcoholic,' Margaret began. 'I feel comfortable saying it here and that's because my right to be anonymous is respected. We all respect each other's privacy, and it is a core tenet of Alcoholics Anonymous that we do not reveal each other's identities outside this room.'

Martin had a feeling she was drawing this out for him. The rest of the group were either looking at the children's paintings of the life of Jesus pinned to the walls, or staring at the red linoleum-tiled floor, which smelt heavily of polish. Some looked into the middle distance, as if bored out of their minds. He guessed they'd heard this spiel many times before.

'This evening our subject is Step One of AA's Twelve Steps,' Margaret went on. '"We admitted we were powerless over alcohol and that our lives had become unmanageable."'

She was a very overweight woman in a top that looked like a floral tent. Martin thought she would do well to admit she was powerless over food, but then looked down at his own expanded midriff and thought about people in glass houses.

The meeting continued as, one by one in a clockwise direction, people stood up, said their first names, attested to their alcoholism and then told stories about what Step One meant to them. Martin could hardly listen. It was as if he was under water and their voices were coming from above him – he barely made out what they were saying. As those nearer and nearer to where he was sitting spoke, his heart beat heavier and heavier. Was he expected to stand up and say, 'My name is Martin and I'm an alcoholic,' then tell some inane story from his life as if it meant anything to anybody here? There was no way he was doing it. No way.

The man next to him, who looked in his seventies, stood up. He was neatly dressed, with white hair parted carefully to the side and a polka-dotted dickie bow that made him look like an eccentric movie professor.

'My name is John and I'm an alcoholic,' he began. 'I took the first step the day I woke up and realised I had reached rock bottom.'

A murmur of recognition rippled through the room and, for the first time, Martin properly tuned in. There was something about the man, a quiet authority in his voice, that commanded attention.

'I was in a doorway, lying on a flattened-out cardboard box. The first thing I thought wasn't that my clothes were wet or that I smelt of urine, or that I was so cold my jaw had locked. I thought about where I was going to get a drink. A young man was passing and I put out my hand to him, begging for money.

He dropped a couple of coins into it, and when I looked up to thank him, I realised he was my son. My beautiful son, whom I hadn't seen in five years.'

He was silent for a moment and Martin felt a stab of sympathy for him. He could sense the same emotion coming from everyone in the room.

'I had lost everything. My career, my home, my family. My son didn't look at me long enough to recognise me, and if he had, he would still have walked away. In that moment, I realised I was powerless. I was completely and utterly controlled by drink. I had done terrible things to my wife and children, things I couldn't bear to think about. I had been to AA meetings before, but I always thought I wasn't like everyone else there. But as I watched my son walk away that morning, I understood the truth. My life had become completely unmanageable.'

'Thank you, John,' said Margaret. 'That was very powerful.' She took a breath, looked at Martin and asked, 'Would you like to share with the group?'

'No, thank you,' Martin mumbled. He wanted to be anywhere but in this church hall surrounded by these lost people.

Not everyone spoke. A few refused with shy smiles, but at the end of the meeting, when Margaret announced there would be tea and biscuits, the entire group shuffled like sheep towards the back of the hall where cups and saucers and plates of custard creams were laid out. Martin tried to make an inconspicuous exit, but Margaret steered him firmly in the direction of the refreshments.

He was standing alone, holding a cup and saucer, wondering how and when he was going to escape this excruciating ordeal, when the old guy with the dickie bow, John, came up to him.

'Is this your first time?' John asked.

'Yes.' Martin nodded. 'It was . . . interesting.'

John gave a small grin, then took a sip of his tea. There was a refinement to his movements, a considered slowness, as if he thought about each and every one. 'I take it you don't think it's for you,' he said.

'Not really,' said Martin, and then some more words tumbled out. 'My sister thought I should come, but I don't think I need it. I haven't had a drink in a month and I don't even know if I had a problem before that.'

John's crinkled eyes met his. He nodded and smiled. 'It's very hard to know,' he said. 'But coming here is a first step towards arriving at an understanding, one way or the other.'

It was like a blessing and permission to leave rolled into one. Martin put his cup down on the table, next to a plate that held some crumbs and a lone biscuit, and smiled back at him. 'Thank you,' he said.

'There's no need to thank me.'

'For telling your story, I mean. It was the best of them all . . . I mean, it was awful . . . I mean . . .'

'I know what you mean. I was glad to share it.'

'Well, I'll be going now.' Martin held out his hand to shake John's. 'It was nice to meet you.'

'What's your name, son?'

'Martin. Martin Brady.'

John's eyes twinkled. 'No second names here, remember?' he said, tipping his chin in Margaret's direction. 'You'll get us both killed.'

Martin laughed, and everyone in the room turned to look at him. Margaret gave him a smile.

'Can I give you my number, Martin?' John said.

Martin felt odd scribbling it on the back of a card for a spare-parts yard he had in his wallet. There was something intimate about it, like they were arranging to go out on a date.

'There may come a time when you need to call me,' John said, as Martin put his wallet back in his pocket. 'If that time comes, don't hesitate to pick up the phone. Call me, night or day.'

Martin thanked him again awkwardly, and turned to leave.

Why would a complete stranger make such an offer? It was a bit too close for comfort.

He glanced over his shoulder as he went out of the door. John was talking to Margaret. She was nodding sagely. They probably had it planned between them, he thought, a sort of intervention for the newcomer, like the quiet plotting of Stepford Wives.

70. The Music Student

Alice had pictured Celia alone on a ward, not really knowing anybody and in need of company; instead she was in a private room that overlooked a bank of trees at the far end of the hospital car park. There were bouquets of flowers on every available surface, and cards from well-wishers were draped over the metal rails at the head of the bed.

She was sleeping when Alice walked in, having told the sister at the nurses' station, as instructed, that she was one of Celia's old students. The sister seemed reluctant to give her the room number, but then the phone on her desk rang and she relented before picking it up.

Alice stood looking at her mother in the feeble light cast by the sun through the room's closed blinds. Her breathing was shallow and there were beads of sweat on her forehead, even though her face was as pale as the pillow she was lying on. Her hands, which again Alice noted for their similarity to her own, were folded on top of each other over the sheets, as Mother's had been in her coffin.

Alice shuddered at the memory and reached over to touch Celia's shoulder. Her eyes flickered open and took a few seconds to focus.

'Hello,' said Alice. 'It's me.'

'Alice,' said Celia, her breath coming slow and jagged. 'Thank you for coming.'

'I got here as soon as I could,' said Alice. Throughout the journey she'd had a flock of butterflies flying around her in stomach, but now she felt strangely calm.

Celia coughed into her chest as she did her best to pull herself into a sitting position against the pillows. Alice wanted to help her, but doing so would bring their bodies close together and the idea was unbearable.

'We don't have much time,' said Celia, looking at the clock above the door.

'I've a few hours until my bus leaves,' said Alice.

'Some people visit me every day. Family members. I don't want them to see you.' Celia patted the bed and gestured for Alice to sit down. 'I'm sorry,' she said, 'but nobody knows about you. They wouldn't understand.'

'*I* don't understand,' said Alice. The question on the tip of her tongue was the one she had been asking her imaginary mother for as long as she could remember. *Why? Why did you give me away?* But she couldn't ask it.

'There's an envelope on the bedside locker,' said Celia. 'It's for you. The letter inside explains everything. Take it away with you. Don't read it here.'

'I want to hear you tell me yourself.'

Celia's mouth twitched. She blinked. 'I don't think I can,' she said.

'If I'd been a better child, maybe it would have been easier for you to keep me.' Alice knew how crazy this sounded, as if a baby could control the way it was, but she thought the answer might be that she had been unwantable.

Celia coughed again and took a moment to catch her breath. 'Since the day I lost you, you've been the first thing I think about every morning and the last thing I think about every night. You were a beautiful child.'

'I've thought about you every day too. I imagined you.'

Celia looked at the clock again. 'There's no time,' she said. 'You'll have to leave.'

'But there's so much I want to say . . .'

'Come again. Maybe a little bit earlier in the day.'

'Why are you here?' Alice said, looking around the sterile room. 'Will it be for long?'

'It's nothing. Just a little infection. I'll be right as rain in no time. Come to see me tomorrow. After you've read the letter.'

'I can't. I've got to get back to work. And my friends are all coming over tomorrow night.'

'You're a good girl. Just as I thought you would be.'

'I'll come at the weekend. I'll take a hotel room and stay overnight. And I'll write down my new mobile number for you, so you can call me at any time.'

'That would be lovely.'

Alice scribbled down the number on a bit of paper, then took the letter from the bedside locker and put it into her bag. She was about to leave when she remembered the strangeness she'd felt at the thought of helping Celia in her bed. The unbearable thought of being so close to her.

'Can I ask you for something before I go?' she said, mustering up all her courage.

'Yes,' Celia said.

'Will you hug me?' she said simply.

Tears came into both their eyes as Celia held out her arms. Alice leaned down into them, her face finding its way into the soft folds of her mother's nightgown. It smelt of rosewater.

'Ssssh, sssh,' Celia repeated in a cracked whisper, holding tight and gently rocking as Alice's body heaved. 'It's okay, girl. It's okay.'

Behind them came the sound of a throat being cleared. Celia stiffened and Alice jerked away, her hands going to her puffed-up eyes to hide them from whoever had come into the room.

A woman of about the same age as Alice was standing at the foot of the bed.

'Claire,' said Celia, her voice clipped and bright. 'Meet Alice. Alice is one of my old students. Alice, this is my niece, Claire.'

Claire looked from Alice to Celia and back again, then held out her hand. 'Pleased to meet you,' she said.

'I was just leaving,' said Alice. 'I have to get a bus back to Dublin.'

'Thank you so much for coming,' said Celia.

'Yes, very good of you,' said Claire, not taking her eyes away from Alice's.

Alice held Claire's questioning look for a moment, then turned to go. The second she looked away, she realised it had been like staring into a mirror. In almost every minute detail, her cousin was identical to her.

71. The Letter

Alice waited through the two-hour bus journey to Cork, the three-hour train journey to Dublin and the half-hour taxi journey home before opening the letter. Even opening it in the kitchen seemed wrong, reading it in Mother's house, or Boo's house, as Alice now thought of it, but it was better than reading it in public, where anyone might see her reaction.

It was written on blue Basildon Bond paper, the neat script bunched close together on the page. In the dim kitchen light it looked illegible to begin with, but slowly the words began to take shape.

Dear Alice,
I don't know where to begin, or where the beginning is. Maybe it's with your birth, or your conception, but

sometimes I think you began long before I even began; that we all came from the same past and this is why things turned out like they did.

The main thing I want you to know is that you were born out of love. You were not a dirty secret bundled off in the shameful night, although you <u>were</u> a secret and have remained my secret all these years. I loved your father and he loved me, in as much as two eighteen-year-olds can love each other, or know of love. Which, I believe, is a lot.

I worked for his family, as a music teacher to his two younger sisters, in the summer after I left school. We drifted towards each other. He had just finished his studies too, home from the boarding school he'd been sent to when he was very young. He knew no one in our town. I was a loner too.

There is no need to explain how it happened, except to say it felt like the natural thing to do and I had no shame. But my father had always said to my sisters and me that if any of us ever got pregnant outside wedlock he would be forced to turn his back on us. Worse, he threatened the laundry in Cork, which everyone knew was like a prison from which some girls did not return.

So I went to your father's mother for help. It may have been the right or wrong thing to do. Even today I can't make my mind up about it. She sent your father away. So far away that I would never see him again and she forbade any contact between us. She got me a job in Dublin in a solicitor's office, and I left home.

When the time came near for your birth, I went to a private hospital, also organised by your father's mother. From there it was arranged that you would be adopted by a suitable family and I would return home, saying nothing of what had happened, except that I gave up the job because it didn't suit me.

I believed at the time that your grandmother had great power. She threatened not only to destroy my prospects but those of my sisters, should I tell anyone about your existence. Wealth sometimes has that blinding effect on the young, and your father's family were Protestants, which had its own influence at the time too.

I had you for three days and two nights. On the second night I stayed awake and tried to memorise every little thing about you. I fancied you looked like my nana, my mother's mother. Your fingers and toes were surprisingly long and I tried to commit the feeling of your tiny hand grasping my finger to the deepest parts of my memory. It would become my only memory of you over time.

The next day, when they came, I did not look as they took you away. A kind nurse had saved me one of the little yellow booties I crocheted for you. She said I should take it as a keepsake, but I did not bring it with me when I left. I could not bear the thought that it would be the only thing I had left of you.

My sisters met me from the bus when I returned and together we walked the two miles home. When they remarked that I looked a little tired, I said nothing. I have said nothing ever since.

I hope you had a good home and a happy childhood. I wished that for you always, and in my mind's eye, you grew up to be the beautiful woman you are today.

I cannot tell anyone about you, not now or ever. When one day I am dead and buried six feet under, I ask you not to reveal our secret to my sisters. They have been my rocks and to think of them knowing I betrayed them breaks my heart.

Sometimes I wished I'd kept that little crocheted bootie. In the dark days when I thought I might lose my mind for grief, it would have been a sign that you existed. There were times when I wondered if you had been a figment of my imagination. I would have been able to give you that bootie when you came to see me, as proof that I once was your mother, that I loved you with all my heart and made plans for you, plans that could not be fulfilled. But I left it behind, as one must do the past.

If we are to see each other again, I would ask you to pretend that you are my ex-piano student. I know this may be difficult for you, but believe me, it is for the best.

With love,

Celia Deasy, your mother

72. Spilled Salt

Barry held on for a few seconds after they'd hugged, squeezing her so close that Katherine almost lost her breath.

'It's so good to see you,' he said, holding her at arm's length when they finally pulled apart. 'You look great. Really great.'

'You too,' Katherine said. 'I like the hair.'

Hair was the wrong word. He'd shaved every last bit of it off, leaving his head bare and egg-like. It seemed out of proportion with his bulked-up body, but his face was more handsome, more distinct.

'Shall we sit down?' he asked, pulling her chair out for her. He was clearly nervous, a novel state for Barry.

They spent a few minutes ordering food and making small-talk – the unusually good summer, Katherine's new position at work, his brother's wedding. Then Barry leaned forward, beckoning her to do the same as if he was about to share some great secret.

He hooked his finger under the knot of his tie to loosen it.

'Look, Katherine, I'll cut to the chase,' he said. 'I think we made a mistake. I think we needed the time apart to realise what we had together – what we have together – how special it is.'

Katherine stared at him, her cup halfway to her mouth.

Not waiting for an answer, Barry went on, 'It's taken being away from you to make me understand how right you are for me.'

A waitress in a crisp silver-grey uniform, the exact same colour as the restaurant's walls, arrived with their brunch order. As she arranged the plates in front of them, Katherine watched Barry without meeting his eyes. There was a bead of sweat above his upper lip that she felt an urge to wipe away. It brought to mind the ease they had had together before it had all gone wrong, the way they had naturally taken care of each other's appearance. There were things like this that she still missed about him.

'It's not as simple as that,' she said, when the waitress had served them and gone. 'It's been five months, Barry. Things have changed.'

'The way I feel about you hasn't.'

'That's not what you said when you left.'

'I was going through a bad patch. I was depressed. I wasn't thinking straight.'

'And you think I wasn't going through my own bad patch? That I wasn't depressed? I needed your support and you weren't there for me. You just walked out when I needed you most. Perhaps the only time I'd ever really needed your help.'

Barry pushed a sausage around his plate. 'I didn't know what else to do. I was just so damned confused.'

'How do you mean, confused?' Katherine didn't think she'd ever heard him use the word before.

'You suddenly needed me, Katherine. After years of being so . . . so unneedy, I guess. That was one of the first things I loved about you, the way you didn't crowd me like other girls, didn't constantly beg for reassurance. You were your own woman. It was like no one could really get to you … To be honest, babes, it drove me wild at first, made me want you more.'

'But I did need you, Barry. Of course I did. Maybe I'm just not always that good at showing it,' said Katherine.

'You can say that again.' Barry flashed her a wounded-animal look.

'What does that mean?'

'Just that, Katherine, you *never* showed it. After a while, I began to feel like you were freezing me out, that you didn't want me to take care of you. So I got used to it – accepted it as your way. And then, when you suddenly turned the tables on me, after all that time, I just … I don't know. I bolted, I guess. I was caught off guard. And I know now I was wrong, I really do, babes, but for a while there, it felt like you were using me.'

Katherine did a double take. 'I would never have used you,' she said, her voice faltering.

'I know, babes, I know. But that's what it *felt* like . . . I'm sorry.'

As Katherine tried to let this revelation sink in, Barry reached across the table to take her hand, knocking the salt cellar over. That was supposed to bring bad luck, wasn't it? What were you supposed to do to counter it? Throw some salt over your shoulder?

'It was my fault,' Barry said. 'I should have told you how I felt, no matter how worried I was. That's why I asked you to meet me today.'

The waitress appeared back at their table to fill their water glasses. 'Everything okay?' she said.

'Yes, thank you,' Katherine said. She was still digesting Barry's words. Lucy had said something similar, that she and their mother had felt she was freezing them out.

'I was a fool,' said Barry, not looking away from Katherine, his hand still clasped over hers. 'I should have told you how I felt. What I wanted for us.'

She hadn't even known she was freezing him out. Had she been that self-deluded?

'Katherine,' Barry said, and there was urgency in his voice. 'I can't go on being dishonest with you.'

For a moment Katherine had the sensation that everyone in the café had turned to gape at her.

'I want you to marry me,' Barry said.

'What?' she heard herself ask.

'I'm not very good at speeches,' Barry replied, gripping her hand tightly, 'but I want you, Katherine, and I want us to be married. I want you to depend on me. You can, you know. Let me in and I'll show you what I can be. What we can be together.'

73. Between the Lines

'The place looks different,' said Jamie, looking around him. 'Where are all the owls?'

'Under the stairs,' Alice replied. 'There was a viewing this morning. I didn't want them putting any potential buyers off.'

'Pity. They lent the place a certain psychotic charm.'

Jamie was the last to come. Lisa had texted them all to apologise that she couldn't make it. Katherine had been ensconced in an armchair with a glass of red wine when Martin had arrived ten minutes earlier. She smiled at him as if everything was just fine between them.

Her hair was pinned up with two blonde curls twisting down each side of her face, accentuating the length of her neck. Martin imagined putting his lips to its soft white flesh, then stopped himself. She'd told him, plain and simple, that she didn't want him. It was time to get over her, to stop imagining there was something between them. It was one-sided: his.

'I wouldn't have put you down as a fan of *To Kill a Mockingbird*,' he said to Alice, when she handed him a cup of tea.

'Why not?' she asked, frowning.

'Well, it's kind of obscure. A classic, yeah, but people know the book more than they do the movie.'

'I haven't seen it before,' said Katherine. 'I haven't read the book either.'

'You can't be serious,' said Jamie. 'Even *I*'ve read the book.'

'My father gave it to me for my thirteenth birthday,' said Alice. 'He always encouraged my reading. Mother said I was a bookworm, that I'd go blind if I didn't take my head out of my books.'

She was wearing a navy dress with little white polka dots and puffed sleeves, one Martin had seen Katherine wear, back when they were working together. It suited Alice, giving her usually shapeless frame some curves. She wasn't wearing any of her coloured plastic accessories and her dark fringe wasn't pinned back at one side.

'It's one of those films that's just as good as the book,' he said, as the opening credits for *To Kill a Mockingbird* rolled, with their haunting childish theme and the cigar box of Boo Radley's gifts to the children. When he saw the first shot of Scout, Martin was taken aback. The child playing her was like a smaller version of Alice: they had similar pixieish features.

'I think the film is like a companion to the book,' said Alice. 'It brings out things that were between the lines. Like children's grief over the loss of their mother.'

'Please don't give it away,' said Katherine. 'I like not knowing what's going to happen before I watch a film. I never even read reviews before I go to the cinema.'

There was a heightened energy about her – perhaps because she'd got her job back and wasn't having to slum it at her sister's any more, Martin thought. It was odd, though, that she'd kept the little yellow Cinquecento, given she was now earning more than ever.

From the corner of his eye, he watched her all through the film. She was transfixed by it, as were Jamie and Alice, but slowly, as the story of the children and their father played out, the court case and Boo Radley, she seemed to deflate.

At the crucial moment, when the townspeople threatened Atticus Finch and Scout stood up for him, Katherine abruptly got up and walked out of the room.

'What's the deal with her?' said Jamie.

'Maybe you'd better go and see,' said Alice.

Martin looked at Jamie, then back at Alice, and realised she had been speaking to him.

Katherine was outside the front door, sitting on the step, her profile illuminated by the glow of the streetlight at the garden gate. Her cheeks, he could see, were wet.

He sat down beside her. 'What's going on?'

'Nothing. I'm tired, that's all.'

'Are you sure?'

'I just want to be alone for a few minutes, okay? I'll be back inside in a second.'

'Was it something in the film?' he asked, not moving from his spot beside her.

Katherine put her face into her hands. Her voice was choked when she spoke. 'I – I just couldn't bear it any more. The film kept reminding me of someone.'

'Who?' he asked.

Katherine turned to him, her eyes searching, and he did his best to urge her on with a smile. Then she looked away again. 'It doesn't matter,' she said. 'We'd better go back in.'

But she didn't move.

Martin reached over and tentatively put his arm around her. 'You can tell me, you know,' he said. 'The world won't end if you do.'

Katherine leaned her head on his shoulder. 'Can I ask you a question?'

'Sure,' said Martin. 'Go ahead.'

'What was your father like when you were a kid?'

Martin hadn't expected this, and it brought up a feeling of

disconnected loss he hadn't been able to put into words since his father died.

'He wasn't around much,' he said eventually, trying to remember something good about the old man. 'I remember he brought me and my sister to the pictures once. To see *E.T.*'

'To me my father was just like the father in the film tonight,' said Katherine. 'I adored the ground he walked on.'

'I wish I could say the same about mine. I was always trying to impress him, but I don't think he liked me very much.'

'How could he not love you?' Katherine asked, lifting her head and searching his face again. 'He was your father.'

Martin had often asked himself the same question, but the only answer he had ever come up with was that he hadn't been good enough. His sisters had blamed the drink for their father's meanness, but Dad had always been nicer to them. Kinder.

She put her head back on his shoulder and, in a very small voice, said, 'Do you mind if we just sit here for a while and not talk?'

'Of course not,' said Martin, and pulled her closer to him. The desire to protect her, which he'd felt when he'd first met her, was almost overwhelming.

74. All about Atticus

When Katherine came back from the bathroom, having gone there to wash her face, they were waiting for her with the film on pause.

'You should have kept watching,' she said.

'Of course we waited for you,' said Martin. 'We're only halfway through.'

Upstairs, in the chilly bathroom, with the smell of Palmolive soap pervading the air, she'd sat on the edge of the bath, hoping they'd start the film again without her.

When she'd told Martin she couldn't bear it any more, she had not been exaggerating. She could not endure another minute of Atticus Finch's love for his daughter. Katherine knew it was a ridiculous overreaction but, try as she might to keep her emotions in check, she was overwhelmed with grief. Watching Atticus through the eyes of his children had brought her right back to her own childhood, when her daddy had been the centre of her world.

She remembered sitting on his knee at Mass, looking up at the black shadow of stubble on his chin. His hand gripping hers tightly as they crossed a street in the rain. The smell of his aftershave when he leaned down to kiss her good night …

To this day Katherine didn't understand why he'd left. Of course, she was aware now of the problems that had existed in the marriage. She'd gleaned as much from her mother as she could, but she'd never been very forthcoming. But just because her parents couldn't live with each other any more, did that mean he'd had to stop being a father?

She remembered polishing the buckles of his policeman's uniform in front of the fire on Sunday nights … Being swung high in the air, looking down at his laughing face …

Maybe, as Martin had said of his own father, he had never really loved his girls. Maybe that was why he hadn't come home.

'Are you okay?' asked Alice, when Kathcrine sat down next to Jamie. 'Would you like a drink?'

'No. Thanks. I'm fine. Let's just put the film back on.'

They watched the remainder in silence, as had become their habit, until the last of the end credits had rolled. It was difficult, but Katherine stayed put, her hands in her lap.

'I have to hand it to you, Alice,' said Jamie, when the DVD finished. 'Ten out of ten for that one.'

Two red dots appeared at the centre of Alice's pale cheeks. 'I'm glad you liked it,' she said.

'Powerful stuff,' said Martin, rubbing his eyes. 'I never saw

Atticus as such a lonely figure before. But when you think about it, he's by himself in nearly every shot.'

'Boo Radley's lonely too,' said Alice. 'And Tom Robinson, because he's hated so much.'

'If Harper Lee was writing that book today, it would be about gay-bashers, not racists,' said Jamie.

'Here we go.' Martin groaned.

'I think that's a bit insulting to black people,' said Alice. 'It's not the same thing, being gay and being black. Terrible things have happened to black people because of the colour of their skin.'

'In some countries they lock you in jail and throw away the key if you're gay,' Jamie protested, his finger jabbing the air. 'In some countries they hang you in the town square. Or lynch you, like they lynched Tom Robinson.'

As the conversation went on around her, the final words of *To Kill a Mockingbird* were still ringing in Katherine's head.

And Atticus. He would be in Jem's room all night and he would be there when Jem waked up in the morning.

Her father had not stayed in her room all night. He had not been there when she woke up in the morning.

But Barry had come back. Barry had loved her enough to come home. No other man had done that for her. And she loved him for it.

October

The Party

'No, it's destiny! You must know how it goes!
The Knight rescues the Princess, and then they share
true love's first kiss . . . '
Shrek
Andrew Adamson and Vicky Jenson, 2001

75. Into the Void

Aaron had been crying from the moment he'd got up, not a steady whimper but an all-out squall. He fell into these crying jags every so often and wouldn't be put down, yet all the time Lisa held him, he wriggled, pushing against her as if he wanted to be anywhere but in her arms. Every so often he calmed down for a few minutes, probably to have a rest, but then he started up again, as inconsolable as before.

Patrick called to say he'd be an hour late home from work, but that had been an hour and forty-five minutes ago. Lisa had been waiting for him to feed Theo and Ben, but they were getting more and more irritable and hungry, so she'd put some chicken nuggets in the oven, hoping Patrick would be back before they were cooked to serve them up. She only had one pair of hands.

'Who'd like to watch a DVD?' she asked, shoving the oven door closed with her leg as Aaron began bawling again, the upper reaches of his shriek reverberating through her entire body.

'Fiona! Fiona!' Ben shouted, running for the sitting room. He'd become obsessed with *Shrek* over the past few weeks. Well, not Shrek himself. Princess Fiona. There were days when no one was allowed to call him Ben. He was Fiona and that was that.

'Maybe he's gay,' she said to Jamie, on the phone.

'Maybe?' said Jamie. 'Try definitely.'

Lisa didn't mind if he was. Most of the gay men she came across had strong relationships with their mothers. It might be a cliché but it was true, and it was kind of comforting to think it might turn out like that. She wished, though, that he could stand up better for himself against Theo. A screaming Ben, clinging to her, tears rolling down his cheeks, trying to tell her about the latest atrocity against him, was not just a daily occurrence: it seemed to happen every five minutes.

At least there might be peace between them for a while with the DVD on, even if above Aaron's cries she could hear Theo making dangerous noises, jumping on and off the couch.

She was trying her best to follow Dr Harvey's directions, praising and rewarding Theo for good behaviour, walking away when he was violent. But it was easier said than done. For one thing, there was precious little good behaviour to praise and reward, and his violent outbursts were increasingly directed at his little brothers. How could she walk away when he was pulling Ben by the hair across the room, or kicking poor little Aaron over when he tried to take baby steps?

Aaron's crying turned into a soft whimper and she took a deep breath of relief, hoping, although she knew it was in vain, that this was the end of it for today. 'Good boy,' she said, stroking the back of his head as after-sobs ran through his body. 'That's it. Calm down.'

Where was Patrick? This was the fourth night in a row he'd said he'd be home early but hadn't made good on the promise. Working late one night a week was bad enough, but every night was something else. He spent more time in that office than he did anywhere else.

Lisa sat down at the kitchen table, moved Aaron on to her knee and re-dialled Patrick's number with her free hand. It went through to his voicemail again. She was listening to his message, contemplating whether to leave another or not, when from the sitting room came a scream that cut like a knife into her brain. Aaron started bawling again, pushing his fists into the side of her breast as Ben came running into the hall, both of his arms waving wildly in the air, his face twisted in pain. Blood dribbled from a gash on his forehead.

'What did you do?' she cried out to Theo, reaching for Ben while still holding on to Aaron, who was trying to dig himself into her and get away at the same time. 'Oh, Ben! It's all right, baby, it's all right.'

Theo walked out of the sitting room, chin held high. He was carrying the poker.

'Theo! Did you hit Ben with the poker?'

'No,' he said.

'He did! He did!' Ben shrieked, his face buried in her thigh, leaving bloodstains on her clothes.

'Go to your room at once, Theo!' Lisa shouted, above Ben's wails and Aaron's cries.

'NOOOOOO!' Theo roared, his voice thick with rage. 'I won't!'

He started walking towards her, the poker still in his hand, pointing outwards.

Lisa got to her feet, still carrying Aaron. She grabbed Ben's hand and backed up towards the patio doors. 'Put that down,' she ordered, but Theo was still advancing with the poker.

How was it possible that a five-year-old boy could terrorise his whole family like this? He was ruining her life, ruining Ben's too. Aaron would be next, and God only knew what was in store for the new baby.

Where the *fuck* was Patrick?

Her back touched the glass of the patio door, and her eyes met Theo's. He was looking at her with naked venom. 'I hate you,' he said. 'I hate you. I hate you.'

'I hate you too!' Lisa cried. Still holding Aaron and clinging to Ben's hand, she slid down against the patio doors, her breath and tears coming fast.

Theo began roaring. He dropped the poker and ran towards her, his head aiming for her like a charging bull's. When he made impact it was with her shoulder, luckily the opposite one to where Aaron was bawling.

'*Muuuummy!*' Ben cried, looking up at her with frightened eyes. The blood from his wound was smeared all over his cheeks.

Theo was still shouting, his low, guttural voice rising above the others in a constant, 'NOOOOO!'

Lisa couldn't catch her breath. It was like the feeling she'd had the first time she was ever on a rollercoaster, with Patrick when they were first going out. 'I want to get off, I want to get off,' she'd yelled, panic overwhelming her as their carriage rattled towards the high summit of the first hill, ready to plummet into the void.

'You can't,' said Patrick. 'Just let go and scream when it goes down. That's all you can do.'

'NOOOOOOOO!' Theo howled over Ben and Aaron's wails, and he aimed his head at her chest.

Lisa placed her head in her hands and began to scream. It was some time before she stopped.

And that was why, when Patrick eventually came home that night, full of apologies and excuses, she picked up her small, freshly packed case and walked straight past him out of the front door, saying only two words: 'Good luck.'

76. Markey and the Little Mermaid

Spurred on by the appearance of her picture framed on the sitting room wall, Kitty was at the kitchen table, working on another elaborate drawing.

'It's a fairy-princess fashion show,' she told Katherine. 'I'm designing all their clothes myself.'

'It's really beautiful, Kit Kat,' said Katherine. 'I think I'll hang it just over there, in the alcove.' Kitty beamed and nudged Laura. 'Auntie Katherine is going to hang it over there,' she said, pointing. Laura lifted her head from her book, gave her sister an encouraging smile, then turned a page.

'At this rate, every available space in your house will be

covered with her artwork,' Lucy deadpanned, but Katherine could tell she was pleased that Kitty's Little Mermaid drawing had been given pride of place. It was true, she thought, how the little things counted, how easy it was to make her sister happy after so many years of thinking nothing she did ever would.

'Are you sure it's okay to bring the girls to the party?' she asked Lucy. 'It won't be too late for them?'

'Are you kidding? It's all they've talked about since you dropped the bombshell. Auntie Katherine's engagement party. Auntie Katherine's engagement ring. Speaking of which . . .'

'Oh, we're not going down the engagement-ring route. A wedding ring will be more than enough.'

'And you're absolutely sure you want to go through with it?'

Katherine bristled. It was the third time Lucy had asked since she'd walked through the door. 'Look, Lucy,' she said, 'I know you don't like him but Barry and I have been together for nearly nineteen years. He's my life partner.'

'But that doesn't mean you have to marry him.'

'We're only formalising it. Putting it on solid ground, for better or worse.'

'Except when it was worse, instead of better, he walked out on you.'

'There were two sides to that story. And, to tell you the truth, I'm glad he did what he did. It put a lot of things in perspective.'

'You're one hundred per cent sure, then?'

'Yes, I am. Bloody hell, Lucy, I wish you could be happy for me.'

'I *am* happy for you,' said Lucy, but she didn't sound too convinced.

'Do you love him?' asked Paolo, speaking up for the first time since they'd arrived. 'Does he love you?'

Katherine wasn't sure why he felt comfortable asking such personal questions. Maybe it was a cultural thing, his lack of boundaries. 'I'll just make another pot of coffee,' she said. 'You all right for juice, girls?'

'Do you have any chocolate biscuits?' Kitty asked, looking up from her drawing. 'Or sweets?'

'I bought Penguins especially for you.'

They spent the rest of the afternoon talking about the wedding. It was going to be a small affair, family and close friends, a registry office, dinner and a jazz quartet in a beautifully restored townhouse by the canal later on.

Lucy insisted on the two of them going to shop for the dress, and although Katherine agreed, she was dubious. If Lucy had her way, she'd be wearing flowers in her hair and floating down the aisle on a cloud of hippie muslin. Instead, Katherine had her eye on a spaghetti-strapped ruched midi-dress from Julien Macdonald's last summer collection. It was perfect, not too showy, not too plain, and although it was white, it didn't scream, 'Wedding!' All she had to do was find the right shoes to go with it, and maybe a handbag. She had decided to wear her hair in a twist, with no adornments.

'We could go shopping on Monday, once the party is over,' said Lucy. 'Town won't be too busy then, so it should be perfect.'

But Katherine had already done the unthinkable and taken a day of annual leave to make the final party arrangements. She couldn't take another so soon. 'We'll do it next Saturday or Sunday,' she said. 'Work is hectic at the moment.'

Laura looked up from her book. 'Can I come?' she asked, her forehead crinkling.

'Of course,' said Katherine. 'We have to get your outfit, and Kitty's flower-girl dress.'

'I've already designed it,' said Kitty. 'I think you're going to totally love it.'

They all left before Barry got home from work, and Katherine suspected it was because Lucy didn't want to see him.

'Jesus, that was some day,' Barry said, taking off his suit-jacket as he walked into the kitchen. 'You know what I need right now? An ice-cold beer.'

'Coming up,' said Katherine. He looked baggy around the eyes, she thought. Although he was only doing nine-to-five days at the moment, he was packing a lot in, reporting to her daily on the goings-on in the Henderson office, which had stepped up a notch since the company's recent redundancies. It was something new, his eagerness to share what went on in his working day. It wasn't the most riveting conversation in the world, but it made her feel closer to him, knowing that he wanted her to be interested.

She poured a bottle of Heineken into two glasses and followed him into the sitting room as he chattered away about something one of his colleagues had said to him at lunchtime.

'God, I'm exhausted,' she said, flopping down on the sofa and turning on the television for *Six One News*. 'Working full-time and party planning is no joke.'

Barry groaned. 'I suppose you've got everything arranged down to the last detail.'

'You know me so well.'

'I wish we could call the bloody thing off. I don't know why I agreed to it in the first place.'

'It's a small party,' said Katherine. 'Just our close friends and family celebrating our engagement.'

'They'll be celebrating our wedding soon enough. Isn't that enough for them?'

'You'll enjoy it. Probably more than the wedding, because you'll be more relaxed.'

'When you put it that way …' Barry said, and took a mouthful of his beer.

The news came on, but the minute the presenter started reading the headlines, Barry pressed the mute button on the remote control.

'Hey, where's my Markey?' he asked, as if he was noticing Kitty's Little Mermaid drawing over the fireplace for the first time.

'I put it in the spare bedroom. It goes nicely with the colour scheme in there.'

'Do you know how much that painting cost?'

'I have a fair idea.'

'And it's in the spare room?'

'I'll bring it back down tomorrow,' said Katherine, taking a sip of her beer. 'I just wanted to see how Kitty's picture looked there.'

77. A Chance Encounter

In the yard of the electronics shop across the dual carriageway from her window, Lisa saw a sign declaring, '50% OFF ALL SMARTPHONES!' She wondered if she'd be able to get a new Sim card if she went over and bought one. If she had a new number, Patrick wouldn't be able to reach her.

She'd turned off her mobile after his last call, but she'd felt so disconnected from the world that she'd thought she might spin off quietly into outer space without anyone knowing.

'At least tell me where you are,' Patrick had begged.

'I can't do that,' she'd said.

'This is crazy, Lisa! The kids need their mother. You can't just walk out on them like this.'

'They have you.'

'What am I supposed to do? My boss is already wondering what's going on.'

'You'll manage, Patrick.'

'Do you want me to leave them with my mother, is that it?'

There was a hint of threat in his voice and Lisa had understood for the first time that he knew it was bad for the boys to be with his mother.

'You can do whatever you want,' she'd said. 'You're their father and I'm sure you'll work out what's best.'

She'd heard his protests as she took the phone away from her ear and pushed the red button. He'd sounded a bit like Theo.

The hotel was squeezed between a car dealership and a McDonald's on the outskirts of the city, one of those faceless €49-a-night places where no one might think of looking for her.

In three days she had not left her room, except to eat in the hotel's restaurant. The buffet was unchanging, plain and flavourless, but it suited her fine. She imagined it was how a deaf person might feel, wandering through the world, seeing everything around them but cut off from it. Much of the time she slept, only marking what time of day it was with pangs of hunger.

She forced the children from her mind every time they came into it. Except last night, when she'd woken up in a cold sweat having dreamed of Aaron alone in the dark, crying to be lifted out of his cot with no hope of anyone coming.

Bar the phone calls from Patrick, she'd barely said three words to another human being since she'd wrestled the door of her car closed on the night she'd left. Patrick had been shouting something at her as she pulled away, but she hadn't heard it properly. When she'd looked in her rear-view mirror, his fist had been punching the air.

Today she thought she might take a little excursion for lunch at McDonald's. She wouldn't make a habit of it, but one Big Mac Meal wouldn't do her any harm. She'd have it with a Coke as a treat.

As she walked out of the front door of the hotel, a sharp blast of autumnal air hit her. She pulled her coat close, looking left and right, and quickly made her way across the car park.

Unlike most McDonald's outlets, this one was strangely quiet – no children shouting about Happy Meals, not even a radio playing as background noise. A few lone customers sat at the plastic tables, and a queue of one stood at the tills, yet the staff looked spruced up and ready to go, rather than the usual laconic bunch.

Lisa was approaching the counter, looking up at the menu,

when out of the corner of her eye, she spotted someone familiar. 'You're just being paranoid,' she told herself, turning furtively to check. But she was right. Sitting, almost hidden, in a corner near the entrance to the toilets was Katherine's fiancé, Barry. Even though he'd shaved all his hair off, she would have recognised him anywhere. He was as handsome as ever.

He sat in front of his laptop in a suit, his tie loosened at the collar. The woman who was emptying trays and cleaning passed him and lifted a paper cup from his table. They exchanged a few words.

Lisa turned her head away. Barry probably wouldn't recognise her, but she didn't want to take the chance that he might. She needed to stay anonymous.

'Poor thing,' said the tray woman, who had appeared beside her, pushing the paper cup into the mouth of a bin.

'I'm sorry?' said Lisa.

'We get them every now and then out here where no one knows them. The ones who've been laid off but are pretending to go out to work. It's desperate, isn't it?'

'Yes. I suppose it is.'

'This one has been here every day for the past month. He just stares into the screen of that computer like it's trying to tell him something, the poor man.'

'Can I help you?' asked the girl behind the till, her smile as bright as a spring day.

'No, I don't think so,' said Lisa and, head down, walked quickly out of the restaurant.

78. No Costumes Allowed

Because the party was on Hallowe'en night, Katherine had stipulated 'no fancy dress' on the invitations, but still a few people turned up in costume – a Wicked Witch of the West, a

Wonder Woman and the Only Gay in the Village from *Little Britain* – some of Barry's friends from his rugby-club days, which were so far back she couldn't remember who was who.

'That's what he thinks,' said Jamie, nodding in the direction of the Only Gay in the Village as he arrived. 'You remember Andrew, don't you?'

'Of course I do.' Katherine smiled, even though she wouldn't have been able to pick Andrew out of a line-up. He looked like a middle-aged Ken doll, receding blond hair, wire-framed glasses and cheekbones so perfectly cut they might have been plastic. His eyes weren't plastic, though. They smiled at Katherine warmly as Andrew said, 'Congratulations. We're very happy for you.'

'Thank you,' Katherine replied, kissing him on both cheeks, then doing the same to Jamie. 'The gang's all here. I've sat everyone together. Come on, I'll bring you over.'

'Is this an engagement party or a funeral?' Jamie said, when they had squeezed through the crowd and reached the table. Lisa, Martin and Alice were all sitting in silence, contemplating three glasses of sparkling water.

'Hey, Jamie,' said Martin, glancing up out of his sulk. 'Hey, Andrew.' He'd barely said hello to Katherine on arriving and hadn't looked at her since.

'Can I get you boys a drink?' Katherine asked. 'They do great cocktails.'

'That would be lovely,' said Andrew. 'Two cosmopolitans, I think.'

'Look! Over here! I'm in the room,' said Jamie, waving his hands at Andrew. 'I can order for myself, thank you very much. I'll have a Jack Daniels and Diet Coke. Actually, make it a double.'

'Can I talk to you for a minute, Katherine?' said Lisa. 'In private?'

She looked like something a cat might have dragged through a bush, her greasy hair pushed back behind her ears, its roots almost completely grown out now, the customary black poloneck creased as if it had just been pulled out of the tumble-drier, its front pushed out by her now very recognisably pregnant belly. Lisa may have a lot on her plate, thought Katherine, but at least she could have made some sort of effort.

'Not right now, Lisa,' she said. Marissa and Jean had arrived and were looking around for her. 'I'll catch up with you later, okay?'

As she walked towards the girls, she noticed Barry downing another whiskey at the bar by himself. She couldn't understand why he hadn't invited anyone from work. The friends he'd added to her list were people Katherine hadn't seen in years. Apart from his two brothers, who had their heads together in deep conversation with their mother at a table in the furthest corner of the room, the rest of Barry's guests were not what you might call bosom buddies.

She'd hardly had time to speak to him today, what with the caterers bringing the wrong food and the negotiations that had ensued, not to mention decorating the room, which had taken four solid hours. A function room was a function room, when all was said and done, no matter how expensive the hotel. She'd wrapped red organza around every chair, tying it in a big bow at the back, and put a single red lily at the centre of each table in stem vases provided by the hotel. The 150 strings of red fairy lights she'd bought online had arrived, by the grace of God, yesterday morning and, with the help of a handyman, she'd plugged them into all the chandeliers and looped them from one to the other around the room. They gave the place a kind of fairytale quality when lit. Kitty and Laura had been enchanted when they'd arrived with Lucy and Paolo, which made Katherine feel all the hard work had been worth while.

'It's beautiful,' said Marissa, giving her a hug.

'Stunning,' said Jean.

'Where's Olive?' Katherine asked.

'Her youngest has chickenpox,' said Marissa. 'It's super-contagious.'

'If you ask me, those children get every infection, rash and airborne virus going,' said Jean. 'I've taken to keeping mine away from them at all costs.'

Marissa hooted. 'You're priceless,' she told Jean, wiping a tear away from her eye.

'I'm deadly serious,' said Jean.

'Can you excuse me for a minute?' said Katherine. Out of the corner of her eye she could see one of the waitresses looking aimlessly about, an empty hors d'oeuvres tray in her hand.

'Oh, you go and mingle,' said Jean. 'Don't worry about us.'

'We can't stay long, though,' added Marissa. 'Babysitters and all that grown-up stuff.'

Katherine made a beeline for the waitress, but Lucy stopped her, grabbing her arm. 'Jesus, will you relax?' her sister said. 'If you're this wound up tonight, I can't imagine what you're going to be like on the big day. Sit down with us for a few minutes.'

'Yes, Auntie Katherine,' said Kitty. 'Sit down with us.'

So, with her eye still on the redundant waitress, Katherine yanked down the skirt of her tulle Christopher Bailey dress – it kept riding up annoyingly – and sat.

Lucy stirred her cocktail. 'I haven't seen Barry all night,' she said. 'Is he here?'

'He's at the bar,' said Katherine. 'I don't know if he's enjoying himself. He seems so . . . so well . . . uncomfortable. It's supposed to be a celebration.'

'Maybe he's nervous. Lots of men get like that before weddings.'

'He looks like this is not where he wants to be,' said Paolo, with his eye on the bar.

Why did he always have to say the wrong thing? Lucy almost imperceptibly squeezed his wrist and changed the subject. 'Mum called. She's worried about the hotel she booked, whether it's too far away from the registry office.'

'I still don't know why she couldn't have stayed with me,' said Katherine. 'It would have saved a lot of trouble.' It still stung that her mother pretended she stayed in hotels when she came to Dublin because she didn't want to put either Lucy or Katherine to any bother, when the truth was she wanted little to do with either of her daughters' lives. She'd stayed depressed for a solid fifteen years after their father had left, withdrawn in a miserable world of her own, and then one day, out of the blue, she'd introduced Liam with a big smile on her face. A year later, she'd sold the house and the two of them had moved to Spain, where Liam's daughter, Linda, and her two kids already lived, in one of the apartment blocks he owned. Truth be told, Mum didn't even like coming back to Ireland, never mind remembering that she'd once had a different family.

'She's a law unto herself, you know that,' said Lucy. 'And, face it, you're probably better off without her. The lovely Liam is coming too.'

'He's not that bad . . .' said Katherine, but she was distracted. At the bar, Lisa was talking to Barry, gesticulating to emphasise some point, while he jabbed the air just above her nose with his index finger. It looked like they were having an argument.

79. Problem-solving for Beginners

'For Christ's sake, have some manners,' Jamie hissed, as Andrew pulled his phone out his pocket for the umpteenth time and started tapping in a message.

'Look who's talking,' Andrew said, not looking up. 'Priscilla, Queen of the Texters.'

'Yes, but we're in company,' said Jamie, smiling with gritted teeth at Alice. Lisa was off at the bar with Barry, and Martin had wandered away despondently. For all Jamie knew, he had gone home. There was one incontrovertible fact about heterosexuals: they did not know how to party. They thought they did but, really, they hadn't the first clue.

'The fairy lights are lovely, aren't they?' said Alice, confirming the fact, and Jamie nodded mutely. It was one thing to listen to small-talk, quite another to get involved with it.

They lapsed into silence again, and watched as the DJ played the opening strains of Abba's 'Dancing Queen' and two women, who should have known better, let out little screams and ran for the dance-floor. Could the night get any more clichéd?

Jamie hadn't wanted to come. He was still reeling from the news about his course. Three days ago, exactly seven days after Jamie had paid the balance registration fees and had his induction week visiting galleries around the city with the twelve other students, the McColgan Private College of Further Education had closed its doors and sealed them shut. They couldn't be accessed via phone or email. Even their website was down.

Jamie Googled 'McColgan Private College of Further Education' under the news filter and found a story that the college had declared itself bankrupt and had ceased trading. It turned out Alice had been right.

It wasn't the money – well, okay, the money was a big part of it: Jamie had all but cleared out his savings account to pay for the first year of the course in advance, which had left him the next best thing to broke. More than that, though, it was the thought of the winter stretching before him filled with nothing for him to do. The course had been a light on the horizon, a beacon heralding a new beginning, a time not filled with crap TV and aimless days wandering around an empty flat in his dressing-gown.

Andrew had promised to do everything in his power to get Jamie's money back, but you could see in his eyes that he didn't hold out much hope. This afternoon he'd literally dragged Jamie out of bed and insisted they go to the party. 'I can't bear you like this,' he'd snapped. 'For Christ's sake, get up!' It had stung in a way nothing Andrew had said had hurt before.

Lisa came back to the table, her cheeks flushed as if she'd run a race. Jamie had never seen her look so bad. 'Seriously, I'm giving

Gok Wan an emergency call,' he said. 'Up the pole or not, you need a complete make-over.'

'Oh, shut up, Jamie,' Lisa said, getting up again and walking off. Between her and Andrew, personality transplants seemed to be the order of the day.

'I love this song,' said Alice, as the closing notes of 'Dancing Queen' led into the Bee Gees' 'Tragedy', sung by Steps.

Jamie turned to Andrew. 'Get your coat, honey, we're going,' he said.

'What?' Andrew blinked, looking up from his phone.

'I said we're going. I can't take this any more.'

'But we can't. Saeed is on his way. He'll be here in ten minutes.'

'What the fuck, Andrew? He can't come here. It's a private engagement party.'

'I doubt Katherine will notice. And if she does, I'll just explain his predicament. He's a little bit drunk and emotional. He needs friends, Jamie. I wish you'd be nicer to him.'

'You can be nice to him all by yourself,' Jamie said. 'I'm going.'

He pulled his jacket off the back of his chair and made for the door. But as he reached it he looked back.

What if Saeed said something? He was drunk. God knew what might come out of his mouth.

Andrew, who had been leaning in to say something to Alice, looked momentarily in his direction, the lights from the dance-floor glinting off his glasses, and suddenly Jamie knew what he had to do.

The solution was simple.

80. This Too Shall Pass

People in the smoking area were staring at Lisa in naked disgust, but she didn't give a damn. 'You think this is bad?' she wanted to say. 'You don't know the half of it.'

At least Martin didn't seem to be judging her. He hadn't batted an eyelid when she'd asked him for a cigarette.

'When are you due again?' he asked, after taking a deep drag of his Marlboro Light.

'The first of January,' said Lisa, dipping the tip of her ash on to the ground. Saying the date made her feel physically sick, so she changed the subject. 'Katherine looks great, doesn't she?'

'Yeah,' said Martin. He looked at the burning tip of his cigarette intently, then took another drag before changing the subject back again. 'Four kids. Wow. That'll be a lot of work.'

Lisa resigned herself. 'It will,' she said. 'It's too much work already.'

'But you're managing okay, aren't you?' Something had entered his voice, a note of concern that brought a sudden lump to her throat.

'I've left them,' she said. 'My children … Patrick . . . I walked out.'

'Jesus. Seriously?'

Lisa began to cry. 'I always thought I'd be the perfect mother, you know. My whole life, I always imagined that's what I was meant to be. I couldn't have been more wrong.'

'Maybe you're being a little hard on yourself.'

'Can I have another cigarette?'

Martin lit one from the butt of his last and handed it to her, then another for himself. A blonde woman with long, pink-painted acrylic nails walked past them, her eyes going from Lisa's cigarette to her pregnant belly. 'You should be ashamed of yourself,' she muttered.

'I am,' Lisa replied, and took another drag.

Martin leaned against the wall. 'I've always wondered how my mother coped,' he began. 'There were three of us and, well, I was fairly wild. And my father was never around. There are photographs of her from that time and she looks younger now than she did thirty years ago. We laugh about it, but back then … The worst of it was that I hated her when I was a kid. For a long time I couldn't work out why, but now I think it was because she was always there. It was easy to lay the blame on her.'

'For what?'

'For my dad. For wanting him around, and then when he was around, wanting him gone.'

'The awful thing is that I'm beginning to think I hate my son just as much as he hates me,' said Lisa. 'That's why I left. What kind of mother doesn't love her child?'

'I think you love him. He's probably a bit of a brat like I was.'

Lisa opened her bag to search for a tissue. She couldn't stop crying. 'I don't know what to do. I can't go back. I can't have this baby on my own. I can't stay in that hotel for ever. I feel lost. Completely and utterly lost.'

Martin put his arm around her and squeezed. 'There's a saying I heard somewhere. "This too shall pass." And it will. I promise it will.'

Lisa leaned into him and tried to take some comfort from his words, but she couldn't imagine her problems passing any time soon. The boys were so young. There was another on the way. It could be like this for another twenty years.

They were standing there, Martin's arm across Lisa's shoulders, both smoking, when Katherine stuck her head out of the door.

'Has anyone seen Barry?' she asked, out of breath. 'We're supposed to be doing the speeches in five minutes.'

Lisa wiped the tears from her eyes and stubbed out her cigarette. 'Katherine,' she said, 'I really need to talk to you. It's important.'

'Can we do it later? I can't find Barry anywhere. His brother is waiting to make a toast.'

'No, we can't do it later. We have to talk *now*.' Lisa had tried to phone Katherine a few times times since she'd spotted Barry in McDonald's, but had kept getting through to her voicemail. It wouldn't have been right to spill the beans on an answerphone message, so she was left with no choice but to tell her here. 'Martin, can you leave us alone for a few minutes?' she asked.

'With the greatest of pleasure,' said Martin, and went inside, walking past Katherine without looking at her.

When she was sure Martin was out of earshot, Lisa took Katherine by the arm and said, 'It's about Barry . . .'

'What about him?' Katherine said, irritation edging through her voice.

'I saw him. In McDonald's, the one near the Red Cow Junction.'

Katherine looked at her as if she had ten heads. 'That's hardly a capital crime,' she said.

'He's been there every day for the past month. He's lost his job and is pretending to go out to work.'

Katherine's face looked like it was falling in slow motion.

'I'm sorry,' Lisa said. 'I just thought you should know.'

81. A Stranger Calls

Alice didn't get to her mobile in time to answer it. She thought she'd never get used to having the thing. Going off importunately in her handbag, asking for her undivided attention. Mostly the calls were from Mrs Silver, who was still playing with her own new phone, like it was a toy she'd got from Santa. 'Alice!' she'd shout. 'Is that you?'

'Yes, Mrs Silver. It's me.'

'I'm just calling to say hello!'

'Hello, Mrs Silver, how are you?'

It wasn't that Alice minded Mrs Silver calling in the middle of the working day, or even that she called to chat about nothing. The problem was that every time the phone rang, Alice thought it might be her mother and she was disappointed when Mrs Silver's name came up.

She pulled the phone out of her bag and checked the number she had just missed, but it was one she didn't recognise. That was hardly surprising. To date, she had only six numbers keyed into her contacts list.

She had been alone at the table for the last ten minutes with Jamie's boyfriend, Andrew, who had smiled and said hello when they'd arrived, but hadn't said two words to her since. Before he'd disappeared, Jamie was being his usual self, looking at her like she was dirt on his shoe. He hadn't even commented on her new dress, which she'd found in a vintage shop hidden on a little side-street in the middle of town. It was blue-checked cotton with a little white bow at the neck and she'd accessorised it with a pair of crimson ankle boots she'd got last week in Brown Thomas. When she'd looked at herself in the mirror before coming out, with her new straight-line fringe cut just above the eyebrows, a different woman from the old Alice had looked back. Alice had decided she liked her.

'This is my first engagement party,' she said to Andrew, after searching for something to say.

'Is it?' he replied, and they lapsed into silence again.

It was a lovely party, though. The lights were twinkling, there were lots of people talking and laughing, and the music was making her foot tap. Alice was determined to enjoy herself. When the DJ had played 'Dancing Queen', she'd felt an almost irresistible urge to get up and dance the way she sometimes did to Abba alone in her bedroom.

She put her phone back into her bag, wondering again who the unidentified caller might have been. Her mother's name came up as 'Celia' whenever she called. It had seemed wrong to key her name in as 'Mother' or 'Mum' in the contacts list.

Since Alice had visited her at the hospital, there had been regular contact. Every Saturday, bar this weekend, she had made the long journey to Ballydehob, and visited Rose Cottage for the afternoon. The last couple of weeks, she'd taken to booking a B&B overnight so she could visit on Sunday too. She didn't feel comfortable enough to ask if she might stay the night at Celia's.

Sometimes there was not much to talk about. Celia steadfastly avoided delving into her own past, asking Alice questions about her childhood and her adoptive parents instead. But there wasn't much to tell. Alice didn't mention 'under the stairs' or much about Mother. Instead she tended to focus on her father in the conversations, telling Celia about their Saturdays watching television when Mother was out with the Brownies, or how he'd come home every Friday after work with a chocolate bar for her and a comic – *Twinkle* when she was little, *Bunty* when she was older.

But even when there was nothing to say and they sat silently in the little floral sitting room, Celia's breath coming in a slow rattle that sounded like smoker's chest, Alice savoured every minute. She knew Celia was savouring it too. Every now and then their eyes met and they exchanged smiles that spoke a thousand words that would probably never pass their lips.

She told Celia all about Film Club and her new friends, and how she and Mrs Silver had decided to move into the same apartment block, now that an agreement had been signed for the sale of the house. They'd still live almost next door to each other.

'You're a very kind woman, Alice,' Celia said. 'Mrs Silver is very lucky.'

'Oh, no. I don't do it out of charity,' Alice replied. 'Mrs Silver is my friend. I wouldn't want to move far away from her.'

'Isn't she a little old for you? As a friend, I mean.'

'I don't think age has anything to do with friendship. She's been very good to me. If it wasn't for her, I never would have found you.'

'Then we both have something to thank her for.'

It was the nearest Celia had come to voicing how she felt about their burgeoning relationship. Most of the time she was circumspect and Alice understood it. She'd inherited that gene.

On two occasions when Alice was in Celia's sitting room, members of the family had dropped in. First, Celia's sister, Lillian, an older version of Celia, who kept looking out the corner of her eye at Alice, but fully accepted the story about her being an old student. The other visitor was Lillian's daughter, Claire, who was just as standoffish as she had been that day at the hospital, interrupting the conversation every now and then to ask Alice questions that were difficult to answer, like: 'What year did you study with Aunt Celia? I must know some girls from your year.' Or: 'How come we haven't met you before now?'

Alice gave evasive answers, not meeting Claire's eye. Once or twice, Celia butted in and steered the conversation in another direction. Alice couldn't imagine that Claire suspected the truth, though. If they'd never known about Celia's pregnancy, how would they begin to put two and two together?

Inside her handbag, Alice's phone began to ring again.

'Excuse me,' she said to Andrew, who barely noticed. He was looking at the dance-floor, where Jamie had appeared and was shuffling around with one of Katherine's friends.

She found the phone just before the caller rang off and answered, 'Hello?'

'Is that Alice?' The voice sounded familiar, but Alice couldn't quite place it.

'Yes,' she said. 'How can I help you?'

'This is Claire Breheny. I'm Celia Deasy's niece.'

Alice's heart plunged. 'Yes,' she said, turning away from the table so Andrew couldn't see her face. 'Hello, Claire.'

'Aunt Celia is asking for you,' said Claire. 'She's back in the hospital. Can you come?'

'Is she okay? I'd have to take the train from Dublin so it's not possible to get there tonight.'

'Alice. Can I be frank?'

'Hold on a minute, I need to go somewhere quieter.' Alice stood up and walked towards the double doors that led to the hotel foyer, her red shoes slippery on the carpet.

'She doesn't have much time left,' said Claire. 'I don't know who you are or where you came from but she wants you. So, please come. We want to make it comfortable for her. We want her to be happy.'

Alice stopped. 'What do you mean she doesn't have much time?'

'She hasn't told you?'

'No,' said Alice, dread rising in her throat.

'I'm surprised,' said Claire. 'I thought she told you everything.'

'Claire, please tell me what's happening.'

'Aunt Celia is dying. The doctors gave her six months, but that was a year ago. She took a turn for the worse on Wednesday. Now they're saying it could be a matter of days, maybe hours.'

Alice turned back towards the table where she'd left her handbag. 'Tell her I'm coming,' she said. 'Tell her I'll be there as soon as I can.'

82. I Will Survive

Now that she had done what she'd come to do, Lisa decided it was time to leave the party. She couldn't bear the thought of sitting with Jamie and Andrew, talking with them as if nothing was wrong. Instead of heading back for the table, she made her way to the cloakroom.

She had pulled on her coat and was going through the hotel's revolving front door when she heard Patrick call her name. He was in the other half of the glass doorway, on his way in.

Lisa kept walking out into the drizzly night, her head down, heels clicking on the tarmac.

'Lisa!' Patrick called, once he had revolved out behind her. 'Wait!'

She stopped without turning. 'What are you doing here?' she said.

'I was hoping to find you. It was the only way I could get to see you.'

'Who's minding the boys?'

'They're with my mother.'

Lisa started walking again. 'Leave me alone, Patrick. I don't want to see you now. I don't want to talk to you.'

He ran in front of her and blocked the way, putting both of his hands on her shoulders. 'This is crazy, Lisa. You have to come home.'

'You came to force me to go back with you? Is that it?'

'It's not like that. I came to talk to you. I don't understand what's happening.'

Lisa let out an involuntary laugh, which sounded bitter. 'Look at us,' she said. 'We're pathetic.'

'We're not. We're just having a few problems, that's all.'

'Why did we have children in the first place? Neither of us was cut out to be a parent. I can't cope with them. You don't want to be there most of the time, palming them off on your mother at the first hint you might have to give them your undivided attention.'

'I do my best for you and the boys. You know I do.'

'You don't, Patrick. You tell yourself you do but, deep down, you know you do everything in your power to get away from us whenever you can so you can pretend you're still one of the lads.'

'I work my fucking arse off for this family. You don't know how hard it is.'

'When was the last time you sat down with your sons? When was the last time you played with Theo, or asked him how he was feeling? We have a five-year-old little boy with serious problems and he's getting worse every day and all you can think about is your next golf trip or your next Lions Club meeting.'

'That's not fair! At least I didn't walk out on him.'

Lisa wrenched her car keys from her pocket. 'I'm not coming home, Patrick,' she said.

The drizzle turned to heavy drops of rain as Lisa turned

the car's ignition on. The radio kicked into life, playing the unmistakable opening piano trill of Gloria Gaynor's 'I Will Survive'.

Patrick was standing where she'd left him, his arms by his sides, rain drenching his hair. Part of her couldn't help wanting to get back out of the car and run to him, to put her arms around him and comfort him. But that was the problem. She had loved him too much. She'd put him first in front of everyone. In front of the children. In front of herself.

Lisa put the car into gear and pulled away into the darkness.

83. The Black Stuff

When Saeed sauntered over to the table, Andrew lit up. He pushed his chair out and stood to greet him.

'Hello,' Saeed said. His eyes took in the whole room before finally alighting on Jamie. 'This is a very good party.'

'It's about as much fun as having your hands chopped off,' said Jamie. 'Which, I imagine, in your country is a regular occurrence.'

'Now, now, mister. That's a bit too much, don't you think?' said Andrew, giving Jamie a knock-it-off glare. 'Can I get you a drink, Saeed?'

'A pint of Guinness, please. The black stuff. Since I came to this country it is my favourite drink.'

'Pity you can't take it home with you,' Jamie muttered.

When Andrew was safely out of hearing, he leaned over the table, getting as close into Saeed's face as he could. 'You think you have one up on me, don't you?' he said. 'Playing your little game.'

'I don't know what game you're talking about. Andrew invited me to this party. I decided to come.'

Under the table, Jamie felt Saeed's leg press insistently against his and a surge of energy bolted towards his groin.

'I miss you,' Saeed said. His eyes were luxurious pools of warm liquid brown. 'I want to make love to you again.'

Jamie turned to look for Andrew. He was making his way back from the bar, Saeed's drink in hand. 'It wasn't love,' he said. 'It was sex.'

'You love Andrew. But you have this sex with me while he doesn't know. In my country that is not love. What we did is love.'

'In your country what we did gets you hanged.'

'Get that down you,' said Andrew, placing the pint of Guinness under Saeed's nose. 'It'll put hairs on your chest.'

'He already has plenty of hairs on his chest,' said Jamie. 'And on his arse. And there's a little fuzzy line just beneath his belly button.'

'What are you on about?' Andrew said, with a nervous laugh.

'You'd better sit down,' Jamie told him.

Andrew sat uncertainly. 'What is it?' he asked, his eyes wide.

'It's about Saeed and me ... We ...'

'Shut up!' Saeed spat. His eyes weren't brown pools any more, they were black and glittering.

'You and Saeed what?' Andrew said. The colour had drained from his face.

Jamie's throat constricted. Hurting Andrew was far worse than he had imagined it would be. But it had to be done. 'We've been having an affair.' Jamie stopped himself reaching out to take Andrew's hand.

Andrew looked from Jamie to Saeed and back again. 'Oh, Jesus,' he said.

'Don't listen to him, Andrew,' Saeed said, his voice wheedling. 'He's jealous because you like me.'

'I don't like you. Not in that way.' Andrew turned to Jamie. 'How long has it been going on?' he asked.

'Since January,' said Jamie, shame filling every inch of him. 'We met on Gaydar.'

Saeed was on his feet. 'Liar!' he shouted. 'I will bloody kill you!'

'Do whatever you want, Saeed. I don't care any more.'

Andrew had taken his glasses off and was rubbing his eyes with his fists, like a child in disbelief. 'You said yes when I asked you to marry me,' he said to Jamie. 'And all the time you were . . .'

He was interrupted by Saeed's fist, which flew past him and into the side of Jamie's face, knocking him off his chair. There was an audible gasp from the people at the next table.

'Get up!' Saeed roared. 'I won't kick a man who is on the floor.'

The ringing in Jamie's ears reminded him of the time he had been attacked on the street, the same night Saeed had first slapped him on the face during sex. Right now, in the middle of Katherine's heterofest, the big gay arrow was pointing down at him, its lightbulbs flashing neon. But he had only himself to blame.

'Right, you, come with us,' said one of the bouncers, who had appeared out of thin air. Saeed struggled a bit, but eventually allowed them to shoulder him out of the room, yelling as he went, 'I will bloody kill you! Kill you!'

Jamie pulled himself up off the floor and dusted himself down. Around him the party returned to stability as people almost instantly forgot what they had just witnessed, the DJ fast-tracking to Michael Jackson's 'Billie Jean' to keep them in the mood. Andrew was sitting with his elbow on the table, his forehead in his hand.

'I'm sorry,' Jamie said. 'For what it's worth.'

When Andrew looked up, his eyes were cold and his mouth was twisted. 'Why?' he said.

Jamie rubbed his jaw, where Saeed's knuckles had made their impact. 'I really don't know,' he answered.

84. Katherine's Choice

Katherine found Barry in the deserted hallway near the men's toilets, leaning against the wall with a glass of whiskey, his face obscured by a fire extinguisher. In profile she saw he'd developed a little belly.

'There you are,' she said. 'I've been looking for you everywhere.'

'Just taking a little a break, babes,' said Barry. He wrenched himself away from the wall, as if it was a mammoth effort, and downed the last of his whiskey. 'Time to do the speeches, yeah?'

Katherine supposed she should be sorry for him, but she wasn't. Instead what she felt verged on contempt.

'Barry,' she said. 'I know you lost your job. Lisa saw you in McDonald's at the Red Cow Junction.'

He bolted upright. 'That's bullshit! She's imagining things.'

'She said you've been there every day for the past month.'

'And what? You're taking anything that flake says seriously? She's a fucking fruitcake.'

'So, it's not true, then? You haven't lost your job? You haven't been pretending to go into the office every day?'

Barry looked away. 'I knew this party was a bad idea, the way you stress out over every little thing. Speeches and table plans and decorations. We should have gone away and had a quiet wedding, just the two of us.'

'You didn't answer my question. Did you lose your job or not?'

After a few seconds Barry said, 'It's just temporary. I'll be back on the horse before you know it.'

'Why didn't you tell me?'

Instead of answering, he raised his glass to his mouth and began to crunch one of the ice cubes.

'Were you going to wait until the wedding was over before you said anything?' said Katherine. 'Is that it?'

He finished chewing the ice and swallowed. 'Let's talk about this tomorrow. We'd better get back out there. People are waiting.'

'You know what the funny thing is?' said Katherine. 'If you'd been honest with me I would have gone ahead with the wedding. I would have married you.'

'I told you, babes. I'll be back in a job in no time. I've already got some interviews lined up.'

'If you hadn't been fired, would you have asked me to marry you?'

'Of course. I love you.'

'No, you don't. You just need me.'

'Look who's talking. Who needed who when you lost your job? Who ended up carrying you?'

'Are you for fucking *real*, Barry? You didn't give me one ounce of support. You washed your hands of me.'

'At least I don't go around whining all the time about not having work. Feeling sorry for myself.'

'No. Instead you live a lie right down to leaving the house every day in a goddamn suit and tie!'

He grabbed her wrist, his fingers pressing hard into the flesh. 'It's your fault I didn't say anything.'

'Stop, Barry. You're hurting me.'

'You want everything to be oh-so-fucking-perfect all the time. The perfect house, the perfect party, the perfect wedding, the perfect husband. Well, I'm not fucking perfect. I never will be.'

Fear surged through Katherine's body as she tried to wrestle her wrist away. 'I don't want perfection,' she said. 'I want a man who doesn't lie to me.'

His hand still crushing her wrist, Barry's face was in hers, nostrils flaring, eyes burning.

'Please, Barry,' Katherine breathed, her heart pounding. 'Let go of me.'

He blinked, the anger in his eyes abating, and released her arm. 'I'm sorry,' he said. 'I don't know what I'm doing.'

Katherine rubbed her wrist. 'You knew what you were doing when you lied to me,' she said, trying to compose herself.

'I was too scared to tell you.'

Katherine gave him a dubious look. The Barry she knew had never said he was scared of anything.

'I didn't want to lie to you,' he went on. 'But after the way I treated you, I thought I didn't have the right to ask for your support. It's been the worst month of my life.'

Her wrist was still smarting as she tried to take this in. He'd been lying flat out to her for a month? Surely he didn't think she'd marry him now.

'I don't think we can go ahead with the wedding,' she said. 'I don't think I can trust you.'

Without warning Barry rounded on her again, pushing her against the wall. 'For Christ's sake, stop whining, will you?' he said, in a low voice. 'We're going out there right now and we're announcing our engagement. You'll smile and you'll act like everything is just fine. You'll do what you're told, understand?'

'What's going on?' said Martin.

Katherine didn't know how long he'd been standing there, but she'd never been more glad to see him.

Barry immediately pulled away and straightened. 'Why don't you get lost and mind your own business, buddy?' he said to Martin.

'No,' said Martin. 'Why don't you get lost? Buddy.' He grabbed Katherine's hand and pulled her towards the fire exit at the end of the corridor.

'I can't go,' she said. 'What about all the guests?'

'They're grown-ups. They can take care of themselves.'

'Where the fuck do you think you're going?' Barry shouted, as Martin pushed the bar to open the emergency door.

Katherine stopped in her tracks. She had a choice. She could go back to party, pretending that everything was great with Barry and her. Or she could follow Martin out into the driving rain without even a coat to cover her dress.

'Are you coming or not?' said Martin.

'Yes,' she said, and they ran without looking back.

November

Brokeback Mountain
Ang Lee, 2005

'Tell you what, we could have
had a good life together!
Fuckin' real good life!'

85. An Out-of-body Experience

When she woke to the sudden noise of a truck blowing its horn, Katherine struggled to remember where she was. Then she saw Martin sleeping soundly beside her, his mouth slightly open, and it all came flooding back.

She sat up and gingerly put her legs over the side of the bed, realising she was completely naked. An orange and black T-shirt that Martin had given her to sleep in lay discarded on the carpet, its Chicago Bears logo half visible in the curtained-off light.

Somewhere in the night it had come off. She had been fast asleep and woken up kissing him, segueing from sleep to sex as easily as if it was something she had been doing with him for ever.

Katherine had found herself going with the flow, despite her reservations about his stubble scratching her face. Martin's mission was not self-fulfilment, but neither was it all about taking care of her every need. He'd struck a balance between the two: he was greedy and giving at exactly the same time.

Still half in Dreamland, Katherine felt his fingers between her thighs and her breath jagged. Her hand automatically reached out to guide him closer, but he held his distance, sucking air in as he watched her enjoy what he was doing before finally moving across her to home in on the tip of her nipple with his tongue. Its motion sent pulses like tiny shocks to every extremity of her body.

There was a moment, just before she came, when everything became suspended in time. The insistent rhythm of his pelvis against hers halted and their faces were jammed so close together she was looking straight into the pupils of his eyes. She had a weird sensation of having left her own body and entered his, feeling his blood rush through her veins and then, as it seemed to pump straight to her heart, she threw back her head and shouted his name: 'Martin!'

'Katherine,' he whispered, and the feeling she had was so powerful that she closed her eyes to bring herself back to reality.

When Martin came, he didn't make a sound, his face screwed up, his arms wrapped so tightly around her it was as if he was clinging to her for dear life. Then, while he was still inside her, he began to cry.

She stroked the back of his head, whispering, 'Sssh.' As she did so, she recalled having heard that the 'sssh' sound replicated the noise an unborn baby heard in its mother's womb, the sound of life flowing through veins.

'I'm sorry.' Martin's muffled voice came from her hair, where his head was buried.

'It's okay,' said Katherine.

'It's the release, that's all.'

'I know.'

They didn't say another word to each other, Martin's breathing eventually turning into little snores against the back of her neck, his body spooned with hers under the duvet. She couldn't remember at what point they'd separated.

Katherine stood up and put the T-shirt back on. It was about five sizes too big so it covered her like a nightdress, which she felt grateful for. On tiptoe, trying not to make a sound, she moved across the room, turning to check if he was still sleeping before opening the door. He was out cold.

In the bathroom she looked at herself in the mirror above the sink. She had panda eyes and her chin was so reddened with beard rash it was difficult to tell where her lips began.

'What the hell are you doing?' she said to herself, rubbing at the mascara stains with a piece of wet toilet paper. 'Stupid, stupid, stupid.'

Her mouth tasted sour, as if she'd been drinking all night, but she'd only had two gin and tonics.

She snuck back into the bedroom where she had spied her handbag atop a bundle of clothes on a chair. At least she had some makeup with her and a comb. On the way back to the bathroom she quietly picked up her dress, bra, tights and knickers, which were strewn in a path to the bed.

She showered and dried herself off, trying not to wonder how often the only towel she could find might have been used before. She ran the comb through her hair as best she could and tied it back tightly with a scrunchie she found at the bottom of her bag, before putting her underwear and tights back on and reaching awkwardly behind to zip up her dress.

Rubbing a clear patch in the steamed-up mirror, Katherine applied her makeup. It was only then that she began to allow herself to think about what she had done.

The party came back to her in snatches. Laughing with Marissa and Jean ... Sitting with Lucy, Paolo and the girls ... Fighting with Barry ... Sneaking out of the emergency exit...

She stopped and searched her shame-filled eyes in the mirror.

Sweet Jesus. On the night of her own engagement party, she'd ended up sleeping with another man. It was a new low in anyone's book. How could she have done it? Barry had probably tried to keep up appearances when he went back to the party, but one thing was for sure: by now everyone knew she'd run away. She imagined the rumours racing through the party like wildfire, from whisper to shocked whisper. The thought of it made her feel queasy.

Katherine took a breath and told herself to calm down. But she was flung back to the moment she'd run out of the hotel's back door with Martin, not even caring about the carnage and confusion she left behind, and then her memory jumped forward to what had happened in bed with him. She had never lost control like that with Barry, never shouted out his name. She pictured herself, sweat-soaked and panting, and she was filled with self-disgust. She had been like an animal.

Trying not to give in to the panic that was rising in her chest, she smudged a bit of colour across her eyelids, not caring what eye-shadow she was using.

The bathroom door opened.

'You're all dressed,' said Martin, materialising bare-chested in the mirror behind her.

'Martin!' she said, fixing a smile into place while trying to push away the animalistic image of herself with him. 'Good morning.'

Martin put his arms around her from behind and she caught a whiff of his morning breath. 'Take off those clothes and come back to bed,' he mumbled.

'No. I've got to go.' She extracted herself from his arms and began to put her things back into her make1up bag.

'What's the hurry? It's Sunday. A day of rest.'

'No rest for the wicked,' she said, turning to face him, her smile still in place. 'Listen, about last night . . .'

'It was unbelievable.'

'I don't know what I was doing.'

'Come back to bed and I'll remind you.'

'Look, Martin, I want to thank you for taking care of me. But I feel awful. It wasn't supposed to turn out like it did.'

'There's nothing to feel bad about. I feel great.'

His stubble looked like it had grown a full inch overnight, there was sleep in the corners of his eyes and his hair was standing on end.

'You don't understand,' she said. 'I had a nice time, but it can't happen again.'

Martin took a step back. 'Why not?' he asked.

'Because it was a mistake. The whole thing, running away like that, doing what we did … I shouldn't have done it. It was totally irresponsible.'

'Nobody in the world would blame you for doing it.'

'It was my engagement party, Martin, for crying out loud. I'm supposed to be getting married!'

'But people will understand when you tell them why you left.'

'It's not as simple as that,' Katherine said, putting her makeup back into her handbag and zipping it closed. She turned back to him. 'Look, Barry left me high and dry when I needed him most. And it was hard, but we got through it and we learned from it. And what have I just done to him? The exact same thing.'

Martin's cheeks fired up. 'What do you mean "the exact same thing"?' he said. 'It couldn't be more different. Fuck it, Katherine, can't you see the guy for what he is? Can't you see how he wraps you around his little finger? You of all people!'

Katherine sighed. 'It's complicated, Martin. I don't expect you to understand. And I never meant for you to get caught in the crossfire. Never.' She looked at him apologetically, but he was shaking his head, his mouth all twisted.

'Katherine, I'm crazy about you, and I'm not afraid to say it. I want to be with you more than anything. But I must be some fool – every time I think we have a chance, you throw it back in my face. And I don't know why I keep coming back for more. Christ knows, I've told myself to forget about you enough times. But then this happens and ... I know you feel it too, Katherine. I know I'm not dreaming about what happened last night. But somehow it's never good enough, is it? I'm never good enough for you.'

'That's not true.'

'It is true, and you know it. Well, you can freeze me out all you like, Katherine, but you're not going to play me for a fool again.'

There it was again, the freeze-word. She remembered Barry with his proposal, telling her how she had frozen him out, and Lucy using it as she blamed her for walking away when they were children, never understanding why she'd had to go.

She put her bag over her shoulder. 'I'm sorry, Martin,' she

said. 'I never meant to hurt you. Or freeze you out or play you for a fool. I know you're not a fool. But my life is one big fat mess right now. And instead of facing up to the right thing to do, I've just gone and done the complete opposite. I'm sorry, but what happened last night was a mistake. And I understand you're angry, and you have every right to be but—'

'Katherine,' Martin interrupted.

'Yes.'

'Get over yourself. And get the hell out of my flat.'

She stopped, opened her mouth to protest once more, then shut it and walked away.

86. A Rose Is a Rose

The night before she died, Celia regained consciousness, albeit briefly. Her eyelids fluttered and an unidentifiable word came out of her mouth.

'What is it, Aunt Celia?' Claire said, pulling herself up from her chair and bending over the head of the bed. Alice didn't say anything, her hands gripping the wooden armrests of her own chair on the other side of the bed, forcing herself not to jump up too. It had been like that all week, holding back every time they thought there might be a hint of life, discreetly leaving the room when the doctors came in to talk to the family, keeping herself to herself as much as she could, pretending for all she was worth that she wasn't one of them.

At the beginning they'd told her to go home. They'd let her know if there was any change, they said. She should get some rest. But Alice smiled, said little and refused to budge. She might have to pretend she wasn't who she was, but in the little time she had left with her mother, she wanted to be there every minute, night and day.

'Rose,' she heard Celia say, and Claire turned to look at her in confusion.

Alice went to the side of the bed and looked into her mother's pale, watery eyes. 'What is it?' she asked, touching one of the liver-spotted hands that rested on top of the sheet.

Celia struggled to lift her head.

'Don't, Aunt Celia,' Claire said. 'You need to rest. I'll ring for the nurse.'

'No,' Celia said, her eyes searching out Alice's again. A tiny tear rolled down the side of her face.

'Claire's right,' said Alice. 'You need to rest.'

'Rose,' Celia said.

'Sssh now, it's okay.'

The words came slowly, punctuated with laboured breaths. 'You were always with me.'

'This is Alice, Aunt Celia,' said Claire. 'You remember Alice.'

'No,' Celia said, and she tried to smile at Alice. 'Rose.'

Somehow Alice had known all along. She was never the girl she had been named on that birth certificate. She was someone else.

'Rose,' she repeated to her mother, the woman who had given birth to her, and it sounded right.

'I should ring for someone,' said Claire, but she didn't move.

Alice reached over the bed and touched her arm. 'I don't think she needs a nurse,' she said.

For a minute that seemed at once like an eternity and gone faster than the speed of light, Celia gazed at Alice, her breathing shallow.

Alice wanted to say, 'I love you,' but she couldn't. Not in front of Claire. So she hoped her eyes were saying it, over and over again, until Celia's closed and her breathing returned to normal.

The next morning, the hospital called the family in. Celia's two sisters and their husbands, her three nephews and four nieces.

'I'm sorry, but this is a time for family only,' the ward sister said, gently steering Alice from the room.

Alice looked back at her mother for the last time, glimpsing her partly obscured face through the clutch of people huddled around the bed.

Claire turned to smile at her, but it wasn't really a smile. It was a warning look, telling Alice to stay away.

For a split second, Alice imagined rushing to the bed, pushing them all aside and gathering her mother into her arms. But then she let the door swing closed. She made her way down the hospital's deserted corridor, her footsteps echoing off its pristine walls.

It wasn't fair. It was her right to be with her mother. She'd been denied her mother from birth and now she would be denied her mother's dying moment.

Alice turned and walked purposefully back up the corridor. Reaching her mother's room she hesitated, her hand on the door handle.

Celia's voice whispered in her head: 'Please don't ever tell, Alice. Not even after I'm six feet under.'

Alice's hand fell to her side. Who was she to deny Celia her dying wish?

The church was full of people who had known Celia far better than Alice ever had, many of them actual former students. A group of them read prayers, queuing up on the altar when the time came. On the way in, Claire had cornered her and asked her to say a prayer too, but Alice had shaken her head. 'I'm not a Catholic,' she said. 'I don't think it would be right.'

'Are you sure? Aunt Celia would have wanted it.'

'No. I'd prefer not to.'

'I understand,' said Claire, and she touched Alice's wrist. 'We'll see you later, I hope, at the lunch.'

'Yes,' said Alice, although the thought of going was unbearable. 'I'll be there.'

She sat at the back of the church through the service, hidden by rows of people, listening to the coughs and sobs that punctuated the priest's solemn eulogy. So many people to mourn Celia Deasy. Alice Little was just one more.

She waited as the family filed out behind the coffin, their heads bent in grief, arms wrapped around each other. She stayed sitting in her pew while the church emptied after them, smiles of recognition being exchanged, conversations sparking up, heads nodding, hands being taken and shaken. And then, when she was sure there was no one left, she knelt down, put her face in her hands and wept.

87. Off the Wagon

The whiskey burned his lips and tongue, its sweet malt fumes hitting the back of his throat, the alcohol instantly entering his bloodstream. Martin downed the rest of the glass in one and ordered another, with a pint of Carlsberg on the side.

If he was going to fall off the wagon, he might as well do it properly.

'No half measures,' he said, raising his glass to a man who was quietly reading the *Irish Times* at the other end of the bar. The man raised his pint of Guinness uncertainly in return, then went back to his paper.

'You're Tom Brady's son, aren't you?' the barman said, handing over Martin's drinks.

'That's me,' Martin replied.

'You're the spitting image of him, God rest his soul. There was never a man more missed.'

Savouring the second whiskey rather than bolting it, Martin tried to imagine his father as a man who was missed by anyone. Even his mother seemed happier now that the old man was gone. A few weeks ago, she'd gone blonde and told Martin she was joining a bridge club that met twice a week in the Gresham Hotel. There was a light in her eyes he didn't remember seeing before, not even when he was a child.

'A good man, he was,' the barman said. 'The salt of the earth.'

'Are we talking about the same man?' asked Martin. 'Tom Brady, the complete cunt?'

The barman's mouth dropped open. His eyebrows shot up and then his pudgy face shut down. 'Shame on you, speaking of the dead like that,' he said, walking away. 'And him your father and all.'

Martin started into the pint, drinking a quarter of it in one go. It didn't taste as good as he remembered, but the feeling of drifting out on its waves was good.

He'd given up the alcohol, he'd done everything he could possibly think of doing for her, yet she'd still shat all over him, leading him on and then pushing him away whenever she felt like it. She played him like a virtuoso, and he fell for it every time.

Well, no more. He was his own man, not a plaything for a stupid woman who couldn't make up her mind. An image of himself following on her heels, tongue out like a slavering puppy's, came into his mind and Martin lifted the glass to his mouth to down the rest of the pint.

'Barman, another pint of your finest,' he called, his glass raised in the air. The barman scowled at him and put a fresh glass under the tap.

It was midnight before Martin fell in through the front door of his building. He'd had trouble finding the main key and was now fumbling for the one to his apartment door.

None of them worked. He knew the right one was on the key-ring – of course it was – but no matter what he did, he couldn't get a fit for the lock. After trying for about ten minutes, he eventually got in.

A letter was waiting on the hallway floor for him, its white-windowed front looking all official. Martin fell against the wall, hitting his forehead as he stooped to pick it up.

A cup of coffee. That was what he needed to sober him up a bit.

In the kitchen, as the kettle crawled towards a boil, he slumped down at the table and opened the envelope. It was from Médecins Sans Frontières.

With great difficulty focusing, he read: 'We are pleased to inform you that you have been accepted into the Médecins Sans Frontières programme. A two-week training period will commence on 23 November at the Institute Goethe in Berlin, Germany. You will be posted to your first assignment on 20 December.'

'Fuck,' Martin said, as the urge to vomit swept through him. He retched over the kitchen sink, but nothing would come up. His tongue felt like sandpaper and his eyes were dripping salty, stinging tears. 'Fuck.'

He slid down the wall and sat on the floor, waiting for the nausea to subside.

When it did, he tried to put a fresh cigarette in his mouth, but his hand was jumping so much, it was near impossible. Steadying one with the other, he managed to light it, but instead of deriving comfort from the first drag, his mind filled with the memory of his father on his deathbed, grey-faced and rubber-lipped, his eyes staring at Martin, not leaving his face as he drew his dying breaths.

'Dad?' he heard himself call into the silence of the kitchen, then a rushing feeling came up from his stomach, taking over his whole body, filling his head with needle-sharp pain. He leaned to one side and vomited what seemed like an ocean of watery puke.

He didn't know how long he lay there before he woke up, jolting his head back so that it smacked the wall behind him. The smell of vomit was overpowering and his brain felt as if it was going to split in two.

He stumbled to his feet and lurched to the sink to pour himself a glass of water. Drinking it in big, greedy gulps he noticed his wallet on the kitchen counter. It was lying open and a card was poking out. The one on which he'd written the number of the guy he'd met at the AA meeting.

'Call me anytime,' the man had said. 'It doesn't matter what time of the day or night.'

The clock above the kitchen door read 2:10 a.m.

It was far too late.

But if Martin didn't ring now he might never do it. And if he never rang, what would happen to him? He'd die unloved and unwanted, like his father had.

Martin managed to get his mobile phone out of his jeans pocket. Slowly and deliberately, he dialled the number on the card.

88. No Goodbyes

It was hard to imagine how all of Jamie's family, his seven siblings and his parents, had ever fitted into the sitting room of their house. It was about half the size of the extension Katherine had put on to her kitchen, with seating for five at a push and all the available wall space taken up with framed family snaps. Jamie's parents, his brothers and sisters, nieces and nephews, aunts and uncles, and some black-and-white shots of a couple Katherine took to be his grandparents. On the mantelpiece above a blazing fire that brought her out in a sweat the minute she walked in was Jamie's First Holy Communion photo, complete with the white rosette on his blazer lapel. The same eyes stared out from behind a flopped-over fringe, half smiling, half wary, and the same full lips framed a gap-toothed say-cheese smile.

'Sit down, sit down,' said Jamie's mother, rubbing her redraw hands on an apron that said, '60 And Still Cookin''. 'You must be perished, you poor love. Take the seat near the fire.'

'For Jaysus' sake, Ma, will you stop fussing?' said Jamie. His accent had taken on a guttural Dublin twang. Katherine had noticed it when he called last week and told her the location for his Film Club night had changed, that he'd explain when he saw her.

He hadn't offered any explanation yet.

'Well, I'll just go into the kitchen, then,' said his mother. 'Shout if you need anything.' To Jamie she said, under her breath but not low enough so she couldn't be heard, 'Come and help me with the food when the rest of them arrive.'

'Sorry about that,' Jamie said, once she was out of earshot. 'She's not used to me bringing visitors home.'

'She's lovely,' Katherine said. 'And the house is really cute.'

Jamie sat down opposite her and poked the fire, releasing another blast of heat into the room. He was uncharacteristically quiet for a moment, then said, 'Andrew and I have split up. That's why we're doing Film Club here.'

'Oh, Jamie, I'm really sorry,' Katherine said. 'I always thought you two were solid as a rock.'

'Yeah, well, appearances can be deceiving.'

'If you ever need any company, you can always call me, you know. We could go out for a drink.'

Jamie laughed. 'Lock up your sons! Two fresh singletons out on the town!'

Katherine was confused for a moment, but then she realised she hadn't seen Jamie since the party. 'Barry and I are still together,' she said.

'But you walked out on your engagement?'

'I know.' Katherine groaned. 'It kind of happened spontaneously. Too much drink, I think. I'm totally embarrassed to tell the truth.'

'Don't be,' said Jamie. 'There are worse things you could do.'

So, everything's back on track for the big fat straight wedding, then?'

Katherine wanted to take her sweater off. It was really too hot. She nodded, although the wedding hadn't once been mentioned since she'd gone home the day after the party. In the intervening weeks Barry had given up all pretence of working – he was snoring in bed when she went out in the mornings and watching TV in his dressing-gown on the sofa when she came home. Late into the night, as Katherine lay wakeful in their bed, he played downstairs on his Xbox, which at least he'd had the get-up-and-go to repair, having pronounced the thing dead more than a year ago.

Once she had woken up in the middle of the night to find Barry standing silently in his underwear in the middle of their bedroom, silhouetted from behind by the landing light.

'Come to bed,' she'd said, and he'd stood there for another minute saying nothing before getting in beside her. She'd put her arms around him from behind, spooning against his body and whispering that everything would be all right, but he hadn't responded. Eventually, he'd fallen asleep and Katherine's arm had got pins and needles under his weight.

He was depressed. And no wonder. Barry had been defined by his success, by his upward trajectory. Now he had no direction but down. She encouraged him to look for a job, but they both knew there was nothing out there at his level. And although he didn't say it, she knew Barry couldn't countenance the idea of working at something beneath him.

'I'll keep the hat I bought, so,' Jamie deadpanned, bringing her thoughts back into the room. 'Just don't be doing a runner at your wedding too. I don't think I could take the disappointment twice.'

Katherine smiled and nodded. She was relieved to hear a knock at the front door. It was probably one of the others, and she didn't want to sit here with Jamie, talking about a wedding she couldn't imagine Barry being able to leave the sofa for.

Ushered in by Jamie's mother, Lisa made her entrance.

'Look at you!' Jamie exclaimed. 'Are you actually the same person?'

Lisa had cut her hair tight into her head, dyed it blonde and peppered it with copper and gold highlights. The effect, along with her dark lipstick and smoky eyeshadow, was startling. She looked a good five years younger, even with her protruding belly in its tight black wrap-top.

'It's me all right,' she laughed, 'only slightly modified.'

'You look amazing,' said Katherine. 'Who did your hair?'

'Sebastian at Chez Cuts on Wicklow Street. I'm officially his number-one fan.'

'Is he good-looking? Single? Loaded?' asked Jamie.

'Not your type. And, anyway, you need to take a breather. You can't just hop from relationship to relationship like some sort of emotional hooligan.'

'Who says I can't?'

None of them noticed Alice arrive until she coughed to announce her presence. 'Your hair's nice,' she said to Lisa, taking her coat off.

As much as Lisa had given herself a makeover, Alice seemed to have regressed in the sartorial stakes. Since her birth mother had died, she'd gone back to her workaday uniform, the grey skirt, the blue cardigan. The pallor was back too, along with the monosyllabic answers.

'Well, that's everyone present and accounted for,' said Jamie. 'I'll just help my mother with the food and then we'll put the film on.'

'What about Martin?' asked Katherine. 'You know how he'll be if we start without him.'

'Did you not hear?' said Jamie, looking at her in surprise.

'Hear what?'

'He's gone to Germany to train with MSF. They're posting him to Chad in a month's time.'

'I've heard it's really dangerous out there,' said Lisa. 'I hope he'll be all right.'

Alice nodded sagely and Katherine looked from her to Jamie to Lisa. How did they all know about it and she didn't? He hadn't even called to say goodbye.

89. On Brokeback Mountain

'Poor Heath Ledger,' Lisa said, the minute Jamie announced he was showing *Brokeback Mountain*, as he had known she would. 'He was so young and so talented.'

'Is he dead?' asked Alice, with equal predictability.

The night Jamie had first seen *Brokeback Mountain*, he'd come out of the cinema making Andrew laugh at his Heath Ledger as Ennis Del Mar take-off, a kind of tight-lipped, half-delivered mumble designed to suggest crippling emotional repression. It was a relief to send the film up, having sat watching it in a cinema full of gay men who had all paid top dollar for the special preview screening.

Although plenty of sniffles could be heard throughout the movie, the atmosphere that had built up was like a pressure cooker. The film had ended with the entire cinema in choked silence, people filing out without saying a word to each other as the credits rolled.

Andrew had argued that the film's ending, with Ennis Del Mar crying over the loss of his lover, Jack Twist, had been the most difficult part to watch, but Jamie wasn't sure. His own pressure-cooker moment had come much earlier when the two men first had sex in their tent on the mountain. Jamie couldn't fully put his finger on his emotional reaction to the moment, but he'd known that everyone in the auditorium was feeling the same weird way. It was like three hundred people were holding their breath in unison.

'I've never seen it,' said Katherine, as Jamie loaded up the DVD. 'Barry and I kept meaning to go when it was in the cinema, but we never got around to it.'

'Same with me and Patrick,' said Lisa.

Jamie was glad he hadn't gone with *Billy Elliot*, his original choice for tonight. The straights never got around to seeing *Brokeback Mountain*.

'What's it about?' asked Alice, scrutinising the front of the DVD box. 'Is it a cowboy film?'

'You could say that,' said Jamie, and pressed play.

The room was deathly quiet throughout the film, no one saying a word except Lisa, who repeated, 'Poor Heath Ledger,' about twenty times until Jamie told her to shut up.

'Yeah, we know, it's an awful waste, but if Heath's looking down, I don't think he's too happy with you interrupting his performance every two minutes,' he said.

Alice kept shifting in her seat, crossing one leg over the other and back again, and at the end, when Lisa and Katherine were wiping away tears, she sat stoically, her lips pursed.

'It's just so sad.' Lisa sighed. 'Why couldn't they have ended up together?'

'Because Hollywood never allows gay characters a happy ending,' said Jamie. 'One of them always has to die, unless he's a screaming drag queen. And even then he never gets the guy.'

'I think you're being simplistic,' said Katherine. 'It's a film about being gay at a time when it wasn't as accepted as it is today. If it were set in modern times, there'd be no story. They'd have bought a ranch together and settled down in the first half-hour.'

'You don't think it's like that for gay people nowadays in redneck country?'

'Maybe you're right, but the film is set in the 1950s, isn't it?'

'I don't know,' said Lisa. 'It looks old-fashioned and modern at the same time, so you can't really tell.'

'I'm not sure,' Alice piped up. 'I didn't really believe in it.'

'Believe in what?' asked Jamie.

'The love story. It didn't seem real to me.'

'I thought it was beautifully done,' said Katherine.

'Like *Romeo and Juliet*,' said Lisa.

'But Romeo and Juliet weren't two men,' said Alice. 'To be honest, the sex in it made me feel a bit sick.'

Jamie couldn't believe his ears. 'It's interesting,' he said, 'that you felt sick when two men were having sex, but when Jack was beaten to death for being gay you thought it was perfectly acceptable.'

'I didn't say that.'

'No, you didn't. But what you're telling us is that you find the idea of gay sex distasteful and would rather not have to watch it. I have to watch heterosexuals get it on every day of my life, in nearly every film and television programme ever made, in almost every film we've watched in this club. You don't hear me complaining, do you?'

'Yes, but heterosexual sex is . . . well . . .'

'Go on, say it.'

'Natural.'

Jamie jumped to his feet, alive with rage. 'I think you should leave,' he said.

Katherine stood up too. 'Relax, Jamie, Alice doesn't mean it.'

'She means it. And she's perfectly entitled to her thick, bigoted opinions. But not in my house. I'm going upstairs and when I come down she'd better be gone.'

90. Catching Up

Alice stood outside the bathroom, her foot creaking on a loose floorboard under the wine-coloured carpet every time she shifted her weight. Through the door she could hear Jamie softly repeating the word 'no' to himself. She wanted the ground to swallow her.

'Jamie?' she said, with a gentle tap on the door.

'Go away.'

'I'm sorry, Jamie. I didn't mean to upset you.'

'Please, just go away.'

Alice turned to go back downstairs, but then stopped. She had to put it right. All these months of making new friends would come to nothing because of this. Both Lisa and Katherine had gaped at her with disapproving faces, then insisted she go upstairs after Jamie and apologise.

'I'm not like other people,' she said, through the door. 'I don't get things the way you do, or Katherine, or Lisa. It takes me longer.'

'How long did it take you to realise you hate gay people?'

'I don't hate gay people. I swear I don't.'

Alice waited for a reply, but nothing came. 'Jamie?' she said. 'Can I come in?'

There was a shuffle behind the door and Alice heard the latch slide open. She found him sitting on the floor with his back to the bath, his eyes red-rimmed, a towel bundled in his lap.

Alice sat on the edge of the bath, careful not to let her leg touch his arm, and took a breath. 'I was brought up in a very religious family,' she began. 'Mother always told me that homosexuality was a sin. An abomination, she called it. Evil.'

'That's me,' said Jamie. 'Evil.'

'No, you're not. You're a bit sarcastic sometimes, but I like you. I really do. And I know Mother was wrong. I just have to catch up.'

Jamie lifted the towel and used it to blow his nose, a big tear-stained honk that, for some reason, made Alice want to giggle. Instead she said nothing and concentrated on the wall they were facing, which was papered with a pattern of swimming goldfish. Eventually Jamie spoke.

'I miss Andrew so much,' he said.

'Has he gone somewhere?' Alice asked.

'We've split up. Didn't the other two tell you?'

'No.' Alice got down on the bathmat beside him. 'What happened?'

'It's a long story and I don't want to tell it,' said Jamie.

'That's fine. You don't have to.'

After a bit, Jamie said, 'We went to see *Brokeback Mountain* together, when it was first out. I remember we had an argument afterwards about what the saddest part was.'

'What was the saddest part for you?' Alice asked.

'The bit where they have sex the first time. It's so awful, like they're doing something that disgusts them but they can't help themselves.'

'And Andrew's saddest bit?'

'The bit at the end, where Ennis finds himself alone because he couldn't be true to himself.'

'I thought the most heartbreaking bit was when they kissed for the first time,' said Alice. 'It was so romantic, but it wasn't like any other kiss we've seen in any of the films. There was something really sad about it as well.'

Jamie turned to her, his chin bunched up. 'They love each other and they hate themselves for it.'

'Is that why you and Andrew split up? Because you're like the two men in the film?'

Jamie pulled back and his face went hard again. 'No,' he said. 'Of course not.'

'Sorry,' said Alice, kicking herself for putting her foot in it again. 'I thought that's what you were trying to tell me.'

'Well, it wasn't, okay?'

'Sorry,' Alice repeated. After a second she realised Jamie was studying her.

'Look at us,' he said. 'Having a heavy, deep and real.'

'I'm not sure what that is.'

'For someone who doesn't, you're very good at it. We'd better go downstairs or the others will think I've murdered you.'

He pulled himself up with the edge of the bath and Alice followed suit.

'"Once more into the breach,"' he said.

'Jamie? Can I give you a hug?'

'Only if you're paying.'

Alice stood still, serious and resolute.

'I suppose so.'

She put her two arms around him and squeezed, feeling his body go a little limp against hers. 'I'm sorry,' she whispered.

'I know.'

Alice couldn't quite believe she was hugging Jamie, of all people.

'Enough already,' he said, after a minute. 'Next thing you'll be having my babies.'

'In your dreams.'

'Alice! I think you're catching up after all.'

91. The Good Memories Only

As had become the routine, Katherine dropped Alice off in a cab before going on to her own house, even though she was still annoyed. Alice had behaved abominably to Jamie, spouting her anti-gay views. It was absolutely unacceptable to say things like that.

Katherine felt like reminding her about it when the taxi pulled up outside Alice's house, but Alice got out of the car, flashing a big smile as she leaned in to say goodbye. She'd perked up plenty, considering her dour state when she'd arrived at Jamie's. And Jamie seemed to have forgiven her, so Katherine decided to let it rest.

The taxi pulled off again, its tyres swishing on the wet road. There had been a change in the air today, that almost imperceptible shift from autumn to winter. A slight chill, the light paler. To think, it was almost a year since Martin had come up with the idea for Film Club. He'd practically forced Katherine to be part of it and now he'd bowed out without so much as a goodbye.

Not that Katherine could blame him.

All through *Brokeback Mountain*, she'd kept expecting him to appear, as if he was just coming back from having a smoke, with some piece of information nobody knew about Heath Ledger or Jake Gyllenhaal. She even missed the burnt-tobacco smell he always brought with him.

Later, after Alice had insulted Jamie and followed him upstairs to apologise, she'd found herself telling Lisa she missed him.

'Me too,' said Lisa. 'It's not the same without him.'

'Do you mind if I ask you a personal question?'

'Of course. Go ahead.'

'Do you love Patrick? The way the guys loved each other in that film?'

Lisa replied without having to think about it: 'Yes, I do. I'm not saying it's perfect all the time, far from it, but there's a sort of chemical connection, like we were designed to be together. Maybe that's why we keep having bloody kids.'

'Barry and me … We were never the we-were-meant-to-be-together type. I've always thought we were just suited to each other.'

'Maybe they're the same thing, being meant to be together and suiting each other,' Lisa said.

'You could be right,' Katherine agreed.

Lisa had given a sad smile. 'The most heartbreaking thing about the film was that Ennis had that connection with Jack but he denied it to himself because he thought it was the wrong thing for him when it was the only right thing.'

'And he ended up alone,' said Katherine.

'What's your house number?' the taxi driver asked, interrupting her thoughts, and suddenly Katherine couldn't bear the idea of going home. Barry would be waiting for her, sitting in his T-shirt and boxer shorts in front of the television, the way she had left him.

'Can you take me somewhere else?' she asked, thinking quickly before giving Lucy's address.

Lucy answered the door in her dressing-gown.

'Sorry for waking you,' Katherine whispered. 'I didn't want to go home. I'm sorry.'

'That's okay,' said Lucy, quietly closing the door behind her. 'I couldn't sleep anyway.'

'You go back to bed. I can sleep on the bed-settee.'

'No. I'll make a cup of tea. Do you want one?'

'I'd love one,' said Katherine, and as she followed Lucy into the kitchen she felt a sudden swell of gratitude. Despite their difficulties, despite the fact that she had walked out on Lucy – it was true – her sister had always been there for her. Katherine hadn't recognised it until this moment.

'How come you manage everything so well?' she asked, as Lucy filled the kettle.

Lucy snorted. 'What are you talking about? I'm a complete mess. No job, two kids, living in this dump.'

'It's not a dump. You've made it lovely. And you're such a great mother, and Paolo loves you so much. I always thought I was the one who held it together after Dad left, but it was you. I completely fell apart.'

Lucy sat down at the table. 'I fell apart too,' she said. 'Just in a different way. Remember what I was like as a teenager?'

'Wild,' said Katherine, smiling in reminiscence.

'Out of control,' said Lucy. 'Seventeen and up the pole.'

'A poet and you didn't even know it!' said Katherine, and they both laughed.

When they were settled on the bed-settee with mugs of tea, Lucy said, 'Maybe I didn't blame myself for Dad going the way you did. I was too young, I think.'

Katherine winced. She remembered Lucy following her home from school the day she'd kicked Sister Aloysius's shin. Telling Lucy their father wouldn't have liked the way she was behaving. Watching Lucy's little figure recede into the distance through the back window of the bus as it took her away to boarding school.

'There aren't words to tell you how sorry I am,' she said. 'I let you down so badly. Mum couldn't take care of you. I knew that.'

Lucy reached across the sofa and took her hand. 'You did the only thing you could possibly do,' she said. 'I knew that, even back then.'

'I'm so sorry,' Katherine repeated. She had begun to cry.

'I know,' said Lucy. She was crying too.

They talked until morning, revisiting memories from their childhood, laughing about the toilet-paper dresses they'd made for the Sindy doll, and Lucy kicking Sister Aloysius, who had most definitely deserved it. They told each other their happy memories of their father, the ones they had held on to after he'd gone without being able to share them. It was like an unspoken agreement between them not to talk about the bad times.

Just as the sun was beginning to rise, Katherine said, 'Have you ever seen *Brokeback Mountain*?'

'Yes,' said Lucy. 'It was on telly last week. Why?'

'We watched it at Film Club tonight. That's why I came here. I was too upset after it to go home.'

'It's pretty depressing.'

'There's a guy in Film Club, Martin ...'

Lucy nodded. 'The girls were going on about him. Kitty said he's gorgeous.'

'I've treated him like shit. I don't think he'll ever forgive me.'

'It can't be that bad.'

'It is, and I feel awful about it.'

Lucy put her feet up on the sofa and hugged her knees in tight to her chest. 'Sounds to me like you have feelings for him,' she said.

'Does it? No, I just wish I'd done things differently. I made such a fuck-up of that stupid engagement party. That's how everything went pear-shaped.'

'But you're back with Barry. That's what you want, isn't it?'

'Yes. It is. I just wish … I just wish I could turn back time, you know? So I could do things differently.'

Lucy stretched out her foot and rubbed Katherine's thigh with it understandingly. A question appeared in Katherine's mind. If she could turn back time, would she go back to before she had ever slept with Martin or to the morning after?

92. Facing Fears

As had become her habit after a night at Film Club, Alice let herself into Mrs Silver's house to check on her before going home to her new apartment.

'Come in!' Mrs Silver whispered urgently, when she popped her head around the sitting-room door. 'Quickly!'

'What? Is everything all right?'

'I knew it!' Mrs Silver cried. 'I knew it was him!'

Alice looked at her in a moment of confusion before realising the television was on full blast.

'They all thought it was the boy who did it, but how could he? He couldn't read. Sometimes these people are so stupid. With all their training, they never see what is in front of their noses.'

'They're not real,' said Alice. 'They're only actors playing parts.'

'I know that. Of course I know that. But they are very stupid actors if they can't see that a fifteen-year-old boy who doesn't know how to read or write couldn't possibly have sent emails to that poor girl and then murdered her.'

'So, who did it?'

'The next-door neighbour. I didn't trust him from the moment I saw him, with his floppy hands and baby eyes. I am good with people. I always see when there is something not quite right.'

'You are,' said Alice. 'Very good with people.'

'So, how was your Film Club night?'

'We can talk about it after your TV show. Finish watching it.'

'Oh, no. Once they find the killer, there is only the part where they smile with their big teeth and congratulate each other on being very good at solving crimes in Miami. It annoys me. They are too big for their boots.'

'Would you like a cup of tea?'

'That would be lovely, dear.'

When Alice had made the tea and settled Mrs Silver's cup and saucer on the nest of tables beside her chair, she sat down and said, 'You will be glad to know I've come to a decision.'

'That's good, dear. Decisions are difficult to come by, but they tend to be for the best.'

'We watched a film tonight called *Brokeback Mountain* . . .'

'Oh, yes. It was on television not so long ago. A very sad film.'

'Yes, it was . . . But the thing is, it helped me make up my mind. It was about a man who never makes the right decision for his life, and he ends up alone and unhappy.'

'Well, that's what happens, isn't it? If we don't take any steps forward, we end up falling behind.'

'So, I've decided to tell them.'

'Tell who what, dear?'

'My family. My cousins and aunts. I'm going to tell them about myself.'

'That's very exciting. And it's the right thing to do. Yes, I'm sure it's the right thing.'

'You don't sound so sure.'

Mrs Silver eyed Alice squarely. 'I am sure it is the right thing to do, Alice. But have you considered what might happen if that's not how they see it? If they turn you away? Not that this will happen. But it is important to think everything through.'

'If I don't tell them, I'll never know. If they don't want anything to do with me, it will be awful, but it would be far more terrible to go through my life wondering. Knowing I have a whole family, while they don't even know I exist.'

Mrs Silver plumped up the cushion behind her and sat back, her hands on her lap. 'Yes,' she said. 'You are right. There are so many regrets about what could have been done. If I had said this, or done that, maybe it would have been different. But we cannot change the past. We can only do our best to make a better future.'

'Will you come with me?'

'No, dear, I don't think so.'

'But I can't do it alone. I'm too afraid.'

'Alice, dear. If there is one thing I have learned in this life, it's that we must face our fears alone. You must go to your family without me. It is a private moment with no place for someone who is only an old neighbour.'

'An old friend. A good friend.'

'Yes, a good friend. And I will be waiting for you when you come back, no matter what happens. But, Alice, this you must do by yourself.'

December

It's a Wonderful Life
Frank Capra, 1946

'You want the moon? Just say the word and
I'll throw a lasso around it and pull it down.'

93. Step One

'My name is Martin and I'm an alcoholic.'

The word 'alcoholic' felt unformed as it came out of his mouth, as if its syllables weren't properly strung together. Before he'd said it, Martin was in a sweat and thought he might choke on his tongue. Now that it was out, he closed his eyes.

A wave of totally unexpected peace washed over him. It was like being on a boat in the middle of the ocean with no oars but not being in the slightest bit worried about where the current might take him.

Martin opened his eyes again. All around the Methodist hall pairs of eyes were staring at him, not in disgust or judgement but encouragingly and with an understanding he knew they shared. In the chair opposite him sat John, wearing his polka-dotted dickie bow. His crinkled eyes locked with Martin's and he nodded gently.

John had been asleep when Martin had phoned him at two in the morning.

'Hello? John? It's Martin Brady here. I met you at an AA meeting a while back. You said I could call you.'

There was a few seconds of silence that rang very loudly in Martin's ear before John, his voice still groggy, said, 'Yes. I remember.'

'I'm sorry it's so late. It's just that I . . . I . . .' Martin couldn't find any more words.

'You took a drink.'

'Not just one. A lot. I started and I couldn't stop.'

'It happens. But you've done the right thing, calling someone for help.'

'I don't think I can manage,' said Martin. 'It's like I lost control. I couldn't do anything except drink.'

'That's the first step, remember? "We admitted we were powerless over alcohol – that our lives had become unmanageable." It's the hardest of them all.'

Martin didn't remember. He'd put that first AA meeting so far out of his mind that, apart from the polka-dotted dickie bow, he couldn't properly recall what John looked like.

'Get some sleep,' said John. 'I'll meet you for a coffee tomorrow at noon at the café in the Stephen's Green shopping centre.'

And somehow, knowing he was going to meet John, Martin calmed down. He got into the shower, washed the stink of alcohol and puke off himself and then, wrapped in his duvet, eventually fell asleep on the couch.

The next day, after coffee, John brought him to a different AA meeting, one with some people Martin's own age. And it was better. Well, he didn't feel the urge to run like he had the first time. After that, John went to a meeting with him every day. There were AA meetings all over the city – you could find one if you needed to at almost any time.

Martin still didn't feel like sharing with any of the groups, but after a while he found he was taking comfort from other people's stories. John said his time would come to speak if that was the right thing for him.

He kept gravitating back to the place where he had first met John, at the meeting where he'd thought everyone was like a Stepford Wife. He didn't know why, but he found himself calmer knowing there'd be small-talk and custard creams with Margaret and the assorted crew afterwards.

All through the MSF training in Germany he called John every evening, and John was always at the other end of the line for him. The other trainees went out at night to the bars and clubs, but Martin stayed in his hotel room rather than be tempted. On the last night he finally gave in to their pleas and went out with them, drinking apple juice while they all got hammered. He was surprised to find it didn't bother him in the slightest.

Martin took a breath. 'I'm not very good at this,' he said. 'I hope what I have to say comes out right.'

There were a few encouraging nods from around the room. Margaret, in another tent-like floral dress, was beaming at him.

'Alcohol has been a problem all my life,' he said. 'My father was a drinker and mostly when he was drinking he was mean. You never knew what was going to happen with him – you always had to be on your guard in case he went for you. He told me I was a waste of space nearly every day of my life.

'The thing is, though, I loved my dad. He died a few months ago and I thought I'd be relieved when he was gone, and for a while I thought I was. But then … it was like there was a big hole left behind, and it couldn't be filled. Even though I'd thought I hated him, I wanted my dad to love me and when he was gone the chance for him to love me was gone too. And it would never be there again.'

Martin stopped. The room was completely silent. Everyone was waiting for him to continue.

'My dad didn't know how to love us,' he said, after another deep breath. 'Maybe he didn't know how to do it before the drink got him, but after that there was no turning back … But you know what the awful thing is? He thought nobody loved him either. It was always like him against me, my mam and my sisters. He was the bad one and we were the good ones. And the truth is we all thought we hated him, when we really loved him and wanted him to love us back. And it was the drink that did that.'

Martin stopped again. His tongue was getting twisted and he wasn't sure if what he was saying made sense to anyone else, but it made sense to him.

'I don't want that for my life,' he said. 'One day, if I'm lucky enough to meet the right girl, I want to get married and have kids. I want my wife and my children to know I love them. I want to know they love me. I don't want alcohol to poison me or them, and fool us into thinking that there isn't love. Because there is. Because I loved my da and I think that maybe he loved me, but he couldn't even go there, and that was because of the drink. And we never got to show each other.

'I know that probably sounds stupid, but it's the way I see it. I know it will be one day at a time. I know there will be hard days. But I know right now that I don't ever want to drink again because I don't want what happened to him to happen to me.'

After the meeting, Martin gave John a lift home as usual. When they got to the apartment building, a development that housed the homeless, he got out and walked his new friend to the front door.

'You did well tonight,' said John, as they walked, his breath coming in clouds in the freezing dark.

'I was shitting it before I started,' said Martin. He was still feeling euphoric after his speech, from having had the courage to say it all and from the reception it'd had. Everyone had wanted to talk to him after the meeting.

'I couldn't have been prouder of you if you were my own son,' said John.

Martin stopped. 'Thank you,' he said. 'For everything.'

'For nothing.'

At the door to the building, John took out his keys, his hand trembling a little in the cold. 'So, when are you off to Chad?' he asked.

'In two weeks, on the twenty-third,' said Martin. 'It'll be weird to be out there for Christmas.'

'You'll be doing good work,' said John. 'And remember you can always call on me if things get rough.'

'I know,' Martin said. 'And I will. Have you any plans for Christmas yourself?'

John's eyes lit up. 'Yes,' he said. 'I do.'

Martin laughed. 'Are you going to tell me what they are?'

'My son called. He wants me to come to his house for dinner.'

'John, that's great news.'

'My other boy will be there, with his wife and children. They'll all be there. My ex-wife too.'

'I'm happy for you, man. You deserve it.'

John gave a shake of his head. 'What was that you said? I'm shitting it. What if I fuck up?'

Martin laughed again. The word 'fuck' sounded incongruous coming out of John's mouth. 'You won't,' he said, noticing that John wasn't laughing along. 'And you can call on me day or night if things get rough. Reverse charges.'

94. Lisa's Choice

Lisa held her breath as the squirt of ice-cold gel landed on her belly and Patrick simultaneously squeezed her hand.

'Now, Mrs and Mr Fingleton, we're just going to have a little look to see how Baby is doing,' said the nurse. 'Just relax, it shouldn't take too long.'

It didn't matter how many times Lisa had a scan, every time still felt like the first. A revelation.

'Look,' said the nurse. 'There's your baby.'

In the green light of the ultrasound screen, amid the gurglings and waves amplified from her womb, she could clearly see the outline of the foetus, one fist jammed against its face, legs scrunched up. It looked bigger than any of the other eight-month scans had, sturdier.

'He's going to be a bruiser,' Lisa said to Patrick, and he squeezed her hand again before returning his concentration to the screen. His eyes were shining.

She tried to picture this baby as part of the family – in one of those studio photographs, posed with her and Patrick, Theo, Ben and Aaron – but she couldn't. It was still inconceivable.

Still, at least the dread had dissipated. She could think about it without feeling sick.

Yesterday Sheila had called her a good mother. 'You need to stop being so hard on yourself,' she added. 'It's not doing you, or your children, any good.'

It gave Lisa a warm feeling to think of Dr Harvey as 'Sheila'. In the days Sheila had been coming to the house, helping her and Patrick work out how to handle Theo, she had become more like a friend than professional intervention. Even Patrick, who had greeted her with suspicion although he had invited her into their home in the first place, was softening.

They weren't out of the woods yet, as Sheila reminded them. There was still plenty of work to be done. There were the house rules to stick to:

No *punching*
No *hitting*
No *biting*
No *kicking*
No *pinching*
No *scraping*
No *head or body slamming*
No *spitting*
No *breaking other people's things*
No *talking back to Mum or Dad*
No *calling people rude names*
Listen and do as you're told
No *shouting or yelling when talking*

These rules were pinned up on the fridge, and even though neither Theo nor Ben nor Aaron could read them, their presence had become part of the household, a daily part of their lives.

The reward for sticking to the rules was a gold star beside your name. For five gold stars, you got an ice lolly, a half-hour of TV time or a mini-Mars Bar. Every time you broke a rule, one star was taken away.

The first to reach ten gold stars would get to choose where to go on a very special day out with Mum and Dad.

The joke was that Lisa had already read about these methods of working with your children in her books about parenting. *Getting Down With Bringing Up Kids* had almost exactly the same template of rules and rewards. Every single episode of *Supernanny* she'd watched had shown Jo Frost implementing a similar system. But somehow Lisa hadn't put two and two together. She was still on the first part of the book, the bit about setting them up to be good children, not the bit about what to do if things went off the rails.

No matter where Lisa was on the parenting continuum, Patrick was the key to making it work. Sheila had confirmed it in so many words from the first house visit, making sure he was part of the solution, calling him on every avoidance of responsibility. When Lisa had finally come home, the morning after Katherine's party, he had promised to be there more for her and the children, and he was doing his best to act on the promise, even though you could see the pull of his other life niggling at him. The need to get away.

Having got away herself, Lisa could understand it, so the first thing she did on returning was to make an agreement with him. He could have either his golf or the Lions Club – one or the other – and in return she could have Film Club and two other occasions each month to get away from him and the children. He would babysit while she was gone and vice versa, and once a month they would get another babysitter and go out together, just the two of them. She had told him that Mrs Doherty from next door would be happy to mind the kids anytime, since she had already done so on several occasions.

Patrick gave up the Lions Club. Lisa joined a tai chi class for pregnant women. She knew everything would change again once the baby was born but, as Sheila said, they had to start as they meant to go on, with all hands on deck.

The rules and rewards, and Lisa's special time with each boy began to take effect, even if there were setbacks of screaming, kicking and biting to get through, with Sheila's help, at first. But storytime was the deal-breaker.

As Theo was the eldest, Sheila had said that he would be last to go to bed in the evening. It was Patrick's duty to be there to put the younger ones to sleep with a story, and then to play with Theo for half an hour. After that he had to take Theo to his room – another development suggested by Sheila – and read him a story of his choice. Sheila said it was an exercise in bonding. At the second meeting with Lisa and Patrick alone in her office she said she felt Theo was seriously lacking in role modelling and that much of his anger was centred on not having enough access to Patrick. He was subconsciously blaming Lisa for driving Patrick away, even though this was not the case.

'He feels your anger, too, you know,' Sheila told Lisa.

'I *am* angry,' said Lisa.

'Or course you are,' said Sheila, but she didn't elaborate.

Patrick hardly opened his mouth at that meeting, but he held Lisa's hand throughout. Afterwards, when they were sitting in the car, he said, 'Is that true? Are you really angry?'

'I walked out on my children. What do you think?'

'I'm sorry,' he said. 'It's my fault.'

Lisa sighed. 'It's my fault too,' she said. 'I think we need to start again, with a clean slate.'

'You know I love you, don't you?'

'Yes. But love is hard work, Patrick. It's not just a case of saying it and then everything's okay.'

'You make it sound like a chore.'

'Sometimes it is. I'm sorry, but that's the truth.'

This morning, as she was sitting with her coffee in the playroom, Ben and Theo intent on building spaceships with

Lego while Aaron crawled and staggered around the floor, trying his best to get in on the fun, Lisa counted the days on her fingers and realised it was a full week since Theo had hit her. She had been under attack every single day for the past year and she felt now as if a thousand heavy chains padlocked around her body had been removed. Despite her enormous pregnant stomach, the biggest she'd ever had, she walked more lightly as she went to put her cup in the dishwasher. Her voice sounded sweeter as she told the boys that Theo had only one gold star to get before he had a whole ten.

Theo looked up at her, his eyes as wide as the cloudless blue sky, and smiled. 'Then I can choose a special treat with Mummy and Daddy,' he told Ben.

95. Andrew's Admission

There was no answer from the buzzer, so Jamie let himself into the apartment, figuring he could wait there until Andrew got home. He was glad of the extra time it afforded him. Although he was determined, his stomach hit the floor every time he thought about saying what he had come to say.

The photograph of the two of them, taken on one of their early holidays to Thailand, was still hanging in the hallway. They looked so young, Andrew's hair bleached white-blond in the blistering sunshine, his arm draped over Jamie's shoulder, the tip of his finger almost touching Jamie's left nipple. It had been taken by a young Thai kid they'd tipped thirty baht, and afterwards they'd had an argument, Jamie telling Andrew he trusted people too much, that the boy could have run off with the camera.

The part Jamie couldn't remember was being as physically connected as they looked in the photograph. They had been at it like rabbits on that holiday, running back to their hotel room at the slightest provocation, desperate to get at each other. There were moments when, their bodies and eyes locked together, Jamie thought he had died and gone to Heaven.

He was walking into the sitting room when a loud sneeze rang out.

'Hello?' he called. 'Andrew?'

There was a silence, then Andrew replied, 'In here. I'm in bed.'

The bedroom was in half-light with the curtains closed. Andrew was propped on a bunch of pillows, surrounded by balled-up tissues. He looked about ninety. 'It's this bloody flu,' he said, sniffling. 'It won't go away.'

'Jesus,' said Jamie, going to the window to pull the curtains. 'It smells like a horsebox in here. How long have you been like this?'

'A week. It's an awful dose.'

'Why didn't you call me?'

Andrew sneezed into his hands and picked up one of the tissues. 'You're not my boyfriend any more,' he said, wiping his wet nose.

'For fuck's sake. We were together for all those years. Who else is going to take care of you?'

For a second Andrew looked as if he was going to cry, but then he slid under the covers and buried his head in the pillow. 'I can take care of myself,' he said, in a muffled voice.

Jamie opened the window to let some air in. 'Yeah, right,' he said. 'You're doing a great job of it.'

He went into the bathroom, found some paracetamol in the cabinet and brought two back with a glass of water. 'Take these. And get out of those pyjamas. They look like the Shroud of Turin.'

Andrew did as he was told, his movements slow and laboured.

'Have you eaten?'

'I'm not hungry. I've completely lost my appetite.'

'You have to eat. You won't get better without keeping your strength up. I'll make some soup, if you have anything in the kitchen.'

'Why are you being so nice?' Andrew asked.

'I'm not a complete and utter bastard, you know,' said Jamie. 'I do have some redeeming qualities.'

Later, when the sheets were changed and Andrew was sitting up in fresh pyjamas, looking considerably less dishevelled, he peered over the rim of his Cup-a-Soup and said, 'What are you doing here anyway?'

'I came to talk to you,' Jamie replied, his voice quavering. Why was he so afraid? It wasn't like the world was going to cave in once it was out of his mouth.

'What about? How you completely betrayed me?' said Andrew.

'No,' said Jamie. 'I've come to talk to you about us. About us and sex.'

Andrew went quiet. Then he said, 'What's the point now?'

'Why did you stop wanting to make love to me?' Jamie asked. He had kept his eyes on the floor as he put the question, but now he looked up and saw that Andrew had paled. His own heart was hammering.

Andrew opened his mouth to say something and then closed it.

Jamie tried again: 'I went with Saeed because I was desperate for sex, Andrew. Absolutely desperate.'

Andrew eyed him. 'That's no excuse,' he said.

'I'm not trying to make excuses. I know now I should have talked to you about what was happening between us. But I couldn't.'

'Why not?' Andrew said.

'Because I was too afraid.'

'Afraid of what?'

'I was afraid that if I asked you'd tell me the truth, I suppose. That there's something wrong with me.'

Andrew sat up, his eyes blazing. 'There's nothing wrong with you!'

'Well, what is it, then? It's been nearly two years, Andrew. We haven't had sex in two years.'

Andrew groaned and lay back down. 'Please, Jamie, I can't talk about this now. I'm too sick.'

Jamie ignored him. 'You know what I've just realised? In all that time you haven't been able to talk about it either. So, you're just like me. You're scared too.'

Andrew groaned again.

'I told you what I'm scared of,' said Jamie. 'It's your turn to tell me.'

There was another silence and then a squeaking sound. Jamie realised Andrew was crying. 'It's okay, you can tell me,' he said. 'I love you.'

'I'm terrified ...' said Andrew, and he gulped '. . . that I might never want sex again. I don't know what's wrong with me. But it's like that part of me has been switched off and I can't switch it back on again.'

Jamie leaned over and used his fingers to wipe the tears from Andrew's cheeks. 'See?' he said. 'You told me and the world hasn't caved in.'

'It feels like it has,' said Andrew.

Lying back on the pillow, Jamie stretched his legs out. 'What about Saeed? Did he float your boat at all?'

'No. Even though I could see he was very attractive.'

'He was a total ride, you mean.'

Andrew gave a rueful laugh and coughed. 'And a complete psycho. Have you seen him since?'

'If I never see him again, it won't be a day too soon,' said Jamie. 'How about you?'

'I emailed to say I'd told the police to keep an eye on him and didn't get a reply. I don't think he'll be bothering us again. Not if he wants to stay in this country.'

'Look, Andrew . . . Saeed was a big mistake. I'll never do that again.'

'And I'm supposed to believe you. Why?'

'Because from now on we're going to talk to each other. About what's going on with us.'

'But what if I can never have sex again? How are we going to get through that?'

'We're going to get ourselves some help.'

'From where?'

'From a sex therapist. I've been looking into it. There are options.'

Andrew groaned again. 'Oh, God. It's hard enough talking about sex as it is. How am I supposed to talk to a complete stranger?'

Jamie hoisted himself up on one elbow and looked Andrew in the eye. 'I love you, Andrew. I've loved you since the first moment we got together. And I'm not going to watch what we have go down the Swanee without putting up a fight.'

'I don't want it to go down the Swanee either,' said Andrew, and his eyes were wet again.

'So, we're going to get help.'

Andrew nodded, but he still looked frightened.

'We have to be brave, honey,' said Jamie, taking his hand. 'Both of us. There's no future for us if we're not.'

Later, when Andrew had fallen asleep, Jamie popped out to the corner shop to stock up on a few supplies.

The woman behind the till, whom Jamie had seen nearly every day since he'd moved into Andrew's five years ago, scowled at him. 'How much are these Lemsip?' she barked, over her shoulder, into the inner recesses of the shop.

A man's voice called back, 'Three fifty.'

The shopkeeper was of Indian origin and had a brusque manner. Jamie had always fancied that she knew Andrew and he were gay and didn't approve.

'They're for my boyfriend,' Jamie found himself saying, pointing at the Lemsip. 'He's got that flu that's going around.'

The shopkeeper gave him a sharp look. 'Tell him to take hot water with turmeric and fresh garlic. It is the very best way to kill a cold.'

'Turmeric and garlic,' said Jamie. 'Sounds delicious.'

'Wait a minute,' the woman said, turning to a shelf behind the counter. 'I think I have some turmeric here. Ah, yes. From Punjab, the very best.'

'How much?' said Jamie.

'Free of charge,' said the shopkeeper, in her no-nonsense way. 'You are a valued customer.'

The little bell on the shop door tinkled as Jamie let himself out with his bag of things for Andrew. Across the street, the woman from the apartment opposite Andrew's passed by and waved. Jamie waved back, took a deep breath, then lifted his face to the white winter sun.

96. Start at the Very Beginning

Mrs Silver had advised neutral territory, so Alice invited Claire to meet her at the tearooms in Bantry House, which she had visited once before when Celia was first in hospital. She liked the calmness of the place, with its white wicker chairs and floor-to-ceiling windows looking out on the stillness of the mountain-lined bay.

She got there earlier than the appointed time, having arranged the meeting for an hour after her bus arrived. She wanted to acclimatise herself to the surroundings, be comfortably ensconced before Claire joined her. Next to approaching Celia that first time at Rose Cottage, telling Claire was going to be the hardest thing she'd ever have to do.

'Put it this way, the only way is up,' said Jamie, when he'd called her out of the blue the other night to tell her about the free portfolio preparation course he'd enrolled for so he could apply for 'real art college'.

'Or down,' said Alice. 'Knowing Claire, she'll probably react very badly.'

'So why are you telling her instead of her mother, or the rest of the aunts and uncles?'

'Because I don't think I could face her mother's reaction. At least Claire's one generation removed. And she's the one I've spent the most time with.'

Alice could see her coming now, walking purposefully up the steps that led to the front of the big house, the wind ruffling her hair. Wrapped in an expensive purple wool coat, with the silver-bright bay stretching out behind her, she looked to the manor born.

Nearing the windows of the tearooms, she spotted Alice and waved, but her expression was impenetrable. She looked neither pleased nor displeased to see her.

'It's windy out there,' she said, when she sat down, without a hello or offering Alice her hand.

'It's beautiful, with the sun shining on the mountains,' Alice replied. 'They look dark blue.'

'I know. It's great to get a break from the freezing cold weather. How has it been in Dublin?'

'Fine,' said Alice. She didn't want to talk about the weather, but hadn't a clue how she was going to find a way into the conversation she had come here to have. She wondered again if Claire had ever noticed the resemblance between them. Since Alice had got her new hairstyle, it was less pronounced, but it was there in lots of little details. Their eyebrows, their mouths, their identical noses. The exact way Claire lifted her hand to get the waitress's attention.

'Will you have some fresh tea?' Claire said, after ordering a coffee for herself, and Alice nodded at the waitress. She had a bitter pain in her stomach, the one she always got when she was nervous, and the tea was doing it no good. But she had to have something to do with her hands.

'So,' said Claire, after the waitress had gone, 'you wanted to talk to me.'

'Yes,' said Alice.

'It must be important, with you coming all the way back down here.'

'It is.'

'Okay, then. Go on.'

'I don't know where to begin,' said Alice. 'I've been rehearsing it for days, but now I can't remember what I planned to say.'

Claire frowned. 'You should start at the very beginning,' she said.

But Alice couldn't tell the whole story. Not now. Instead she burst out, 'It's Celia. She was my mother.'

Claire was perfectly still. Her eyes wandered to the bay, where two boats were passing each other, their sails little white triangles against the blue. When she turned back to Alice, she was crying. 'Oh, Alice,' she said. 'I knew.'

Alice began to cry too.

'That day in the hospital, when I first met you . . . you looked so like her . . . And then, when you kept turning up . . . I didn't want to believe it, because of Celia. I didn't want to think she'd lived her whole life without telling a single soul.'

The waitress arrived with their order, putting their cups in front of them without a glimmer of expression, as if two women openly crying was part of her everyday customer experience. When she had gone, Claire picked up a napkin and dabbed at her eyes. 'Why didn't you say anything?' she asked.

'She didn't want me to. She invented the story about me being an old student. She didn't even want me to tell you after she was gone.'

'I don't understand. Why did she keep it a secret?'

'She never said anything at the start, and then, as the years went by …'

'And your father?'

'I don't know much about him. He was from the same town, about the same age as her. His mother sent him away.'

'Have you looked for him?'

'Not yet,' said Alice.

Claire digested the story slowly, asking Alice question after question, many of which she couldn't answer. Alice began to realise the gaps Celia had left, the unexplained bits that would never come to the surface now that she was gone.

'What about the people who adopted you?' Claire asked. 'Did you have brothers and sisters?'

'No, I was an only child. Both my parents are gone now. My mother passed away in January.'

'So you have no one.'

'I have friends. Good friends.'

'It could have been so different,' said Claire, when she ran out of questions.

Alice's eyes went out to the bay again and the two little boats that were now a mile apart. 'Maybe not,' she said. 'It was another time when Celia had me. Lots of girls kept the same secrets.'

'No. What I mean is that her death could have been so different. I turned you away.'

'You did what you thought was best.'

'It was a terrible thing to do.'

'I don't blame you,' said Alice. 'You did right by Celia, and that was the most important thing.'

Claire picked up her coffee cup, then put it down again. 'Was it?' she said. 'I'm not so sure.'

'It's a relief telling you, at least,' said Alice. 'Even though you may not feel the same.'

'I don't feel the same.'

'I understand. I was prepared for that.'

'I can't begin to fathom what you went through. I still have my mother. You've lost two.'

Alice hadn't put the picture together like that before, but it was true. First Mother, then Celia.

'What time is your bus home?' said Claire.

Alice looked at her watch. 'In an hour and a half.'

'You'll have to miss it. We're going to my mother's house.'

'I'm not sure that's a good idea,' said Alice. She didn't think she could go through it a second time today.

Claire glanced out of the window again and then her eyes met Alice's. 'You're part of our family,' she said. 'We're not going to let you go again so easily.'

97. Getting to Know You

The heating wasn't on when Katherine let herself into the house and she shivered as she took her coat off, wondering if the timer was broken. On the hall floor there were a few envelopes – a Christmas card with her mother's handwriting, the gas bill, her credit-card statement with 'Mastercard' stamped on the envelope.

'Barry?' she called, walking into the kitchen, but she knew he was out. In the past couple of weeks his mood had shifted a little for the better and he'd taken to spending more and more time away from the house. Katherine asked him where he went, whether there was any news on the job front, when he would be back – but he revealed very little. The last time she'd questioned where he was going, he'd told her, with the expression of a parent admonishing a child, to stop nagging him. She'd felt a prick of annoyance as he'd walked out of the door, yet she was glad that at least he seemed to be getting a life again. It took the pressure off her a bit.

In the kitchen she checked the central-heating timer, which had been switched off. She turned it on and boiled the kettle for a cup of tea. She'd wait, she thought, until Barry was home to cook dinner.

At the table she opened her mother's card. There was a picture of an angel playing a trumpet on the front, with the words 'Feliz Navidad' coming out of its bell. 'A very happy Christmas, Katherine, from your ever loving Mum,' the inside said. The gas bill was much as expected – huge. It had been an unusually harsh winter so far.

The Mastercard envelope was weightier than usual. She tore it open and took out what amounted to a small sheaf of pages. Unfolding them, Katherine went straight to the last one, to see November's total. It was €1,430.20.

She was confused. She'd hardly used the credit card at all last month. She went back to the beginning of the bill.

The first item was for €120 and it came from Il Primo restaurant. Katherine hadn't eaten there in at least a year. She looked through the pages, alighting on charge after charge that wasn't hers: €225 to the Merrion Hotel Spa, €73.99 to HMV, €165 to Burton's Suits, €345 to Games Stop …

Games Stop … Katherine's mind went to the sitting room and Barry's miraculously repaired Xbox … Surely not.

She dropped the pages and went to the kitchen counter to get her bag. She opened her purse and looked in the card section. Her Mastercard wasn't there. Neither was her Visa.

Katherine stayed in the kitchen for the best part of an hour, waiting for him to come home, hardly moving except to go to the toilet once. While she sat there she imagined what Martin would have to say about this. Probably that he'd told her so. But then she realised that Martin wouldn't even think of saying such a thing to her, or to anyone else for that matter.

She thought back to that night, to the moment when they were having sex and she'd come and he'd brought her face close to his, whispering her name. What had she felt then? Katherine closed her eyes and went inside herself to see if she could bring it back.

It had been a feeling of safety. Deep in the fibre of her being, in that moment with Martin, she had known that this man would never, ever do anything to hurt her.

And then she had rejected him. For a man who lied to her and stole from her and manipulated her for his own ends.

When Barry eventually walked in he was pulling a wet Christmas tree behind him. He dragged it through the hall and into the kitchen.

'Look at what I picked up, babes,' he said. His cheeks were rosy red from the freezing weather and his words were slurred.

Katherine didn't reply. She pushed the credit-card bill across the table and sat back in her chair.

Barry didn't notice. 'It's a lovely one,' he said, surveying the tree, its damp pine smell pervading the room.

'What did you pay for it with?' Katherine asked. The house had warmed up, but she felt utterly cold.

Barry looked at her, looked at the tree, then noticed the credit-card bill on the table.

'So much for the Christmas spirit,' he said, shrugging. 'I should have known you'd start nagging the minute I got in the door. Nothing I do is ever good enough for you, is it?'

'Do you have my credit cards, Barry?'

'Fuck, I need a drink. Did you get any beer in?'

'I said, do you have my credit cards?'

For a moment Barry was motionless. Then he sat down at

the table. 'Katherine,' he said, his voice suddenly filled with concern, 'are you okay? What's going on?'

'You stole from me. That's what's going on.'

'No, I didn't.' Barry shook his head vigorously. 'I bought a few things, that's all. I was depressed, babes. I hardly knew what I was doing.'

Katherine felt revulsion rise in her. 'You stole from me,' she said again.

'Look, babes. We're supposed to be getting married, aren't we? That's what married couples do. They share. You have to learn that.'

She had the urge to laugh, but then she saw that Barry had his hands out towards her, as if he was pleading. She stood up. 'You think I don't know who you are,' she said.

'Sit down, babes, will you? You're overreacting.'

'It's taken me a while, Barry, I'll admit, but I've got the measure of you now,' Katherine said. 'Every last selfish, miserable, lying, cheating inch of you.'

'What are you talking about? I bought a few things, that's all. It's no big deal, babes.'

Katherine's hands made fists. 'We're selling this house,' she said. 'It's just about worth the mortgage we took out on it now, so neither of us should have any debt. And after that I never want to see your face again.'

'No fucking way! We'll lose all the money we put into it.'

'I don't care about the money.'

Barry stood up and moved towards her. 'You're not going anywhere,' he said. 'And we're not selling this house.'

Katherine had the urge to back away from him, but she stood her ground. 'If you won't sell the house, I'm walking out on it,' she said. 'I won't pay a penny more of the mortgage and we'll see how far you get on a pair of stolen credit cards then.'

Barry grabbed her wrist and twisted. 'I'll sue you,' he said. 'I'll screw you to the fucking wall.'

Sharp tears of pain sprang into Katherine's eyes and, with one swift movement, she brought her knee up hard into his groin.

'Fucking bitch!' Barry gasped, falling away and grabbing his crotch. 'What did you do that for?'

'Because I can't stand bullies,' she said, and walked away.

As she clicked the front door closed behind her, she could hear him shouting, 'You won't get away with this, you fucking bitch! I swear you won't get away with this!'

98. Delayed Gratification

Lisa thought no one would agree to a Film Club meeting on Christmas Eve, but to her surprise they all jumped at the idea, Katherine and Jamie agreeing with her that they couldn't watch *It's a Wonderful Life* on any other day. She was even more surprised that no one cancelled, given that it had started to snow two days ago and had virtually not stopped since.

Jamie did express his wonder about the sanity of a woman who was about to pop a baby out hosting an evening on Christmas Eve of all nights, but Lisa assured him that Patrick would be doing all the hard work and she'd just be sitting around 'like a pregnant sloth'. She had resolved to keep going to Film Club once the new baby was born, but you never knew what was coming your way with an infant. Theo, Ben and Aaron had all been unpredictable in their own ways, and if the new one slept anything like Aaron, or didn't, as the case had been, she wouldn't have the energy to go out for a while. So tonight might possibly be her last Film Club attendance for a while, and it was her turn, so she'd told Patrick she wanted to do it.

Alice asked hesitantly if she could bring a friend along, which was fine by Lisa. Patrick would be joining them too, after he'd put the boys to bed. All the Santa shopping was done and, once everyone was gone, they'd lay it out on the sitting-room floor, ready for the morning.

She'd emailed Martin to let him know, but he'd replied giving his apologies. He was being posted to Chad on 23 December, he said, asking her to wish everyone 'a very happy Christmas' in his absence.

'PS,' he'd added. 'Turn up the sound to full volume for the bit near the beginning of the film when George goes to his father's office. There are two lines of secret dialogue nobody ever catches.'

Lisa loved that about *It's a Wonderful Life*. There was always something new to find in it.

Alice's friend, who was eighty if she was a day, claimed to have seen *It's a Wonderful Life* when it was first released in the cinema.

'I'm not so partial to black-and-white films nowadays,' she said, manoeuvring herself into the chair nearest the fire. 'I prefer everything in colour.'

'Now that's what I call a philosophy,' said Jamie, who was clearly enraptured by Mrs Silver.

'Well, you're both in luck,' said Lisa. 'I have the colour version. It's very beautiful.'

Theo was hovering, watching Alice, Jamie and Mrs Silver from behind Lisa's legs.

'Come here, little boy,' said Mrs Silver and, as if summoned by the Queen of Sheba, Theo dutifully walked over to her side. She opened her handbag and took out something wrapped in tissue. 'This is for you and your brothers,' she said. 'Go and share it.'

'My brothers are in bed,' said Theo, screwing up his face with shyness. 'I'm the older one so I get to stay up later.'

'And so you should,' said Mrs Silver, pressing the tissue-wrapped thing into his hands. 'You are a very big boy indeed.'

Thrilled with himself, Theo ran off into the kitchen where Andrew was preparing drinks. Lisa was tempted to go after him to see what the old lady had handed over. She looked a bit unhinged, with the flower Alice had once worn pinned to the lapel of her jacket, her blue-rinsed hair and magenta-painted nails.

'Don't worry,' said Mrs Silver, her eyes twinkling like those of a mind reader's. 'They are *Weihnachtsplätzchen*. Christmas biscuits. I made them especially.'

'Thank you, Mrs Silver,' said Lisa, though she was still dubious.

'You can call me Ilsa, dear. "Mrs Silver" makes me feel my age. It's a very old-sounding name, don't you think?'

'Nonsense. You don't look a day over fifty-five,' said Jamie.

He had been first to arrive, bearing gifts for the boys. Lisa insisted he put the parcels under the tree without saying anything, not wanting Theo to get too excited by opening them tonight. She planned to eke out the presents over the next few weeks, rather than shower them all on the boys on Christmas Day. She and Patrick had carefully picked one special thing for each of them from Santa, sticking to Dr Harvey's delayed-gratification rule. That would be enough for tomorrow.

Katherine was the last to turn up, bringing a gust of frosty air in with her, again laden with presents. 'I can't stay late,' she informed everyone immediately, pulling off her green beret and shaking her hair out. 'I promised my sister I'd go to the midnight mass with her and my nieces.' She was wearing an uncharacteristically simple red turtleneck jumper and denims under her coat.

'Time for the oldest boy to go to bed,' said Patrick, arriving in with Theo. 'Santa won't come until all the children are fast asleep.'

'Say good night to everyone,' said Lisa.

'Good night to everyone,' said Theo.

'What a lovely child,' said Mrs Silver. 'As good as gold.'

'That's what you think,' Jamie muttered, under his breath, and Lisa shot him a look.

'I told you, mister, things have changed a lot around here,' she said.

'More than you can imagine,' Patrick added, kissing her cheek and leading Theo out and up the stairs.

'To the Forced Redundancy Film Club, and all who sail in her!' toasted Jamie, with the bottle of champagne Lisa uncorked when they were left alone.

'It doesn't seem right toasting without Martin,' said Katherine. 'Has anyone heard from him?'

'He's already in Chad,' said Lisa. 'He called in with presents for the boys the other day. He sent his apologies.'

'How was he looking?' Katherine asked.

Lisa thought she sounded a bit over the top. 'Like a different man,' she replied. 'He's totally off the drink now, you know. He seems more ... grown-up or something.'

'To absent friends, then,' said Jamie, still holding out his glass.

'To absent friends,' they chimed, clinking their glasses against each other's. The sound was like the tinkle of Christmas bells. Lisa thought of *It's a Wonderful Life* and angels getting their wings.

She always found the opening scenes of the film a bit surreal, with the prayers going out for George Bailey from the houses in Bedford Falls, especially the one from his little girls, and then the conversation in the night sky between the stars.

'Weird,' agreed Jamie, as the film began. 'But very modern when you think how ancient this film is. What year was it made?'

'Nineteen forty-six,' said Mrs Silver. 'Just after the war. I saw it here in Dublin. In the Theatre Royal, I remember.'

'My mother loved *It's a Wonderful Life*,' said Alice. 'I remember it came on television one Christmas Eve and I watched it cuddled up on the couch with her. She was crying at the end.'

'I always cry too,' said Lisa. 'No matter how many times I watch it.'

About half an hour into the film, Patrick came back downstairs. 'All quiet on the western front,' he whispered to Lisa, as he took a seat on a cushion on the floor beside her. From there on, he watched it with everyone else, laughing at the funny bits, going quiet at the sad bits, as if it was his first time too.

He turned to catch Lisa's eye once during the film, towards the end when George's daughter Zuzu had a fever and asked him to paste the petals back on a rose for her.

When the nurse who had been giving her the scan had asked them if they wanted to know the sex of the baby, Patrick had said an outright no. But Lisa had hesitated. She'd been through the surprise-baby thing three times now. What harm would there be in knowing? So she'd said to Patrick, 'Let's find out this time. I'd like to be prepared.'

He'd put up an argument for about ten seconds, then capitulated and turned expectantly to the nurse.

'You have a healthy baby girl,' the nurse had told them, and for a split second, you could have heard a pin drop in the ultrasound room.

'Really?' said Patrick. 'A girl?'

Lisa winked at the nurse. 'I suspect she's going to be a daddy's girl,' she said, while inside her head she began to imagine all the things she might do with her daughter in the years to come.

99. It's a Short Life

'The film is totally anti-capitalist,' said Patrick. 'I'd say if they'd tried to release it ten years later, it would have been banned in America.' He was taking part in the post-screening discussion vociferously.

'No way!' said Jamie. 'It's as American as Mom's apple pie.'

'Maybe Patrick's right,' said Katherine, doing her best to contribute to the discussion even though her mind had been elsewhere for much of the film. 'It's clearly saying that money doesn't matter. That you don't need it to be happy.'

Jamie snorted. 'But what about the end, when everyone piles the cash in front of George? That makes him *very* happy.'

'I think the money is meant to represent generosity of spirit,' said Alice.

'It's still money,' said Patrick. 'And it's a film about money, one way or the other. The underlying message is that the gathering of wealth is evil. The wealthy guy is the bad guy.'

'But what about Sam Wainwright?' asked Lisa. 'He's wealthy and he's not a bad guy. He uses his money for good.'

Mrs Silver gave a little snore. She'd nodded off long before George Bailey had made his Christmas Eve suicide attempt and discovered how wonderful life really was.

'I'd better bring her home,' said Alice, getting to her feet. 'We've got an early start tomorrow.'

'But it's Christmas Day,' said Lisa. 'Surely you can allow yourself a little lie-in.'

'We're flying to Cork at eight a.m. To spend Christmas with my family.'

Katherine noted the hint of pride in Alice's voice. 'Good for you, Alice,' she said. 'I'm so glad.'

Alice sat down again. 'It's a bit scary, actually,' she said. 'They don't know me very well. And Mrs Silver can be a handful. I didn't want to leave her on her own at Christmas, though.'

'I'm sure it'll be fine,' said Lisa. 'And Ilsa's a hoot. They'll love her.'

'*I* love her,' said Jamie. 'Ilsa Silver. It's like a silent movie star's name. She's Greta Garbo in Miss Marple's body.'

'Pardon?' said Mrs Silver, opening her eyes. 'Is the film over?'

'You fell asleep,' said Alice. 'I was just saying it was time for us to go.'

'But we haven't had the discussion. That's the bit I was looking forward to.'

Alice gave everyone an apologetic smile as Mrs Silver searched around the floor beside her chair for her bag and, having retrieved it, took out her glasses and a piece of paper. 'I made some notes,' she said, pushing her glasses up on her nose and reading what she'd written. 'Now let's see . . . Oh, yes. George Bailey. What do we think of him?'

'He's a stock Hollywood character,' said Jamie. 'The guy next door. James Stewart always played him in the forties and fifties, Tom Hanks in the eighties and nineties.'

'Who plays him now,' asked Katherine. 'George Clooney?'

'No, George is the guy at the cocktail party. The one Cary Grant used to play. The guy next door is just an ordinary bloke.'

'Yes,' said Mrs Silver. 'But in this film George Bailey is not just an ordinary man.' She read from her notes again. 'There is an angel in the film, but I think George Bailey represents God.'

'Just like the Wizard in *The Wizard of Oz*,' said Lisa.

'Except the Wizard was a fake god,' Jamie reminded her.

Katherine thought back to Martin's theory about Dorothy searching for God on the yellow brick road. How many months ago was that? So much had changed, it seemed like a lifetime.

'It's a religious film,' Mrs Silver said. 'Its message is to have strong faith so that you can stay strong when life twists and turns.'

'I thought you saw *It's a Wonderful Life* in nineteen forty-six, Ilsa,' said Lisa. 'You certainly have a very good memory.'

'Oh, no, dear. I saw it last night. I bought the DVD on the internet. With my phone. Can you believe it?'

'I think the film is about making mistakes and learning from them,' said Jamie.

'Oh, yes,' agreed Mrs Silver, emphatically. 'We all make mistakes in our lives, and we all must learn from them.'

'We most certainly do,' said Patrick, getting up from his place beside Lisa and stretching. 'One for the road, anyone?'

'One for the road?' said Jamie. 'We've only just begun.'

'I'd like a whiskey, if you have any,' said Mrs Silver.

'But we've got to be going,' said Alice. 'Our flight's at eight.'

'Alice, dear, relax. If there is one thing I have learned in my time on this earth, it's not that it's a wonderful life – it's that it's a short life. When you get a chance to spend time with friends you should not hurry it.'

Mrs Silver took her notes up again and began to talk about the film's theme of friendship and community, but Katherine was no longer listening.

All through the film, George Bailey had reminded her of Martin, even though he looked nothing like him. The resemblance was in George's fundamental decency, the way he looked after other people before he looked after himself, the way he was flawed but willing to admit it, and it was in his devastated expression towards the end of the film, just at the moment he discovered he had lost everything. Katherine had watched the same expression dawn on Martin's face the last time she had seen him. The morning she had told him she was going back to Barry.

'It's a short life,' Mrs Silver had said and Katherine was instantly floored by regret. She had made such a huge mistake and now it couldn't be rectified.

She stumbled to her feet. 'I'm sorry,' she said. 'I have to go.'

'But it's an hour and a half until midnight,' said Lisa. 'Stay with us for a while.'

Katherine looked around the room at the rag-tag bunch the Forced Redundancy Film Club had brought together and felt an outpouring of genuine affection for each and every one of them. For Alice, who had blossomed beneath her very eyes into a whole new person. For Jamie, who was a big softie at heart, for all his sarcasm, and for Lisa, who was as kind as she was loyal.

But the one person she cared about most among them was missing, and she was the one who had driven him away.

100. The Great Pretender

On the way home, Katherine called Lucy and told her she wouldn't be coming to Midnight Mass. That she was too tired.

'Are you all right?' Lucy asked. 'You sound like you've been crying.'

'I'm fine,' Katherine lied, trying to make herself sound cheerful. 'You have a good time with Paolo and the girls. I'll be over in the morning with their presents.'

'Okay,' Lucy said, her voice tinged with doubt. 'We'll see you tomorrow then … if you're sure.'

Barry had moved back to his mother's, although he was still calling to the house regularly, letting himself in and lying in wait to beg her to take him back or threaten legal action or both. The last time had been in the middle of the night, and he'd forgotten his keys. He'd banged on the door until Katherine was forced to open it, then insisted on sleeping in their bed. Katherine had taken the spare room, eventually nodding off under Kitty's painting of the Little Mermaid.

Katherine was relieved not to find him there when her taxi finally got through the snow to bring her home. She went upstairs and lay curled up on her bed, feeling pain in her heart that was like nothing she had ever experienced before. She could hear a heavy thumping bass and sounds of revelry from next door, where the neighbours were having their annual Christmas Eve bash. She cried and cried.

Somewhere after the Church of the Holy Name chimed midnight she remembered she was Martin's Facebook friend. He had returned none of her calls in the past few weeks and the email she'd sent to his gmail address on Monday, wishing him luck in his new job with MSF, had bounced back so she'd realised the account was dead. But she'd be able to send him a message on Facebook.

Katherine sat up and ran her fingers through her hair.

What could she say? 'I'm sorry, please come back?' She knew there was no chance of that. But at least she could explain herself. At least she could take back the hurt she had caused him.

She took her laptop off the bedside table, opened it and logged on to Facebook, searching for Martin's profile. His photo showed him fully shaved and smiling widely. He looked impossibly handsome. Katherine clicked to send a private message and began as best she could:

Dear Martin,

I know this comes too late, and I know that anything I can do or say now will always be too little. But nonetheless I still feel compelled to write to you. I want to explain myself, not because I expect you to forgive me or take me back into your life, even as a friend. I know it's too late for that.

But the truth is, I know now that when I had my chance with you, I blew it. I could not admit what was staring me straight in the face. And because of that, I treated you badly. And you, of all people, don't deserve to be treated badly.

It's taken me a long time to see some home truths about myself that, no doubt from the outside looking in, are pretty obvious. But for lots of reasons, I've been scared. Scared of letting someone truly in. Someone good, that is.

Once, when I was eleven years old, I had this fight with my dad. It was over something stupid – finishing my homework. I used to wish I could turn back time to just before that fight. It haunted me for years, because just a few days later, Dad left. He never came back and I never had a chance to say sorry. For a long time, I thought I was the reason he'd gone.

It took me quite a while to figure that one out.

And now I find myself once more wishing that I could turn back time. If I could turn back the clock, Martin, I would go back to the Christmas party two years ago, when you kissed me. I would tell you that I had never felt anything like what I felt in that moment. But I was a coward and I behaved in the lowest way possible. I blamed you and rejected you instead of admitting the truth to you or myself.

The truth is that I am a pretender. I put up a front, or at least I try very hard to, but it's just that, a front – and I have been pretending for so long I can hardly remember who the real me is. The problem was that you kept reminding me of that person, and it scared me.

If I could turn back time, I would also go to the morning after we made love and I would tell you that are an amazing man, a wonderful, strong and honest man. I would tell you that you make me feel like myself. That you make me feel safe enough to be myself.

The funny thing is that I was afraid that by being myself I would drive you away, but the truth is that, by putting on a big pretence, by not being myself, that's exactly what I ended up doing.

I hope that everything works out well for you in Chad and that one day you can meet someone who won't be afraid to leap at the opportunity to love you and be loved by you. I wish you all the love and happiness you deserve.

I'm sorry for how I treated you, Martin. And I will always be grateful to you. Thank you for your unconditional kindness. It has changed my life. If you ever need anything in return, I will always be here for you in whatever way you want. All you have to do is ask.

I love you.
Katherine

101. You Learn Something New Every Day

At two thirty a.m. Katherine woke to the sound of Barry jamming his finger hard on the front-door bell. She'd fallen asleep in a foetal position outside the covers and was shivering. Her hair was plastered to her face and her makeup, which she hadn't had the energy to take off, felt caked in.

'Go home, Barry,' she moaned, pulling herself off the bed and putting on her dressing-gown. She shoved her toes into the pink bunny slippers Kitty had given her last Christmas and dragged her feet down the stairs.

The bell rang more urgently.

'Okay, okay, coming,' Katherine said, unhooking the chain. Why couldn't he have left her alone, tonight of all nights? She couldn't bear the thought of waking up on Christmas Day with him in the house.

She opened the door and muttered, 'Please go away.'

'Katherine, I love you too,' he said.

'What the fuck, Barry . . .'

'Barry?' He tilted his head. 'Try Martin.'

For the first time Katherine's eyes focused properly on the bulky creature wrapped to within an inch of his life in a big coat and scarf, wearing a hat with ridiculous floppy ears.

'But . . .' said Katherine. 'I thought . . .'

'My flight was cancelled . . . The snow . . .'

Katherine looked at him in amazement.

'Any chance of a cup of tea?' he said. 'I'm freezing me bollocks off out here.'

Katherine didn't care what she looked like – the bird's nest hair, streaked makeup, puffy eyes, her ridiculous bunny slippers and old dressing-gown. She reached out, pulled him into the hall and, taking his head in the stupid hat between her hands, she kissed him.

He'd lost a lot of weight since she'd last seen him. His belly was gone, and he was completely clean-shaven, his hair cut so tight to his head it appeared auburn instead of muddy ginger. This, combined with the weight loss, gave his chin and cheekbones a kind of carved appearance. His face was less boyish.

She made him a cup of tea to warm him up and they sat together at the kitchen table, hardly saying a word. More than anything she wanted to feel his lips against hers again. When she'd kissed him on the doorstep, she'd felt like she had at the Christmas party and when she'd been in bed with him. But now it wasn't scary. She searched for a word to describe the feeling – freedom, maybe.

'Do you mind if I go out for a smoke?' he said, pulling his Marlboro Lights out of his pocket.

'Of course not,' she said. She'd put an ashtray out on the garden table for him already and when he saw it he turned back to her and smiled. As he lit his cigarette she put on the pair of garden shoes that sat by the door and pulling up the hood of her dressing-gown, followed him out on to the deck.

The night was as still as a baby sleeping. Not a car could be heard on the road beyond the walls of the garden, not a siren in the distance. It was as if the world had been completely muffled by snow.

Katherine shivered and pulled her dressing-gown around her as Martin emitted a plume of grey smoke.

'Go back in,' he said. 'You'll catch your death out here.'

'I want to be outside,' said Katherine, noticing how the bed of snowflakes on the back garden glistened in the moonlight. 'It's so beautiful.'

Martin jammed his cigarette between his lips, took off his coat and put it over her shoulders.

'I feel like I shouldn't be smoking with you here,' he said, dipping his ash.

'Go ahead. I'm too judgemental for my own good.'

Martin took a deep drag and looked up at the sky. 'I hate the things myself,' he said. 'I'm giving them up on New Year's Day.' After a moment's silence he added, 'I don't think there'll be any more snow tonight. It's so clear up there, you can see the Milky Way.'

The moon was three-quarters full, a shimmering silver-white amid the constellations. It seemed so close you might reach up and pick it out of the sky.

'Where's the Milky Way?' said Katherine. 'I can't see it.'

Martin pointed, guiding her eye. 'See there, just beneath the moon, where there's a whitish colour flowing through the stars?'

'Yes, I see it,' said Katherine, after a moment. 'That's the Milky Way?'

'It is.'

'Well, you learn something new every day.'

'That you do.' Martin took another drag of his cigarette. 'So, how's Barry?' he asked, exhaling a mouthful of smoke.

'We split up. We're selling the house and going our separate ways.'

'I'm very glad to hear it,' Martin said, and then stopped. 'I mean, I'm sorry to hear it. I mean, are you okay?'

'I couldn't be better,' said Katherine.

Martin pulled in the last of his cigarette, looking at its orange tip before stubbing it out in the ashtray. 'So, Lisa said the club watched *It's a Wonderful Life* tonight. Did you go?'

'Yes,' said Katherine. 'I couldn't concentrate, though. I could only think about you.'

'The thing I like most about *It's a Wonderful Life* is that it's messy like reality,' said Martin. 'It's about a man who has great courage, but doesn't get what he dreamed of. His life is full of loss and disappointment. But at the end, he understands that only one thing matters in the grand scheme of things.'

'Love,' said Katherine.

'Yes,' said Martin. 'Love.'

From the party next door, the strains of Judy Garland singing 'Have Yourself A Merry Little Christmas' started up.

'I adore this song,' said Katherine. 'It's so melancholy, not like all those pretend-everything's-perfect Christmas songs.'

'Everything is perfect.'

'You're right, it is,' she said, and little bubble of joy exploded in her belly.

'Do you know what I'd like to do?' she said, after they had quietly listened to the song for a few seconds.

'Walk off into the sunset?'

'Maybe later,' said Katherine. 'But right now I'd like to dance.'

Martin held his arms out to her. 'My pleasure, madam,' he said.

Close together, their heads resting on each other's shoulders, they danced by the light of the moon.